ROAR

Volume 10
Community

Edited by Mary E. Lowd

Bad Dog Books

2019

ROAR Volume 10
First publication 2019

Edited by Mary E. Lowd

Cover by Teagan Gavet
Copyright © 2019

Published by Bad Dog Books
www . baddogbooks . com

BAD DOG BOOKS

TABLE OF CONTENTS

For the Furry Writers' Guild and the community it fosters.

FOREWORD

This is the fifth volume of ROAR I've edited, and every year, I've learned a lot from the stories I received in the slush pile. Over the last five years, the authors who've been generous and brave enough to submit their stories to me have taught me about Scoundrels, Legends, Paradise, Resistance, and now... Community. They've shown me what these words mean to them, and I've learned—through the act of selecting which stories will compose the final anthologies—about what these words mean to me.

And yet, I don't need to read a pile of stories to know what community means to me: this book that you're holding; this is community. All of the writers, all of the readers, and all of the characters in the stories meet at a point in time and space, encapsulated by these pages. When you read these stories, you are part of that community, and this is your invitation to step in.

Go on a hike with a fisher. Learn magic with a dragon. Attend a family reunion full of gregarious cows. Face a mystery among meerkats. And celebrate Colony Day on Mars.

You're invited to it all.

-Mary E. Lowd

Let us begin our journey with a young fisher, Preston, embarking on a journey of his own to hike the Appalachian Trail.

BOURBON JACK
Linnea Capps

Flames danced in the campfire before him, but Preston could hardly enjoy the sight nor its warmth. The hissing, crackling wood had taken years to soak up the energy from the sun and grow. Now it was burning so briefly to warm the mustelid's weary paws. After only four days on the Appalachian trail he couldn't seem to muster the strength to go much further.

The fisher sighed, leaning against the heavy backpack he had been toting throughout the hike. It had sounded like such a grand adventure before embarking on his college education: hike the entire Appalachian Trail. He had bought all of the equipment the article online had said to, or more accurately his parents had bought it. He had printed off a map for directions. He had been ready for an epic tale to tell of a grand adventure in the wilderness.

He looked across the fire towards the man he was sharing it with, Tucker Hill. Preston had met the portly beaver on the Appalachian Approach Trail, both of them starting the hike together. Preston had bragged with the bravado only the young truly could to his new hiking buddy about how he would conquer the entire trail.

His boldness was quickly crushed by the Amicalola Falls, famous for the 425 steps that had to be climbed to pass. "Strenuous" the sign had warned before they started the ascent together. The sign had been an understatement. Preston had been sure he was in good enough shape for the hike. He proudly displayed the letterman jacket he had earned playing high school Lacrosse in his room at home. How could walking be so difficult?

Unfortunately the confidence he once had was now shaken and the fisher was considering his way out. He missed his bed with the warm fluffy blankets. He wondered what his friends online had been up to; he hadn't been able to send them so much as a text since he started the trip. He craved cinnamon French toast the way his mother made it, the very thought of it causing his mouth to water. He knew he could reach Neels Gap hiking the next day. It was the perfect place to sell his gear and bail as many hikers had done before him. A pang of guilt shot through him as his thoughts turned to Tucker.

The beaver had been so excited to have a hiking buddy to keep him motivated on the trail. He had been kind enough to gnaw through some logs and start the fire that night when the mustelid had been too tired to do much more than sit down. Not to mention he had even made them both dinner. Even if Tucker was technically a stranger, could Preston so easily leave without saying a word?

Preston lost himself in thoughts of somehow running into Tucker in the future after he abandoned the hike, and considering his chances of ever having to face such an awkward, unpleasant situation. He barely caught the intoxicated southern drawl of a third voice ringing loudly through the night air.

"Man whose house is on his back, town to town, around and back, give me nothin' cuz it weighs me down!"

Preston's small round ears perked up, and he turned his head towards the singing that grew louder, closer, and more rambunctious with every passing second.

"I already carry weight, of my mem'ries of the date, where my whole life got flipped upside down!"

"Tucker," Preston hissed as his tail lashed behind him. "Grab your knife, there's a drunk coming our way!"

"Relax Preston," Tucker chuckled, making no attempt to quiet his husky voice. "Not everyday you meet a legend after all!"

Tucker's comment left Preston perplexed. He had always been told to steer clear of drunks as they might try to take your money, rough you up, or worse. Did Tucker have some death wish? A dream to be part of a legendary story of a murder in the forest?

Preston was too busy being a jittery mess to fully notice the jack rabbit doing a strange combination of hopping and limping along the trail, beside where they had camped.

"Scuse' me," the jack rabbit belched around the cigarette butt hanging loosely in his maw. "Forgive my manners, can I share your fire for the night?"

Before Preston could open his own maw to say no, Tucker quickly belted out, "Of course! Not often you get to camp with Bourbon Jack!"

"Wait, you know me?" the jack rabbit queried, blearily searching for a flat spot near the fire

"Who on the trail doesn't know Bourbon Jack?" Tucker replied.

Preston certainly had no idea who this 'Bourbon Jack' was that flopped completely at ease on the ground next to him. He first noticed how the glow of the fire shone through what looked like chunks ripped out of the rabbit's long ears standing straight on his head. Preston then caught a strong whiff of alcohol, and noticed the bottle of the rabbit's namesake clutched almost desperately in his paw. The rabbit drew the bottle to the graying scruffy fur of his muzzle to take a sip.

Preston's puffed and twitchy tail was a clear signal of his discomfort to anyone with eyes. He looked down and away from their new guest, trying his best to ignore the intrusion.

"You're out from California, ain't ya?"

Preston turned to look at the jack rabbit, baffled that he had guessed so perfectly. "How…?"

"I figured if your stompin' grounds were around here, you'd be SOBO like all the other fishers, with em' livin' in Maine and all."

Preston was taken aback by how knowledgeable their new campfire mate seemed to be. He had been born and raised in California, and never had a clue he would run into others of his species during the trip. If the drunken hare was even right about that of course. Still he had no idea what SOBO meant.

"Oh yeah, we're both northbound, NOBO!" Tucker was eager to join the conversation and his voice carried with jovial enthusiasm.

Preston was secretly thankful he could figure out SOBO likely meant southbound from the beaver's comment. Once again something that it seemed everyone knew had gone completely over his head. He worried again that he had taken on more than he could chew on this hike.

"Well, if that's the case you're lucky. That sleeping bag you got looks right warm, but your friend's wouldn't last an early spring in Maine!"

Preston hissed softly under his breath. Who was this random drunk to criticize the gear so much of his parents' money had gone into?

"You think my gear is good?" Tucker cut in before the mustelid could rally a retort.

"I can only see so much by firelight, but I reckon it looks fine. Chat me up if ya meet me in Neels Gap, I can getcha the full shakedown at a discount."

Shakedown? Preston once again was quite confused, but Tucker seemed more than delighted at the offer. "It would be an honor to have your help with it. What is this, your seventh, eighth thru-hike?"

"Naw, it's my ninth!"

Tucker punctuated an impressed whistle by slapping the tree behind him with his wide tail. "Gosh, and I haven't even made it halfway, and I'm on my third try!"

Preston gently placed his paws on his temples, massaging them with a digit on each side. Hiking expert or not, he wasn't about to listen to the drunk rabbit's ramblings, especially not when he was this exhausted. Besides, he had all but decided to give up the journey after the next day anyways.

"Hey guys, if you want to talk it's fine, but I'm exhausted, probably going to try and get some extra sleep."

"Hey, don't worry son, it strikes hiker's midnight different for everyone. Not to mention it takes some folks longer gettin' their trail legs than others. Sleep! I might even promise to not start singin' again!"

His two campmates chuckled at the joke while Preston crawled over on his knees to a flat spot on the other side of the fire. He then let his heavy pack slip from his shoulders, took the sleeping bag from it and rolled it out. It hadn't looked like it was going to rain so they hadn't bothered to set up their tents. As he removed his hiking boots, he remembered that Tucker had called it 'cowboy camping.'

The fisher slipped into the sleeping bag, the sound of synthetic material slick against his fur. Despite the noise of the two older men jabbering on so close to him, the warm cocoon around him lulled him into comfort. Exhaustion won out, and Preston quickly drifted off to sleep.

A chorus of bird song accompanied by calling wood frogs formed the Appalachian alarm clock which finally roused Preston from his slumber. Sunlight had begun to fill the sky, warm orange and pinks blanketing the landscape in a call to rise. The trees shone as if they wore golden crowns, kings surveying the mountains they claimed as their own.

The fisher drowsily rubbed the sleep from his eyes, his blurred vision eventually focusing on Tucker. The beaver seemed to have remained fast asleep despite the tempting calls from nature to wake. A thought broke through the sleepy fog in Preston's mind. His ears raised, head turning to survey the camp for Bourbon Jack. There seemed to be no jack rabbit nor a spare pack of equipment in sight. As a cool breeze ruffled through Preston's fur, he breathed deeply through his nose, trying to catch the hare's scent.

He gagged, finding himself choking on an acrid combination of lingering bourbon, ashy smoke, and overpowering ammonia. He shoved his muzzle into his elbow, beginning to cough. It was quite apparent the jack rabbit had relieved himself to put out the fire the previous evening. Preston logically comprehended the idea of not wasting water in some way. However, with the strong sense of smell many species possessed, the idea of urinating so close to camp, not to mention on something warm, was incredibly rude.

The loud coughs stirred Tucker from his slumber, sleepily grumbling, "Preston you alright? Not choking are you?"

Preston was rubbing both his paws over his snout, trying his best to clean his whiskers and rid himself of the offending scent. "Fine, that damn jack rabbit pissed out the fire…"

Tucker chuckled, "Hey now, Bourbon Jack's good people. You just gotta understand he doesn't always know how to act. Doesn't really do normal society you know?"

Preston sighed, wanting to do anything to distract himself from the smell. He reached into his pack for a roll of spicy summer sausage he had stored away, and sliced through its plastic casing with a claw. While he had appreciated Tucker's meal the night before, the mustelid was no vegetarian. The beaver had cleverly rehydrated some vegetables, keeping them in a bottle full of water during the entire previous day's hike to make them cook faster. They had been quite delicious, but couldn't settle a carnivore's craving for meat.

Preston opened his maw wide, taking chunk after chunk out of the log of meat. He had given up on the idea of conserving food now that he had planned to abandon the journey. What was the point of not digging in, with only a day of hiking left ahead?

"I take it our new rabbit friend started off without us. So you ready for the hike today? If we hit Neels Gap we can get that shakedown, maybe even sleep at the hostel for the night to spoil ourselves!"

In ways, Preston envied Tucker, who had been able to simply find a bit of fallen wood near the camp to gnaw for breakfast. The beaver wouldn't need to buy food once they reached their destination later that day. Thinking of how he would be abandoning Tucker so soon, guilt tinted Preston's reply. "Oh yeah, we could probably do that."

"You sure you're doing okay?" Tucker eyed his younger trail companion, genuine concern showing across his features.

Preston's ears flattened slightly, nose twitching as it always did when he was about to lie. "I promise, Tucker, I'm okay, just that disgusting smell still has me distracted is all."

"Alright, if you say so." Tucker's eyes made it clear he was not convinced and that the fisher hadn't been confident enough in his response. Preston tried to ignore the beaver, focusing on chomping through the rest of his morning meal. He was eager to get his boots on and get to the end of this mistake of a journey.

The pain of his foot paws as they were forced into the boots made him reconsider. It reminded him how much his legs had burned the day before; the aching still radiated through his body even as he sat on the forest floor. He didn't want to deal with how heavy his backpack would be once hoisted onto his shoulders.

"Come on, Preston, roll up your sleeping bag, we gotta get going. Blood Mountain won't hike itself!"

It didn't look like Tucker was willing to let him stew in misery any longer. Preston did as he was asked, rolling up and then attaching the bag to his pack before strapping it to his back. He wasn't ready to face the ominously named summit they were due to cross. All he could remember was it was the highest mountain in all of Georgia, which did nothing to raise his spirits. With a grunt Preston stood from the ground to begin the hiking day.

Several miles into the day's hike and after Preston had replied with enough one word responses, Tucker gave up on making conversation and steadily pulled ahead of his companion. The fisher kept his head tilted down, his tail tip dusting the dirt behind him.

It didn't take long trudging at a steady pace to begin the slow rise above the tree line. The sun drenched the mountainside in dazzling light. The surrounding mountains lined the horizon like the spine of the land, as if a great unknown creature had chosen to lay there eons ago and had never risen again. From the highest points of the peak, the trees below looked almost like matchsticks scattered out onto the horizon. None of this majesty broke into the mind of Preston, who simply was not present enough to enjoy it.

The two hikers stopped, put down their packs, and ate their lunch in silence. When they were done, they picked up their packs to continue down the trail. The fisher had tried to fill his belly only to find an unfillable hole of remorse from his treatment of Tucker that day. If this was to be the last day he ever saw the beaver, being polite was the least he could do.

"So Tucker, how exactly did you know that… Jack guy?"

"Burbon Jack!" the beaver's entire body practically lit up at the chance of good conversation. "See, there's some legends on the trail. Like Long Beard, the oldest man to thru-hike. Or Yo-Yo, who did the trail back and forth without stopping twice! You read and hear about them all the time online or when you hike."

"So where did you hear of… Bourbon Jack?" the odd name felt strange leaving Preston's mouth. "And why do they all have weird names?"

"You don't like my trail name, boy?"

Preston's fur shot up on end as he jolted back, screaming in the signature way only his species was known for. The fisher's claws fully extended, his arms trembling while the racket echoed across the mountaintop.

"Good lord!" Tucker gasped, paw clutching his chest. "You nearly scared me half to death!"

"Sorry, Tucker, and put them weapons away, boy. I was just playin' ya! Heard ya coming up the trail durin' a rest and couldn't help but play possum to spook ya!"

The familiar southern drawl snapped Preston out of his instinctual fear and returned him to reality. The dusty brown of the jack rabbit's fur with the soft greens of his gear had made him blend so thoroughly into the brush that neither of the hikers had noticed him.

"What the hell!" Preston was shaking, now more out of fury than fear. His claws refused to retreat into the chocolate brown of his paws.

"Settle..." The concern was clear in Tucker's voice, slowly inching between the fisher and the hare.

"Now he's got every right to fly off the handle. I reckon that really was a bit much. Beg your pardon, wait, I never got your name!"

After their encounter the evening prior, the honest display of politeness caught the fisher off guard. "Preston... My name is Preston..."

"Bourbon Jack! But you already knew that. Look I'll make it up to ya. Just a few more miles to Neels Gap. Want a shower and dinner on me?"

Preston took a few deep breaths, his fur slowly returning to its usual state. He figured less money out of his pocket couldn't end up hurting him, right? "Fine..." he grumbled. "Just seriously, never again okay?"

"Scout's honor! Though I never was a scout." The jack rabbit mimed crossing his heart, but Preston barely noticed as he walked past his sitting form, trying to work out his anger by marching forward on the trail.

Bourbon Jack bounced up from the brush, tossing his backpack over his back before continuing down the trail, Tucker right on his heels.

"Goodness, that kid goes fast when he wansta' huh?" the rabbit commented softly so only the beaver could hear.

"Honestly never seen him at that speed before." The beaver chuckled under his breath.

With an angry Preston setting the pace, the three hikers were in sight of Neels Gap before dusk had even begun to settle in. The mustelid slowed slightly, surveying the picnic tables occupied by various species sharing meals together, their jumbled voices carrying enough that he could catch snippets of conversations. As they drew nearer he saw a stone building, he assumed to be the shop that was printed on his map. Seeing actual cars in an actual parking lot made his ears lift. He had worried he would have to hike into town, and while he had never hitchhiked before, he planned to avoid walking any further than necessary.

He found himself suddenly jerked to the left, the jack rabbit having hopped up and wrapped an elbow around his neck to pull him in close. "If you're doin' a lookie, loo take a gander at the boot tree!"

Preston's annoyed sigh was stopped in its tracks upon spotting that very tree. What must have been hundreds of boots tied at the laces hung from the thick branches of the giant oak, strung like decorations on a cobbler's strange Christmas tree. The mustelid, despite his misgivings about the old hare, couldn't help but settle his curiosity on the sight.

"Why is there such a thing as a boot tree?"

The jack rabbit cracked a grin, removing his arm from the fisher's neck. "Ya see, you go through a lotta boots on the trail if you choose to wear em.'" He pointed down at his long feet, which Preston noticed lacked any footwear. "Folks who've done the whole trail come back, toss their last pair of boots up in that tree. It's supposedly good luck. Big trail tradition, ya know?"

Preston nodded before Tucker piped up, "How did you miss stories about the boot tree reading up on the trail?"

The mustelid's ears fell, feeling too embarrassed to admit how little he had studied the trail before starting out. He kept silent, thinking about how it wouldn't matter. Soon he could slip away and return to civilization.

His pack slapped against his back, snapping his focus back again. "Get those legs kickin' up dust, boy!" the hare said, punctuated with a slap to his backpack. "Gotta getcha shaken down and see how ya look in clean fur. Get that trail stank off ya!"

The comment made Preston suddenly self-conscious, and he leaned his muzzle over, trying to inconspicuously get a sniff of his fur. He couldn't quite tell if he had gone smell blind to his own musk or if the jack rabbit had a better sense of smell than he had known.

Before he thought to ask what a shakedown even was, he was yet again jolted forward, with another slap to the back, this time from Tucker. "Come on Preston, we're almost there!"

In spite of his large frame, Tucker practically skipped ahead of the fisher on the trail; Bourbon Jack quickly did his weird limping hop to join him. For the first time in days Preston truly smiled. Their enthusiasm was strong enough even he trotted a bit faster to keep up.

Before he knew it, Preston was being pushed into a door by the old jack rabbit, into a store called Ruffin' It.

"Rusty! These boys need a shakedown, give em' the ol Bourbon Discount!"

A booming laugh cracked through the store. The bear whom Preston assumed must be Rusty stood up from behind the counter and made his way towards them. His muscles bulged under a flannel shirt, making him look like the living stereotype of a lumberjack.

"If you keep giving people discounts, I won't let you work here over the winter again!"

The hare cracked a mischievous grin. "Aw, come on now Rusty, my buddies here need a shakedown, and this one," he said, hiking a digit at Preston, "Needs himself a shower!"

Rusty chuckled, pretending to slap his palm to his brow. "Alright Jack, if you insist. Come on boys, get your gear to the counter."

Preston did as he was told, and Tucker followed suit. As they hefted their bags onto the counter the jack rabbit cut in. "Hold onto my bag too, would ya? Till my shower anyways."

"Hey can I pay for a shower too?" Tucker asked, reaching into his pants to find his wallet.

"Of course you can! Costs four bucks for the shower, six if you want your laundry done," Rusty replied. "We'll keep your gear safe, you can pick it up after the shakedown tomorrow."

Tomorrow? Preston was becoming concerned that he would have a harder time time slipping away than planned. "Excuse me…" he tried to say timidly, but he was cut of as clean clothes were shoved into his chest.

"I dug ya out some clean duds from your pack, get that grime off ya so we can get dinner!"

Preston couldn't manage another word; the old hare was pushing him towards what he assumed was the showers faster than he could get his thoughts straight. He found himself shoved into a stall. A plastic bag was dangled over the door.

"Come on now boy, getcher' dirties off, I'll pop em in for laundry."

Preston realized the rabbit wouldn't give him a moment to even consider being self-conscious and resigned himself to follow orders. He set down his clean clothes on a counter where he was surprised to find shampoo and conditioner waiting for him. He stripped, and tossed his clothes into the bag before lobbing them over the stall door.

"I swear I'd better get those back!"

He heard nothing but a whistle and big jack rabbit's feet walking away as response. He shook his head, turning to face the old metallic dial and showerhead. He turned the dial with a paw, the other paw tried to muffle the squeak that was starting to escape his maw in shock at the cold water.

He was worried he'd be embarrassed yet again by making such a noise, but soon the never ending waterfall of warm water cascading over his fur relaxed him. The steam seemed to float his troubled thoughts away, the warmth seeping into his bones. He lost himself in the warm relief, muscles that had not felt good for days seeming to finally cease aching.

"Hey, you finishing in there soon?"

Preston jumped slightly, the unfamiliar voice startling him from his stupor. He realized more time had passed than he had thought. "Oh sorry! Just rinsing out the shampoo!"

He hadn't even begun to actually clean himself but quickly grabbed the bottle and got to work. A paw full of shampoo quickly became a thick lather rubbed over his water-darkened coffee-colored fur. He ran his paws over his slick form, his lithe body being fully revealed once again as the suds sank down the drain.

A few minutes more to condition, followed by a minute in the walk-in blow drier later, his fur was fluffier than he had seen it since the beginning of the trail. His fur splayed where the sleeves of his clean t-shirt met it, the fur of his legs almost cushioning himself against the denim of his jeans.

"Hey boy!"

Preston had barely been able to step out of the stall before the old timer had somehow found him once again. Properly relaxed, he was ready to deal with the hare's antics. "Yes, Jack? Where's Tucker?"

"*Bourbon* Jack. Jack's for those close. He's fine, I wanna show ya somethin!"

Preston found himself being dragged out by a wrist firmly grasped in the rabbit's paw. "Hey slow down, what about my boots?"

"They need replacin' anyways. Now come on boy, you don't wanna miss this!"

As they headed to the front door, Preston looked back pleadingly toward Rusty only to find the bear shaking his head with a smile that said he'd be giving no help to stop whatever was happening. Once they gotten a few feet out the door, Preston noticed the jack rabbit looking suspiciously left to right, eyeing the other hikers as if the two were spies in a foreign land.

"Now listen up boy, we're walkin' nice an' casual-like. When I give the say so, you're runnin into the woods to follow. Gotcha?"

Preston's ears laid flat against his head, concern growing. He attempted to act casual while being dragged past the other hikers who were enjoying meals at the picnic tables. His stomach growled in protest at the sight.

"But…" He paused, remembering he had been asked to use the full, if awkward name. "But Bourbon-"

Once again he was interrupted. Before he had time to remind the old hare that he had been promised dinner, Bourbon Jack limped at full speed into the woods. Preston hesitated. Did he really want to follow what he had the sinking suspicion was a crazy old man? He surprised himself, finding he was putting one foot paw in front of the other, some inner instinct pushing him into a sprint to catch up.

"No one's following us, right boy?"

Preston turned his head to look, ears at full alert. While there seemed to be a trail ahead of them, the entrance had been whatever brush he had just crashed through. There would be no chance of being seen now that it was behind them.

"Why the hell would anyone be following us, old man?"

Bourbon Jack flashed a thumbs up behind him, keeping up the quick pace. After several minutes of running, the hare finally began to slow down as they approached what looked to be a large rock face ahead.

At this point, Preston felt sure he'd been lured here to die, only to be found as bones years later by some poor hiker lost on the trail. But then he saw the rabbit find a small paw hold, then a narrow foot paw hold, before starting to slide across the rock. The hare was headed over a ledge to his right that Preston, too focused on keeping up, had completely missed before.

"Come on, boy! Just a bit further!"

Preston carefully looked over the ledge without stepping closer. A chill shot down his spine to the tip of his tail at the sight. If the old hare were to fall from this height there wasn't a remote chance of surviving.

"Old man, you're going to die up there! What the hell are you doing!"

"Call me old man one more time an' I'll climb right back over there and whup ya! Now come on! Fishers have been the best climbers in the Appalachian woods for hundreds of years. You gonna let an' old hare beatcha at the game you were built for?"

Preston's entire body trembled. He feared if he didn't stop Jack—no, Bourbon Jack—now, the old man would plummet to his death while he watched. Yet he was frozen, unable to move.

Bourbon Jack was slowly closing around the corner of the rock. "Stop lookin' as lost as last years Easter egg. You followed me this far, didn't ya? Come on boy, let those instincts kick in!"

Preston didn't know how the hare knew what had driven him to the forest to begin with. It all seemed insane to him. He looked over to the hare and saw nothing but the fullest of confidence, not only in himself but also in the fisher he was looking so intently at.

Before Preston could stop himself, he ran forward. His claws sank effortlessly into the moss on the rock face, foot paws slipping with perfect ease into their holds. He found himself climbing the rock face as if he had done this thousands of times, losing himself in the focus of the task to abate the fear of falling.

Once he rounded the corner, he pounced to land on a large stretch of flat rock in front of a cave, panting desperately without taking in his surroundings.

"Boy, you're gonna miss out on life if you keep closing your eyes to it like that."

The mustelid looked up and found his jaw dropping outside his control. The clouds looked as though they blushed at the warm touch of the setting sun. The fiery orb had inched close to the horizon, cut into by the mountain ranges in view. From those wounds the sun seemed to dye the heavens in a swirling sea of oranges and reds, tinted with a hint of violet. The silhouettes of birds soared over the trees, branches dancing gently in the breeze.

"Come on, sit down proper boy. I got the dinner I promised."

Preston slowly made his way over to the hare who procured a ziplock baggie packed with sandwiches from his jacket pocket. "Here, The Beast gave me these. Peanut butter, bacon, and dried cherry sandwiches. Claimed they're the best meal the trail has to offer! Peanut butter sticks to the roof of your maw like no other though. Of course no bacon for the veggie eatin' creature, so I took mine and put it in yours."

Bourban Jack held out the two packed sandwiches in his paw. Preston took them eagerly, popped the bag open and started to stuff the stacked sandwiches into his muzzle.

"Finally got your trail legs I see. Not hurtin' so much now are they?"

Preston paused, pulling his meal from his maw. It was the second time the hare had seemed to read his mind that night. While his legs were sore, the pain was slight, perfectly manageable.

"How did you…?"

"It just takes longer for others than some. Don't you worry bout' it."

They both dug into their meal. The mustelid found it as difficult as suggested to get the peanut butter from the roof of his maw and smacked his lips together loudly.

The two hikers enjoyed the view in silence until a realization drifted into Preston's mind. He was reminded of a question he hadn't got answered earlier.

"Bourbon Jack? What *is* with all the weird names people have around here?"

The old hare looked thoughtful. "The gal who made our dinner, The Beast? I hear tell she earned her trail name by being able to hike faster an' farther than most boys your age in their prime. The woman's turnin' fifty soon! She's a beast on the trail, so she's The Beast to those that hike it."

Preston chuckled softly at the story. "So I can name myself whatever and people will call me that?"

The jack rabbit guffawed. "You really didn't read a thang before hikin', didja boy? A trail name has to be given, earned by doin' somethin' on the trail. Comes with a good story, somethin' to reminisce over. It's the biggest favor I ever done you that your name ain't Screamer for that gawdawful racket what came from your maw when I frightened ya!"

The fisher felt the heat rise in his cheeks, but the confidence he had gained climbing alongside the rock face gave him the courage to tease the hare back. "So how'd you get a name like Bourbon Jack then? Is it because you stumble through the woods with a bottle of it every night like how we met?"

The hare was briefly taken aback by Preston's newfound confidence, but it didn't stop him long. "Boy, you think my parents were cruel enough to name a youngin' after their species? Can you imagine the teasin'? Naw, Jack ain't my real name." He paused, scratching behind one of his long ears. "You're only half right. You see, the bottle has been a friend to me for many years. One day I was hiking with some strangers and a big ol bottle full of bourbon somehow fell out of my pack an' by some miracle didn't break when it rolled down into the rocks below. I was right determined not to waste my hard earned liquor and started climbin' down to get it. *'It's only bourbon, Jack!'* one of em yelled at me, not knowin' my God given name. After grabbin' the bottle it stuck like crazy glue and I've been going by Bourbon Jack ever since."

Preston couldn't help but chuckle. He had barely begun to know the man he shared this impressive view with but the name seemed to fit his personality perfectly. "So Bourbon Jack, when are we headed back to the store? We gotta sleep sometime, right?"

The old hare cocked an eye at the fisher. "Even I ain't crazy enough to climb them rocks with night comin' in."

"So how are we supposed to keep warm and sleep? Do we light a fire?" the mustelid queried.

The hare looked as though Preston had killed a close relative. "If you light a fire an' folks find my secret spot from the smoke I'll make sure your name is listed as a trail murder." The old hare seemed so serious for a brief moment Preston was unsure if he was actually kidding.

"Alright, no fire! But how the hell are we staying warm then?"

"Cave's warmer than you'd think, keeps most of the wind out. Moss makes a pretty soft bed there too. Don't be worryin', I've slept here during four of my thru-hikes. I don't feel the rain comin' in my knee, we'll be fine."

The old hare stood and shuffled into the cave. Preston knew he should follow while there was still enough light left to find a comfortable spot to sleep. He saw Bourbon Jack settle in, likely the spot where he had slept in those four hikes prior. With a bit of experimenting, the mustelid was able to wiggle himself into a comfortable position. His head rested on an angled rock, giving him a perfect view as the sun gave way to velvety darkness dotted with an uncountable number of stars.

"Neath' the shinin' of the moon, in a warm a gloomy June, hangin' there in that Kentucky sky…"

Preston's keen ears heard the old hare faintly singing the rest of the words to the very song he'd sung when they had first met. The jack rabbit sighed softly before continuing. "Says she's gone and been untrue, sends me 'way and packin soon, nothin left than to move on and cry…"

The final notes of the verse drifted weakly into the night. Before Preston could gather the courage to ask the old hare why he kept singing that same song, he heard the steady breathing that only comes with sleep from across the cave.

Preston sighed softly, another question left needing answers. This time however, he felt comfort knowing that he could ask tomorrow. He closed his eyes, the backdrop of crickets and wind rustled leaves lulling him into slumber.

The sunrise rivaled the beauty of the sunset from the night before, and somehow that crafty jack rabbit had breakfast hidden in another pocket of his jacket. It was simple, cheddar cheese, sunflower seeds, and dried pineapple for dessert.

"Calories," the hare put simply. Preston wasn't about to argue. Salty and sweet played jovially over his palate, the tang of cheddar a perfect complement to their flavors. When the meal was done, Bourbon Jack carefully made sure all of the baggies and wrappers were collected. Then the two hikers confidently returned across the rockface and walked back into Neels Gap.

As they entered Ruffin' It, they were met by a familiar beaver, whose face turned from crestfallen to beaming upon seeing the two enter the store. "I couldn't find you guys anywhere! I thought you must have abandoned me until Rusty here told me your gear was still in the shop!"

Guilt overwhelmed the young mustelid, having forgotten his plan to do just that. The idea of leaving his buck-toothed hiking companion almost crushed him on the spot.

As it seemed to be his fate in the shop at this point, Preston's thoughts were interrupted. He felt a pack being pushed at him over the counter.

"Come on, now!" Rusty's voice was filled with pride. "Learn why Ruffin' It has the best shakedown on the trail!"

Preston looked over his gear, or what he had assumed was his gear. It wasn't the bag he had been carrying; the sleeping bag seemed to have been replaced, and he could only imagine what had happened to the gear inside. Not to mention the hikers poles he hadn't owned before, attached to its side.

"Excuse me, I don't think this is my bag."

The jack rabbit gently tapped the fisher on the back of his head. "Yes it is, boy. Now Rusty, no forgettin' to give him his money!"

Money? Preston found himself even more confused as a small stack of bills was placed in his paw. "You had some very expensive gear," Rusty explained. "It was heavier than anyone should need. We replaced parts of it with lighter equipment that's just as good of quality. It should hold you over well. We'll sell the other gear we can, which is why you get that cash. Oh yeah! I noticed you were way too low on food, so I scavenged some things from the hiker's box and packed them in for you."

"Aw, come on now, no more jabberin', try it on boy!"

Preston carefully slid his arms into the backpack and hoisted it on his back. He audibly gasped, bending and unbending his knees to marvel at just how light the pack had become.

"See there, boy? You'd be amazed what weighs you down. Say good riddance to the things you don't need, it makes you truly lighter."

Preston eyed the hare as Tucker tried on his own pack, discussing the new contents with Rusty. He saw the jack rabbit with a serious expression that looked unusual on his rugged features. Preston was waved towards the door by the old hare, and almost reached it before Rusty's resounding voice filled his ears. "Hey now, don't forget your new boots!"

Preston sat down on a bench just outside the shop and busied himself with trying on his new boots as Tucker and Bourbon Jack chatted alongside him.

"You know, we could make Unicoi Gap today if we put on the hustle and the creek don't rise!"

"At my size? Come on, Bourbon Jack, you must be going trail crazy!" Tucker chuckled, rubbing his rotund belly.

"Aw, come on now, where's your spirit? Whatcha' think, boy?"

Preston stopped flexing his foot paws in what might be the most comfortable pair of boots he had ever worn in his life and looked up at the knowing eyes of Bourbon Jack. The hare knew just as well as the mustelid that if he were going to bail, this was his last chance.

Preston looked behind him towards the parking lot. Civilization was a mere awkward conversation followed by a car ride away. The temptation crept into his mind. No more nights slept in sleeping bags, though the views were beautiful. No more strange trail meals, but deep down he craved another sandwich from The Beast. On that note, he had never even gotten a proper trail name.

Preston returned his gaze to his companions, the words the jack rabbit had spoken just moments before in the store playing through his mind. *You'd be amazed at what weighs you down.* He thought of all his fears, the uncertainty of the journey, the guilt he would feel from thoughts of Tucker, the disappointment he would feel giving up, and the burning curiosity of just why Bourbon Jack sang that same song every night. He realized they would weight heavier than any pack he could ever carry on his shoulders.

He sprung up from the bench, stretching his arms out wide over his head, before grabbing onto the hiking poles he had so recently acquired. "What are we waiting for?" he said, taking his first confident stride back towards the trail.

Wendel has his hands full with a dragon and collection of eager forest animals who all expect the overwhelmed wizard to teach them magic.

Squonk and the Horde of Apprentices

Pete Butler-Davis

On his first day as Wendel the Wizard's apprentice, Squonk the Dragon was learning his first lesson:

Fire was *beautiful*.

Fire glowed red and orange and yellow and danced around and smelled nice and went "Crackle!" and "Pop!" and was, by far, the most fascinating thing Squonk had yet seen in his young life.

Most dragons learn to love fire as soon as they come out of their eggs, when their parents celebrate their birth by spitting great gouts of flame into the sky; dragons often use fire to express joy. Or anger. Or surprise. Or boredom. Or the fact that they're still breathing. Dragons *really* like fire.

But Squonk didn't even know he *could* breathe fire. That's because his adoptive mother, a little blue bird named Mrs. Tweedle-Chirp, didn't know he could breathe fire, either—and even if she did, she certainly would have forbid him from ever doing it. Like most forest creatures, Mrs. Tweedle-Chirp didn't like fire one little bit.

But her not-so-little boy was, indeed, a dragon. And while there are some things you *can* teach out of a dragon...

"Isn't it beautiful?" Squonk asked a raccoon named Slowfingers. Slowfingers was Squonk's best friend, which was why he was currently sitting on the edge of Squonk's hat.

"Uhm," Slowfingers said as the pile of logs snapped and sizzled and burned, "dunno if I'd say 'beautiful,' exactly. There's another word. Can't think of it, it's right there on the tip of my snout…"

Like Squonk, Slowfingers was Wendel the Wizard's apprentice. Wendel stood behind them in the glade near the largest tree in the world with all his other apprentices—Whitepaw the Wolf, and Miss Pounce the Bobcat, and Mrs. Honeylog the Bear, and Bristletongue the Raccoon, and… and a whole *lot* of animals, all of them wearing the wide twiggy upside-down-nest hats that showed they were learning how to be wizards.

Squonk and Slowfingers were in charge of "building the fire" so they could all "brew a potion." Wendel was explaining to his new apprentices just what this meant, and what it had to do with being a wizard. He was starting with what he called "Lesson 1: What Is Magic?"

Squonk had no idea what magic was; so far, he only had a list of what it *wasn't*.

"No," Wendel said, "the cauldron won't actually catch on fire!"

"And that's because it's magic, right?" asked Mr. Snuffles, a badger.

"No!" Wendel said. "It's not magic; it's metal! Metal doesn't burn!"

The fire got bigger. Squonk put another log into it.

"But the *fire*, that's magic, right?" asked a sparrow named Flit.

"No," Wendel grumbled. "Fire isn't magic. We've been over that already. Several times."

"Oh, come on!" said a raccoon named Bristletongue. "I've never seen anything like that before! It's gotta be magic!"

Squonk didn't like Bristletongue; he was mean and liked insulting Slowfingers. Squonk would have told him to shut up, but the fire was so beautiful he forgot how to speak. Fire got bigger the more stuff you put into it! This fire had started from nothing, and had already grown as tall as Wendel! He put a few more logs in.

"Fire isn't magic!" Wendel said. Again. "Fire is perfectly natural! Magic is—"

"'Perfectly natural?'" asked an old bear named Mrs. Honeylog. "I've seen this 'fire' thing before, Mr. Wizard, and I assure you it's bad news. Not 'natural' at all!"

Squonk had no idea what Mrs. Honeylog could possibly be talking about. So he started feeding more logs into the fire one after the other, and it grew, and grew, and grew…

"Can it kill you?" asked Despairing Nevermore, a raven with blue feathers around her eyes. "I bet fire can kill lots of things, can't it?" Ravens were weird.

"When it gets out of control," Wendel said, "then yes, it's a lot of trouble. But that's not—"

"AreWeAllWizardsYet?" ChpChpTkTk and his squirrel friends were back. They'd been running in and out of the glade all afternoon, listening to Wendel until they got bored—which didn't take long.

Wendel made a kind of growly-whimpery noise.

"Say, Squonk?" Slowfingers said as Squonk piled more logs into the fire. "I think I figured out what word I was looking for."

"Eh?" Squonk said, barely hearing him.

"'Terrifying.' Fire is terrifying. I'm, uh, gonna run for my life now and hide in a hole, okay?"

"Uh-huh," Squonk said, his mind deep within the flames as Slowfingers scampered down his neck and off his shoulder to the ground. Wow, how big could a fire *get*? He wanted to find out!

"Where are you going, DUMBfingers?" asked Bristletongue.

"Hey!" Wendel said from behind him as Slowfingers ran off. "Where do you think you're—GYAH!"

And at that moment, Wendel's gathered horde of animal apprentices got their very first demonstration of an actual magic spell, and Squonk learned his first actual lesson about magic:

Magic is *wet*.

***

Once the fire had been extinguished, Wendel the Wizard bade his 'apprentices' good day and stepped inside the largest tree in the world, where he'd carved-out a home for himself. He was calm and dignified, the way a powerful wizard ought to be. He walked into his living room and put his voice in his pocket.

And then, he started shouting.

He didn't make a sound—that was the point of tucking his voice safely in his pocket, after all.

He threw his pointy wizard's hat (a *real* hat made from *cloth*—faded, worn blue cloth that had seen much better days, but *cloth* just the same and not grass and twigs and mud and other such nonsense) across the room. He pulled at his hair, stomped his foot, and smacked his head against the wooden wall. He said… well, it's hard to say precisely what words he was shouting, his voice being in his pocket and all. But whatever he said, it was probably very, very rude.

After carrying on like this much longer than a wizard who was either calm or dignified ought to have gone on, he took a deep breath, flopped down into a wooden chair, and put his voice back in his throat where it belonged.

"It's madness," he moaned. He hadn't even wanted *one* apprentice, let alone… merciful gods, how many 'apprentices' had he just saddled himself with anyway?

His brain realized that counting his 'apprentices' would just make Wendel very depressed and refused to work on the subject any more. (Wizard brains are often that annoying kind with minds of their own that think about what they *want* to think about and are tough to persuade to do anything else.)

He could quit. He *should* quit. Tomorrow, he should just march out there and tell that infuriating menagerie that the very notion of a bunch of… of birds and raccoons and bears and wolves and things being wizards was just too absurd to even discuss, and they should just be on their way and do… whatever it was they did when they weren't annoying him.

"But Wendel," his colossal green neighbor Squonk would say, "why not? They did all the stuff you said *I* had to do to become a wizard! And each and every one of them is my bestest friend in the whole entire world, and if you don't give me a good reason why they can't become wizards too, I'm going to get very angry and set you on fire and eat you! Grr!"

To be fair, Squonk would never actually say anything like that last bit, and Wendel knew it. But Wendel had met other dragons; the threat of Squonk growing angry, setting him on fire, and eating him always felt very real to him, even if Squonk's mother had raised him to not eat anything that could talk back.

Ah, yes. Mrs. Tweedle-Chirp, Squonk's belligerent twittering little adoptive mother. "Blah blah blah," she'd say. "Wizards are nothing but trouble and blah blah blah and that makes you a very bad person because you *promised* you'd teach him wizardry and reading and arithmetic and history and geography and a whole bunch of other things that I didn't even know I was asking for because I'm just a stupid tiny blue bird—who keeps outsmarting you! BLAH!"

Wendel knew perfectly well that Mrs. Tweedle-Chirp sounded nothing like this, either. But imagining her saying "blah" a lot soothed him, for some odd reason.

Wendel was tired of being outsmarted, and far too proud to go back on his word.

"If you can't go around something," his own teacher had once said, "go through it!" So, what was the way through this?

Wendel had no idea.

But he hoped that if he sat in his chair long enough, the answer would find him.

***

In the upper branches of the largest tree in the world rested a bird's nest built for a dragon. The tiny blue bird responsible for the nest fluttered around within it. She hadn't built the nest herself, of course—she'd been the one who taught its builder, her son, everything he knew about nest-making.

Mrs. Tweedle-Chirp was so excited. Squonk would be back soon from his first day of learning to be a wizard! Was he actually a wizard yet? She had no idea if learning to be a wizard only took you a single day, or two, or even ten!

She heard the enormous whooshing noise of her little boy's wings. She flew over to her tiny corner of the nest and tucked some twigs back into place, as though she'd been tending to it all day.

"Hey, Mom." The enormous branch bent as Squonk settled in. When she'd been a young bird, Mrs. Tweedle-Chirp would never have imagined a branch this big bending for any reason! You learned all sorts of things when your son was a dragon.

"Hello, dear," she said, calmly. Funny, Squonk didn't look nearly as excited as he'd been when he left that morning. In fact, he looked very wet. "How was your first day of learning to be a wizard?"

Squonk adjusted the silly upside-down nest on his head. "Not so good."

Mrs. Tweedle-Chirp frowned. She had her suspicions about that Wendel! "And why do you say that?"

And Squonk told her all about his day, about how he and his friend Slowfingers had spent all their time building a fire and how Wendel had put it out all at once, and had seemed very upset doing it.

She didn't like fire, not one little bit; fire was nothing but trouble. But she'd long believed much the same about wizards; maybe they had something to do with each other?

"So, what does fire have to do with being a wizard?" she asked.

"Dunno," Squonk said. "But it's not magic. It *looks* magic, and beautiful, and pretty, and dancey, and goes 'pop' and has the most wonderful smell—"

"Dear," she said, "are you sure Wendel is really teaching you magic? That he's not just fluttering you around?"

Squonk nodded. "He's trying, I think. You know how he looks when he's unhappy?"

"I believe I do. All red and scrunched?"

"Yeah. He looked like that a lot. And him turning all red and scrunchy isn't magic, either. I asked."

Hmm. Mrs. Tweedle-Chirp couldn't abide trickery, but saw no shame in honest failure. Unless it was trickery *disguised* as honest failure... which that Wendel was no doubt sneaky enough to think of. Still, she wasn't *certain* he was breaking his word...

"Well," she said, "perhaps it's a bit harder than he thought."

"Yeah, probably," Squonk said.

"Then we should be patient," she said, as much to herself as to her boy. "He's a very clever fellow; I'm sure he'll figure something out."

"I think it's 'cuz there are so many of us 'prentices and just the one of him," Squonk said. "I bet..."

And all of a sudden, Squonk's face had that funny look he got when a particularly interesting idea hit him in the head, all bug-eyed and puckered.

"That's it! Wendel just needs some help! Gotta go, bye Mom!"

And he was gone, leaving behind a gust of wind and a gently swaying nest.

Mrs. Tweedle-Chirp had to give Wendel credit for one thing: her son seemed to do an awful lot of thinking on account of him. She suspected this was a very good thing.

***

As Wendel sat in his chair all night and all morning, pondering just what the blazes he was going to do the next day, a good answer did *not* find him.

A really nasty headache, however, did.

The headache dug-in its claws as he fixed himself some coffee, put his hat back on, and stumbled out into the glade outside his home, where his accursed horde of apprentices sat waiting for him under the noonday sun.

The headache gave his brain a playfully cruel swat.

"Hi, Wendel!" Squonk said. The other animals made growly, chirpy, chittery greetings as well.

Perhaps I could forget the spell that lets me understand what they're saying? he thought. *Surely I've got a forgetting spell lying around somewhere in my library—how dangerous would it be to use it on myself? All right, 'extremely,' but still...*

"Good afternoon." Wendel sighed. Any moment now he was going to think of something that would prevent today from being the same flaming disaster as yesterday. Any moment...

"I've got some great news!" Squonk said.

Wendel's headache twinged; hoping the news would actually be 'great' seemed like a waste of perfectly good hope. "Yes?"

"I got you some assistants!" Squonk nodded to a nearby shrub with three owls perched on it.

Wendel didn't know *why* things were about to get worse, just that they were.

Squonk said, "I asked them if they'd like to help you teach magic, and they said yes! Isn't that great?"

Wendel pinched the bridge of his nose while his headache cackled. "Squonk, what makes you think they know any magic *at all*, let alone enough to help me teach it?"

"Because owls know everything!" Squonk said it as if it were the most obvious thing in the world.

"*Everybody* knows that owls know everything," said the annoying not-in-Squonk's-hat raccoon.

"How wonderful," Wendel said.

"This is Mr. Horribly," Squonk said, nodding towards the screech owl. "He can see the future!"

"I have seen your future!" Mr. Horribly proclaimed.

The entire glade fell silent.

"And you… shall DIE!"

The gathered creatures gasped.

"HORRRRRRRRIBLY!"

"Whoa," Squonk said. "I'm so sorry, Wendel."

Wendel now feared that if he took his hand away from his nose, the headache would thwack his brain clean out of his skull. "Thank you, honored oracle," he said. "I'm sure—"

"WhatsAnOracle?" came a chittering voice. Oh merciful gods, the squirrels were back.

"An oracle is somebody who can see the future," Wendel said. "Squonk, please—"

"AnOracleIsSomebodyWhoCanWHATNow?"

Wendel glared at the squirrels and gave serious thought to setting them on fire—but turned back to the owls instead. "And you two? I suppose you also have names and alleged areas of expertise?"

The snowy owl, Mr. Treespeaker, claimed to know all there was to know about trees. And the barn owl, Mrs. Loudwater, specialized in everything.

Hoping that they at least wouldn't make the situation any worse, Wendel swallowed his pride and got on with it.

"All right," he said. "No practical demonstration today. Let's just focus on the basics. Lesson 1: What Is Magic?"

"Flying is magic," Mrs. Loudwater proclaimed. "And you should never think about flying while you're doing it. You'll forget *how* you're doing it, and that hurts."

"Trees hate you when you're flying," Mr. Treespeaker said. "They get jealous. That's why they hurt you when you crash into them."

"They'll hurt you... HORRRRRRIBLY!"

Wendel's headache doubled-over laughing at him.

***

Mrs. Tweedle-Chirp had long believed that wizards were nothing but trouble, and actually meeting a wizard had not done a lot to change her opinion. So when she went to check on Squonk that afternoon, she was disappointed—but *not* particularly surprised—to find Wendel missing. In his place, a trio of owls babbled their usual owlish balderdash to her son—and to some of his friends. And many of their neighbors. And—goodness! There were going to be an awful lot of wizards in the forest when Wendel was done.

She found him sitting on a root with his back to their tree, hat in his hands, staring at a little patch of plants he grew—he called it his 'garden.'

Wendel started speaking as she perched on a beanstalk. "In some lands," he said, "the bluebird is a symbol of happiness and contentment. I honestly have no idea why."

Mrs. Tweedle-Chirp chose to pretend that *wasn't* an insult. "A good day to you too, Mr. Wizard. May I ask what you're doing here and not teaching my son, as we agreed?"

"Because I don't have to!" He gave her a smile so big and fake that she took a startled hop backwards. "The owls have taken over for me! I just stepped out for a quick rest while they instruct your son—and half the forest. I'm sure they have everything well in hand! Or well in beak. Or wing. Whatever."

Mrs. Tweedle-Chirp, who was *not* accustomed to sarcasm, wasn't sure what to make of this. "Did you actually... *listen* to what the owls were saying?"

"Pure genius, every word!" he said. "Why, I had no idea that green mice taste exactly like frogs! Or that fish stay in the water because they're afraid of what the trees might do to them! Or that when when the sun rises tomorrow, it shall rise... horribly!"

"*Why* have you left my son's instruction to owls?"

Wendel sighed. "Because they cannot possibly be doing a worse job of it than I was."

Mrs. Tweedle-Chirp cocked her head at Wendel. "Mr. Wizard, I think you're exaggerating."

"Mrs. Tweedle-Chirp, I think you're mistaken. Taking on all those animals as apprentice wizards… it's just not possible!"

Mrs. Tweedle-Chirp glared at him without a trace of sympathy. When you raise a dragon as your son, other peoples' notions of what isn't possible tend to sound rather lazy.

"Perhaps there's some piece of magic you could use," she suggested.

"Won't work," he said. "If you're going to teach somebody something, you have to do it the hard way. You can't just magically pound ideas directly into somebody's head. The ideas don't stay. And it's bad for the head."

"Well, I'm sure you'll think of something." She used the voice she used to let people know that she was giving them an order, but being polite about it. "You gave me your word, and I expect you to find a way to keep it."

Wendel scowled at her. "I'm sure I will," he said.

"Perhaps you're going about this the wrong way," she offered. "Not that I mean to tell you your business, but maybe teaching them *all* to be wizards at once is a bit more than should be asked of one fellow."

"And how do you propose I do it, then?"

"Why, a few at a time, of course!" she said. "Then once you've got them all wizarded-up, you instruct the next bunch."

Wendel gave her a look that was downright strange. His eyes were wide, and his mouth hung open. He looked quite silly.

"Mrs. Tweedle-Chirp," he said, "how long do you think it will take me to teach your son—or anybody else—to become a wizard?"

"Well, never having learned to be a wizard, I'm certain I don't know," she said. "A few days at least. Maybe even as many as ten."

Wendel's eyes got huge. "As many as…?"

"That's not including the time it will take to teach him of the world at large, of course," she said. "Don't think I've forgotten about *that* part of our arrangement. I expect teaching him that may well take even longer than the wizard-y bits."

Wendel gave her a whole lot of that strange look before finally saying, "Yes. Maybe even *twenty* days."

He got to his feet. "Thank you, madam." And he strode back towards the clearing where her son was waiting.

"You're welcome." She flew away not entirely certain of what he'd been thanking her *for*, but Wendel was so bad at being polite she though she ought to encourage him.

***

Squonk learned many interesting things that day. He learned that trees are shy and will only grow bigger when you're not looking at them. He learned that if you hoot at the moon long enough, it will get scared and hide. He learned that anything that happens is probably going to happen horribly.

But he didn't know how any of this related to being a wizard.

"Perhaps," Slowfingers suggested, "trees hate magic?"

"Or magic hates trees?"

"Maybe magic makes things happen horribly?"

Squonk thought about that one; it certainly would be consistent with Mr. Horribly's teachings. "But then why are we learning it?"

"Dunno," Slowfingers said. "This is like chasing my own tail. Whenever I get closer, it just gets further away!"

Squonk, who had a chaseable tail of his own, knew exactly what Slowfingers meant. "Magic sure is tricky."

Wendel walked back into the glade with a determined look on his face. Squonk opened his mouth to ask if magic was like chasing your tail, but remembered Wendel didn't have a tail of his own. And then Wendel was talking.

Loudly.

"All right!" Wendel said, cutting off Mr. Treespeaker's lecture on deceiving oak trees. "Thank you *very much* for your help, but I think I can handle things from here. Fly along now."

"I'm not done speaking," Mr. Treespeaker said, "and I don't like being interrupted."

"And you have been interrupted... HORRRRRRIBLY!"

"Did you know," Wendel said, "that Mrs. Tweedle-Chirp thinks owls don't know what they're talking about?"

The entire glade gasped—especially Squonk!

"Doesn't that *offend* you?" Wendel asked the owls.

It most certainly did! Squonk could tell from how their feathers were ruffled.

"Doesn't that offend you *so much* that you want to *fly off* and have a few words with her?"

Why yes it did! Though Squonk couldn't help but notice the three owls flew south instead of towards Squonk's home, which was a long ways straight up.

"All right, apprentices." Wendel rubbed his hands together. "I have a question for you. Who can tell me what a *year* is?"

"I can!" Bristletongue said. "A year means the same thing as 'forever.'"

"Wrong!" Wendel shouted triumphantly.

Bristletongue folded his arms. "Am not. A year is—"

"I said WRONG, you smarmy little ring-tailed rodent!" Wendel's voice sounded furious, but his face looked like he was overjoyed. "*This* is a year!"

Wendel drew a circle in the air, and because it was magic, it stayed there. He pointed and a little glowing dot like a firefly appeared at the bottom of the circle.

"Now this," he said, "is where we are right now. Summer! Middle of summer!"

"That's not summer," Bristletongue said. "That's—"

"SHUT. UP." Wendel gave Bristletongue a long look; Bristletongue got embarrassed, and tried to make himself smaller.

"Summer!" Wendel returned his attention to the circle hanging in the air. He moved a finger, and the little glowing dot started following the circle. "Nice, warm, sunny summer. Day after day of it until—"

He made a gesture, and all of a sudden all the leaves on the trees around them slowly turned all different shades of orange, yellow, red.

"Autumn," Wendel said. "Days get shorter. Weather gets colder. Leaves change colors, and fall." And indeed, the leaves started falling. It was so impressive that not even Bristletongue had anything to say.

"And then it gets even *colder*," Wendel said, "because it's winter, and the snows come." And it started snowing! Though it wasn't actually cold—and Squonk couldn't feel the snow, not even when there was suddenly a layer of it on everything. Must have been part of the magic.

"But the snow stops, and it melts." The snow stopped falling and vanished as suddenly as it had come. "And then all the leaves grow back." And they did! "And it's spring." And it was!

The little glowing dot was still going around the circle. "And it gets warmer and warmer," Wendel said, "until we're back to *exactly* where we started from—middle of summer." And the little dot stopped right where it had started. "*That* is a year. Now then, who can tell me what a 'year' has to do with learning magic?"

Nobody said anything.

"What?" Wendel said. "Nobody? But yesterday, you all had so *much*—"

"Is that how long it takes?" Slowfingers asked.

Wendel's head snapped towards Squonk. "Who said that?"

"I did," Slowfingers said meekly from Squonk's hat. "I'm sorry, I thought you wanted somebody to say something."

Squonk knew that *couldn't* be the answer... could it?

Wendel said, "You're not quite right, Mr.... hat-raccoon."

Whew! Squonk thought. Of course magic didn't take a year to learn! Nothing could take—

"Learning to be a wizard," Wendel said, "takes *yearsssss.*" Wendel held on to the 's' like a very happy snake.

The creatures in the glade gasped.

Squonk couldn't have heard that right! "*Years?* As in, like *a* year, but even more than just one?"

"Yes," Wendel said. "What, did you think I'd just say some magic word and, poof! You'd all be wizards?!"

"Well," Squonk said, "actually, yeah, kinda."

Wendel opened his mouth to yell some more, then snapped it shut. "It doesn't work that way."

"Then how does it work?" Slowfingers asked.

"You have to *learn,*" Wendel said. "You have to think. I'll show you how things work, you'll help me with spells and potions and such, and then you'll have to do them yourselves. And guess what? You'll do them wrong! Because *everybody* does them wrong on the first try! And on the second, and usually on the third, too! And eventually you'll run out of ways to do it wrong and maybe—just *maybe*—you'll actually start doing it right!"

"Whoa," Squonk said. "That sounds hard!"

"Yes it is," Wendel snarled. "And guess what? It's even worse than you think! Because your mother asked me to, because of a promise I made to a *little blue bird*, I'm going to be teaching you *all kinds* of other things! I'm going to teach you history! Geography! Teach you about the world and the creatures and the people outside of this forest! I'm going to teach you math! And…" His chest heaved. "I'm going to teach you how to read. May the gods help me, I'm actually going to teach you mad creatures how to *read.*"

"WhatsTeachYouHowToRead?" asked ChpChpTkTk.

"Nothing you need to worry about," Wendel growled, "because in order to learn to read, you actually have to listen to somebody *without* getting bored halfway through. And so help me, if you ask me another question I just answered *five seconds ago*, I'm going to set your tail on fire."

"WhyDon'tINeedToWor—" ChpChpTkTk stopped, thought about it for a second, and then ran back into the trees, followed by his squirrel friends.

"Becoming a wizard," Wendel said, "requires more than just a silly hat. It takes work and lots of it. And after all that hard work, it might turn out that you don't like it, or that you're not any good at it."

"So why bother?" asked Mrs. Honeylog, the bear.

"Because if you *do* like it, if it turns out you *are* any good at it… you get to understand how a piece of the world works. And you get to *do* things, *create* things, instead of just having to watch things happen around you."

Wendel's face wasn't so red now, and his voice sounded strange. In fact, he sounded… happy?

"Becoming a wizard," he said, "will be, *by far*, the hardest thing any of you have ever done. Now run along and think about whether or not you really want to do it. And if any of you do, I'll be here tomorrow at noon." And with that, he made an opening appear in the tree, which closed after he stepped through it.

The creatures of the glade sat in stunned silence for several long minutes.

"Well," Slowfingers whispered to Squonk, "I guess we finally know what magic is."

"Really?" Squonk said. "I think I missed that part."

"Magic," Slowfingers said, "is hard work."

***

That night, Wendel slept instead of banging his head against the inside of a tree and staying up all night obsessing over a problem he didn't know how to solve. Disappointed, his headache slunk off sometime after midnight and looked for somebody else to torment.

When Wendel got up, he half hoped he'd solved *all* his problems. He'd promised to *teach*, but if Squonk decided it was too much trouble to *learn*, then he was off the hook.

Sadly, when he stepped out of the tree at noon, he found Squonk waiting for him… along with a few of the creatures who'd once infested the glade. A raccoon, a bear, a wolf, a raven, and a bat.

"You all heard what I said yesterday, right?" Wendel asked. "Years. Hard work. I wasn't joking about any of it."

Squonk nodded. "Yes, we did."

"Believed every word of it, Mr. Wizard, sir," said a raccoon down by Squonk's feet. At first Wendel thought it was that one annoying little twerp, but…

"You're that hat-raccoon, aren't you," Wendel said.

The raccoon nodded.

"What's your name?"

"Slowfingers, sir."

"And why do you want to do all that work to become a wizard?"

"Well, I, uhm…" Slowfingers held his hat in his paws and was fidgeting with it—and Wendel couldn't help but notice how much raccoon paws looked like human hands. "I've been thinking about it a lot, sir. At first, I wanted to be a wizard 'cuz I'm a lousy raccoon. Raccoons are smart and clever and fast and… well, I'm not. Maybe I'd be good at being a wizard. But what you said yesterday about understanding how a piece of the world works… that sounded really great. I'd like to understand something like that, too."

Wendel recalled the reasons he'd heard from the normal human apprentices he'd had:

"'Cuz me da says I'm a useless lump and I'm not cut out for *real* work."

"Because if I know magic, girls will like me."

"So I can be the most powerful wizard of all time and rule the world!"

Compared to all that, teaching a raccoon who wanted knowledge for its own sake sounded almost—*almost*—reasonable.

"And what about the rest of you?" he asked.

"Because," Squonk said, "I've *seen* you do stuff, and it's really great! Like, that thing where you showed us what a year is! Or that thing you do where you can make yourself look like other things! I wanna be able to do stuff like that, too—being a wizard looks fun!"

"It has its moments," Wendel conceded.

The bear—Mrs. Honeylog—said "Because my children are all grown and I'm too old to have any more. I'm tired of laying around doing nothing."

The wolf—Whitepaw—said "Because this all sounds simply *fabulous*, and I know I'll be biting my own foot later if I don't give it a sniff now while I have the chance."

The raven—Despairing Nevermore—said "Because magic sounds incredibly dangerous, like fire! I'd like to hear about all the ways you can die from doing it wrong."

And the bat—Mr. Nightfang Slayer of a Thousand Insects—said "Because bats are perfect at everything we try! And if a bat learns to become a wizard, he'll be the most powerful wizard ever and take over the world!"

Oh, well. There was one in every class.

And to his amazement, Wendel thought that trying to teach these animals sounded… *interesting.*

Wizard brains think about what they *want* to think about. And what they usually want to think about is problems. When the problems are too big, they get frustrated. "How can I move a mountain with a soup spoon?", or "How can I build a stadium out of leaves and leftover twine?", or even "How am I going to teach several dozen forest critters and a dragon to be wizards?" Giving a wizard brain that kind of problem is just cruel.

But give that brain a problem that's small enough to be solved but *just* big enough that the solution isn't obvious…

"I have to point out," Wendel said, "I honestly *don't know* if it can be done. You'd be the first-ever wizards of your kind. First raccoon wizard, first bear wizard, first wolf, first raven, first bat. There are going to be some problems."

"Like what?" Mrs. Honeylog asked.

Wendel held up his hands and wiggled his fingers. "A lot of wizarding requires hands of some sort. I know dragon paws are enough like hands that Squonk can fake it, and I suspect raccoon paws are close enough, too. The rest of you…" He shrugged.

"I'm ready to try." Whitepaw licked his chops. "You don't know if you can catch the rabbit until you chase it."

"Why do you chase rabbits?" Squonk asked.

"Wolf game."

The rest of the animals were willing, too.

"All right," Wendel said. "Everybody have a seat. Or a perch. Or… whatever. Lesson 1: What Is Magic?"

Nobody said anything stupid. Pleasantly surprised, Wendel kept talking.

And that's how Wendel the Wizard wound up with a dragon, a raccoon, a bear, a wolf, a raven, and a bat as his apprentices. It turned out that teaching them magic wasn't as hard as he expected.

It was actually a great deal *harder*.

But that's another story.

Head into the heart of New Mexico, surrounded by longhorn cattle.

THE WIDEHORN HERD
Madison Keller

Sam waddled out of the airport and into the depths of hell. The heat washed over her like a wave and she stopped walking. The sun beat down from a clear blue sky overhead, forcing Sam to lift a webbed paw to shield her eyes from the glare. The silver and turquoise engagement band slid down her arm.

Behind her the automatic doors whooshed shut, cutting off the glorious flow of cold air. Sam took a deep breath and forced herself to take another step. The dry air seared her nostrils and she swore she could feel the skin on the top of her flat tail shriveling in the heat.

"Here," Oscar, her miniature Longhorn Texas Steer boyfriend, said, slipping a pair of sunglasses into her raised paw. His matching silver bracelet clinked against hers. "These will help with the glare."

"Thanks." Sam pulled her suitcase upright so she could use both paws to put on the sunglasses.

Next to her, Oscar gave her an encouraging smile and placed a hooved hand on her shoulder. His wide horns stuck out from underneath a worn cowboy hat that was almost the same color as his tan fur. The cowboy hat, which came off as a hipster affection back in Portland, fit right in at the El Paso airport. In fact, Sam had never seen so many cowboy hats in her life.

"So, when do I get to meet your mom?" Sam asked, once again grabbing her suitcase handle as Oscar began trotting off across the sidewalk towards the curb where a line of cars waited to pick up passengers.

Oscar had told her a lot about his family in preparation for this trip. Although he assured her that they would love her, Sam was still nervous. Interspecies couples were not unheard of, but a steer marrying a beaver was still a bit of a stretch for most people to accept. Sam's own mother had taken it in stride, although the first question out of her mouth had been

47

when they planned to adopt grand-kits for her to spoil. Sam had assured her that they planned to soon, but failed to mention that they planned to try to adopt both a kit and a calf.

They stopped at the curb and a black SUV pulled away to reveal a small herd of full-size longhorn steers crossing the blacktop. Traffic was stopped in both directions as the group pounded across the street. Sam didn't pay them much mind, at least until Oscar backed up into her with a groan.

"Oscar, darling!" The lead cow of the group stopped directly in front of Oscar. Sam almost shrieked as the rest of the herd surrounded the two of them. All Sam could see was knobby cow knees and udders. The massive cows and steers seemed to block out the sun as they loomed over the pair of them. Sam dropped her suitcase handle and grabbed hold of Oscar's arm, burying her head into his side. Oscar had warned her that his family was not miniature, like him. Sam had assured him that she could handle being around a few full sized cattle, but the reality was a bit more overwhelming than she'd imagined it would be.

"Hi, Mom," Oscar said grimly, wrapping his arm around Sam's shoulder and pulling her forward. "I'd like you to meet my fiancé, Samantha Digger."

Emboldened by the familiar weight of Oscar's arm on her shoulders, Sam pulled her snout out of Oscar's shirt and stared up, and up, and up, at the massive Longhorn cow that loomed over them, more than twice Oscar's size. The cow had the same tan-colored fur as Oscar, although hers was speckled with white spots, with a distinctive white blotch on her muzzle between her eyes. Sam's eyes went wide as she recognized Oscar's mom.

"Well, we're all happy to welcome you to the Widehorn Herd, Samantha." Oscar's mom squatted down, but she still had to bend over to get her hoof-tipped hand down low enough for Sam to reach.

In a daze, Sam reached out and shook. "Call me Sam, Mrs. Widehorn."

"Sam, of course. I'd be honored if you call me Goldy." Goldy gave Sam's arm a gentle shake. "Or Mom."

"Uh, thank you, Goldy."

Before she knew it, Sam, clinging tightly to Oscar, was swept along with the herd. Along the way to the parked truck a whirlwind of Longhorns introduced themselves to her. A few she recognized from Oscar's photos, like his older sister Lucy, a tan cow with a smattering of white spots; his older brother Holster, a dusty brown steer; and his youngest sister Betty, a black cow. The rest flew by in a flurry of names.

"How many siblings do you have again?" Sam whispered to Oscar as they buckled themselves into the front seat of Goldy's truck. Sam was grateful that Goldy's truck only sat three, allowing her to escape the press of Oscar's enthusiastic family.

"I guess it depends how you define 'sibling,'" Oscar said, waving out the window at yet more Longhorns as Goldy pulled the truck out of the parking spot. The half-a-dozen Longhorns that had accompanied Goldy crammed themselves into the bed of the truck behind them.

Sam blinked. "It does?"

"Of course. Are you counting every child born into the herd around my age or after? Or just those I grew up around?" Oscar put his hooved-hand over her paw and gave her a reassuring gentle squeeze.

The herd. She'd known, intellectually, that cattle were a herd species, but it was quite a different thing to be *surrounded* by that herd. "Oh." She pondered for a moment. "I guess when I say sibling I mean those who have the same biological parents as you."

"Well, Goldy had six other calves besides me, but only three of them are still with the Widehorn Herd." Oscar smiled at her.

"Really?" Six? But she hadn't seen any other miniature cows in the group at the airport. "Um, forgive me for asking, but uh, why—"

"Are they all so much bigger than me?" Oscar snorted and stared at the dash, refusing to meet her eyes. "Sometimes it happens, that a full-size cow breeds a miniature like me."

Sam gave him a smile and turned her paw over, so she could squeeze his hoof back. "Well, I'm glad you're the size you are." Oscar glanced at her and flashed her a grin.

They came to a stop at a light and Goldy leaned down to pat her son's shoulder. "We are so happy to see you again, Oscar."

Oscar shrugged. "Sure." His grip on Sam's paw tightened and he kicked a back hoof like he was pawing at grass. However, on these seats sized for a full-size cow his hooves didn't touch the floor.

Sam frowned, but didn't want to ask him what was wrong with his mother right there. She'd wait until they got back to the house and were alone in their room together. Instead, she tried to change the subject. "So, Oscar, when do I get to meet your father?"

Goldy let out a peel of laughter. "You might have already, deary!"

"I might have?" Sam blinked at this non-answer.

"Most cattle aren't monogamous," Oscar said with a shrug. "We usually take a herd-name instead of a family name, and relationships are with the herd as a whole, not with any specific individual within it."

Sam's eyes grew wide and she glanced down at her silver-and-turquoise engagement bracelet. Why hadn't Oscar said anything when he proposed to her? "But—"

Oscar brought her paw up to his muzzle and kissed it. "I said most." His eyes danced with amusement as he smiled down to her. "I know beavers mate for life with their partner. I wouldn't have proposed if I didn't mean it."

Sam relaxed against him and spent the rest of the ride watching the desert scenery fly by outside the window, while Oscar pointed out local landmarks. Sam was fascinated. So much sand. And cactuses. And sage brush. In the distance mountains towered over the flat landscape.

"I always thought cactuses were taller," Sam said, staring out of the truck window. They'd stopped at a light and she got a good look at one of the cactuses. It looked like a dinner plate set on its side, with only a few visible spikes. The typical cactus she'd always seen in pictures was tall with bent arms coming out of the side.

Oscar laughed and leaned over to plant a kiss on her head between her ears above the sunglasses. "There are hundreds of different types, Sammy."

"I'll give you a tour when we get to the ranch!" Goldy mooed happily. "I have a cactus garden out back. Some of them have the most brilliant flowers."

"Cactuses have flowers?" Sam leaned into Oscar, sitting in the middle seat, so she could stare up at Goldy.

Oscar fell silent while his mom told Sam all about her garden, her hobby when she wasn't at her lawyer job. Sam sat listening in fascination. Growing up in the Pacific Northwest, Sam knew next to nothing about desert plants. Before she knew it, Goldy pulled off the main highway and they bumped down an unpaved road. Plumes of dust trailed in their wake.

Goldy stopped the truck in front of the biggest house Sam had ever seen. It had clearly started out life as an old human ranch house, which she recognized from her work in Portland's human neighborhoods, but had been added onto over the years. Several additional stories, the wood construction clashing with the brickwork of the original house, rose up above her. To either side, wings jutted out of the house at odd angles, every one built in a slightly different style than the last.

"Welcome to Widehorn Ranch!" Goldy and all the rest of the cattle in the truck-bed mooed.

"Wow," was all Sam managed to get out before the passenger door was opened by Betty, one of Oscar's sisters recognizable by her distinctive black fur, the only black Longhorn she'd seen in the huge gathering. Up on the truck's seat, she was about five feet off the ground. When she unbuckled her seatbelt and stood on the seat, that almost put her at eye level with Betty.

"Come on, Samantha, I want to give you the tour!" Betty held out a hoof-hand. A long line of Longhorns in every coloration, size, and shape streamed away from the bed of the truck, sending up more dust as they went. A dull roar of conversation followed the pounding thuds of their hooves on the dirt.

"Thanks," Sam yelled over the noise, gratefully wrapping a paw around one of Betty's hoof-like fingers and allowing the cow to help her down from the truck. Climbing up here with her short legs had been hard enough that Sam had honestly been wondering how she was going to get down. Unlike Oscar's hoof-hand which was only slightly larger than her own webbed paws, Betty's hand was almost twice the size of hers.

Once she was down, Sam turned around intending to offer Oscar some help, but he shook his horned head and just jumped. He landed next to her with a thud of his back hooves on the ground in a puff of dust.

"Show off," Sam whispered to him, and Oscar grinned and winked back at her. By now most of the herd had passed by, and Sam could finally hear herself think again.

He opened his muzzle, but before he could respond his mother Goldy's voice called from the other side of the truck, "Oscar, come help me put away luggage while Betty shows your fiancé around."

"Coming, Mom!" Oscar called back, giving both her and Betty another fleeting smile before clopping off.

"Wait, I'll come help. It's my luggage, too." Sam waddled after him.

Betty stepped between her and the retreating Oscar, a scandalized look on her long face. "You're a guest. Guests don't do work. Besides, I'm excited to meet my new herd-mate."

Sam squeaked. "Herd-mate? What does that mean?"

"It means that you're now officially part of the Widehorn Herd." Betty grinned and leaned over to hug Sam.

Sam uncomfortably got up on the toes of her webbed paws and stiffly accepted the embrace with Betty.

Betty finally let go and stood. "Come on, I can't wait to show you the house."

"Alright," Sam said, reluctantly following Betty.

Up close the house looked less like a human house. The doorway had been expanded to almost twice its original size to accommodate the cattle's wide horns. Sam struggled to keep up with Betty's huge strides as she burst through the door.

Just inside, a group of cattle were lounging around on couches in what looked like a living room area, watching a soccer game on a screen that took up most of the far wall. Framed photographs of Longhorns covered every other speck of wall space available.

As she and Betty walked in, one of the lounging cattle picked up a remote and muted the TV, and then the entire group turned to look at them.

Betty waved to the group as they walked through, names spilling from her lips like a torrent of rain drops. "This is Bob, Rick, Steve, Irma, Torn, and Ally. All, this is Oscar's fiancé, Samantha."

"Hi, Samantha!"

"Nice to meet you!"

With all the cows and steers bellowing their hellos at once, the noise was tremendous. Sam stepped back, her paws lifting to cover her ears before she could stop herself. She turned the motion into a double-pawed wave at the assembled cattle.

Betty gestured for Sam to follow her. They went through one of the three extra-wide interior doors into a dining room. More cattle sat in here, playing a game of cards at one end of the longest kitchen table that Sam had ever seen. Poor carpentry work revealed where a wall of the original house had been removed and the room extended. Some of the beams were visible behind the badly set dry-wall sheets.

Again, Betty did introductions, but Sam's head was already so full of names that she couldn't keep up. Like before, happy bellowed greetings came from all of the cattle. All of them looked excited to meet her. Sam waved and followed Betty into the next room.

The tour seemed to go on for hours, room after room, and all of them packed with cattle. Sam started to feel like she'd fallen into a dream, reliving her traumatic experience of last summer, again lost in the Winchester Mystery House, only this time with cattle instead of hares. Sam's family was flying in for the wedding in a few days. They were staying at a hotel, thankfully, but she realized she better call and warn her few family members about the sheer size and overwhelming nature of Oscar's family so they weren't caught by surprise.

They entered yet another room, but this one had a normal-sized door that Betty had to turn sideways to enter. Inside the room was blessedly empty. A big bed took up most of the floor space. Her and Oscar's bags sat inside the open closet.

"Finally, blessed silence." Sam would have collapsed on the bed right then except that Betty was still with her. In fact, the only thing she wanted more than a nap in an empty room was a swim. It had been over twenty-four hours since she'd been in the water, and her fur felt dust-coated and too dry.

Betty gave her a curious look. "You *like* silence? It always makes my fur crawl to be in a room by myself."

"I love it," Sam said, waddling further into the room, headed for her luggage. Oscar had warned her about the dust, and she'd packed the biggest package of fur-wet wipes that she'd been able to find at the store into her suitcase. "Honestly, there are so many of you, it's a little overwhelming."

"Well," Betty smiled. "I'm sure you'll get used to it quickly. After all, you're part of the herd now."

"What?" Sam stopped, clutching her engagement bracelet as she turned to stare at Betty, her eyes wide. "You said something like that earlier. What do you mean?"

Betty gave her a puzzled blink of her wide brown eyes and sat down on the edge of the bed. "The herd is both a family and a community." Betty scuffed a broad back hoof into the carpet, a move that Sam often saw Oscar do when he was nervous or thinking. "Aren't you and Oscar moving into the house after the wedding to live with us? That's what usually happens. The bride and groom pick one of their herds to live with and after the wedding they move in with the rest of the herd. Oscar didn't tell us he was leaving our herd for yours, so that means you're moving in after the wedding." She hesitated. "Right?"

Sam stared at Betty, eyes wide and mouth gaping. It took her a few moments of opening and closing her mouth before she could get words to come out. "I… Guess I just assumed we were flying back to Portland?" Had Sam misunderstood Oscar? Is that why he'd wanted the wedding to be in New Mexico, rather than Portland? This was too much to think about right now. Sam shook her head and turned her back to Betty. She waddled over to her suitcase, unzipped it, and pulled a few wet-wipes from the package.

When she turned around, Betty had her front hands balled around the edge of her t-shirt, which she was twisting nervously.

Sam snapped open the first wipe and began scrubbing at the fur of her neck.

"I wonder…" Betty's ears drooped down the side of her head. "Herd is family, yet I always felt like Oscar thought he wasn't as welcome as the rest of us, because of his small size. Although we always tried to treat him just like everyone else." Betty shook her head. Sam nervously eyed the big horns as they swung around.

Betty's confession made Oscar's less than enthusiastic greeting to his mother make more sense. "But he always seemed so happy when he was telling me about his family when we were back at home. I can tell he loves all of you."

"I thought so, but then he left us and moved to Portland." Betty sighed. "I'm sorry. I shouldn't be bothering you with my problems."

"No, it's—"

The door creaked open and Oscar walked through. Goldy ducked, turning her head sideways and leaning down slightly to fit through the door. It was surreal seeing them together like that; the top of Oscar's head only came up to his mother's navel, yet other than that they looked so similar: same tan colored fur, same long cow face, same wide brown horns, even their horns curved up at the same angle. She hadn't realized how much variation there could be in Longhorn horn shape until she met some of Oscar's herd. Even Goldy's white splotch was in the same place as Oscar's white diamond would have been if it wasn't covered with fur make-up.

"Hi, Oscar." Her relief was palpable. She had so many thing she wanted to talk with him about alone. She walked up to give him a hug, which he returned, enveloping her in his familiar and comforting scent.

"Oscar," Betty said, "Sam says you'll be going back to Portland after the wedding, but you didn't warn us all you are leaving the herd." Her big, brown eyes filled with unshed tears.

"Beavers don't have herds," Oscar said, turning to face Betty and draping his arm over Sam's shoulders. "I'm not leaving the herd, but we won't be living here." Relief washed through Sam at Oscar's words.

"It won't be the same." Betty dashed tears from her eyes and pushed past Goldy out of the room. "I have to get to work, nice meeting you, Sam," she called back over her shoulder as she retreated down the hallway.

"Betty—" Sam began, but it was too late; she was gone.

"Son," Goldy said. "Betty has a point. Won't you feel more comfortable moving back home with your family after the wedding?"

Oscar shot his mother a slight frown. "Sam and I hadn't discussed moving."

Goldy knelt to look Sam in the eyes and placed a large hand on Sam's shoulder. "Please consider it. It doesn't matter that you're beaver, the whole herd will accept you since Oscar does. We all miss him and would love for him to move home. We'd all do our best to make both of you welcome."

Sam nodded, but privately thought it was far too dry here for a beaver to survive.

"We'll talk about it." Oscar glanced at Sam. "But for now, Sam's looking a little overwhelmed." Sam bobbed her head, her eyes wide. "We'll be down for dinner, and we can discuss the rest of the wedding plans then. In the meantime, I think Sam needs a little alone time."

Goldy smiled in understanding and stood back up. "Of course, dear. And please, do discuss my offer too." With that, Goldy turned and ducked her way back out of Oscar's tiny room.

Sam gave him a grateful squeeze as the door shut behind Goldy.

"Your family is nice, but there are just so many of them."

"Yeah, sorry."

"You don't have anything to be sorry for." Sam loosened her arms and stepped back to regard him. "Well, ok, yes, you should be sorry for not warning me I'd be considered part of the herd because of this wedding."

Oscar ducked his head, the insides of his wide ears turning red. "Sorry, I just didn't even think about telling you. It's one of those things that everyone knows, I mean, something that everybody Southwest knows. I can see how it caught you by surprise though, since Portland doesn't have any of the herd family like the Southwest."

Sam got up on her tip-toes, using her wide, flat tail to balance, and grabbed one of his horns to pull his head down to her. She pecked a kiss onto the side of his nose, right where the snout began turning into hair. "It's fine. I love you. I can understand why you didn't think to warn me."

"So, um, what did you think of them?" Oscar turned his head, leaning down towards her so that she could drop back down to stand flat while he nuzzled the side of her neck, making her glad she'd cleaned with the wet wipes.

"They're loud," she said honestly. "But everyone seemed so excited to see me. It was weird."

"It's always like this when the herd expands." Oscar grinned and ran a hooved finger down her back in the way she liked.

"So, what does being a part of the herd mean, exactly?"

Oscar stepped back and took both of her webbed paws into his hands. "It's like…" His voice trailed off and his eyes went distant, flicking back and forth as he struggled to find words. "Well, you know how we're friends with the Doberman couple in the apartment next to ours?"

"Yes." Sam smiled. Oscar had met the Dobermans while moving into the apartment. They'd hosted a welcoming dinner when Sam moved in with him last year, and were house sitting the apartment for them right now. That was something that Sam loved about Oscar. One evening as she and Oscar had gotten back from a date, they'd rode up in the elevator with the dingo that lived a few floors above them. By the time she and Oscar had gotten off on their floor, he and the dingo were best friends and he'd convinced the dog to join their weekly tabletop role-playing game.

"Well, having a herd is like having an entire community of best friends."

"I thought it was just you and me?"

"Well, yes, it'll be you and me. But, also us and the herd."

"If its so wonderful, why'd you leave it to move to Portland?" Sam slapped her tail on the carpet. "And you didn't seem very excited about your mom and sister's offer to move back."

At this, Oscar's wide eyes filled with tears and he turned away. "I have missed them, but also, at the same time, I didn't feel like I fit in here. I felt smothered. I wanted to prove to myself I had what it took to make it on my own." Sam barked out a laugh, remembering what it felt like at the airport to be surrounded by the bigger cattle. "Smothered is one way to put it, yes."

Oscar sniffed and turned back to her. He rubbed his forehead, where the white triangle of fur was hidden by fur make-up. Sam smiled as she remembered their first date, where everything had seemed to go wrong and how she'd found out about it in the first place. "No one ever made fun of my size. But, I don't know, sometimes I don't feel like a Longhorn. What kind of cattle am I, living away from my own herd? But at the same time, I don't want to move back."

Sam waddled forward and threw her arms around his chest. "We'll make our own herd, together in Portland."

"What? But, I'm part of the Widehorn Herd."

Sam lifted her arm, showing him the bracelet he'd given her and then touched his matching one. "Of course you are, that will never change. They'll always be your herd, too. But, you said that a herd is like a community. You've also been building your own community in Portland, with your neighbors. Your friends. Me."

"Be part of more than one herd?" Oscar's soft, brown eyes went wide as he stared down at their matching bracelets.

"Why not? I understand not feeling like you fit in. My entire family are carpenters. It's the family business. All of my brothers and sisters joined the family business when they were old enough, except me. I like being a cop, but I struggle with that, too. Did you know I'm the only beaver on the force?" She took a big breath. "Anyway, what I'm saying is that community is what you make of it."

"I never thought of it like that…" Oscar trailed off and then leaned forward, pulling her into a tight hug. "Part of the Widehorn Herd, but also part of my own herd in Portland."

Sam grinned up at him, and on a whim got back up on her tiptoes, grabbed the cowboy hat from his head and plopped it on her own. Much too big for her, it promptly fell down to cover her eyes, and she had to hold the brim up with her paw to look up at Oscar. "So, if I'm an honorary cow, does that mean I have to wear one of these now?"

He laughed and pushed the hat back farther so that he could lean in and kiss her. When they broke apart several minutes later, the hat was on the floor, and was quickly buried by the rest of their clothing.

Goldy called out on the other side of their door, "Oscar, Sam, time for dinner!" and the knob rattled.

"MOM, no!" they both shouted.

The communities we build for ourselves are every bit as meaningful as the ones we're born into.

OUTSIDERS
Kyell Gold

Tryk rode a thermal down the cliff face, the cloth wings attached to his arms and midsection providing plenty of lift for his light-boned fox's frame. He pivoted, turning a lazy half-circle in the air, and angled his wings toward a small recess about halfway down.

As he approached, he brought his arms forward to cut his momentum, turning to glide parallel to the cliff and then folding his wings when he reached the cave entrance. His feet touched the ledge at a run, bringing him just to the cave before he skidded to a halt. The sun warmed his dark brown wind-blown fur and he gave himself a moment to reflect on his near-perfect landing before leaning around the entrance to the cave. "I'm here," he called, and smoothed down the orange fur on his sides and chest to the black and brown on his stomach.

Movement inside, and then a fruit bat's head poked out of the shadows. "I'm ready," Flit said. "I was waiting for the cry of pain."

Tryk let his tongue loll out in a smile and pulled his tail around to groom it as well, even though they were just going to fly again. "I know! I had a good landing this time."

The bat emerged fully, adjusting the straps of a pack Tryk had made for him some months back. Like the fox, he wore little else to cover his grey and russet fur, but the two were familiar enough with each other to dispense with modesty. "Do you need a moment?"

Seeing the bat always gave Tryk a little burst of warmth, as much because of their friendship as because Flit was the closest thing to another fox down here in the southlands. The warmth faded into a mild disappointment as the bat passed over his good landing so quickly, but then he noticed his friend's distracted posture. "Did you have a bad riberry?"

"I'm fine." Flit moved to the outcropping he used to take off. "Mango Landing, right?"

"That's what we said last time. They should've left from the plateau at sunrise." Tryk squinted at the sun, an hour above the horizon. "We might get there before them."

"Then let's go." Flit stretched out his natural wings, catching the sun so the pattern of blood vessels showed through them, and leapt gracefully.

Tryk liked to think that he was getting more graceful with practice even if his clumsy cloth and wood wings couldn't match Flit's lovely real ones. At least he could now keep up reliably when they flew, which was one of his favorite things to do. His arms were equal to the challenge of holding his wings level and he could steer well enough to follow the bat through the air.

If Flit hadn't had a bad fruit, then likely he'd just come from visiting his family. It had been many days since they'd seen each other and now that Tryk thought of it, the last family visit had been close to a month ago, so that fit. That meant that Flit would snap out of it soon, and maybe a bit later would talk to him about what had happened.

So he let his mind wander as the jungle passed slowly below him, scents of fruit and animals stronger now in the rainy season. The last two visits from northern ships hadn't brought any of the dried fruit he'd hoped to find for Flit, but if his calculations were correct, winter was drawing to a close up in Divalia, which meant that perhaps there would be surplus of apples, starfruit, and other things. The bat had to go harvest fruit about every other day, and if he had a store of dried fruit that would keep, he could rest one day or another.

Then there were Tryk's other friends, the jaguar Silence (properly his name was "the sound of a paw crushing a blade of grass," but he didn't mind the shortening outside of his tribe), the capybara Sunny, and the Pampas deer Cherron. All of these southlanders had been incredibly generous, making his exile here much more comfortable, and so he looked forward to Trade Days, because it was the one time he could be the expert around them.

Ahead of him, Flit banked and slowed to let Tryk pull even with him. The bat's ears had come up and he seemed in better spirits. Flying did that for Tryk, too. "Have you figured out what you're going to get for Sunny?"

"He already has so much jewelry." Tryk kept his eyes on the silver thread of the river ahead.

"Never enough, though."

"I guess not. But I'd like to find something else for him this time if I could."

"He likes jewelry."

Tryk grinned. "Maybe I'll get you some jewelry. How would some silver rings sound when you're flying?"

Flit grimaced and fluttered his wings, making them rattle a bit in the air stream. "I don't want to put anything through my wings."

"I didn't say through," Tryk said, but Flit had already moved ahead of him again. The fox sighed. It wasn't often, but when Flit was in these post-family moods, sometimes an innocent word could put him back into a funk. He'd snap out of it.

That left Tryk even more determined to find some dried fruit for him. At the same time, he could get some dried hot peppers for Silence, and maybe find another book for Cherron. A few weeks ago, his friends had helped bolster his cabin against a rainstorm like he'd never seen in his life, not only finding every crack in his walls and roof, but also flooding the area and nearly washing Tryk's house off the cliff it sat next to. Without their help, he might be homeless or dead, so he was determined to get something good for each of them this time.

Up ahead of them, the river grew wider, bluer, and louder as they headed toward it. Flit usually caught the right air currents to keep their altitude, but today either he'd missed a few or the air just wasn't there, as he said. He called something back over his shoulder, but the wind took most of the words; Tryk's large ears only caught "the river." The bat's meaning became clear as he cut toward the river and angled upstream when he reached the shore, where the trees were lower. Still, they had only just sighted the simple wooden platform some distance away when Tryk had to land on the muddy riverbank. Flit could have glided farther, but folded his wings and dropped to follow the fox to earth.

In trying to avoid the trees, Tryk lost his balance and stepped down in the shallow river water, then hurriedly scampered up to dry land. A few ripples showed where the *chori* fish that lived in the shallows had hurried over and then meandered back, disappointed.

"Almost lost that foot for good," Flit seemed to have recovered his good humor again.

"I've been bitten by one of them once." Tryk followed him up the riverbank, waving at the gnats that clustered around his face. "It healed up well."

"The best kind of encounter: painful enough to learn your lesson and not enough to leave a mark."

"Like a visit to your family?" Focused on getting out of the mud, Tryk said it without thinking and immediately regretted it. Fortunately, Flit hadn't heard (he was facing forward and Tryk had spoken down toward his mud-covered feet), because the bat turned and said, "What was that?"

Tryk cleared his throat and said a quick thanks to Canis for second chances. "I said, uh, really? Is that best? Wouldn't it be better if I'd caught it and eaten it?"

"For you, maybe. Don't make me sick."

"All right, then." The fox stepped carefully where Flit had already stepped. "Best lesson for you isn't best lesson for me."

"True enough."

They walked in amiable, comfortable silence for about twenty minutes and then came around a gentle bend in the riverbank some fifty feet from a simple wooden dock upon which rested a capybara, a jaguar, and three more packs like the ones Tryk and Flit carried. Sunny jumped up when he saw them. "Ho!" he called. "We're here!"

"They can see that." Even the jaguar's low tone traveled over the water to them.

Tryk called around Flit, "Where's Cherron?"

Sunny dropped his arm, his round shape sagging. "Isn't she with you? She went to meet you."

Both fox and bat looked around, but nothing looked or sounded like a deer around them. The mango trees by the shore bent toward the water, heavy with mangoes, and the underbrush around them, though dappled with shadows, contained no deer-sized silhouettes that they could see. "She's getting better," Tryk said to the bat.

Flit nodded. "Can't see or hear her at all."

They continued on to the dock, and as they were hugging Sunny, but before Silence stood on his wooden leg to greet them, a deer splashed in mud from head to toe emerged from the forest.

"I'm not hugging you like that," Tryk said.

"I followed you for fifteen minutes." Cherron tossed her head. "You wouldn't have known I was there at all if Sunny hadn't said something."

"I didn't know it was a secret!" The capybara clapped his paws to his muzzle.

"I put camouflage on and slipped into the forest, and you couldn't figure out that I was being a spy?"

"You did very well," Tryk said. "As good as Marina de Mustela, I dare say."

Cherron's dark eyes glowed at the mention of her favorite heroine from the books Tryk had traded for over the last few months. "I don't know about that. I'm still getting better."

"How did you keep so quiet?" Tryk asked.

"Oh, you just have to watch where you step and make every motion small and deliberate."

"The real question is," Flit said, "where are you going to wash that mud off?"

The deer's smile vanished. She eyed the water and sighed. "Maybe it'll dry by the time we get there."

They did take half an hour to walk down the river to the outskirts of the small trading post, waving river bugs away from their eyes and noses, and by the time they'd gotten to the river mouth, the mud that covered Cherron's handsome tan fur had not really dried at all in the humid air. She managed to scrape most of it off, and gathered leaves to wipe her fur mostly dry while the rest of them put on tunics and pants from the packs they'd brought.

"I don't care if they get dirty," Cherron said to the others' looks as she pulled the tunic over her dirty fur. "I hate these things anyway and I don't see why we have to wear them."

Putting on clothes felt strange to Tryk now, almost nostalgic. "So the traders—"

"I know." The deer yanked on her pants backwards. "They're in our land. Why don't they have to take off all their clothes?"

"That would bother them more than it bothers you to put clothes on." Tryk stashed his wings in the lower branches of a mango tree and sniffed the fruits until he found a few ripe ones to add to his pack. "You've got those on backwards."

"Looks the same to me." The deer skipped away from him. "Let's go."

Tryk fell in alongside the jaguar as the others forged ahead. Silence got along well on the wooden leg Tryk had made for him, but usually walked slowest, and Tryk didn't want him to feel left behind. "What are you looking for this time?" he asked.

Silence huffed in amusement. "I'm just coming to carry things back for you all. I have everything I need."

"Of course we have everything we need," Tryk said. "But what about things you want?"

The jaguar considered that. "Can your traders sell a quiet day with the sun in your fur and no bugs around your ears?"

"We used to have an oil that would keep bugs away," Tryk said. "It smelled terrible, but when everyone wore it it wasn't so bad."

"Everyone on those ships smells bad." Silence paused a moment. "You don't, though."

"All right, I won't buy any oils or perfumes this time."

The jaguar shook his head. "If you like it, buy it."

"I don't really miss it," Tryk said. "Just sometimes, like when I'm covered in mud and even though I wash it off I can still smell it."

"You smell fine with mud." Silence fidgeted with his tunic.

The path led them over a small rise and through a thicket of bushes where they had to go single file. On the other side, Tryk said, "Do you have any idea what kind of jewelry I could get Sunny that he doesn't have already?"

"He wears too much as it is," Silence replied.

"Is there something else I could get for him?"

The jaguar shook his head. "No, jewelry's really all he wants. But still."

"So what should I get?" Tryk asked more to make conversation and to talk it out than because he thought the ascetic jaguar would really offer ideas.

"You'll find something nice." Silence caught his pants on a thorn bush. "Claws and blood, why would any one invent these things? And then make other people wear them?"

Tryk smiled. "Do you want to wait at Mango Landing and we'll just meet you at sunset?"

"No, no, I'll come along." The jaguar looked ahead at the others. "I'll keep quiet about the cloths."

"'Clothes'. Go ahead and complain if you want. You've listened to me enough times."

Silence made an amused noise. "If you buy food, get something that isn't so bland this time."

"Noted." The fox congratulated himself on already having selected hot peppers for the jaguar. "Thanks for coming with us. Don't worry, it'll be over before you know it."

"So many people." Silence sighed. "I don't know how you bore it."

***

It had been over two years since Tryk had seen the seemingly endless buildings of Divalia, the Grand Cathedral, the Palace he'd visited exactly twice, and the market. Compared to any one of those wonders, the trading post would necessarily come up short. How could one put the three-year-old wooden building up against hundreds of years of architecture and history?

And yet, after two years with no other gathering larger than fifteen people, the trading post felt as active as his birthplace. This time, no fewer than three ships sat in the harbor at the mouth of the river, visible through the clouds of gnats in the thick salt-smelling air. The trading post must be full, for several unlucky merchants had set up their stalls outside the building, glancing up at the threatening clouds.

None of them had anything Tryk wanted, but Sunny had to stop and look at each stall, and Silence took any excuse not to go into the main building, so the two of them remained outside while the others walked in through the wide doors.

Well over a hundred people, by Tryk's estimation from the noise and smells that greeted him inside the building, made their way through rows of merchants who'd come down from the ships. No other bats, but many jaguars, capybaras, hares, and at least two of the great slow sloth bears. A few wore shirts and trousers, but many wore nothing more than a loincloth. "Let's go see what's come in," the fox said, already craning his neck to see if there were any foxes among the merchants.

Flit and Cherron exchanged glances. "We know you have a lot of things you want to get," the bat said. "Go ahead and we will meet you back here soon."

"Oh," Tryk said. "Sure, okay. If you need help with something…"

"We'll wait for you." Cherron smiled and patted the fox's shoulder, leaving a dirty mark. "Go on, we always feel like we slow you down."

Truthfully, it was relieving to be able to shop for gifts for his friends without them around. Tryk hadn't planned on surprising them—he'd thought he would just walk around and when he found something, would buy it and give it to them—but this worked too.

There weren't any fox merchants, at least not immediately visible. So he followed his nose to a merchant with dried fruit and peppers and haggled to get a good load for one pot of his numbing salve. The rabbit touched a little to his lip to prove its effectiveness, and then Tryk had to use some himself to prove it wasn't poison.

Finding something for Sunny was a more difficult matter. Several merchants had brought small silver trinkets, but most of them were religious and featured either an avatar of one of the Circle or the abstract sign of that member of the Circle, and he didn't want to get Sunny anything religious even though the capybara probably wouldn't care. Several merchants had brooches and pins that they had not yet realized were unlikely to be useful to people who wore little clothing, so that left necklaces and wristlets. Tryk looked around for Flit and Cherron to help him, but he couldn't spot them, so he followed the smell of silver polish to several different merchants.

He'd just found a silver wristlet in a leafy vine pattern that he thought Sunny would like and was haggling over it when a voice said over his shoulder, "Don't believe anything this huckster tells you."

Startled, he turned and found a grinning red fox in a green velvet cap and matching cloak facing him. For a moment his mind went blank, even with the shock of species recognition and a familiar sweet scent of amber filling his nose. "What?" the fox said, "forgotten me so soon?"

"Well," Tryk said, recognition dawning, "there are a thousand red foxes in Divalia, after all. It's much easier for you to recognize me, Salian."

Salian laughed and pulled Tryk into a hug that made the cross fox very aware of his dirty tunic and trousers. Behind them, the tall mink held out the wristlet awkwardly. "If this is some bargaining ploy…"

"Not at all." Salian reached into his pouch. "What more would you need to give my friend this bauble?"

The mink's eyes flicked to the paw that emerged full of silver pieces, and then up to the brooch that marked Salian's family. "Er, the pot plus three royals would be more than adequate, sir."

Salian counted out three coins and dropped them into the mink's open hand. "There you go, Tryk. Take your piece and let's move along."

Tryk placed the pot on the merchant's table and made a quick bow, putting the bracelet into his pack before hurrying to keep up with Salian's green cloak. "What on earth are you doing here?" he asked, catching up.

"I came here to look for you, of course," the red fox said. "But let's get outside first."

They passed through the wide doors and out to the docks and landings. Salian pointed to the farthest of the three ships, a three-masted carrack flying a flag that fluttered weakly in the breeze. From the color, it would have to be one of the Fox houses, but Salian's family hadn't been rich enough to afford a ship, not when Tryk had known him. "I'm aboard the *Mirage On The Water*, that one, property of the Wilkyres."

The Wilkyres: a grey fox family, but foxes were foxes, grey or red (or cross-phase red), and unless they fell foul of one of the First families, they'd support each other. "If they'd been sailing down here two years ago," Tryk said, "I might have some royals left."

"Whose ship did you get on?"

"The Southland Trading Company. They told me to be wary of pirates but I didn't realize they meant themselves until they'd taken all my coin and most of my clothes and left me on the savanna."

"We can get you some better clothes." Salian's paw touched Tryk's tunic and pressed in, more familiarly. "I'm not sure your old ones would fit anyway."

The touch brought back memories of more than just dalliances with Salian: he remembered perfumed salons and silk sheets and wines and meads, drinks that weren't water or fruit juices, scents like amber that weren't just the flowers and people he lived among. Other foxes, more often than once every few months, a community around him that he was born into. He steadied himself. "Oh, I don't use them much, not anymore. Only for coming down here to be presentable. But tell me, what have you and the others been doing these past two years?"

Salian smiled. "You might need clothes more than you realize."

Tryk looked again at the ship. "Is one of the Wilkyres on the ship? Are you inviting me to dinner there?"

His friend laughed. "Same old Tryk. I confess, I'm rather amazed to find you in such good health after two years. Canterphil told me there was a cross fox who came around the trading post and I thought it had to be you, but I expected you'd have lost an ear, or run afoul of one of the savages here, or contracted some tropical disease. You look in excellent health." He put a paw to Tryk's stomach. "Better, even, than when we last met."

"They're not savages," the fox said, but he leaned into the touch with some pride. "It's hard, living here, but there are rewards as well."

"Oh ho, so you've tamed some of them." Salian winked and elbowed Tryk in the ribs. "I should've known you'd turn your tinkering to good use."

"It's not taming—" The cross fox took in a breath; he was remembering now the tricks one had to use in conversation with Salian, skirting around some of the things he said and turning the conversation back to better topics. "So tell me about the last two years."

"It's been dreary." Salian's sparkling eyes indicated a secret he was going to get around to eventually. "The same people spouting the same gossip. Oh! Lord Black got sick and vomited at the King's feast, and all over Lord Dewanne, too. The Jackal's Staff is still there, but your favorite rabbit is gone. Nobody knows where, just up and disappeared one night. And nobody, as far as I know, has had their fur fall out in patches since you left."

Tryk laid his ears back. "Sounds about right."

"Oh, yes, and one more thing." Salian perked his ears. "The Circle's turned."

"What?"

The red fox nodded, grinning wide. "King Barris passed away peacefully so now Lord Montnight is King, and he's taken the name Alain, if you can believe it, but I suppose you know rabbits better than I do. At least, you used to."

"So that means that Prince Berniss—"

"Is no longer prince."

The cross fox searched Salian's dancing eyes. "And I can…"

"Yes, my friend." The red fox clapped him on the shoulder. "You can come home."

Home. Soft beds, Madame Coban's spiced cakes, a fully stocked apothecary, music, all the company he'd been missing, the graceful curves of the Cathedral and the bountiful scents of the market. "With you?"

"With me."

Tryk looked out at the carrack, which seemed lit by a heavenly glow now. "When do we leave?"

***

Salian returned to his ship to prepare a berth for Tryk while the cross fox went to meet his friends outside the trading post. Sunny had a silver ring he'd traded ten mangoes for, Flit had a wrapped package, and Cherron, the last to arrive, ran up to Tryk with her arms full of black cloth.

"I had to bargain forever for it but finally he let me have it," the deer said. "You'll help me make a cloak from it, won't you?"

Tryk took the cloth and examined it. "Another one?"

"They keep tearing." The deer's tunic and pants also had several tears in them. "But this should be enough for two."

"I…" The fox poured the cloth back into the deer's arms. "I met a friend here."

"Yes, I saw." The deer's eyes narrowed. Sunny looked interested, and Flit very neutral, as though the bat suspected what was coming. "He didn't look like a nice fox, not like you."

"We were friends up north, years ago. He told me—you remember the prince I made angry? Well, he's not a prince anymore so he doesn't have as much power, and now it should be safe for me to go back."

The three of them looked at him silently. Cherron fidgeted with the cloth, and Sunny turned the ring on his finger. "I see," Flit said. "So you're just going to leave? Right now?"

Tryk shifted from one foot to the other, tail curled against him. Overwhelmed with the excitement of returning to Divalia, he'd not thought at all about how hard it would be to say good-bye to the friends he'd made here. "I'm a fox." He gestured to himself. "I wasn't born here."

"I thought you were happy here," Cherron said softly. Flit and Sunny echoed the sentiment silently with pained expressions and flattened ears.

"I was, but—I mean, I am. It's just—it's home, you know?"

"Isn't this your home?" Flit asked.

"You don't understand." Tryk gestured. "All of you have others like you around. I'm the only fox here, the only one. You can all go to your tribes and there are plenty of people like you. I can't do that."

They stared back at him, and right away he got the gnawing feeling that he'd said something wrong, jumped into words without thinking about them again. To cover, he asked, "Where's Silence? I have some things for him and for the rest of you, too."

"He got bored and went back to Mango Landing to wait." Cherron folded the cloth clumsily over on itself. "Are you coming back there or should we say your good-byes for you?"

"They're sailing tonight," Tryk said, pointing to where some of the merchants were already loading their wares onto small boats to be rowed back to the third ship, the carrack. "I might be able to make it up and back."

"But if you miss the ship, it's gone forever." Flit waved a wing. "We'll say good-bye for you."

That didn't feel right. The more he thought about this, the worse he felt. "I can't just leave without saying good-bye. If we set off now…"

Sunny, cheerful Sunny, turned his back. "No," he said. "We wouldn't want you to miss your boat."

Tryk wavered. Divalia was far away and years ago, and these friends were here. He'd taught them their facility with his language, and in return they'd helped him survive—not just survive, but settle—here in the south. From Silence he'd gotten meat; from Sunny he'd gotten furniture; from Cherron he'd gotten stories in trade; from Flit he'd gotten fruit and the chance to study his wings, to refine his artificial ones. From all of them he'd gotten friendship, companionship, and more.

Cherron put an arm over Sunny's shoulders and walked toward the river with him. Flit remained behind, Tryk's oldest friend in this area, the first one really to welcome him rather than just tolerate him. There were no bats in Divalia, not that he'd ever seen.

"Hey," he called. "Hey wait! Why don't you all come with me?"

Sunny and Cherron stopped but didn't turn. Flit shook his head. "We belong here. You belong there. That's all right." He held out the package to him. "Here. I don't suppose you'll need them in the north, but we won't have much use for them."

The package surprised Tryk with its weight. He unwrapped it and found inside two gleaming silver knives, small but solid, probably sharp, exactly the kind of blades he'd been hoping for to carve his wing struts and other wooden pieces more precisely. "I didn't see these in there," he said.

"We got to them early. We've been planning it for a little while, ever since a few months ago when your bone knife broke. Sunny checked all the merchants outside while Cherron and I went separately to the inside ones. I was very pleased when we found them, and I'm glad we have a chance to give them to you as a gift before you leave, I suppose."

"Oh, Canis," Tryk breathed, turning the knives over. They were perfect, exactly what he needed—would have needed. "Thank you. Thank you all." He took a step toward where Sunny and Cherron were retreating and then stopped, ears flat. "Tell them for me, would you?"

Flit glanced at the other two and then came over to hug Tryk. "It's been my great pleasure to know you. We'll miss you, but we know this is what you have to do. If things changed for any of us so that we could go back to our tribes the way you're doing now, I'm sure we would all do it."

The bat's wings enfolded him. Tryk couldn't hug back, but he rested his muzzle against Flit's and his paws against the bat's stomach, the way they'd learned to hug over the last year and a half. "Mmm," Flit said. "What do you have in your pack? Smells good."

"Oh." Tryk disengaged and stepped back. He put the knives in the bottom of his pack and took out all the fruit. "This is for you. It'll keep so you don't have to go out if you don't feel like it some days. And the peppers are for Silence. Can you give them to him?"

"Of course." The bat took the fruit and curled one wing around to make a pouch to hold them.

The bracelet he'd gotten for Sunny lay in the bottom of his pack. Could he leave that with Flit as well? How would Sunny take that? Now he might associate the bracelet with Tryk's departure and not get the enjoyment out of it that he should. So Tryk left it there and stood awkwardly, knowing that this was the time when he should turn and leave, and yet more and more unwilling to. "I'll… I'll come back. There are ships now and I can get passage down here."

Flit lifted his free wing. "We'll be here waiting if you decide to."

All adventures had to come to an end. He missed not having insects in his fur all the time; he missed not worrying about whether a storm would wash his house off the cliff; he missed the days when he and his friends could sit around and talk philosophy and make jokes; he missed the buildings and activity of Divalia.

He could come back with better clothes, better equipment, and he'd have more presents to bring them, better ones that really showed what Divalia could offer. So he pressed his paw to the fingers on the end of the bat's wing, said "Good-bye," and turned around.

Every few steps, he looked back. Flit had turned to walk away a moment after Tryk had, and by the time the fox was halfway to the ship, the bat had disappeared into the undergrowth. The knives his friends had gotten him bounced against his side as he walked, solid and reassuring, and reminding him with every step of what he was leaving behind.

At the part of the beach where one merchant was loading small packages onto a rowboat, a bored-looking mouse sat on a stool drawing designs with his sword in the wet sand. He looked up as Tryk approached, and the fox made out an unfamiliar crest on his cloak, likely that of the merchant family that owned the ship. The cloak, like the sword and the mouse's tail, trailed in the sand. "How much stuff you got?" the mouse asked without raising the point of his sword.

"Just me and the pack." Tryk curled his tail to keep it off the sand. "I'm, er, Salian's guest."

Now the mouse examined him more closely. "Ah, right. Step on in, then, we'll get you over there."

Another mouse, who'd been helping the merchant load packages into the boat, took the oars when Tryk and the merchant were seated in the boat. The mouse with the sword pushed the boat into the water and then jumped in as his fellow started to row.

The trip out to the carrack took a good twenty minutes, during which Tryk kept looking back toward the shore. At the time Salian had told him he could return, there'd been no question that he would go back to Divalia with the other fox. Now that that journey had started, the fox saw in the darkening skies over the jungle the peaceful nights, the pleasant company of his friends, the solitude in which he could work on creating new things, and the delight those new things brought to the people here. He'd jumped at the chance to return to his old life without taking the time to realize that his new life suited him better, though it might have been less comfortable.

He found this plain tunic and pants confining and itchy now. Storms wouldn't wash his cabin over the cliff, not really, and being in their raw power was a little scary but that fear was exhilarating. He missed his friends back in Divalia, but had he ever belonged with them? How many of those foxes had so much as sent inquiries about him through traders? He reached into his pack to feel the shape of the knives again through the cloth wrapping. His paw there brushed the bracelet he'd gotten for Sunny.

What had Flit said? "If any of us had the chance to go back..." But Tryk was the only one who'd been wholly kicked out of his "tribe." Silence couldn't hunt but still lived with the other jaguars; Sunny didn't participate in a lot of his tribe's activities but still lived with one of his brothers; Cherron's situation was different but still she roamed the savanna with her herd. Flit was the only one who lived apart from his family, and that was by his choice. So that comment had been directed only at Tryk, meant to reassure the fox that they understood his departure, but Tryk now turned it around and saw the other side of it: that they had all chosen to be part of a group, and that group had included him, and he'd now turned his back on it.

The small rowboat bumped the side of the carrack, startling him out of his reverie. The mistake he'd made loomed over him as obvious as the great wooden ship, but fortunately so did the means to fix it. "I'm sorry," he said to the mouse with the sword. "Can you take me back to shore?"

A rope ladder had dropped over the side and the mouse secured it to the side of the boat. "We have to go back at least one more time," he said, "but we'll be sailing after that. You not going to see Salian?"

Tryk looked up the ladder at the mouse silhouetted against the evening sky. "I suppose I should go tell him I won't be coming with him. Can you wait for me?"

"A short time. Captain wants to be under sail by the time the moon's up to there." The mouse jabbed a finger at the sky, about two inches above where a ghostly moon hovered.

"I'll be fast," Tryk promised, and scrambled up the rope ladder.

One of the mice on crew directed him to Salian's cabin, down a ladder toward the stern of the ship. The terms he'd learned on his month-long trip years ago came back to him slowly: the forecastle in front of the ship, the stern at the back where the captain and officers slept (he'd slept below the forecastle with the crew on his trip down), the mizzenmast at the stern, the mainmast in the middle, and the foremast to the fore of the ship. This carrack bore light cannon to guard against piracy and cross-hatched rope rigging from the deck to the crow's nests—they were called "shrouds," he now remembered. But just because he knew his way around a ship didn't make it home any more than Divalia was his home any longer.

The smell inside the ship brought back memories, too, although here the rank smell of months of people living in close quarters mixed with perfumes and old laundry soap, making Tryk pinch his nose. He knocked at Salian's door, and the fox opened it as quickly as if he'd been waiting on the other side.

"Tryk! Welcome. Please, come in."

There was scarcely space for the two of them in the small cabin, so Tryk sat on the bed while Salian took the chair on the other side of a small table. "Unfortunately, as you can see, I can't offer you a place to stay here, although if you wanted to spend some time before sleeping, I would very much enjoy your company."

The room smelled thickly of Salian's sweet perfume, so even if Tryk had wanted to do what Salian undoubtedly was hinting at, he wouldn't have been able to stay in this space long enough to do it. "As it happens," he said, "I only came back here to tell you good-bye."

The red fox stiffened, and then regained his smile. "What's this? We'll be on the same boat for a month, we will certainly see each other again."

"No. I am quite grateful you came to tell me the news, but I have..." He gestured to the small window. "I have some obligations here. Perhaps in another six months, or another year, I might want to return."

"I see." Salian rose and turned to open a small chest. "There's nothing I can say to convince you?"

The amber perfume that had enticed him earlier now felt overwhelming and dizzying. He'd been too long without it, he supposed. "Nothing."

"Will you have a cup of wine with me, then? One taste of wine to remind you of what you've left behind?"

"It won't change my mind." Tryk rose from the bed.

"Then as a personal favor to me. I did come all this way," Salian said, holding up the bottle. "It's not one of the better vintages, but on this ship I promise you it is the best I have to offer."

The cross fox steadied himself with a paw on the table. "Half a cup," he said. "I have not much tolerance for it anymore."

"I imagine." Salian set two cups on the table and poured. "Out there, what do you drink? Water?"

"Fruit juice sometimes." Tryk took a step to the window and looked out at the distant jungle, growing harder to distinguish as the sun crept downward.

"It's a nice view from here, though boring during the voyage, I admit. Here." Tryk turned to Salian holding out a cup, half full of wine.

"Thank you again for coming all this way." The two foxes toasted, and Tryk drank the wine.

The sharp taste seared his tongue in a familiar, pleasant way. He smiled at the light rush to his head and the memories that evoked as well. "I'm just sorry that I can't convince you to come," Salian said, putting his cup down. The fox reached out and touched Tryk's paw. "It would be a much more pleasant return journey."

"Yes, well, I'm sorry." Tryk put his own cup down.

"Your father is anxious to have you back." Salian regarded him intently.

"My father?" Of all the people Tryk would have thought interested in his return, his father wasn't among them. "Why didn't he come himself, then?"

"His leg is worse, I hear, and at any rate, this is a young fellow's journey to make." Silian cleared his throat and his tail swished. "But he did offer a generous reward for your return."

The cross fox flattened his ears. "What?"

"If you come back..." Salian gripped Tryk's wrist. "I'll share the reward. After my expenses for this voyage, of course. There'll be enough for you to tinker with for a while, if you like."

"What does my father want with me?" His fingertips tingled with how tightly Salian was holding him.

"Wants his son back, I assume. Is that so strange?"

They hadn't been estranged, not exactly, but Tryk hadn't missed his father and given how little they'd talked, had assumed his father hadn't missed him, maybe hadn't even known he was gone. "No," he said, "I mean, it's not strange, but..." His friends here. Cherron had taught him about poisons, about the first signs that you might ignore if you weren't alert for them. Why had that popped into his mind? Tingling in your fingers and toes. Clouded thinking.

He stared at Salian. "You poisoned me."

The red fox laughed. "Not poison, dear. I'd hardly collect the reward then. Just a sleeping powder I used to relax me on the trip. I thought it would keep you nicely quiet until we were on our way. Well, I'm generous enough. My offer to split the reward stands."

Salian tried to push him down to the bed and he pushed back. Silence had worked with him a little bit on fighting, in case someone came to attack the lone fox in the cabin by the cliff, and Salian was no savanna raider. With a twist of his arm, Tryk freed himself from the other fox's grip and pushed him hard into the wall.

"Hey!" Salian called, and swiped at him as Tryk jumped for the door. "They won't take you back!"

Of course his friends would take him back. Ignoring Salian, Tryk landed in the tight hallway outside and ran for the ladder. He'd almost made it up onto the deck when a paw grabbed his foot. He kicked free and was rewarded with an oath from Salian.

On the deck, it took him a moment to orient himself, and then he ran to the side and searched for the rowboat. The two mice looked up as he called down to them, and one stood and gestured for Tryk to climb down. He set a foot on the rope ladder, but before he could go any farther, Salian had reached him and yanked him back onto the deck. "Push off!" he yelled to the mice below. "He won't be returning with you!"

Oh, he'd meant the *mice* wouldn't take him back. Tryk scrambled to his feet and looked over in time to see the small rowboat heading away from the carrack. "You can't kidnap me," he cried, hoping one of the crew would hear, but the ones in earshot all kept their heads down.

"I'm not." Salian leaned back against the deck, confident. "You'll realize this is the right thing to do sooner or later. Once you do, you'll already be home, or on your way. Much better than having to wait for months."

"This isn't right." How long before the poison—sleeping powder— took effect? Fifteen minutes? Ten? Tryk scanned the ship, desperate for ideas. Nearby, a mouse mopped the deck. Could he steal the mop, knock out Salian, swim to shore? The water was deep, the sky darkening, and the mice out there in the boat could bring him back easily. "I have friends here, friends who don't need a reward to come find me."

"Oh?" Salian made a show of looking out toward the shore. "Where are these friends? Have they a boat? Wait, I think I see them! Are they all white fisher-birds?"

While the red fox mocked him, Tryk formed a desperate plan. He covered the deck to the mouse with the mop in three strides, seized the mop, and ran for the mainmast shroud.

Behind him came a cry from Salian: "Stop him!" But none of the mice seemed particularly interested in stopping Tryk, and he made it unhindered to the webbing of ropes.

The ship hadn't set sail, so the crow's nest was empty when he reached it. He fell inside—the sleeping powder was beginning to drag at his muscles and eyes—and pulled himself up to look down.

Salian paced on the deck, looking up, and when he saw Tryk, he laughed. "Stay up there by all means!" he called. "It won't be as comfortable as a bunk, but perhaps the captain will pay you for your trouble!"

In the bottom of his pack, there was the package with the knives. He unwrapped it—good, his paws still worked—and applied one to the base of the mop. After some deep scoring, the wood parted with a snap, leaving Tryk with a body-length piece of wood. It might be a little short but should work.

The other important part, the part he'd gambled on finding, lay at his feet. As in the ship he'd taken south, the crew kept a blanket in the crow's nest for the watch to bundle up in on cold nights. All he needed was rope, and that was available to him just over the side. But he'd have to work fast, before the drag on his muscles became too much to overcome.

Below him, an officer, maybe the captain, asked Salian what was happening, and Salian said, "My passenger is up in the crow's nest, but he'll fall asleep presently and then your men can go retrieve him."

The captain seemed to think that either Tryk had to be retrieved now or that he would be left there until he woke, and in either event that it was Salian who would do the retrieving because his men all had jobs of their own, and Salian had told him that his passenger would be no trouble. Tryk took pleasure in the captain's refusal to accommodate Salian's demands and regretted the necessity of poking holes in the blanket, and even more the necessity of cutting and unraveling part of the shroud. He'd hoped it would pass unnoticed below, but Salian had a small crowd around him now, several pairs of eyes glimmering up at Tryk, and the flash of his knife caused a small stir.

"What's he doing?"

"Cutting the ropes?"

"Ho!" This was the captain. "Don't cut those ropes."

"Sorry," Tryk called down. "My kidnapper will pay for them."

This, as he'd hoped, bought him a precious minute during which the captain said, "Kidnapper?" and Salian protested that Tryk was being dramatic and repeated his assurance that Tryk would be asleep in a few moments. The captain said, "A few moments can damage a ship and make us miss the tide," and that drew his attention back up to Tryk. "Bo'sun," he ordered, "climb up there and put a stop to this."

A mouse leapt to the shroud. Tryk wouldn't have time to finish, not before he arrived, so he leaned over and held his knife to the rope anchoring the shroud, which he had not yet touched. "Stay down there!" he called. "I'll cut the whole thing down if you come any closer!"

The bo'sun kept climbing, so Tryk sawed at the rope, and the mouse stopped with a quick look down, both questioning his captain and gauging how far he would fall if Tryk made good on his threat.

"Don't be a fool," the captain said. "You've nowhere to go."

"Then leave me alone and I won't damage your ship any further." As he talked, Tryk unwound the rope into its component cords.

The bo'sun hung for a moment, still looking down, until the captain said, "Bo'sun, return to the deck."

By this time, Tryk had threaded thin ropes through two of the holes in the blanket, focusing on the activity to keep himself alert. He scored rings in the mop handle a paw's width from either end. Properly they should be deeper grooves, but he didn't have time. He tied as tight a knot as he could manage around each ring with the ropes attached to the blanket, hoping the grooves would keep them from sliding off. The longest length of cord he had went around his waist like a belt, leaving just enough to tie it to the middle of the mop handle.

The handle now lay across the base of his tail. He looked out again to the shore, and as he did, his eyes drifted shut.

"Still awake up there?" Salian called.

Tryk's eyes snapped open. He would have to reduce his weight as much as possible to make it to the shore, as he wasn't sure this makeshift wing would work at all. He stripped off his tunic and pants, and weighed the knives. He wanted badly to keep them both, but would their weight drag him down? He slid them inside the rope around his waist, hoping he'd tied it tightly enough to keep them there. And last, he took Sunny's bracelet and slid it over his wrist.

With his paws through holes at the top two corners of the blanket, he stood and tested the blanket's lift against the wind. It wasn't great, but with his light bones and the stiff breeze from the shore, hopefully it would be enough. The knives might even help, weighing down his back half to keep the blanket puffed to the wind like a sail.

"Hey." Salian's voice, sharper. "What's he doing? Hey! Tryk! Don't jump."

"What?" Tryk couldn't resist calling back. The red fox paced back and forth below him, the white tip of his tail showing its lashing back and forth. "If I die, you don't get paid, is that it?"

"That's not just it. I don't want to see you die."

"Neither do I," Tryk said, mostly to himself, and leapt.

He had enough lift to clear the ship, he was sure, and there was a heart-stopping moment where the dark sea came rushing up to meet him, but before he'd even got to the level of the deck, the wind jerked the blanket upward, the rope yanked at his waist, and he was gliding some thirty feet over the surface of the water.

The glimmers of white where the waves broke seemed an impossible distance away. Tryk kept himself pointed toward them, stifled a yawn, and tried his best to glide the way he'd learned. But the breeze blowing from the land toward the sea, though it kept him aloft, also slowed his forward progress. He passed the rowboat; the two mice in it stopped rowing to stare at him as he passed by.

"Get him! Stop him!" Salian's cry came clearly enough that the mice definitely heard it as well. Tryk, beyond them now, couldn't see their reaction, but the splash of oars picked up. The crash of waves breaking grew closer, but still far ahead of him and rising toward him as he lost altitude.

All the flying he'd done served him well, and if he'd started fifty feet higher, he might have made it. When he dropped to ten feet over the water, the wind became less regular, with gusts that lifted him half a foot and stalled his forward progress completely, and lulls that dropped him closer to the water. His feet trailed into a swell, and he tried to lift them clear, but that was the beginning of the end. In another ten seconds, his legs were soaked, and a moment later he was splashing in the water, trying to swim. The blanket soaked up water quickly and pulled him down, but the one saving grace of the cool ocean water was that it shocked him awake enough to remember the knives. He seized the handle of one, turned it, and cut the rope around his waist easily.

Water soaked his fur as he struggled away from his makeshift wing, and currents pulled him away from the shore. Swimming should be easier than flying, he thought, but every time he looked at the wave crests ahead of him they did not seem to have moved, while the oars behind him drew closer. His muscles protested and his eyes closed. The shore was so far still, and he couldn't feel ground under his feet.

Something bumped his foot, something heavy, and paws grabbed his arm.

Tryk struggled and pulled, but the mouse holding him had better leverage and lifted him partly out of the water. Desperate, he snapped his other arm across, aiming the knife out of reflex (thank you again, Silence). The short blade sank into the mouse's forearm, eliciting a loud curse. The mouse released him and stood up in the boat, a long metal length gleaming in his paws.

The fox flailed in the water, ineffectually. The sword hesitated at its apex, and then the mouse seemed to fall backwards. Another shouted curse came from somewhere—Tryk flicked his ears. Was it behind him? In front of him? And then paws grabbed him again, this time around his chest, under his arms. Again he struggled, and a voice growled in his ear, "Hold still."

He tried to spin around, gulped salt water, and spit it out. "Silence?"

"Shh," came the answer, and paws pulled him away from the boat, away from the sword.

He floated on his back, and powerful legs beneath him kicked, stirring up the water around his tail. The water wasn't so cold now he was used to it. It was nice, in fact. "Can I sleep now?" he murmured.

"Not yet."

"The boat," he said. "The mice."

"Cherron's taking care of them. I'm taking care of you."

"Oh." He considered those words. "So why can't I sleep yet?"

"Because I'm not carrying you to shore. Now be quiet, this isn't as easy as it looks."

Stay awake, he told himself. How do I stay awake? Eyes open. Look up. Are there stars? There are stars. Count the stars. One, two, three, four…

He got up to twenty-three, and then the churning of Silence's legs stopped, though their progress backwards didn't. "You can stand now," the jaguar said. "Walk to shore."

Tryk lowered his legs and found sand under his feet. Silence let him go, and he staggered, then tottered through the waves. His body felt very heavy and his tail splatted wetly against the backs of his legs, but he made it out to the narrow band of sand, the jaguar at his side.

Once there, he turned to look for the rowboat, but his eyes couldn't find it against the white glimmer of waves. The smell of the sea filled his nose.

Another shape rushed forward to help him, metal and gems glinting on him. He leaned on the shorter capybara. "Sunny," he said, and held out his arm, the bracelet still somehow hanging there. "I got you this."

Sunny patted him. "I love it," he said. "You want to go back to the landing?"

"Can I sleep there?" he asked.

"Why are you so tired?" The jaguar slipped an arm under his other side to support him.

"Drugged," Tryk said, and the knife fell from his fingers to the sand.

***

Bright sun on his fur and eyes, thick humid air, the feel of gnats humming around him. He took a moment to process all this and then sat up and instantly regretted it.

"Ow. Ow." He pressed a paw to his head. But he was here, sitting on the dock at Mango Landing, and mango trees surrounded him and he wasn't on a carrack bound back for Divalia. And sitting by his side with a smile on his face was Flit, wings spread to catch the sun.

"From the drugs?" the bat asked.

Tryk nodded. "I suppose. I don't know what sleeping powder he used but it worked pretty well. Are the others here?"

"They're gathering fruit and making a shelter. Apart from the drugs, are you all right?"

The fox nodded. "I feel stupid though. I did it again, jumped into something and then realized it was wrong. Almost too late."

"Oh, good." Flit's smile grew. "So you did decide to stay. We were mostly sure when you jumped off the ship and tried to swim back, but Sunny said you might not be in your right mind after I explained to him and Silence what 'drugged' meant."

"It was just a sleeping drug. My father offered a reward for my return and Salian, that's the other fox, he wanted to collect it even after I told him I wanted to stay." Tryk slumped over. "I'm sorry I said I was leaving, sorry I made you fight some mice when I came back."

Flit snorted. "Don't apologize for making Cherron and Silence fight. They loved it." He paused and folded his wings in. "I'll tell you this before the others come back."

Tryk perked his ears and crossed his legs to sit more comfortably. The bat looked out over the river, away from him. "I visited my family two days ago. They asked me to come back. They say I can do the things I want and have my friends and they won't interfere."

"Really?" Tryk groomed the salt from his tail, his eyes fixed on Flit. This explained the bat's morning moodiness.

"They ask me every time I visit. This time they grew angrier when I said no."

"I thought they didn't approve…"

The bat clucked his tongue. "We have an expression, translated it is something like, 'you only need to serve one ripe *kimsha* to bring guests in.' I know them, you see. The ripe *kimsha*, the sweetness, was offering me that freedom if I came back, but once I was back, they wouldn't be able to leave things alone. I like the freedom I have, and I always turn down their offer. But having the decision…" His fingers closed over the fox's paw. "It makes the choice more meaningful."

"I see that." Tryk sighed. "I just wish I'd thought things through a little faster." He looked around the dock. "Why did you all come back for me?"

"Mmm." Flit smiled. "I reminded them that you sometimes jump into bushes without checking for thorns. This was a big jump. Once I said that, we all thought you might reconsider."

The cross fox inclined his head. "You know me pretty well." He glanced back at his old wings; his new knife sat atop them. "I lost my other knife."

"We can go look for it when the ships are gone, if you want."

"I'd like that." Tryk leaned against the bat's light form and watched the river go by in front of them. "You know, I don't know why my father wants me back, but other people are sure to try to get me."

"Let them." The bat wrapped a wing around his shoulder. "We'll be here."

War is hell.

No Choice About It
Mikasi Wolf

People always say we have a choice, that everything that happens to us is on account of our actions in the past or present. That we reap what we sow. I take a look around me at the soldiers in the cramped "armored" personnel carrier and see how big a crock of shit that is, each and every bump on the shell-ravaged ground driving the point further home.

Take the binturong with the SAW on the left side of the door, for example, whose scent makes up most of the interior's smell. Syed had a great life, great job, great everything in a city far from here. School and his childhood were hell for him, so he'd studied his way up through the best local university, and furthered his education in a much better university elsewhere. He kept in contact with his Mum, and soon got into a well-paying research job in one of the top ten research companies. He wasn't one to shirk his duties, so when his ma fell ill, he came back to care for her, despite the fact that war had just arrived in his country. He figured a son's duty was to care for his mother.

However, the government believed it was every man's duty to fight for his country, not for their family. So they had him drafted with everyone else. Never mind that lone surviving sons aren't actually allowed in combat roles. Sure, he was allowed to submit a letter of deferment, as long as he served with the unit while they processed his application. It's been a year since then, not that it matters anymore, especially with Syed's mother already dead from pneumonia. And now Syed's in the war only because he tried doing what's right. Only what's right may not be what's best, especially when the world's gone to shit.

Then you have Taro Kinjashima, the nervous otter at the front carrying all our spare ammo. Hailing from another country altogether, this isn't even his fight. But the law says Permanent Residents have to serve in the army, and even defend in times of need. Being posted at a foreign engineering firm merely gave the army an opportunity—a one-stop recruitment of ready-made engineers to keep their shit running. Taro worked in the car radio industry, so naturally the army assigned him to the radio and comms unit. Only to realize how different entertainment devices are from military communications. Not having a use for him anyways, rather than posting him in Administration or even sending him back home with a "thanks for trying", they saddled him up as a pack mule in a combat unit. Our unit. His job is carrying whatever needs carrying, from food, ammo to other crap like a spare GPMG tripod. As if the MG team needs more than one. His role isn't born of necessity, it's born out of no one knowing what to do with him, one of many miracles of Army Administration.

See that small-clawed otter with the glasses over there? Typical bookworm, you must think? Stereotypes do come true more often than not. That's Nu-Li, one of the rifleman. He started off as a born loser in school, always bullied and with shit grades. When he finally passed his Ordinary levels after the 5th try, he came to the realization that he wanted to put his country on the map, not just be a footnote in it. He completed his Advanced levels, got his Bachelor's Degree, and enrolled in a PhD program alongside the smartest and brightest of the nation, making new discoveries every year. Nu-Li believed he could make his mark on the world, and I've no doubt about his abilities. But the country needs guys who can hold a gun more than those who can solve equations and run experiments, so his entire cohort got enlisted. Except for his damn professors who'd been benefitting off his discoveries, but were far too old to do morning PT and route-marches. Nu-Liwas a fucking wreck during and after Basic Training with the others; his mind couldn't believe life could do this to him. Even now, he keeps muttering something under his breath; whether it's a religious mantra or mathematical equations I haven't yet figured. Tough luck; you can respect life by living it to the fullest, and not committing suicide when things get tough. But like any self-righteous bastard, life takes it all and spits at you in both eyes.

What about me, you ask, the tough-looking wolf who doesn't smile? I must be real leadership material for the brass to appoint me Lieutenant of this motley array, after all. Never mind the gang tattoos and affiliations, never mind my troubled past with my parents and the law. As the philosophers say, even the low-born and downtrodden may make something of themselves. Nope. No such luck. I happened to be reservist corporal when my Sergeant died, and happened to be Sergeant when my Lieutenant got himself blown up trying to be all gung-ho, showing us how to advance even when the bullets and bombs started flying. That guy was a real showoff, but at least he never acted like he didn't have to do the same as us. But because of his bullshit, I ended up getting promoted to acting Lieutenant; with all the responsibilities, but none of the benefits. Being a wolf might have something to do with it; people think all of us want to play the leader when it's really only a few of us with such ambitions. Again with the stereotypes. But they don't always come true.

And as our transport shakes with every missed shell and deflected round as we near certain death, you might think I must be pissed, being thrust into a war I don't believe in, being forced to lead others just because someone decided to up and die. But the truth is, with all the shit I've experienced in life, with all the beatings and bitings that parents, gangsters, and police have given me; with all the rejections and heartbreak as friend after friend, boyfriend after girlfriend left me, with all the shit life and society have thrown at me, I don't really care. We are all going to die, but unlike the many others with me, I accept my life for what it is. We survive every battle and accident in the hope we can live a few years more, but the truth is, it's all a waste of time if you can't enjoy it. We live our whole lives hoping to make use of others, and be made use of. Like now. Like later. Like in the future.

And as the next 120mm shell rips open the roof of our half-assed transport, explosion and shrapnel shredding flesh, cotton, steel and Kevlar alike, I don't regret this one bit. I know our deaths will prevent our enslavers from making use of us for another day more, for only through death is there true freedom.

The voice of a single individual can help steer a community, towards good or ill.

The Hero of Brambleward

Frances Pauli

Osef Thornmantle pushed a wooden handcart down the cobbled street. The Brambleward market waited at the center of town, and he'd gotten a later start than he liked. The cabin had been cold when he'd awakened, and Osef had kindled a small fire and banked it before loading his vegetables for the day's sale.

He preferred to return to a warm house. His bones practically demanded it.

The in-town homes bore shale roofs, baked clay walls and quaint, twig-framed windows and doorways. As he trudged forward with his load, heaving with one shoulder or the other when a wheel would stick on a particularly high cobblestone, a few pointed faces peered out between the curtains. In less than an hour the animals of Brambleward would be up and about, and he still had to get his goods to the stall.

Osef let his long ears sag against the back of his head. He twitched his nose irritably and pushed until the scar running across his furred back pinched and throbbed in complaint. He wore rough trousers with suspenders embroidered by Brambleward's best seamstress. His cotton shirt had a soft, grassy hue that contrasted with his gray fur in a way he found pleasing. And though his long feet had once spent every moment stuffed into a pair of marching boots, these days, Osef preferred to go unshod.

The carrots smelled of freshly turned earth. Even a long scrubbing couldn't erase the touch of his garden upon the finest vegetables he'd ever produced. The season had been long and lovely, and today's crop should bring him a fine amount of coin if he ever wrangled it to market.

Osef grunted, pushed, and freed the cart from another rut.

"Good morning, General," a high-pitched voice squeaked from a nearby doorway, Widow Dashwood, sweeping her front step before the sun was fully up.

"A fine morning, indeed." Despite his tardiness, and the irritating way Dashwood continued to call him General, the statement proved true. The morning was, in fact, delightful.

"Lovely carrots today."

The widow's husband had fought with Osef in the Vulpine war. The field mouse had not returned, and Mrs. Dashwood brought up their three daughters on her own. Osef reminded himself of her loss as her prattle delayed him even further.

"Thank you, Mrs. Dashwood."

"I've got something for you."

"Perhaps…"

The diminutive widow had already vanished back through her doorway. Osef considered continuing on, even prodded the cart forward another pace, but his memories of a fellow soldier, his compassion for the family, would not allow him the rudeness.

The field mouse reappeared, this time scampering out into the street. She carried a small clay pot in her paws, and when she reached Osef, held it up so the rabbit could retrieve it without too much bending.

"My thanks." Osef shuffled his large feet until the cart wheels creaked.

"It's a salve," Mrs. Dashwood squeaked. She reached one paw up to her left eye, tracing over her fur in the exact place Osef's was missing. "For your scars, General. T'will ease the aching."

"You're too kind." He blinked, cleared his throat. As if to shame him further, the scar on his back twinged. "Much appreciated."

Widow Dashwood's large eyes shone up at him. Osef cleared his throat again, dipped into a bow, and managed not to cringe when she saluted him. He smiled instead, tucked the salve into his leather satchel, and pushed his carrots down the street. The war was long since over. He wasn't the hero of Brambleward anymore, and Osef wished the town would let him forget it.

***

He returned home with a full purse. The country lane wound away behind him, disturbed only by the double rut that marked his cart's passing.

Dragonflies buzzed overhead as he approached the thatch-roofed cabin, and the dense forest beyond his garden yawned dark and silent.

After the bustle of town, home brought a welcome peace. The rabbit parked his cart just inside the garden gate and scanned the rows for any sign of weeds. The onions poked their bald heads through the soil, nearly ready for market as well. His turnips and radishes had been harvested down to a single line each, and those he would have to pull soon and store for his own use. He'd eaten the tender lettuces early in the season, but the vast bulk of his rows were occupied by carrots.

Osef admired the fuzzy green tops, lined up in perfect order, and frowned. He stepped between the empty lettuce patch and the flourishing onions, and approached the scene of his morning's picking. In the packed dirt beside the row, three fat carrots lay withering in the afternoon sun.

The rabbit scowled at them as if they were snakes. He'd never been so sloppy. The waste of it pressed his ears flat. His tail twitched annoyance, and he shuffled between the rows to pick up the lost veggies. Another lay at the edge of the garden. Osef glared at it. Had he driven the cart so recklessly that some of his goods had tumbled free? Where had his head been not to notice?

He retrieved the carrots, which could only feed his compost pile now, and stood staring into the thicket that fringed the wood. A breeze shifted the branches—moving shadows and a dance of light. Another thought flickered through the rabbit's mind, but he dismissed it as quickly as it came. He lived too far from town to fear delinquents, and the forest had been vacant as a tomb ever since the war.

As if on cue, his back pinched. Osef placed his free paw against the spot where a fox's sword had found its mark. He narrowed his gaze, searched the dark trees and felt a shiver creep across his shoulder blades. No foxes in the woods for years, and all the civilized animals lived in town or on farms too far from his for idle visits.

Exactly how he liked it.

He carried the vegetables to the compost pile, tossed them on the heap and turned back to his pride and joy. Tidy lines. Freshly turned earth. No weed or insect lived long inside his heavy twig fence. No neighbors haunted his doorstep, and no...

Osef stared at the dirt. He bent forward, ignoring the complaining of his back, and squinted at the packed soil beside his carrots. His paw reached out, dragging a finger around and around while his heart quickened and his other hand reached for the hilt of a sword that no longer hung from his hip.

He might have known he hadn't dropped a thing. Careless, Osef wasn't. The wind whispered to him now, singing in one long ear as he stood and surveyed his home. Secluded, perhaps, remote certainly. He kept himself apart from the animals of Brambleward, kept to himself. But today, he hadn't managed to hold the world at bay.

Today, someone had been in his garden.

***

"What did it look like?" Pfaff Oakenwall leaned against the side of Osef's stall, chewing on a nub of tobacco root.

"What do you think it looked like?" Osef snapped and then smiled for the shrew perusing his carrots. "It looked like a paw print."

"Fox?" Oakenwall lowered his round head and peered at Osef from under his heavy eyebrows. It was a conspiratorial look, one to match the note of both fear and excitement in the woodchuck's voice. A secret between soldiers, that look said. A warning to be on watch.

"No." Osef snuffed out the moment and shook his head. "Rodent for sure, but slender, long toes."

"Worse than a fox, then," Pfaff said. "Sounds like you've got foreigners in your woods."

"Rubbish." Osef shrugged off the idea and reordered the carrots that had been rifled by customers so that they lay in tidy orange lines. "Most likely some farmer's son."

"Who'd have his own carrots to pilfer." Pfaff nodded sagely, as if he'd even seen the print, as if he'd peered into Osef's forest boundary and spied the exact culprit. "No. Most likely refugees from Fernsglen."

"Refugees? In my garden?"

"From Fernsglen." Pfaff gave a grim look, nodding as if it were certain now. "Running from *their* fox problem. Not fighters, the Fern folk."

"They'd have to cross the Gash to get to my forest." Osef imagined trekking over that terrain and shook his head. The open plain between Fernsglen and their northern border bore nothing edible. It would take days to cross for the nimblest rabbit, and the lack of cover would make anyone who tried a fast meal for even a slow fox. "My money's on some bored farm boy."

He ignored the woodchuck's snort and shook off the idea of immigrants. Some kid had been at his garden, and that was that. The morning wandered into a much slower afternoon, but Osef had sold all of his carrots an hour before the market closed. He began packing up even before the final sale, and after bidding Pfaff a good afternoon, scrambled out of the square and back up the lane at a faster trot than his cart wheels, or his back, appreciated.

If he hurried, he reasoned, he might catch the culprit in the act. But when the rabbit rolled his cart against his fence and examined the garden rows, nothing was amiss. The onions stood in solid lines. The carrots marched like soldiers along the front. Osef squinted at the trees, listening to the breezes play with the slender branches.

Perhaps the kid had only wandered too far from his own farm and had grabbed a quick snack from Osef's carrots. It was thievery, just the same, but it didn't mean the perpetrator would return. His wide shoulders lowered. His long ears perked. The sense of violation faded, and the rabbit twitched his tail and wandered down his garden pathway looking for weeds.

He stooped and pulled, cradling the cringing in his back with one paw and plucking a thistle sprout with the other. Thistle made good tea, and Osef let it grow wild around the borders of his property. The penalty for that was the occasional stray in his garden, but he considered it a fair tradeoff. When the onion rows were bare of interlopers, he carried a sparse armload of unwanted plants to the compost bin.

And found more prints overlaying the first one.

Osef squatted beside his compost bin and squinted at the dirt. Long prints, rodent in shape and light of foot. They tracked from his bin to the forest, from the rows of carrots to the bin. He pinched the dirt between his fingers, sniffed it, and then let the grains fall like seeds on the wind.

Pfaff's words echoed in his mind. *You've got foreigners…*

He stood and returned to his carrots, this time examining the rows with a more critical eye. Whoever had been at his vegetables had taken extra care this time, plucking only every five or six tops in and smoothing away their paw prints everywhere except by the compost bin. If they'd caught those as well, Osef would never have known a thing was missing.

As it was, it took him a good five minutes to find the holes in his rows. It took him twice that long to decide what he meant to do about it. Osef rubbed the small of his back, let his ears droop toward the back of his skull, and marched for the front porch of his sanctuary. There would be no market tomorrow, though it meant he'd waste more carrots than he liked. Tomorrow, he would pack a meager cart, wheel it to the edge of his property and then circle back through the thickets to keep watch on what was his.

Osef had a thief all right, and tomorrow, he meant to catch him in the act.

***

He brought as many of the carrots as he could carry, abandoning only a few dozen to wither in the cart. No help for it, leaving with the thing empty would have looked suspicious. If the thief was keeping an eye on his movements, Osef had to at least appear to begin his day as usual. But once he'd parked his produce beside the thorn bushes along the road, he couldn't bring himself to waste it all.

And so he trudged through the brambles with his arms overflowing with carrots and his old saber dangling in its sheath from his hip. Circling back, Osef stalked to the border of his own property, picking his footing so as to go in silence, and ducking through the thorn bushes and under branches rather than snapping them. When he neared the garden fence, he nestled the carrots into a nook in a fallen log and crept forward with his body held low and his nose twitching for any scent that his interloper might be about.

Nothing in the garden moved. The onions and carrots remained neatly in line, and Osef settled himself into a spot where he could see the spread of his rows without being visible himself. He watched through the leaves, listening to the breeze playing overhead and nibbling on one of his plump carrots.

A meadowlark joined in the wind's song, and the forest became a symphony, leaves fluttering, the whistle of the bird's fellows, and the subdued buzzing of a dragonfly nearby. Osef leaned back on his paws and listened. He finished off the green tops of his snack and considered reaching for another until the thicket on the far side of the garden rustled.

His heartbeat revved in his broad chest. His paw hovered near the hilt of his sword, and he eased his body forward, rocking onto his wide feet and then holding as still as a stone. The meadowlark called again, sharp and lilting. The brambles near the compost bins shifted, rippling in a wave while someone eased along behind them. Osef held his breath and fixed his gaze upon the moving brush.

The soft rustle of the leaves stilled. For a moment, nothing moved and he feared he'd been spooked for no reason, a bird perhaps, something native to his garden border. Then, the thicket parted all at once and a cloaked figure stepped through. They ducked between the twig rails of the garden fence and stepped gingerly toward Osef's carrots.

Moving like a thrush when the hawk is about, the thief turned their head from side to side between each step, placing one foot here and the other there as if to intentionally scatter their prints. The rough cloak and hood obscured them from view, and Osef leaned forward and to the side, trying to catch a glimpse of paw or muzzle, anything that would clue him into the manner of creature he dealt with.

His paw wrapped around the sword hilt, cool and strong in his grip. The thief reached his produce rows, stepping carefully over the first three before lowering to a squat and reaching for one fluffy green carrot top.

Osef eased forward while the thief plundered his carrots. He took slow steps, squeezing below branches and around thorns. Without a sound, he reached the fence. His heart beat high and fast. His nerves tightened, preparing for conflict, and his mind flickered between the current crime and his long months on the front, battling the foxes back from Brambleward's border.

The breeze shifted, carrying his first scent of the stranger's pelt. Osef stepped through the twig rail with Pfaff's declaration fresh in his thoughts. *Foreigners.* He ducked under and through, and though the brushing of his ears against the wood seemed loud enough to wake the dead, the thief remained too absorbed in their pilfering and showed no sign of alarm.

Until Osef drew his sword.

The ring of steel he couldn't mask, and the thief reacted as if lightning had struck the carrots. They sprang straight into the air, twisted, and fell back in a tangle of cloak and fuzzy limbs. Osef leapt forward, two bounds that brought him within range of the stranger. He pinned the corner of the cloak beneath one of his long feet and raised the sword point in a gesture that should have told the owner not to move, not one inch.

But panic had gripped his thief. They twisted and flailed, oblivious to his weapon. When the cloak would not come free, its owner abandoned it. Quite suddenly, Osef was staring into the terrified eyes of his foreigner. He towered over her, sword in hand, and yet it was he who froze. It was Osef, who found he couldn't move.

The squirrel woman had a soft gray pelt, but it was poorly groomed and dirty as the rags he used to oil his cart. She might have been as tall as him, or close to it, but her whole body was gaunt and as thin as a reed. Osef knew many squirrels, and none of them had a line of bones along their ribs, a protruding collar or a tail that barely had the muscle it needed to lift itself above the dirt. This squirrel was starving, and the rabbit suffered a twinge of guilt at the pathetic, single carrot clutched in her right paw.

Her cheeks sank inward, dark and hollow. Nothing about her was puffed or round except the two, over-wide eyes blinking up at him through a sheen of tears.

His impression was made in the matter of a breath, and before he could register it fully, the squirrel had sprung to her feet again. She abandoned the cloak beneath his toes, dropped the precious carrot, and bolted for the far fence.

"Wait," Osef called after her, and she flinched to the side without slowing. He watched, dumbstruck, as she dived through the fence and vanished back into the thicket. Beyond that was the deep woods, and though it would have been an easy pursuit, Osef only stood and stared at the brush where she'd disappeared.

He trembled from ear tip to tail, and only after his heart had stilled to a normal rhythm did he realize he still held the sword, point out, wavering in the air like a compass needle. He still held the squirrel's cloak, trapped beneath his big foot, and despite the churning footprints on his garden path, despite the wreckage her thrashing had caused among his carrots, Osef could think only of the night to come, of the crisp chill that had already taken hold in the wee hours, and about the warm cloak the squirrel would not have to keep the cold away.

***

The next morning, he filled his cart for a full day's sale. He filled an old egg basket that had been collecting dust in his rafters, too. When the carrots overflowed the woven vessel, Osef draped the squirrel's cloak over it and set it all at the very edge of his garden, as close to the spot where she'd emerged as possible.

She might not return at all, but Osef believed the cloak would bring her to his boundary at least one more time. The carrots were easy to spare, easy to forgive when he had so much surplus. When the fat around his middle completely obscured his ribcage.

With his apology in place, the rabbit left it, pushing his cart from the garden, down the lane, and only glancing back once or twice before the hills had taken his cottage fully from view. His thoughts swirled, replaying his encounter with the hungry squirrel over and over as he went. He pictured her, skeleton poking through her fur, and could easily guess what had brought her to his garden.

How long had she been living in his woods? Osef was certain that she was, in fact, living there. He tried to imagine why and came up with too many horrors. Had he scared her away for good? How would she survive without her cloak, ratty as it was? Even a little barrier from the cold could make all the difference.

He rolled into the market late. The other vendors had set up shop and already a few early customers drifted between the stalls. Pfaff eyeballed him sideways as he unloaded the carrots, but Osef ignored him, arranging his produce into neat lines and then parking his cart behind the counter where he could lean upon it. By the time he'd settled behind his wares, Widow Dashwood appeared to purchase a bundle of carrots and ask him how the salve had worked.

"It's lovely," Osef said, despite the fact that he hadn't tried it yet. If his scars had pulled at all on the journey to town that morning, the preoccupied rabbit hadn't paid them any notice. "Thank you, Mrs. Dashwood."

When she'd tottered away, Pfaff abandoned his stall and trundled over to Osef's. He leaned against the carrots, mussing a line with his elbow, and tried the suspicious look again. "A bit late today. Not like you at all."

"Cart gets stuck on the blasted cobbles." Osef scowled at the mess and shrugged, but Pfaff wasn't letting him off easily.

"And a day off yesterday. Your carrot thief come back?"

Osef grunted and pushed the carrots back into line.

"I suppose it was just some farmer's kid." Pfaff's eyes narrowed. He puffed out his cheeks and gave Osef a too-knowing look. "Fernsglen folk have been pilfering like crazy over in Meadowdown."

"Why?" The rabbit sagged back against his cart and let Pfaff have his moment to gloat. "Why are they here, Pfaff? What would drive them to risk the Gash, to go without, go hungry?"

"Foxes, same as we had." Pfaff shrugged. "But they had no standing army in Fernsglen. Not much for fighting at all."

"So they just left?" Osef frowned and stared out at the rest of the market. What would Brambleward do if all of Fernsglen showed up, hungry and desperate for somewhere safe? What would *he* do, if the squirrel did come back? If she didn't?

"It's a real mess, sure enough," Pfaff said. "But they ought to go straight back and fight for their land, if you ask me. No good coming here, causing trouble for us folk that already beat our foxes out of town."

"Maybe they can't go back," Osef argued. "Maybe they're starving."

"Plenty to eat back in Fernsglen." Pfaff would give the refugees no quarter. He crossed his stout arms and squinted at Osef. "That's exactly what I'd tell 'em too, if they were sniffing around my crops."

"I've the surplus," Osef said. "No harm in sharing a few carrots."

"Doesn't sound like the General Thornmantle I know," Pfaff said. "The General was all, 'run the bastards through or send them packing.'"

"Foxes," Osef mumbled. Talking about the war made him uncomfortable. His pelt itched all over, and his nose tightened as if it could still smell the musk and the blood. "Foxes that attacked first, Pfaff. Not hungry women and children."

"Nobody made 'em come here," Pfaff insisted. "Nobody invited 'em. Mark my words, you let one of them off easy, and you'll have five more by the end of the week."

He'd adopted a tone Osef had come to recognize and avoid at all costs. Letting the subject drop would convince the woodchuck he'd won the argument, but it would be no good continuing the conversation either. Pfaff had already decided he was right.

Osef grunted, smoothed his ears with one paw, and waited for the woodchuck to get back to his own goods. The market crowd thickened, and they managed to avoid the topic of refugees, his garden, and the thief for the rest of the afternoon. When his carrots sold out, Osef packed quickly and slipped away while Pfaff was busy with a customer.

All the way home, the rabbit heard his fellow soldier's argument like an echo. He rolled along the lane with the dragonflies buzzing overhead, and tried not to imagine his garden overrun with squirrels. He grew a hearty surplus, certainly, but there had to be some for market, too. There had to be enough to put up for winter, and unless he expanded the plots…

By the time he'd reached home, his nose twitched non-stop and his mind shifted between ideas for a better fence or a design for expanding the garden. If he cleared even a few feet of bramble around the edges, he could plant a lot more rows.

He approached the gate with a belly full of nerves, and immediately found the basket by the fence, the cloak missing. Osef sighed and felt a rush of relief he hadn't expected. She'd be warm at least, warm and possibly less terrified of him. He parked the cart and crossed the garden. The carrots were gone as well, apology accepted. In their place, Osef found a slip of parchment, dirty and crinkled as if it had been salvaged from someone's trash heap.

There was writing on it, letters scratched in haste and barely dark enough to make out. Not that that helped him. Osef didn't recognize any of the words. He held it in his paws, stared at the paper with an ache building behind his eyes. The squirrel had written him a note in her own language. She'd left him a message, but Osef couldn't read a bit of it.

***

The next morning, Osef knocked on Widow Dashwood's door. He parked his full cart beside her stone pathway, and stood on the doorstep with his hat in his paws and the squirrel's note tucked into his shirt pocket. He'd seen the curtain shuffle before coming up the walk but still feared he might have woken the field mouse.

"General!" The squeak at least *sounded* delighted. "What a surprise."

"Good morning, Mrs. Dashwood." Osef dipped forward into a polite bow. "I wonder if you might have a moment?"

"Of course." She shuffled farther into the house and motioned for Osef to come in. "Looks like a good market day, General. Lovely sun."

"Yes." Osef scooted inside and stepped from the narrow entry into the cozy parlor to allow the widow room to close the door. "Almost time to put things up for the year."

"Oh, I've already been at the jam." Mrs. Dashwood smiled and pressed her little paws together beneath her chin. "Can I offer you some tea, General?"

"No. Thank you, but I have to get my wares set up." He paused, shifted his weight from one foot to the other, and then drew the note from his pocket, smoothing it as much as possible. "I wonder if you might know someone, Mrs. Dashwood. You're very well considered in town, and I could use some help with this. I mean, someone who might be able to read it."

"Read it?" The mouse's eyes shone in the light from her hall sconces. Her whiskers twitched. "Let's have a look."

Osef suffered a momentary reluctance to part with the paper. He smoothed it again, and when the widow reached for it, sighed and placed it in her paw. "It was written by someone from Fernsglen."

"Oh my." Mrs. Dashwood nodded fiercely. "I see."

"Can you read it?"

"Oh no." Her ears drooped to the sides, and she shook her head sadly. "I might know someone who can, though. General, I do hope you haven't been unduly bothered by our recent influx of foreign animals."

"Not bothered." Osef watched her brighten. He'd left a full basket of carrots by the garden fence again, with the addition of a few turnips, but he wouldn't call it a bother at all. "I only wondered what it said."

"The mayor is in quite a state about it, you know."

"Is he?"

"Oh yes. They'll have to do something, of course. That or wait until the weather turns and nature sorts it out for us."

Osef flinched. He couldn't help it, nor did he mask his reaction if the widow's expression were any indication. She fluttered her hands, shaking his note like a handkerchief and lowering her long tail to drag on the floor.

"It's sad, of course, but what are we to do? We've enough to worry about just getting by ourselves."

Osef looked around the parlor, nicely appointed, warm and comfortable. He tightened his lips and nodded for her. "You said you knew who might be able to translate it?"

Widow Dashwood clapped her paws together, rumpling the note in the process. "I'd say Geraldine down at the bookstore could do it. That or she'd have a reference on hand that might help."

"Thank you so much, Mrs. Dashwood." Osef sighed. Of course Geraldine could do it. If he'd let himself think farther than the safety of Mrs. Dashwood, he might easily have gone there first.

"Would you like me to take it down there? You've got produce to deliver."

"Thank you, but it's no problem. I'll stop by after market."

He bid the field mouse good day, bowed three times on the way out her door and then gathered his cart, his note, and his resolve and marched directly to the bookstore. Geraldine was an elderly hedgehog who'd owned Brambleward's only literary shop for as long as Osef could remember. Though he didn't relish another discourse on the current immigration problems, he agreed with Mrs. Dashwood's assessment. If anyone could help him read the note, it would be Geraldine.

***

"It's a bit faded." The hedgehog leaned over the counter, rolling her shoulders so that her prickles became a halo of spikes. "But it's definitely the language of Fernsglen."

Osef braced himself for the next confrontation. He'd left his cart in the shade of a dogwood tree outside the shop, but at this rate, doubted he'd get the load to market today. The bookstore was dim, crowded, and as messy as his own bedroom. Piles of volumes blocked many of the aisles, and Geraldine appeared to be trapped behind the counter by a tower of boxes.

"Can you read it?" He held his breath.

"No." The pointy face scrunched up, beady eyes riveted to the paper. "Fascinating. I've always wanted to pick up another tongue."

"Excuse me?"

"I've a book here somewhere that can help us."

Osef's heart leapt. He'd expected another argument against the animals of Fernsglen, but Geraldine's attention had fixed and stuck to the academic issue of translating the note.

"Let me think. Yes. In the back stacks, history and social sciences. Just a… minute."

It took Geraldine two full minutes to extract herself from behind the counter. In the end, she climbed over the boxes and then waddled down one of the far aisles, muttering to herself in a tone Osef couldn't follow.

She returned with a smaller book than he'd expected, one with a tatty cloth binding and pressed gold letters on the cover.

"Here we are." The hedgehog joined Osef on the customer side of the counter. She lay the book down beside his rumpled note and immediately began rifling through the pages. "Very interesting. This part here."

"Yes?" Osef leaned closer, avoiding the prickles by inches but eager to know the squirrel's message.

"This word is 'gratitude' or possibly 'thanks'. *Much gratitude.*"

The knots in Osef's shoulders unwound a little. He blinked away the relief and held his breath while the hedgehog went to work on the rest of the note.

"And this verb is 'work', 'I work.'"

"Work?"

"Yes. I believe it's conjugated in the first person. 'I work', but then this is 'you.'"

"I work you?" Osef frowned.

"I work of you, actually," Geraldine said. "Much thanks. I work of you."

"That doesn't make any sense."

"Hmm." Geraldine rubbed her muzzle in the spot directly between her eyes. "It's possible the conjugation is wrong. Then there's colloquial nuances."

For a moment, they both stared at the note, then at the book, as if the squirrel's meaning would somehow manifest on either page. Finally, Geraldine sighed and closed it. The cover read: *Abroad in Fernsglen- A Traveler's Guide.*

"My apologies, General. I fear that's the best I can do."

"No apology required. You've done far more than I could." Of course, he hadn't had the book. Osef eyed it and the way the hedgehog tapped the cover absently with her paw. He might need to translate more letters, and he'd wasted a good portion of his market day on this one. Pfaff would be suspicious already, but if Osef had the book for his own use… He smoothed and re-folded the note, sliding it back into the safety of his pocket before asking, "How are you set for carrots this year, Geraldine?"

He left the bookstore with an empty cart and a carefully wrapped copy of *Abroad in Fernsglen*. Skipping the market entirely would get him home a few hours early and spare him whatever comments Pfaff had prepared for the day. Osef pushed his cart out of town, past the cobbles onto the dusty lane. He whistled as he went, using his large front teeth to sharpen the notes and feeling for the first time in ages a great deal younger than he had any right to.

His thoughts fixed upon the note, specifically on the part he understood. She'd thanked him for the carrots. Perhaps that meant she wasn't afraid, that she'd come back for the basket he'd left her today as well. That in time her bones might protrude a little less, her tail lift a little higher.

I work of you. Osef contemplated a half dozen things that might mean. Perhaps, she'd only meant to thank him for his work. Or it might be that the word 'work' was incorrect, much as Geraldine assured him the translation was accurate. Nuance mattered when dealing with other languages. Perhaps it meant the squirrel would function again with his help.

He'd almost settled on that interpretation when at last he parked the cart inside the garden gate. Osef took the wrapped book in his arms and, forgoing his usual inspection, made directly for the basket he'd filled and left for the squirrel before leaving.

It was there that the note's meaning became perfectly clear. I work of you. The carrots had been accepted as before, but in their place, the basket was filled with weeds, *his* weeds from *his* garden. The squirrel had worked *for* him. She'd taken his offering, but paid for it with her paws' labor.

A proud thing to do. Osef nodded as if she were there to see his approval. He carried the weeds to the compost bin and, after checking that none were in seed, dumped them on top of the heap. His rows were clean as a whistle, which combined with his early arrival home to give him a solid two hours of idle time.

He set the basket beside the bin and collected an armful of firewood for the cabin. He liked a warm house, and tonight, he had some extra time and a new book to study.

***

"Someone set fire to Macland's haystack." Pfaff crossed his arms and tilted his round head to one side. "Nearly spread to the barn before they got it out."

"Someone's haystack always catches fire this time of year, Pfaff." Osef arranged his carrots and bit his tongue. "The heat builds up is all."

The woodchuck grunted. It seemed the immigrant situation had seized the attention of all of Brambleward. Rumors spread from the market outward, ripples of hostility and fear that no reasonable argument could assuage. In the week since the foreign squirrel had been weeding and tending to Osef's garden, the townspeople had begun to have their own encounters with the fleeing population of Fernsglen.

That these were only reported as negative experiences worried him. The suspicion had turned to panic when one of the shops downtown had been broken into. Despite the fact that it turned out to be the work of a disgruntled customer, somehow, the initial blaming of the refugees never quite abated. Even proven innocent, the animals of Fernsglen were somehow twisted into the culprits. The actual crime was dismissed in favor of the more exciting fiction.

It worried him for certain. Almost as much as the chill in the air each morning and the fact that a frost was most likely only days away.

He'd spent every night pouring over the language book, and he'd left a note in the basket every morning, along with a selection of his produce that he hoped would put some meat on the squirrel's bones. Despite his messages in her own language, the squirrel had not replied. Not when he thanked her for her work, and not when he asked her what she needed, if she were in danger, or getting cold.

Perhaps his translations were entirely wrong, but Osef had simplified each request, hoping the gist of his words, at least, would be understood. This morning he'd changed tactics and written a message he'd been working on for several days: "How did you get here? Why have you come?"

In hindsight, he hoped it didn't sound accusatory. In light of all the rumor mongering going around, Osef imagined the squirrel might take his note the wrong way. But he'd hoped a direct question would spur her to answer. Now, staring at Pfaff's fat, nasty expression, Osef feared he'd drive the squirrel away instead.

"Thinking of rounding them up, you know," Pfaff said. "Send the whole lot back across the borders and be done with them."

"Feed them to the foxes, you mean." Osef growled and flattened his long ears to his skull. "What has happened to our sense of mercy, Pfaff? Have we no compassion left?"

"Perhaps I lost it in the war." Pfaff scowled at him. "If you'll remember, those same foxes took enough Brambleward lives to paint the fields in our blood."

"Exactly why I wouldn't wish them upon our neighbors," Osef said.

"And what's to keep them from following the Fernsglen cowards right back into Brambleward?"

Osef stared into the woodchuck's eyes. Behind the bravado, he caught the flicker of something else, something he could finally relate to, if not forgive. He sighed and lifted his ears to a more relaxed position. "I don't want another war, Pfaff. No more than anyone would. Maybe you and I want one even less than those who haven't… who didn't do what we did.

But there has to be another way to solve this. There has to be a solution that helps us all."

"And if there isn't?" Pfaff's voice lowered but didn't soften. His eyes might hold a shimmer of fear, but there was accusation there as well. "If there's no other way to avoid a war, *General*, what will you do then?"

"I'll do my duty, Pfaff." Osef let his anger tinge the words, and the woodchuck had the sense to back up a step, to lower his gaze. "I dare say you of all animals wouldn't doubt that."

The woodchuck nodded and left him alone, the conversation having come to a place neither of them cared to pursue further. If Pfaff had meant to question his loyalty to Brambleward, he'd be a fool to press it openly. They both knew who the hero of the Vulpine War was. It would take more than a rumor to change Osef's status with the townspeople. But he felt the tension between them for the rest of the day, and he knew better than to write off Pfaff's hostility as harmless.

If the refugees became a serious problem, Osef would have to take a stand, could already see his opinions on the matter would be neither popular nor well received by his community. He finished his market day without further engaging the woodchuck, and though they exchanged a curt goodbye, it did nothing to ease his sense of dread. That built with each step he took toward home, adding to the worry he'd already wrapped around his garden helper.

By the time Osef wheeled his cart into the cabin yard, he was so distracted by his anxieties that he'd entered the garden and closed the gate before he even noticed the squirrel.

***

She refused his offer to enter the cabin, so Osef brought the book outside. They sat on his porch steps, passing the thing back and forth while the afternoon waned and the air turned too cold for staying out of doors. So far, they'd accomplished introductions and a few confused attempts at discussing the coming frost.

"But the weather, Seffia," Osef pointed to the words he'd cobbled together on a fresh piece of paper. He believed it said, winter is coming, but couldn't be certain from the way she shook her head. "You must have a warm place to stay."

"No, Osef." She tapped long fingers on her own note. It read, "Too much. I work for food."

She'd latched onto that phrase and said it so many times he wanted to cry. Her ribs still showed beneath her pelt and as far as he could tell the days of good eating had done very little for her condition.

"Here." He took the book again and searched for the right words. His frustration pressed his whiskers into a downward arc, and his ears fell limp and sad against his head. "Just a minute."

But she pulled the volume from his hands and flipped through the pages like a mad thing, fast and with long fingers that had grown knobby in her malnourished state. Finding whatever she sought, she began to write again, one word after the other, and Osef leaned over and read as she worked.

No work for cold.

Osef shook his head and tried to extract the book, but Seffia clung to it until he relented. She flipped and wrote, and Osef read each word as it came, with his heart in his throat.

No weeds in winter.

"But…" he choked on it, had to start over. "But there has to be something."

Seffia's large eyes grew soft and she shook her head, pointed to her repeating message. "Too much."

"But you could clean." He took the book as gently as possible from her fingers and chased the new thought through its pages. With painstaking care, Osef translated and wrote what he hoped was an invitation and not an insult: *You could clean the house.*

Seffia read it almost as slowly as he'd written it. She sucked in a breath, closed her eyes tight, and folded her long-fingered paws in her lap. He gave her a moment, and made no move that might spook her again. When she finally looked up at him, Osef felt they'd come to an understanding at last.

The squirrel smiled, and the rabbit let a week's worth of worry slip away in a relieved breath.

***

Three days later, Osef came home to a basket still full of carrots. No new paw prints decorated his garden rows, and not a single carrot had been tampered with. He stood, staring at the overflowing basket, with his heart pounding like a bass drum.

Something had happened to her.

His paws clenched into fists at his sides, and his vision narrowed until all he could see were the plump orange carrots that should have fed Seffia today. Osef tried to breathe the panic away, tried to rationalize the squirrel's absence. Perhaps she'd only skipped a day to rest. Maybe, he'd offended her with his offer after all.

His gut told him both possibilities were rubbish. Seffia's visits had been as reliable as his pocket watch. Her condition wouldn't allow her to skip a day. Osef's tail twitched. His whiskers flickered up and down, and he sniffed the air as if he might find the squirrel there.

Only a trace of old scent answered, and Osef bounded for the house, strapped on his saber, and bolted back across the garden. He slipped through the fence beside the compost bin, and he searched for the trail he knew Seffia's coming and going should have made.

She'd been careful, though, and it took him too long to find the traces of her passing. Cursing her skill, Osef found a broken branch at last, a good ten paces from his garden border. He found another a few feet farther in, and certain the trail was Seffia's, he followed it. One paw hovered over his hilt and the other reached for the next break in the foliage, the next trace of a print that would lead him onward.

The wood opened up as the brush thinned, but the squirrel's trail followed along the edge of the brambles. Rather than enter the dark trees, she'd kept to the thicket for shelter. Osef would have approved if he hadn't been terrified for her. If he could discover her tracks, his panic reasoned, so could someone else. He would have been relieved, if the trail hadn't ended abruptly.

Osef looked up. The boughs overhead were undisturbed. He retraced his steps forward and back. Beginning with the last broken twig, Osef began to search the brambles, moving each tendril aside and looking for any sign he might have missed. He bent low to the ground and sniffed. He reached into the stickers and pried the thicket apart.

Something smacked him on the nose. Though the impact stung, there was little force behind it. Osef blinked, shuffled backwards and stared into the brush at a pair of shining, wide eyes.

"Seffia?"

The thicket rustled. A low voice whispered, fast and wholly in Seffia's language. It was answered by a high-pitched squeaking and a great shaking of the bush.

"Hello? Seffia?"

A stout stick poked out of the brush. With a flurry of leaves, a squirrel boy followed it. He held the weapon in one paw and was followed by a smaller squirrel, so like him that they could only be siblings. The two of them stopped just outside the safety of their hiding place and began to chatter simultaneously.

"Wait," Osef tried. "Slow down a moment."

The bigger boy stabbed the air with his stick and then pointed it at Osef.

"I'm Osef," the rabbit said. "Is Seffia—" He stopped mid-sentence. At the sound of his name the boys began chattering again, heads together and upright tails flicking madly. He heard his name more than once, and seized upon that fact. "That's me, Osef. That's right."

When they looked his way, he tapped his chest and repeated it. "Osef. Please, where is Seffia?"

They considered him. The little one tugged on his brother's hand. Osef noted that, though thin, both the boys' bodies were in far better shape than Seffia's. He noted, and he understood at last why the carrots he gave had not improved her condition much. She'd been feeding three with the basket's offerings, and from the looks of it, taking the lightest share.

Osef cleared his throat and waited for the squirrel boys to trust him. It took moments only—they had so little choice. Alone in a foreign forest at their age. He made his smile gentle when the larger boy said his name again. This time, the little squirrel pointed up the line of thicket and scurried along it, half dragging his younger brother behind him.

They rediscovered Seffia's trail a ways up. Osef found the point where she'd emerged from the thicket and stared into the tunnel. They'd made a warren inside the brambles, a maze of tunnels that allowed them to vanish in one spot and reappear somewhere else.

A tug on his arm got him moving again. The boys led him to a gap in the thicket, and there a thin trail wound outward until it broke on a patch of blackberries that still held a few, sad, late berries. Not much nutrition, but Osef supposed it would be a nice break from carrots. He also guessed the squirrel had come here to glean after leaving his place the night before, and that thought put a ball of lead in his belly.

He motioned for the boys to remain behind the bush and then crept around, finding Seffia's prints and reaffirming his theory that they were long hours old. When he found the basket, his heart sank. It lay upturned against the ground, and the bushes around it were shredded and smashed. The lane which passed his house continued north here, and only a thin strip of brush lay between the berries and the road.

Osef retrieved the basket, clutching it in his paws with enough force to bend the stout handle. He carried it to the very side of the road, and examined the tracks etched in the dust knowing full well what he'd find. Knowing just as surely that Seffia was long gone.

*** *

It took little coaxing to get the boys back to his cabin. Once they'd accepted him as Osef, they'd both relaxed. He settled them in at his dining table with a bowl of soup each, a loaf of bread between them, and firm orders to lock the door and not let anyone in. He could only hope they understood him in the end, and he marched from the cabin armed with his saber and an overpowering sense of urgency.

What if they left while he was out? What if he found Seffia only to lose her boys? What if he was too late?

Osef sprinted up the lane with his white-tufted tail bobbing. He found the spot where Seffia had been accosted—and judging from the state of the brambles and the interwoven tracks leading to a cart rut, she had absolutely been accosted—and bounded on, loping now and using his front paws to add speed.

The vehicle was easy enough to follow. Four wheels and an overloaded bed had made deep cuts in the dusty surface of the road. But the hour was fading fast, and the sun already flirted with the distant hills. It wouldn't be long before the dusk made following the trail a job for noses better suited to tracking than his own.

He sniffed anyway, picking out the flavor of the cart in case darkness fell before he caught it up. Then Osef sprinted, churning legs that hadn't done more than push a cart back and forth to town in years. His back twinged and throbbed. His scars pulled tight, reminding him of other moments when he'd been a hair's breadth too late. His eyes teared, and Osef ran, ran with every ache and stutter pushing him onward.

The road branched again a quarter mile further north. Here he feared to lose the trail. The darkening sky already made the ruts blend together. When he crowned the last hill before the split, however, his prayers were answered in the horrific sight lain out before him.

They'd made a camp of old Stewardson's farm. Lights glowed inside the rickety barn. Tents sprouted like dirty mushrooms across the wide pasture, and additional wire, barbed and twisting, had been strung above and between the rails. Animals from Brambleward patrolled the fence, armed with sword or pitchfork, and inside it… Inside it the last of Osef's faith in his community died.

He spied the cart, or one like it, that had taken Seffia. Three of them parked beside the barn, lined up like a train delivering cargo to the depot. That cargo milled about the pasture, moving in and out of tents or sitting against them. The refugees of Fernsglen huddled around campfires and clustered together as far from the newly barbed fence as possible.

Osef stormed down the hillside. He marched through the farm gate and straight for the pasture fence. Two guards intercepted him. The chipmunk wore overalls and held a four pronged potato fork. The beaver carried a saber not unlike Osef's.

"Stop right there." The beaver moved directly into his path and then stopped short. "General?"

"Move aside, Higgins."

"But, sir."

Both of them moved with him, not exactly barring his way, but not getting out of it either.

"What the devil have you done here?" Osef set his heels together and pushed his chest out. He lay one hand on the hilt of his sword, posing, not exactly threatening.

"The mayor passed an injunction," the chipmunk stammered. "We've got clearance to round 'em up and hold them here until the law passes."

"Which law?" Osef caught the glance they exchanged and decided he didn't care. Not tonight. Not when he was surrounded and outnumbered. He shifted gears. "Never mind. You've made a mistake."

"How's that, General?" Higgins let his sword dangle toward the farmer's grass.

"You've abducted my housekeeper," Osef said. "Whilst she was picking berries for my supper."

They looked at one another again, frowning and shifting their feet. He didn't have time to convince them. The sun was nearly down and they'd already drawn the attention of more guards. A few drifted in their direction. Osef shook his head and stepped forward as if he were on the way to inspect the troops. As if he'd every right to be there.

"Her children are hungry. I've no time to waste here, boys. If you'll excuse me."

They parted for him. Higgins even gave a salute as Osef passed. Sam Wolton, the town butcher, rounded on him as he approached the pasture gate, but his hooves stalled when he recognized the intruder. Osef let his reputation carry him forward. He set his shoulders back and waved the guard aside before sliding through the gate and into the camp.

"Seffia!" Osef called for the squirrel, and a family of rodents huddled beside the first of the tents shook their heads. He nodded to them and marched on, weaving between the makeshift shelters and around the campfires. "Seffia? Have you seen a squirrel?"

The rabbit wandered among the refugees with his heart in his stomach. He watched the fence line for any sign the guards had decided his reputation was not currency enough, and he watched the immigrants' faces as he pleaded with them to understand. Suspicion, fear, dark sorrow.

As the night deepened, Osef's teeth ground together. His ears drooped. His calls became desperate and weaker as his throat dried. A tent flap fluttered to one side, and he turned toward it. A family of shrews stood beside a tiny fire. The parents made a protective wall in front of the children, but the woman nodded to Osef and spoke in her own language.

"I don't… Have you seen Seffia?"

The father scowled, but the mother shrew gestured with one paw. Osef stumbled in their direction, rounding the fire in time to see the children vanish back inside the tent. Their high-pitched voices chattered behind the canvas wall. He waited, gaze flickering from the tent flap to the shrew couple to the far fence.

He didn't belong here, not according to the whispers from the camps around them, and not according to the scowling from the nearest guard. But when the canvas moved again, and a familiar squirrel limped into the firelight, Osef rushed forward. Her ankle was swollen and matted, and she leaned on the larger of the shrew children. Osef ducked in, slipped an arm around her waist and whispered, "I have the boys."

If she understood him or not, the rabbit couldn't have said, but Seffia leaned into him. She came along, one wincing step at a time, back through the tents. Halfway there her ankle gave out entirely. Osef scooped her up and carried her in front of him. The faces they passed were far less grim this time. The whispers had grown soft, held a question more than an accusation now.

The guards, however, had shifted in the other direction. They'd added to their number as well, and a crowd of angry animals with makeshift weapons waited outside the pasture gate. A torch, held in the fuzzy brown paw of a familiar woodchuck, cast them all into garish caricatures of themselves.

"What are you doing, Osef?" Pfaff's voice had lost all trace of friendliness.

"What am I doing?" Osef tightened his grip on the squirrel and glared at them. She felt like a leaf in his arms, too thin and far too frail for their abuse. "What the hell are you doing? What is this nonsense?"

"The mayor's orders." Pfaff placed his free paw on one hip and raised his torch high. "We're gonna round up every last one of 'em."

"This woman is in my employ." Osef stepped forward, and though he felt the weight of the moment, no one moved in to stop him. His heart pounded. If they meant to take him, they'd have to do it all at once, and his nerves perked to attention, ready for the rush he'd be unable to stall with his arms full of Seffia. "She works for me, and I am taking her home to her children."

"Works for you?" Pfaff whistled through his front teeth and then spat on the ground. "She's no more than a thief."

An unkind whisper swirled through the guards. The animals of Brambleward narrowed their eyes. Their paws drifted absently to their weapons, but Osef saw farmers there; he saw shopkeepers and young men who'd never seen the Vulpine War. He thumped one foot against the hard ground and watched them flinch.

"Has the mayor passed a law that dictates who I can and cannot hire to wash my socks? Has he?" He pressed forward, snarling the words and earning a gap in the ring of guards. "Will you come to my door next? Come and get the children, too?"

"They've no place here." Pfaff shouted it, but the crowd looked at their toes now. They grew quiet, and when the woodchuck whistled again, no one moved. "No good can come of this. The mayor—"

"I'll be having a word with the mayor," Osef said. "Make no mistake about that."

Pfaff glared at him. The flame from the torch made a mask of his usually soft round face. In Osef's arms, Seffia shivered. Her long tail dragged against his ankles. He lifted her higher and shook his head, shook his head at each and every one of them. Then, without further argument, Osef marched toward the road.

The guards parted and let him pass. Pfaff said no more, but Osef heard the whispers start again before he'd even reached the gate. They had a long walk still, and a long road. Once he'd seen the squirrels safely reunited, then Osef could plan his next move. As he marched beneath the waning moon, he relived each campfire he'd passed, each downtrodden huddle of animals with nowhere safe to go.

How had it come to this?

Osef carried one injured woman to safety, but he'd left a sea of them behind. He'd *let* it come to this, somehow. There might have been a way to sway things sooner, to avert the whole calamity. But he'd removed himself from the town's business, hadn't he? Ever since the war.

Osef had hidden away from the world, and in doing so, he'd left it in the hands of men like Pfaff Oakenwall.

***

Seffia rubbed the widow's salve into her ankle and raised one eyebrow at him. She sat at the dining table, clean, fluffed, and at last beginning to show signs of health again. Her tail curled gracefully behind her and her cheeks had rounded out into a pleasant, less skeletal shape.

"Osef?" She spoke his name with a heavy accent, but he enjoyed the sound of it.

"I'm going to town."

Her eyes stretched wide. She reached for the back of the chair.

"Don't get up." He held up his hands and waved her back down. "I'll get them."

Osef crossed to the door and pulled it open, letting a blast of cold air invade the toasty cabin. He poked his head out and called, "Nica, Holt!"

The door pushed in before he'd finished, and two squirrel boys half scrambled and half rolled inside. They'd been swaddled in wool scarves until they'd lost their shape, and began peeling off the layers as he closed the door again. The weather hadn't turned quite enough to warrant the extra caution, but Osef couldn't blame their aunt for being a little overprotective.

"Stay inside. Keep the door locked." He didn't have to remind them but said it anyway. Maybe for his own comfort.

When he left them, he wore his emerald overcoat and his saber hung from his hip, as it always did these days. He'd managed to keep these three safe, to keep them here, but Pfaff's wagons still rolled north across the Gash, despite Osef's many conferences with the mayor.

His attempts to influence the community had gone better. Osef's integration movement had taken root among the older farmers, those who could use a few extra paws, and landlords who had vacant rooms in need of renters. It wasn't enough, but if they kept at it, in time… He had to believe the rest of them would come around.

In the meantime, he would continue to press the mayor, to make his argument against Pfaff's hatred. He would continue to try. Osef marched toward town with his head high and his steps long and full of purpose. A deep fall wind ruffled his gray fur. The dry lane had turned moist and soft in places. The cold was coming, and the hero of Brambleward had work to do.

A terraforming crew faces a mystery in the nights of an alien world.

ONCE WE WERE MEERKATS

Huskyteer

The suns were at their highest point when the alarm went off.

Some of us were on sentry duty, some minding the children in the nursery. The ones lucky enough to have their rest period during the hottest part of the day were sleeping or sunbathing. Most of us were digging and building.

We scrambled for the shelter of the underground complex, scooping up kids and the infirm as we went, while the sirens screeched.

Our leader, Mo, quietened us down. She got hold of the sentry who'd raised the alarm and took him aside so he could give her a statement. The rest of us took stock of who had tagged in. There were two missing: a surveyor, out checking the area for the best place to extend our site, and one of the engineers, who'd been working on the irrigation system out near the fences.

Mo made a statement to the effect that it was probably a false alarm, and the missing just hadn't heard the siren. We were to carry on with our work, maintaining extra high vigilance just in case. But the rumours were already flying; it's impossible to keep a lid on anything around here. Some kind of monster—vast, stealthy, unseen—stalking around the outside of our walls and fences. Plenty of us had heard it or smelled it, now we came to think of it (it smelled of meat and ice), but none of us could say what it looked like.

We already had sandbugs, pricklemouths, and jumping snakes to contend with. We didn't need invisible monsters too. We were just trying to build a city.

Once we were meerkats. We've seen pictures in the database.

They made us human-sized, so we can build human-sized homes for them, and we lost our tails. We still have the fur that keeps us warm in the cold nights and cool in the heat of the day, with a dark mask to protect our eyes from the sun. We still have strong hands and nails designed for burrowing, even though we also have tools. We're still tough enough to deal with predators, and immune to some types of venom. We need little water, and we can eat almost anything. Most of all, we still look out for each other. That's how we survive.

We used to be cute.

Our missing two didn't come back, and search parties headed out to look for them. We returned with nothing to report: no prints, no scent, no sign of a struggle. We concluded that our surveyor and engineer had run off together; it happens sometimes that one or two of us decide to leave and start a new life according to their own rules. It's not exactly encouraged, but there's nothing any of us can do to prevent it, and perhaps it's best to be rid of any dissatisfied element. We wished them well and forgot about them. We were *busy*.

The city was behind schedule. The terrain was tricky, and we were having problems setting up the water supply. It was the diggers' fault. No! The engineers! No, the planners who'd picked the site!

The human ships had already left Earth, bound for their new colony, and even if we'd been able to get a message to them, they could not have turned back without a great deal of trouble and expense. We would have thousands of souls incoming, and not enough space and food for them. Or for us.

We worked extra shifts, and those of us usually assigned to other jobs pitched in with the building work. We often found ourselves working alone to put in extra time on a project, rather than sticking in the groups that kept us safe from attack. Tired ears and eyelids drooped. All of us were tired and all of us were preoccupied.

We were not as vigilant as we should have been.

Our nights were short, but black and cold. One cold, black night a group of our teenagers chose to sneak out beyond the fences, looking for a kind of cactus that some among us were always willing to swear got you high. When they didn't find one they teased a sandbug out of its burrow and poked at it a while, trying to flip it over with sticks while avoiding the stingers. It was while they were dancing around their prey, giggling and shrieking, that they noticed the starlight fade and the night become blacker. They fell silent and looked up to see a patch of darkness blotting out the line between sky and desert. Still shrieking and giggling at the adventure, they fled for the safety of home, where they found an unamused sentry waiting at the exit point they'd cut in the fence.

We thought they were just making up a story to slide out of the trouble they were in for breaking bounds. Then we noticed another of our number was missing.

We're designed to cope with hostile environments and predatory wildlife. Our whole purpose is to turn desert planets into human homes. But this was outside our scope and way beyond our skills.

The building work fell ever further behind. More of us were assigned to guard detail, but even so we worked with one eye on our current job and the other glancing over our shoulders for danger. We got jumpy, and we made mistakes that cost us precious time and materials to fix.

The kids who'd run away from the desert night and left their friend behind began to drift away from the rest of us.

Arguments began between those of us who wanted to get on with the job and those who wanted to arm ourselves, the whole lot of us, and sweep the desert for monsters. Some of us wanted to pull out altogether. There's a protocol for when a planet reveals a hidden danger missed by the initial surveys. We'd never needed to activate it, nor had we heard of any crew who had. It's a serious matter.

The rest of us asked, what were we so afraid of? Ghosts? Stories? Funny smells? Kid stuff.

We were divided.

That never happens. Unity is in our genes. Sure, we have our spats and squabbles, but they don't last. In the worst case Mo has to knock a few heads together, or someone bops someone else on the nose, and it's all sweet again. Because we have purpose. Together.

We don't just blindly follow instructions. We might have a vast bank of plans to work from, but every planet is different, so we often need to improvise and substitute. Each city we create is unique, built in response to the particular problems and advantages of the landscape and climate.

Not all of us are solid muscle, built for labour and protection. We are architects, technicians and scientists. Some of us are record-keepers, adding to the sum of knowledge that our crew and others can draw from. Some of us describe ourselves as artists, or even visionaries.

We scientists and visionaries set to work on this new problem.

Our research and discussions led us to the conclusion that there was no such thing as the invisible. Just because we, ourselves, could not see something did not mean it couldn't be seen. So we adapted the goggles we use for night work to help us see beyond our usual range.

We argued over whether the aim of our exploration should be to investigate or to kill. Either way, we concluded, we would need to defend ourselves. Our sentries already had electrical weapons as well as firearms, and to these we added a type that used sound to disable and disorientate.

Some of us secretly fashioned our own armaments: knives and clubs, crude but reassuring. One of us made a helmet of wires to protect his brain from what he described as alien mind-rays, and we teased him without mercy.

Then we went hunting.

Split into groups, weapons on our shoulders, we divided the desert surrounding our base into squares and we patrolled.

Nothing.

We tried at different hours of the day and night. We looked for tracks, and for burrows where a large creature might lie low if it heard us coming. We lost one of our fighters to a jumping snake, but this, at least, was the kind of loss we could understand.

One of us had an idea. We had done our patrolling in groups, of course. The ones who were taken had been isolated, working remotely or left behind. What if someone tried going into the desert alone?

One of us kept their idea a secret, so as not to be prevented, and executed it privately. One of us walked out into the night weaponless, without a word of goodbye to friends or family, and sat atop a dune with the cold wind ruffling their fur, and waited for the unknown.

It came. It came as a rush of meat-scented air, and a distortion in the line of the horizon. The goggles showed a glowing blur, vast and wavering. A formless cloud without recognisable features like legs, eyes, or teeth.

One of us spread furred hands out wide to demonstrate a lack of weapons, and looked at the monster, and did not faint or run away.

The cloud moved forward and settled in the sand around the dune, filling each wind-carved hollow. One of us touched a soft nose to something less than solid, more than gas.

Our little kids were first to figure out there was something going on, and cluster around the fence. Then our teenagers slunk out of the shadows, trying to look as if they were there by accident and found the whole thing boring. The rest of us came in pairs or groups, looking for our young or our friends. We huddled up to the fence and peered over each other, passing our pairs of goggles around.

"I think you should come out here. All of you," one of us called.

We debated. Was it a trick? Had we lost another to a monster that was now puppeting one of us to lure the rest into its maw? We raised our voices, and some of us scuffled in the sand, pulling towards or away.

Mo ended it. She stepped forward to do her leader's duty, and we would not let her go alone. Our strongest and bravest went first, but the rest of us were not far behind. None of us intended the kids to come, of course, but they sneaked along anyway, dropping to all fours, skittering between our legs and racing through the fence before we could grab them.

We would confront the unknown for ourselves, and for our lost, and for our human employers when they arrived.

We swarmed the dune together and stood in a mass. Parents held children in their arms. Mo drew herself up tall, at the very front, as if she could shield us all. Nobody whispered or chattered. We were never this silent.

Our silence, our stillness or our concentration allowed it in. We all took it in at once: the knowledge that the cloud creature was alone and dying on a world that no longer held life, and so could not sustain it by renewing its cells—until we came.

Now we had questions, and we yelled them all at once.

"One at a time," Mo called, but we drowned her out.

We became aware of shapes forming in the foggy cloud, and we craned forward. Those of us with goggles, and the youngest of us, could see most clearly.

Our missing. They lay curled up, eyes closed and unresponsive, but none of them looked hurt, and they were breathing. Some of us broke away to run down and hold them. Eyes blinked open.

These two are too old, and this one too young, we now knew. For what? we wondered. We'd seen movies. We'd scared each other, as kids, with stories of crews who'd ended up as exhibits in some alien zoo.

The answer sent ripples through our minds, and raised the fur on our spines. We felt the strained gaps between atoms barely held together and we knew what would become of this planet when the force could no longer hold.

I need one. I take one.

"No deal," Mo said. "We're family. We stick together." We heard her words, but we also felt them as the alien felt them, broken down into emotion and sensation. It was a new kind of togetherness.

We considered the offer. We did not bicker or fight. Each of us turned the thought around silently, each in our own mind.

This city we're building with such care isn't for us. It's for them.

Their eyes aren't as good as ours, so there are lights all along the tunnel walls and in the subterranean spaces. Really they prefer to be above ground, in the sunshine, so as well as setting up the solar panels we have to pour a

117

lot of time and resources into houses with air-conditioning for their elite, and into safely fenced parks and sports arenas.

When it's done at last, they arrive in ships and move in to their new world. Those ships then carry us to the next unclaimed planet, to start all over again. There's no place that we can call home. It's a life that most of us like, but it isn't for everyone.

One of us said: "I'll do it."

One of us was scooped up into that cloud, and felt the planet fade away. One of us had our mind enveloped by another.

Tell me, it said.

So I began my story.

Celebrate Colony Day!

YEAR FORTY-FOUR
Lloyd Yaeger

Arrival

***

Joyce is ready for Colony Day. She has her decorations up, but only because she never took them down from last year. And why should she? Oh sure. They all make comments. She's one of *those*. But Joyce doesn't pay them any mind. At the very least, she has the excuse that she's an old duck, and shouldn't risk hurting herself by trying to move them. And anyway, they make her happy, and they give her something to look at while she sips her tea.

"We are, of course, anticipating that the N.A.F. supply Frigate Blue Beacon will land any day now with provisions," says the newscaster, a fox with a velvet voice.

She likes to listen to her radio app in the morning. The fox's voice is soothing, like her tea and her decorations. There's the replica flag from first landing, with "Year 0" printed on it. And the scale model of the good ship Photon, which brought her here, to Argyre-II, forty-three years ago.

Then there's her lucky geode, the two halves of the earth rock she keeps in her purse, which she brings out every so often to admire. In fact, that's what she's doing now. The pieces are small enough that she can hold one in each feathered hand. The burnished surface of the flat side reveals a blue-ish pattern of sedimented layers, running from indigo to sky. It reminds her of foamy sea waves, and it's the only thing left on Mars to remind her of what oceans were like.

The fox continues and the duck listens. "The Beacon, we're being told, is still in high orbit, with no indication of when or if it will land, pending the ongoing authorization process on Earth. We will, of course, keep everyone updated as the situation un—"

She mutes the app, sighing, and returns to her tea and vitamins. How many pills today? Twenty two. Standard regimen, plus the six extra supplements, now that she's "getting up there," as Doc Bradshaw puts it. She takes one pill with each little sip, savoring the fragrance. Same tea for forty-four years.

But that doesn't bother Joyce. Very little, in fact, can bother her today. Because tonight is the party, *her* party, the one event she looks forward to every year. Colony Day is her excuse to make her famous (or infamous) Photon cake, a layered simulacrum of sponge, buttercream, and rice krispies, constructed to resemble the good ship herself. Her cake is the talk of the colony. Or at least that's how she imagines it. Sure, there were naysayers. Too sweet, Alice would say. Just like Joyce.

That one always stings. But this year, she plans to add an unconventional touch. She will make it with carrot. Eat your heart out, Alice. And then have a slice of cake for dessert.

The rattling knock at the door of her habitat breaks the duck out of her favorite fantasy (in which Alice, brought to tears by the sheer rapture of the cake, is begging her for the recipe). It's the kind of urgent knock one associates with either someone desperate to get out of the cold, or someone with a search warrant.

She sighs, because she knows who it is. "Him again, no doubt. I wonder what it is this time."

When she drags the door open, the mouse on the other side gawks and begins biting his nails. He looks surprised and embarrassed, as if not expecting an answer, even though he's always received one before.

"Hello Kevin. Come inside, won't you?"

***

"I'm sorry. I'm really sorry." He sits across from Joyce, his paws between his legs, eyes fixed on a tea-stain that she hasn't bothered to clean up. He taps his fleshy foot paw on the floor with the rhythm of a woodpecker. "I know it's weird. I just show up at your door unannounced. Again. That's weird, right? Creepy even."

"It's… unconventional," says Joyce. She likes that word because it's true, and it applies just as well to an odd duck who loves her Colony Day decorations as to the mouse who now occupies her living room.

Joyce is a therapist. Or at least, she was, before she retired. It's not a role she has taken on because of her qualifications (on Earth, she was an English teacher) but rather by default, when among the first wave of converts, her ability to encourage and comfort became a necessary resource in the cramped conditions of long-term space travel, and subsequent life under the dome. With each new wave of arrivals, she has acted in good faith as grief counselor, marriage counselor, child psychologist, and a host of other jobs.

That is, until Doc Schaefer arrived, and began the more professionalized practice. But even after her retirement, Kevin prefers talking to Joyce, a decision she partly understands. A psychiatrist and medical doctor by training, Schaefer has little faith in the talking cure. That, and her bedside manner is, as Joyce describes it, clinical.

Kevin is a recent convert. He's somewhere in his twenties, short, even for a mouse, wearing secondhand thermals under a plaid shirt that's seen better days. Mars has been his home for about a year now. The whole process has been, as Joyce would gently put it, an adjustment for him.

"You could have called me."

"I know. I just… sometimes I get so focused on something that I forget. I don't think about the things I could do because all I want to think about is what I'm actually doing. Have you ever felt that?"

"Sometimes, yes." The habitat's ceiling, with its scuffed plastic panels, gives her something to look at while she thinks about the best response. "But I wish I did it more, to be honest. That kind of focus can be very useful. It's what makes you very good at what you do, isn't it?"

"You mean being unemployed?"

"I mean your engineering work, back on Earth."

He shrugs.

"Would you like some tea, Kevin?"

"No thanks. I just wanna talk."

It's what he always wants, thinks Joyce. "Why don't we talk about this little episode here. What motivated you to come today? Were you afraid of something?"

He rests his head in his paw. "It's like this. I blew it. I had another chance to meet someone and I threw it out the window."

"Slow down for a moment. Walk me through this."

He takes a deep breath. "Okay. So there's this guy. He's here in Argyre, and we start chatting over the network. Follow? He says we're connecting. I think so too! But then he asks me to meet him for lunch. And well—"

"You declined?"

"I accepted. But then I just… don't show up. I flake on him, and then he messages me like what the fuck. And then I just stop talking to him."

"Now why was that, do you suppose?"

"I don't know. I just feel lost. I can't find work, and I feel like I have no friends."

"I'm sure that's not true," says Joyce.

He sighs. "People are so stupid," he says. "They're all so slow. Everybody's always wringing their paws. Navel-gazing. I don't want to be like that, so I push them away."

Joyce finds it both interesting and productive that Kevin says "paws," because it indicates he is adjusting. "I understand that. It was like that, on Earth, with some of the humans. Not all of them. Some are awful, some aren't."

"But I feel that way about everyone, not just the humans."

"What I'm hearing," she says, "is that, in the past, you've felt disappointed in some people. You don't like the idea that you could disappoint someone in the same way, so you alienate yourself. Because you know what that's like."

"That sounds about right."

"I have an idea," says Joyce. "I'm holding a party tonight, for Colony Day. Why don't you drop by? It's a perfect laboratory to try out meeting some new friends. It's just a small get together. But we're a small community, so you'll know at least someone there. And…" She says this last part like it's a secret. "There'll be cake."

He chews on his nails for a moment before saying "I guess I could."

"After our session, I'm going out to get some supplies. You're free to come with me, if shopping doesn't bore you. I think it might benefit you to try some of that slowing down you find so irritating. When was the last time you took a day to rest?"

"It's been awhile." He fidgets in his seat, scratching at his shirt collar while he stares at the tea stain. "Alright, sure. Why not? I'd be happy to go with you."

***

Vendors

***

The rain in the colony of Argyre-II comes from a series of sprinklers that line the upper areas of the dome. Joyce remembers when they were used only for crops in the early days, when water was scarce. But years later, after all the water reclamation efforts and resupplies, they have enough for a bit of rain, a few times a year. It turns out, in spite of the complaints, that most converts like the rain, if only from time to time, because it reminds them of places on Earth. It's a comforting kind of inconvenience.

Joyce waddles along the muddy path that joins the habitats to the market hub, holding her parasol nice and high, so Kevin can walk next to her beneath it. But for some reason he keeps on ahead. Perhaps he likes the brisk drizzle against his fur (that she understands, how like an old duck) or maybe he's trying to keep a distance. Or she's just walking too slow for him.

"I can only walk so fast, Kevin."

He nods and pauses while she catches up, paws buried in his pockets. He stares off in the distance, a look of concentration on his features. Joyce wonders what he's staring at, but when she turns east and looks where he's looking, all she can see, through the rain-flecked polyethylene surface of the dome, is the butterscotch haze of dust outside.

"Sorry. I just like to, you know, get places."

"Webbed feet change the way you walk. The gravity doesn't help."

It's about noon, Mars time. On Colony Day, the market hub is busier than it might have been on any other holiday. It's covered by a canopy of canvas sheets stretched over a PVC skeleton. There are gutters for the runoff, but a little water always seeps through, and it doesn't get much warmer as they step onto the damp cobblestones. It's about the size of a large flea market on Earth. The long rows of stands are stocked with produce, dry goods, clothing, art, and anything she might need. The aisles are filled with converts of all species, each going about their business.

"We need shortening, dairy powder, sugar, self-rising flour, and carrot. Oh, and puffed rice," she says. It takes her a moment to dig in her purse for the extra coupons that she's saved up over the last month or so. She hands two of them to the mouse. "Why don't you find me the shortening and dairy powder? And the cereal."

Kevin eagerly snatches the papers from her hands, nearly pulling out a few feathers with them. He looks apologetic but doesn't say anything, and they part ways, traveling in opposite directions in the huge market.

She makes her way to the dry goods, but on the way, her attention is snagged by a little shawl hanging from one of the designer clothing stands. It's pink satin, embroidered with an intricate green William Morris-esque design, and would have fit her nicely in her younger days.

"I don't know, Joyce. It's a bit gaudy for you."

She recognizes the voice that pulls her away from the fabric, and so she's unsurprised to see Alice looking up at her. They're both in their seventies, but Alice is the kind of rabbit whose fur hides any sign of aging, still so soft and downy, unlike her own thinning feathers. Alice's eyes still have the warm energy that Joyce only finds in cups of tea nowadays.

Turning back to the shawl, Joyce says "I suppose so," and hangs it back on the rack. She knows Alice means well, that her comment is her way of dismissing the reality that it wouldn't have fit Joyce anyway. "It might look nice on you, though. Why not give it a try?"

"I would, but I'm tapped out on clothing coupons." Looking at the shawl, she sighs, as if reconsidering the idea. "That's what I get for being a shopaholic."

"Addicted to shopahol, are we?"

"Oh, don't be such a cliché. I got enough of that from my English teacher way back when."

They laugh the way old friends do. Joyce has known Alice since year zero, aboard the Photon, where they were bunk mates and confidantes during the long trip.

"Will I be seeing you tonight?"

"Oh, of course. I wouldn't miss your cake for the world. Though I know I shouldn't indulge. Doc Bradshaw says my blood sugar's too high as is."

Another dig. But then that's Alice, always finding new ways to talk with the back of her paw. Joyce smiles. Because what else is there to do? And anyway, she hasn't revealed anything about the carrot. That's the ace up her sleeve.

"Well, I'll see you when I see you, then," she says as they smile and part ways.

Joyce has most of what she needs when Kevin returns with the wet ingredients. He's holding out a plastic bag filled with cereal, shaking it triumphantly.

"It took some asking around, but I found it!"

She smiles at him. "You're an angel."

"We're making good time too. Need anything else?"

"Just carrots."

"I haven't seen any. The produce is slim pickings"

"I know someone who might have them."

She's referring to a deer named Sidney, who has a tiny stall thrown in among the stalls of cleaning supplies, easily missed if one isn't looking. He's there because nobody knows exactly where to place him. His stock is a hodgepodge, acquired, as rumor has it, through vague and enigmatic connections. How his stuff ends up on the supply ships is anybody's guess. But he always seems to have the thing Joyce needs.

The deer leans back in his chair, supported by stacks of styrofoam crates, his hooves up on his table. There's a daydreamy look in his eyes, which disappears as he leans forward and recognizes the duck.

"You're looking spry," he says as she lumbers up to him. He stands and slides his chair out from behind the table. She knows him well enough to take it without seeming rude.

"Thank you, Sid." She lets herself fall into the seat, groaning, and begins rubbing her calf.

"How's the knee?"

"Ready for a replacement when you've got one. This, by the way, is Kevin," she says. "Have you two met?"

The mouse stands aloof, holding his tail in his paws. Sidney smiles and holds out his hand, and they shake in that nervous way. They might be blushing, thinks Joyce, if she could see beneath their fur.

"Pleasure."

"Um, likewise," says Kevin. Following this, there's a pause, filled with the busy sounds of the other vendors, kilograms being weighed out, coupons changing hands. Kevin isn't the type to smile often, but there are traces of something in his expression that Joyce hasn't seen in a long time.

A pity she has to interrupt them.

"Sid," she says. "I don't suppose you have any carrots? It's for the you-know-what."

"Gee, Joyce. You know that's a tough one, what with the Beacon fiasco…"

"Don't be coy with me. I know you have them."

He sighs, turns, and starts rooting inside one of the crates. After a minute or so, he returns, holding a bundle of Martian carrots by their thick greens. Their roots are slightly darker than Earth carrots, more reddish, like the color of the planet itself. And fresh, too, their surface still glistening with reclaimed rainwater.

"What can I give you for them?"

"What've you got?"

She's now in the realm of unauthorized bartering, a practice not so much expressly forbidden as gently discouraged. Argyre-II's economy is delicate (hence the coupon system), but a certain degree of trading and borrowing is mostly expected. The problem is that Joyce has very little that most of the merchants would want. The coupons themselves are only desired insofar as they, per a standing agreement with the N.A.F., can be converted into Earth currency, allowing more supplies to be purchased.

She stares at the carrots and considers the question at hand. When the moment passes, there is no more question. The cake, right now, is everything.

"What about an earth rock? You know they're rare."

"You have one?"

She reaches inside her purse and draws out the two halves of her lucky geode. The deer takes them in his hands and quietly sniffs at them, smiling.

"I don't know if I can accept these, Joyce. They're worth a lot more than a bundle of carrots." He makes as if to hand them back, but Joyce shakes her head.

"Well then," she says, shoving them back at him. "I guess you'll owe me. A few freebies each month ought to square us, don't you think?"

Looking more guilty than happy, he nods and hands her the carrots, which she snatches and quickly conceals under the other ingredients, as if afraid someone might see them (and for a moment, she really is afraid, though she isn't sure why).

"Wonderful. You'll be at my party, yes?"

Sid nods, half-smiling, his eyes trained on Kevin. "I'll see you tonight."

**

Parade

**

The Colony Day ceremony involves a trip out to Photon, whose retired hull lies a few miles due southwest of Argyre-II. It's close enough that it can be seen through the dome, if your vantage point is high enough to get a view over the edge of the barrier at its base.

Going to Photon means leaving the dome. But there aren't enough vac-suits for everybody, nor is there enough space in the Omnibuses for the entire population. Tickets for a viewing are handed out via lottery. For those who aren't able to get a seat on an omnibus, a camera crew is on-hand to broadcast live-ish footage of the ceremony back to the dome. This year, Joyce, lucky duck that she is, has a ticket. She hasn't told anybody, because this is the first time in a decade that she's won. The omnibus passengers are allowed a plus one.

"We've got time. Why not come with?" she asks. They're back at her habitat, loading the groceries into her locker-sized fridge. Kevin looks at her askance. Outside, the rain has stopped, and even further, beyond the dome, the dust is beginning to settle. Through the lone window, it finally looks like daylight outside the habitat.

"Why are you asking me?"

"I'd ask Alice, but she went last year. And I'm guessing you've never been there in person, have you?"

"No. And to be honest with you, I didn't watch the footage last year. Too depressed."

"Well let's enjoy it together then."

An omnibus is basically a long rover with flexible tank treads, like a rolling centipede, the inside of which resembles a segmented airplane cabin, but with much larger windows. There are four total, though one of them is being repaired, leaving three for this year's trip. The passengers board single-file, past the uniformed fox standing near the hatch who scans their tickets. Joyce hands him the coupons, slides her way through the too-narrow entrance and finds her way to the nearest open pair of seats, taking care to choose one on the left-hand side of the cabin.

"Take the window seat. You get the best view that way."

Kevin nods, and Joyce can tell he's annoyed. She guesses that waiting in long lines is unbearable for him. Maybe this will be good for him, she thinks.

The airlock is designed to fit only one bus at a time, so the process of getting all three out of the dome – the de-pressurizing and re-pressurizing – feels like an eternity. Their bus is last in line, and so by the time they roll past the airlock door, Kevin is fidgeting in his seat and tapping his foot on the floor.

"Everything okay?"

"I just wanna get going is all. I know it takes a while, but it's just… never mind. I'm fine."

The buses rumble slowly through the crater, single-file, a long, slow parade of metal and plastic. The driver is careful not to allow them to sink into any loose pockets of dust that may have accumulated. The trip is mostly smooth, save for the occasional bump as they pass over some of the bigger rocks that have the audacity not to be pulverized. Kevin makes a point of showing how bored he is, and Joyce wonders whether she ought to have come alone.

But when Photon comes into view, everybody starts climbing out of their seats and crowding the windows on the left side of the bus. And now the mouse can't help but look. Directly ahead is the ship, which lies prone, its massive train of compartments lying one after another in a line, like vertebrae, joined by the connective tissue of wide cables and tubes. The three rings, the tori, where its passengers used to sleep, lie flat along their length.

A few feet in front of the ship is the ceremony site. It consists of a series of flags, each numbered, arranged in a spiral that extends from a central point, where (so the story goes) the captain of the Photon, James McClay, planted the very first flag. The most recent flag, at the outer edge, has "Year 43" printed on it in bold white. Each flag before it is so numbered, though the lettering seems more and more faded as they spiral toward the center.

"You arrived on that tin can?"

"Back then, it was the Cadillac of ships."

Staring at the site, Joyce wonders at the irony of how she got here. The captain, McClay, was, in his pre-fox years, a tycoon of privatized astronautics, specializing primarily in low-earth orbit flights for the ultra-wealthy. Had someone told him, before the conversion, that he was to be at the forefront of the formation of the first Martian communes, he probably would have died laughing on the spot, and there would be no homesteads. She's thankful that nobody told him ahead of time about the whole turning-into-a-fox thing.

On the loudspeaker, a woman's voice echoes through the cabin.

"Airlock One de-pressurized."

"Go, Airlock One."

"Roger. I'm going out now," she says.

"Watch," Joyce says to Kevin. But Kevin doesn't need to be told. His eyes are trained on the wolf in the vac-suit outside the omnibus, who is now headed toward the spiral.

"Who is that?"

"Her name is Laila. She won this year's essay-writing contest, so she gets to do the honors."

Outside, Laila, holding the flag over her shoulder, takes long, bounding strides toward the outer edge of the expanse. When she's about a meter or so away from Year 43, she stops. A moment or two passes. Then with both hands, she hoists the short pole up and jabs it down into the dust, twisting it back and forth until its height is in line with the others.

The voice chimes in again. "Forty-four is down."

Then almost in unison, everyone in the bus starts to clap and cheer.

***

The walk back from the airlocks to the habitats feels like the uncertain calm that comes after a marsquake, when everybody is waiting for the aftershock, even if it never comes. Joyce and Kevin walk side by side now. The weather is clear, and beyond the dome, the sky is pale violet. They're quiet for awhile, and then Kevin chimes in.

"I became a mouse on my twenty-fifth birthday," he says. "It happened fast. The whole thing took two weeks."

"It was like that for lots of people," says Joyce. "There were humans on board the Photon, too. Not just converts. They had dreams of going to Mars. But one by one, just like us, they started changing. There wasn't a human left by the time we arrived."

"How does it happen? I don't understand. Nobody ever told me how or why I changed, or why I became a mouse and not some other animal. Why doesn't anyone ever talk about it?"

Joyce stops and turns to look at him, then places a wing on his shoulder. Her expression is grave. "To a lot of people, it's a touchy subject," she says, and leaves it at that. Because what else is there to say? Probably more, she thinks. But then, it's not easy, remembering what it's like to go to sleep one night as a human, and to wake up the next morning with feathers. Not many at first. Just a few odd patches of down, here and there. But she remembers vividly how fast they would grow. How it always happened at night, every day waking up a little different. How she would always dream, night after night, about growing wings and soaring above the earth.

But the truth about Kevin's question is this: she doesn't know why. Nobody does. Not after all the theories, the quarantines, the hastily-assembled papers on contagions and epigenetics and the physiology of metamorphosis. Maybe, for all she knows, someone back on Earth really did figure it out. But after nearly half a decade, she's long since ceased to care. Even so, Kevin isn't ignorant. He, like all the others, is a separatist. What else could motivate a bunch of converts to live out the rest of their existence in an air bubble on a dead planet, with little more to their name than a pot of earth soil and a desire for something beyond the ordinary? Turns out, a free ride helps.

***

Room Party

***

To make a cake on Mars is not such a hard thing. There are lots of kinds one can make. Some are flaky, some are spongey. Joyce's recipe has a perfect crumble to it. The main thing is to get the leavening just right. They've been working all afternoon in the rented rec hall, which Joyce manages to reserve every year. In the kitchen, the cake pans slide in and out of the oven. It's a special forced convection model, which allows pastry to rise more predictably under low gravity conditions. Now the Photon is emerging, piece by piece.

Kevin shapes the puffed rice into the ringed torus that surrounds the hull, taking care not to burn himself on the sticky marshmallow confection.

"A little thinner there. They get smaller toward the bow," says Joyce. "Perfect."

She lays the layers, one atop the other, spreading a healthy amount of buttercream in between each one, and shaves off the excess to make the tapered sections before adding more frosting around the whole thing. Finally she carves in the little meticulous details with her thin spatula. She slides the rings down the length of it, and holds them in place with wooden dowels, like the spokes on a wheel.

"The Photon."

"It looks great," says Kevin. "You do this every year?"

"This is my forty-fourth cake. And it's my best."

At around seven, the guests start to trickle in. There's Laila, who wears a sequined cocktail dress. The wolf bows as she enters, and Joyce hugs her.

"That was beautiful. You were incredible."

"Oh. Um, thank you."

Behind her are a pair of crows: Doc Bradshaw, the physician, and Doc Schaefer, the psychiatrist, waiting to have their turn at overly-affectionate introductions, each double-fisting unopened bottles of liquor in their wings.

"We ready for this?" says Doc Bradshaw, who has already begun drilling a corkscrew into one of the reds. He pulls it out with a satisfying pop. "Isn't that just the most festive sound?" He pours everyone a glass and they clink.

"To good health and sound mind," says Schaefer.

***

Alice, in her loud polka-dot skirt, giggles a lot when she drinks. It's the kind of laugh that's so cute that it makes Joyce's blood boil with that rare combination of envy and wrath reserved only for her good friends. She finds herself imagining that somewhere, in another life, she and Alice are cartoon characters, locked in an eternal struggle over which hunting season it is—duck or rabbit.

Here she comes, skipping across the tile. "Isn't this grand? I haven't felt this funny in months. What's in this wine?"

"It's wine, Alice."

"Oh yes. That's true. You should have more. Catch up with me."

"I'm working on it."

"When do we get cake?"

"You just wait. It'll knock your socks off."

Alice bites her lip the way some people do when they flirt, and she swirls the liquid in her tumbler.

***

Sidney slides into the room about a quarter past nine. The drinks are flowing, and the energy in the room has swelled, by now, to that perfect hurricane of bitchy comradery that great parties are made of. So the deer knows he doesn't need an excuse to help himself. He goes for the bottle of Terran chardonnay (it's been long enough for them to grow and ferment their own grapes, but Martian wine still tastes like it came out of an Orson Welles commercial, so most prefer the imported stuff) and pours himself a glass. When he turns around, who should be standing there but Kevin, newly sloshed and ready to tango.

The deer smiles. "If you give a mouse some wine, will he want some harder stuff later?"

"I got something to say to you," says Kevin, ignoring the comment.

"Well, aren't we direct?"

"Yeah, I'm direct… It's a thing with me. Sorry."

"No problem. What is it?"

"It's like this. I uh…" The mouse pauses and considers a moment. Then he says, "I think you're cute. That's basically the thing. Tada?"

"Well thanks," says Sidney. "You're pretty cute yourself. You look different than I pictured you."

"Different?" His tail starts to coil around his leg. "Have we met before or something?"

"Oh," says Sidney. "Well this is awkward. You don't remember?"

Kevin stares at the deer, head tilted, for what seems like an eternity. Then a spark of recognition passes over him. His ears stand upright, and his eyes widen.

***

Doc Schaefer has managed to corner Joyce in the kitchen. Try as Joyce might to escape, she has no option but to brave the whirlwind of the crow's drunkenness. She's seen it before. One year, Schaefer got smashed on cider and collapsed on the floor, crying, because she thought she would change back into a human someday. She kept going on about how sad it was that somebody should get to know what it's like to be a bird, all covered in shiny, black plumage, and then, after all that, to have to give it up and be human again. Wasn't that just the most awful thought? Having turned it over in her mind, years later, Joyce can't pretend to disagree.

But this year, it's Kevin the crow wants to talk about.

"Look at him. Scared out of his wits."

"He's fine. I see a guy talking to his crush. Now what's wrong with that?"

"Why do you insist on doing this to him?" asks Schaefer. "Your bootstrap theory of social phobia is going to hurt him. Can't you see he needs real therapy, not affirmations from an armchair amateur?"

"Really, Judy," says Joyce. "I don't see why you need to be so insulting."

"I'm just saying. You're not a doctor. You're not even a trained therapist, and here you are playing pretend psychoanalyst."

"I've done nothing of the sort."

"You write on people, Joyce," Schaefer says. "You think you're reading them but really you're just writing."

"You're drunk. And you're projecting."

"Call me whatever. I don't care. That's the difference. You say what people wanna hear. I tell the truth."

"The truth is, he's a grown adult. He can make his own decisions about who he wants to be."

"I can't agree with that. None of us chose what we are. Did you choose to be a duck?"

"No, and in that sense, he's not unique either. We all change. As if turning into a bird and spending thirty years under a bubble doesn't do something to a person."

"Now who's projecting?"

"Still you."

"Fine." The crow tips her tumbler upside down and knocks back the last of her cabernet. "Thanks for the terrible party." She storms across the tile, though the drama of her exit is lessened somewhat by the way the gravity affects her gait. Pausing in the door-frame, she turns around. "Sooner or later, you'll have to face it. You're a quack, Joyce!" This last comment she yells, as if announcing it to the room.

Joyce is mortified. How many people heard? But when she turns around to look at the others, she realizes they're distracted by another scene entirely. Some few yards away, a crowd has gathered around Kevin and Sidney, whose argument is only now starting to get loud.

"You didn't have to bring that up," said Kevin. "You didn't."

"I'm only saying how it is." The deer folds his arms over his chest. "I'm not mad or anything. Why are you?"

"You didn't have to bring it up. And now you won't even apologize. You think this is easy for me? It's not." The mouse is trembling.

"Look, Kevin. I'm honestly confused. I thought maybe you didn't want to talk to me anymore. Can we forget it? I didn't mean anything by it."

"Of course you didn't. People like you never *mean* anything, do you? Because you don't *think*. That's why you're all stuck here like me!"

"Easy there…"

"You think you're better than me because you're a deer? Well so what if you've got those stupid, sexy antlers. And what do I have? Nothing. I didn't want this. But *you* did, didn't you? You just love those antlers. You love waking up every day on this stupid rock—"

Sidney's drink is on the mouse before he can finish his diatribe. The majority of it lands on his vest, but a good portion happens to fall, as all rogue liquids inevitably do, on his crotch, and seeps slowly onto the inside of his thigh and down his leg. The shock of the cold wine is enough to stop his train of insults. And for a moment, the room is silent, staring at the wet spot on his slacks.

Kevin looks around as the other guests begin murmuring to one another. Joyce can almost see tears welling up in the mouse's eyes. He pushes past the deer and through the crowd, shouting "Move!" to anyone in his way. He walks by Joyce but doesn't look at her, and grabs his coat before walking out the door.

For some reason, everyone now turns to look at Joyce. Something about this makes sense to her, though she wishes it didn't. The silence continues for a few seconds. She searches desperately for something to fill it.

"Well… who wants cake?"

***

Joyce portions the cake and arranges the slices on plates for people to take and enjoy, and it's weirdly quiet. She's too focused on passing out the cake to notice the odd, uncomfortable lack of reaction to it as people begin eating. The carrot was meant to be a surprise, but it doesn't seem to have the effect she anticipated. When she looks around, people are quietly chewing, but nobody is talking about it. Smiles are nowhere to be found.

Even Alice, with her boundless politeness for things she dislikes, seems put off.

"Is something the matter?"

"I think you may have… overcorrected with this one."

Joyce takes a forkful of cake into her bill, savoring the crumbly texture and the smell of the warm spices. But then, as she chews, she begins to understand the look on everyone's faces.

Then it hits her. Somehow, after all that time fiddling with the recipe, she's managed to forget the sugar.

***

Pass Out

***

There are lots of ways for a party to fall apart, and Joyce has experienced the rare treat of witnessing most of them in a single night. As the duck sulks back to her habitat, she can't help but return over and over to her conversation with Doc Schaefer. Mean drunk though she may be, the crow could have a point after all. All those years, helping homesteaders through grief, pain, and hopelessness - after all that, is Joyce nothing but a soft, feathery collection of pop-psychological affirmations?

It's midnight, and Colony Day is over. The narrow cylinder of her habitat is dark, and she finds herself fumbling through the shadows to find the ladder leading to her bunk. She isn't thinking. The model of the Photon stands between her and the ladder, but she can't see it until too late. She trips. The model goes down, and her with it.

"Ouch! Damn it..."

The kindness of low gravity leaves her uninjured from the fall, save for a small cut where one of the ship's rings scrapes her knee. But the model has not fared as well. Joyce pulls herself to her feet and finds a light switch. When she can finally see again, it's clear that the model is broken, split into three chunks, along with smaller bits of debris scattered around it.

Sighing, she collects the larger segments and gathers them on her table, and then sweeps the smaller bits away with the webbing of her foot. It's been a long day, and she doesn't want to deal with this right now. So she finds her way back to the ladder, turns off the light, and settles into her bunk.

***

'Til Next Year

***

The Blue Beacon will not land. The news of the ship's return trip to Earth arrives in the form of an official communique from the N.A.F, which states bluntly that a recent referendum, having declared Argyre-II a sovereign nation ('earnest congratulations from North America'), has therefore reclassified any and all provision-runs and related transactions as a form of foreign aid, subject to any and all relevant restrictions and statutes.

Meaning essentially that, assuming future supply runs will occur, the next one will not reach them for at least another year, and even then only after a series of lengthy and delicate negotiations.

Joyce learns this by overhearing it, which is the way she learns most news now, for she hasn't turned the radio on since Colony Day.

She's sitting alone in one of the communal dining centers, enjoying a warm slice of bread and carrot soup. The news feels like the culmination of something, like she always knew.

It's been a few weeks since she's seen Kevin, and now she wonders whether he's avoiding her, or whether he's decided to start seeing Doc Schaefer instead. That would be just as well, she thinks. Better Schaefer than an old quack.

But no sooner does she think of him than the mouse appears before her.

"Hey, Joyce. Mind if I sit?"

She looks up at him, standing with his tray, which contains a half-sandwich and a glass of water. She nods and he seats himself across from her. Rather than say anything more, he bites bit after bit of his sandwich, and follows with a few loud gulps of water. They eat for a while in silence. Kevin works through his meal in a matter of minutes, while Joyce very deliberately savors each spoonful of the smooth, red soup. Her bowl is still half-full when he's finished, and he begins talking again.

"I got something for you," he says.

"Oh?"

He reaches into the front pocket of his sweater and digs out what looks like a wadded up paper bag. He passes it across the table to Joyce.

"You're not going to tell me? I've never known you to be much for build-up."

"It's your geode," he says, as if to confirm her understanding of him. "Half of it, anyway."

Sure enough, as Joyce reaches into the sack, she feels the feathers on her fingertips brush against the rough texture of her earth rock. She brings it up to look at it, at the flat side, where it was bisected, its polished surface like a window to the blue layers of compressed sediment below.

"How did you manage to get it back?"

Kevin looks oddly surprised, like he didn't expect the question. "I found Sid. I told him I was miserable and embarrassed about what happened, about what I said. I said I was sorry. Then I told him how much it meant to you. He said he'd give me half now, half later."

"Half later?"

Kevin's face has that familiar flush from when he met Sidney in the market. He stares down at his empty plate and smiles.

"Well, he says I can have it. But he also wanted to 'hang out' with me, and said he'd hold onto the other half so I wouldn't flake on him again. Kind of like an insurance policy."

"Hang out? You mean he wants a date?"

His eyes snap back up. "What? No. I mean—I don't know. He said 'hang out.' Oh god, is this a date? Is that what I agreed to?"

They laugh, and for a moment she thinks it might be the first time she's ever seen the mouse this happy.

"I mean," he picks up the thread again. "I do like him. I think. This is all very new to me."

"Is this the last of our sessions, then?" she asks, her voice thinning near the end of her question.

"Nothing's that simple. I'll still visit. I mean, if you want me to. I have some thoughts about the structural integrity of your cake under Martian gravity."

"I have a feeling, given the recent declaration of our sovereignty, and the new likelihood of food rationing, that there won't be any more Colony Day cake."

"Well maybe there's something else I can work on."

The first image that springs to mind is a daydream, in which she and Alice are sipping tea, and Kevin is there too, fixing her broken model of the Photon. But then she imagines the dome itself, seen from high up in space, nestled in the crater, alone, at least for now.

"Yes. There's a lot of work to do."

"Did I tell you I got a job? I'm working on a new project to create multi-level vertical agriculture, to produce greater yield."

"Congratulations, Kevin." She says it very quietly, eyes still on the soup.

"Well, what about you? What'll you do?"

"I think I'll have a cup of tea, and maybe a nap. I'm supposed to be retired."

"You should write an essay," he says. "For the contest."

"What's the point? No Colony Day anymore. No ceremony. No more contest."

"That's just it," he says. "We'll need a new thing."

She thinks about this for a moment as she finishes the last of her soup. It's uncharted territory, familiar in a way, like when she first stepped on board the Photon, that Cadillac of ships. Or like Argyre-I, that flimsy, overcrowded habitat they lived in for the first two years while the dome was being built. Yes, things were difficult then, and they'll be difficult now.

There are always adjustments. But then, Joyce thinks, if they made it back then, anything can happen.

It's year zero again.

*Sometimes the very shape of the world changes, depending
on the eyes it's seen through.*

FOLDING IN THE WOLF
Bill Kieffer

The horse stood, straddling the bike. The drafter was just a few inches over ten feet tall. The gray leather jumpsuit he wore was well-worn from a time when the equine's body had been heavier, dumpier. Its color was a close match to the natural coat on the backs of his currently gloveless hands. The matching gloves went into the long triangular helmet, along with the pink mesh nose sock that he wore when riding to keep bugs from stinging the inside and outside of his sensitive and flexible lips and nose.

His ears cocked with mild amusement as he looked down into the side cart where an embarrassed Apennine wolf with black fur sat like a student in a corner with a dunce cap on.

Trucks rumbled past, a constant roll of thunder across the four lane highway. The sound barely disguised the horse's deep chuckle. The wolf slid a mild glare across the motorcycle, but didn't say anything. The policeman was coming back.

"OK, Mr. Hertsmere," the uniformed dog barked deeply enough that they could both hear him over the traffic. "Here are your license, registration, and insurance cards. I'm not going to write you a ticket for speeding; but please slow down next time, instead of trying to outrun a double trailer. They ain't known for stopping quickly. I am, however, going to ticket you for a passenger without a helmet. $75, no court appearance needed. Just mail it in to the address on the back."

"Thank you, officer," the wolf said. His amber eyes twitched as they met the husky's blue eyes. He reached with black-furred hands toward the ticket but canceled his attempt to take it as the cop's ears went back suspiciously. The trooper made a point of giving the ticket to the horse he'd been addressing.

The horse took the paperwork with the same amused look, as if enjoying the fact that the young canine had to look up at him. "I appreciate that, Sir. I'm terribly sorry, Sir, and I appreciate your discretion. My friend here had been up this way several years ago, and he insisted that he hadn't been required to wear a helmet then."

The canine turned his well-shaved muzzle toward the dark lupine. "The helmet law went into effect about five years ago. You do have a helmet that will fit your head, or do I need to have your friend make a big round trip to get you one?"

The wolf sighed and reached around to get the helmet from the compartment behind the seat. He did not notice the officer twitch and unholster his weapon. "Slowly," the dog barked, making the horse nearly twice his height gasp. A rainbow helmet covered in a blinding coat of glitter was in the black furred hands of the passenger. The wolf's ears rocked back in apology and the policeman re-snapped his gun in place.

The cop turned and tried to glare intimidatingly into the horse's chin. The horse looked down as soon as his ears locked into neutral. With wide innocent brown eyes, the stallion simply said, "That's my sister's."

The dog held up the distinctly shaped helmet, much too small for a draft horse. "He means, MY sister."

The horse nodded quickly. "Yes, Sir, sorry, aphasia."

A canine eyebrow rose over an otherwise expressionless face. "Get your gear on and get off my highway as safely – and as quickly – as possible."

"Yes, sir," they said as if they were of one mind.

***

An hour later, the two pulled into the Richlin church parking lot, already crowded with trucks, vans, and trailers designed for the drafter set.

The wolf pulled off his rainbow helmet before anyone of the normies could see it. "I can't believe you wore this helmet all the time."

The horse took off his gloves and nose guard as the engine cooled beneath him. "I needed color in my life, Leon."

The wolf's ears went alert and he glared at the taller creature. "You're Leon. I'm Preston. You can't slip up today."

A giant equine shrug rocked the bike. "I already told CC to warn everyone that I have memory loss and aphasia. From the accident that we don't like to talk about." The drafter pulled off his long helmet, revealing tall ears standing forward in a smile that betrayed the serious line of his lips. "Don't worry, Wolfie. The Hertsmeres seem like nice people from what you told me."

The wolf climbed out of the side car and began stretching. "Well, they're your family now, so I hope so for your sake."

"Brush out my tail." The horse pulled out the pale blond mass from his leather outfit.

'Preston' hesitated only long enough to free his own tail from his pants. The wolf tried to hide his smile but the happy wag betrayed him. "You're going to have to learn to do this yourself one day."

White fingers with brown and black hoof tips fluffed up the blond mane that matched his tail. "Pshaw." The motorcycle side mirrors were adjusted up so the horse could review his work. "You know my tail better than anyone, puppy."

***

Great Auntie May greeted the wayward colt, as she called him, with a hug and shared breath. The wolf was amused at his wide eyed friend's reaction. Leon had never liked the sensation; it had always felt like an invasion to him. The dappled stallion leaned into the old mare and closed his pale eyes so tightly that he appeared to tear up.

He likes it. He would have been shattered if he hadn't.

The new wolf made a mental note to add this to their journal, just as 'Leon' turned to introduce him to Great Auntie May. Luckily, she had a nametag on her Hertsmere Herd Reunion 2019 sweatshirt, so his stallion spoke as if he'd known her all his life. "May-May, this is Preston Altabef. Wolfie, this is my Great Auntie May."

He expected a hug, but in an instant, he saw that bending down a yard to the wolf's height was a bit too much for the ancient mare. "Pleased to meet you, Mrs. Hertsmere." He offered a handshake that she accepted with all the grace her ninety years on God's Green Earth had instilled into her.

"It is a pleasure to meet you, Mr. Altabef. Thank you for bringing our colt back to us."

The wolf stared awkwardly at the mare's hands embracing his right hand. The hoof tips looked dried and brittle, and the frogs felt lifeless and cold against his black pads. The knuckles looked larger than he remembered, although that just might be the size difference. He wanted to ask after her health, but that was the horse's job now. He looked up at the stallion, confused by the strange morbid emotions stuck in his throat.

"Preston is my boyfriend, May-May."

The wolf flinched, because this was not how they'd agreed he'd be introduced. A wave of dread got his fur up, and he felt his tail hide between his legs. But May-May merely squeezed his hands, her ears in a gentle surprise of polite pleasure. "I'm so happy to hear that. This colt's been needing to get laid since he hit the six foot mark."

He nearly bit his long pink tongue as the mare straightened up and tossled his black head fur as if he were a child. His ears didn't know what to do with themselves. Stallion and mare shared a laugh and some words, but the wolf could not hear them over the ringing of his ears. He wondered if wolves fainted but told himself he was just hearing the blood rushing into his ears as he blushed.

The mare took his shoulder and steered him towards an equine-sized card table where cousins Bobby and Gene manned a greeting table. Unlike most of the Hertsmeres, the brothers were mostly-white drafters. They were younger than Leon, yet they had teased the dappled horse mercilessly when they'd been colts. The horse greeted them as if that had never happened.

And it hadn't.

At least, it hadn't happened to the returning stallion. The adult versions of the bullies returned the favor of acting as if nothing had ever happened. But of course, bullies were like that.

The table came up to the wolf's shoulders. He watched the horse sign into the book that had tracked the last three years of guests and recipes.

"You signed my name, Leon," the wolf said, standing on tip toes to read what was in the book.

The stallion's ears flicked as he realized that his mate was right. "You can sign mine, Wolfie."

The stallion offered to lift the wolf by his scruff to help him sign-in. "Don't you dare," the wolf growled to Cousin Gene's delight.

Cousin Bob stayed all business as he collected an additional twenty bucks from each of them because they hadn't brought anything for the potluck. Gene looked down at the wolf, his ears friendlier and more sincere than expected. "There should be some things you can eat without much of an issue. If nothing else, there's always beer and lemonade."

Black-furred fingers tapped a jacket pocket full of jerky. He started to say he had emergency rations when Bob moaned. "The last thing we need is a belching and farting doggo. Go easy on the booze."

The wolf yipped, trying to make a scoffing noise. He growled with his head as far over the table as he could manage. "At least I'm not the one who burned his tail off trying to light his own farts."

Bob and Gene gave the stallion equally betrayed looks and missed the wolf belated clamping his black hands on his muzzle after the fact. 'Leon' was off-balanced for a moment, but recovered quickly. "It was a funny story," he said with just the right amount of lameness that it was as much an apology as an explanation.

Bob did not laugh, but Gene did, nodding in agreement.

"I hope the fur grew back," the stallion said in another attempt at the male non-apology apology that he'd gotten pretty good at.

This sent Gene into hysterics. Bob stewed deeper. Neither seemed to have noticed that 'Leon' had said fur instead of hair, as horses do, but maybe CC had coached everyone as promised. The wolf pulled his hands off his muzzle and wrung them under the table. Bob told his brother to shut up three times. Both wolf and horse backed up a little as a fight seemed about to break out.

Gene told a story about a nineteen-year-old Bobby... "OK, a nameless colt, who's still Bobby." His brother's ears set back with the long sufferance that comes with having a twin like Gene, but the gelding eventually gave in. Preston and Leon gave equally appalled gape-mouthed expressions of horror as farts, lighters, and fireworks in the story accidentally conspired to geld the white drafter.

"Ooo," the horse said with more sympathy than Gene evinced. "That's... not going to grow back."

That comment sent Gene into further hysterics. It took him over a minute to spit out something about space age plastics. Now that the worst was over, cousin Bob reached under the table and took out a Stile-Mart bag with LEON PLUS ONE written in marker on it. "CC set aside this for you."

Inside, the wolf found a light cotton shirt that loosely fit him over his button down shirt. It read Hertsmere Herd 2019 on the front and FUTURE FAMILY MEMBER on the back. He wondered if the stallion and CC had conspired against him when he hadn't been looking. Gene and Bob were trading quiet, almost pleasant barbs when the wolf noticed that his other half hadn't tried on his sweatshirt yet.

Instead, the leather clad stallion was flipping through the book. "I'm checking to see if my father's here yet."

The white cousins paused as if the stallion had mentioned that he'd invited Satan to his wedding.

The wolf jumped in before the drafter could figure out what he'd said wrong. "He meant Howard. His step-father."

They relaxed as the stallion nodded his head in agreement. Leon's biological sire had gone missing when he was five. Since he'd never bothered to marry Leon's dam, she'd been free to marry Howard when he was widowed and Leon was ten. Leon had spent most of his early childhood waiting for the man who hadn't bothered to leave his last name behind. His mother's marriage to Howard had squashed those dreams.

"Uncle Howie is running late. He might not be here until tomorrow morning."

Gene nodded. "After this weekend, a couple of us are going to help him move out of his house into a trailer."

The wolf opened his mouth to decline out of habit, but the stallion cut him off with a warm smile as if he'd never been invited to move furniture. "I'd like that. I'd like that a lot."

Even Bob smiled warmly at the stallion's eagerness. The wolf cocked his ears into something close to a smile.

It is his family. I have to let him reach out.

I have to let him risk getting hurt.

The stallion noticed the sweatshirt in his hands. He peeled off his jumpsuit, and the wolf found himself admiring the stallion's body. Leon had never been so lean and muscular before the treatment, and the last few months, the drafter had worked hard to get the body he'd wanted. Bob and Gene were pop-eyed with awe as the dappled gray chest and the pinto swirled belly glistened in the sunshine. The stallion had a very defined six-pack that few drafters ever saw. It was almost a shame to put a sweatshirt over it.

The stallion bundled up the gear and asked the wolf to put it in the side car. The wolf pulled the horse's big gray head down to kiss him with a little leap at the blond mane. Leon whispered urgently into the fuzzy ear that cocked his way. "Don't flirt with your homophobic cousins."

The stallion gave a mischievous smirk, and the wolf padded off leaving his mate to figure it out for himself.

***

The wolf had folded and wiped down the inside of the jumpsuit to get rid of most of the musky horse sweat the stallion had left behind before spraying the inside with disinfectant and then a deodorizer. The gray leather outfit was expensive; anything nice in equine sizes was costly. He had learned to take care of his things years ago. He applied conditioner to the outside as was his habit before folding it up and putting it into a clean plastic storage bag. That would keep it supple.

He should have headed back to his mate's side the moment the outfit was locked away properly, but there was road dirt on the bike. Against his better judgment, the wolf selected a tacky cloth from the compartment he kept stocked for just such moments. He sighed, accepting that this was just him avoiding dealing with his anxiety.

He had buffed only a small portion of the chrome gas tank when an equine hand grasped the scruff of his neck firmly. Despite himself, his black hands dropped the cleaning supplies and folded partially in front of his chest. He was on his toes when his weight pulled out his underarm pits painfully, and he mewled in protest, a childish unexpected sound that scared him more than anything.

"How's it feel to have the scruff you always wanted, Leon?"

He spun around to face CC as soon as the mare let go off his scruff. "What the hell?"

His heart pounded as he looked up at Catherine Christina Hertsmere. She was almost four feet taller than he was, and if she hadn't been bent over to glare at him, he would not have recognized her from this new angle. "Before you ask me what I'm talking about, try to remember that I'm the only one here that knows both of you. From before 'the accident,' before you both went to Gunther University… which just happened to announce that clinical trials had begun with the Janus Cerebral Exchanger… a 1930's invention thought only to exist in pulp fiction."

"That really hurt," the wolf blurted. It was half a stall. He'd forgotten that one of the reasons that CC was a renowned gossip was that she didn't listen to or repeat gossip. She was simply supremely observant and not afraid to step in to manage a situation directly… or indirectly, as the case might merit.

"I'm sorry," but the mare wasn't quite. He could tell from her flaring nostrils and flattened ears that she was really angry with him. "Also, the hand wringing, Preston never did that. Then you let… or rather Preston let you handle his gear and his precious motorcycle."

"I can't talk about it." The wolf whispered, although they were alone in this end of the parking lot at the moment. "We signed an NDA."

"Did the mind-swap make you an idiot?" The mare came close to imitating a lupine growl. "You had me lie to everyone. I don't like being made a liar."

Leon almost responded that she was an unrepentant gossip. Luckily, self-preservation overrode that impulse. He kept his mouth shut. The black wolf moved his shoulders as he weighed his next words. The pain – and the scare from nearly being pulled off his little clawed feet – had thrown him off. It was a sensation he'd never experienced as a ten-foot-tall draft horse, and he didn't like it much.

After a moment, the hurt bird routine began to soften his older cousin.

"I'm sorry we made you lie," he said when it seemed safe to talk. "But it wasn't much of a lie. Preston and I do have some memory loss, and we both say the wrong thing sometimes."

"Because you forget you're not a horse anymore?"

The wolf nodded. "Preston really likes being a horse. More than I ever did."

The mare shook her head. "So, the self-loathing horse and a self-loathing wolf just happened to hook up and then get into the most controversial clinical trial ever?"

She is smart. Leon realized that she knew him too well to lie to her further, wolf body or not. Non-Disclosure Agreement or not. He leaned against the side car heavily. "No. GU hooked us up after we did a body image poll for money. Right away, we realized we were attracted to each other."

"You literally wanted each other for your bodies, you mean. *Literally.*"

For the second time that day, the sound of his ears blushing nearly overwhelmed him with the sound of rushing blood. "It was more curiosity for me, but yeah. Later, after the swap… the connection grew closer. We… completed each other." He spoke over her eye rolls. "You don't get to judge us… we had to learn how our new bodies worked… and we both knew our old bodies better than everyone else."

"OK, but I have to ask you—"

"You can't ask me about our sex life," the wolf barked firmly, surprised by his own irritation. He softened his voice. "Not with that disgusted look you had on your face."

"Fine, but I have to know—"

"Is this question about my genitals?"

CC opened her mouth and closed it again. For a moment she seemed to still be angry. Then her lips twitched with a smirk. "It is… knot."

Leon face-palmed, but had to force himself not to laugh. "OK, what's your question?" He growled softly, although he was pleased to see that she was about ready to forgive him.

"Why are you just giving your family away?" She gestured to the card table where a bunch of stallions were having a friendly chat with Preston in his horse skin. "I get why you couldn't be here for Aunt Thelma's funeral… everyone would wonder how this balling wolf got into a funeral for a horse."

"The week that happened, I couldn't understand written or spoken words. Even colors were… wrong. It was another two weeks before I even understood that Mom had died. I never even had that much of an option to be here."

"I'm sorry, I didn't know."

Leon caught himself wringing his hands again and forced them apart. "No one knew… that's what happens when you sign an NDA, I guess. Can I count on you to keep my secret?"

"Yes, but I won't like it. Just like I don't like you passing Preston off as you coming home to people who love you."

Loved me? Leon almost barked his objection, but he caught himself. The therapy GU had required him to take kept him from over-reacting. Of course, the herd had loved him. Just as they would love any other hoofer related to them. But in failing to understand him, they had failed to support him.

"They don't just think Preston is me. Legally, that horse is *still* Leon Hertsmere. His flesh is still the flesh of the herd. His breath is still the air of the herd." Amber eyes darted back to his mate, softening as a mare he didn't recognize introduced a pair of young fillies to their long lost cousin. Judging by the set of the stallion's ears, he was head over hocks in love with them already.

"He is someone who actively needs the support they offer. And this mind-swap thing is just experimental. We don't know how long it might last. That mole who invented this… he always did mole to mole swaps. It never occurred to him to move across species. Or genders. At least, not that we know of. We're in uncharted waters."

"So… you could just wake up back in your own bodies tomorrow?"

That horrible thought pulled Leon's tail between his legs and visibly swept his ears back, although he tried to hide it. Another couple in the trial had supposedly twinned within hours of their mind-swap. One subject with a new persona and the other subject with their old persona and reduced motor skills. One of the identities had been lost. "It wouldn't likely be that neat."

"Why would you take that chance?"

"The chance to be the best me?"

CC gestured broadly at the wolf body. "This is not the best you."

Leon growled, and enjoyed how deep he could feel the vibration. How right it felt to express his anger without words. How pure, without stomping hooves. How wonderful it was to focus like this.

"You think you get to judge what the best version of me is? OK, look at my big, clumsy, dappled butt talking with our cousins. They think Preston is the best version of me. A version of me that grew up proud and comfortable in his skin. Except, they don't know he didn't… they don't know what he risked… and is risking to be one of them. Did you ever see my ears standing so tall? That lovely stallion is the best Leon. The best stallion ever."

"That could have been you."

"That confident? Maybe. But never that proud; never as a horse could I ever have been so proud."

"If you hate horses so much, if you hate your body so much… how can you sleep with…" CC cut herself off, realizing that she was getting angry.

He took her hands. She was much stronger than he was, but she let him. "It's a lot better when that body isn't in a mirror. Preston freed me with this exchange."

"That is the stupidest thing I ever heard. Sure, you had terrible self-esteem – a lot of young colts are like that when they have absentee fathers… and your father was no great shakes when he was around either."

The wolf shook his head, grateful she hadn't taken her hands away. "I was never a horse. Yes, I had hooves. Yes, I towered over almost everyone that wasn't a horse. But every time I shared breath with a horse, I was repulsed. It hurt me. Crushed me. I don't know why, but its a fact." Now it was his turn to check his anger. He softened his voice. "Every morning since this happened, I wake up looking at a myself in the mirror. The real me. This is a face I can live with. The real me."

CC shook her mane and flicked her own tail in annoyance. "I don't understand any of this."

Leon caught himself from snapping back at her. So much emotion and passion danced in his chest, looking to get out. He took a deep breath and let his hands wring themselves. "Maybe we could skip the understanding part and just try acceptance? I promise to share as much as I can; as soon as I can. It would mean a lot to me if I could still be part of this family."

"Just not part of the herd? I –" CC stopped herself. "Look, your boyfriend is bringing a bunch of our idiot cousins over. We'll talk about this later, Leon."

"Call me Preston, please. Or Wolfie. I like that."

The mare rolled her eyes one last time, unhappy but no longer angry. That was more progress than he probably had a right to.

She slipped away before any of the other stallions noticed. The four cousins with his other half only had eyes for the bike and side car. 'Leon' introduced the four, although the wolf had grown up with all of them when he had been a dappled gray colt. They shook hands making the lupine webbed fingers feel smaller each time. The thought made him smile. He liked feeling small.

"Wolfie, the guys wanted to know about our bike… but I kept losing my words."

The black wolf beamed with pride. He'd always been interested in mechanics, but it had never seemed like a good career choice for a bulky and brawny drafter. Once upon a time, maybe, with large hulking diesel guzzling engines, but the modern, delicately balanced, computer-enhanced motors were the realm of smaller creatures. Normal sized creatures.

The new horse, the real Preston, hadn't the slightest bit of interest in engines, but he'd listened to Leon talk about the bike enough. He could have recited its entire history if he wanted to. Instead, he brought this small herd to Leon… to listen to him.

"Well, after the accident, the doctors recommended I take up something to work on. Motorcycle repair is actually good eye-hand co-ordination… and I found this little fixer-upper in the classifieds." The wolf totally skipped why a little wolf like him would be interested in a huge monster of a bike sized for someone almost twice his height and massing about four times as much. Machines like the Endless Vista were works of art.

The cousins listened and asked questions about the bike. Richlin wasn't a rich area. Bikes like this were the best way for large creatures to get around on roads built for creatures of 'normal' size. Everyone had a bike story, and Leon was amazed to enjoy swapping motorhead stories with them. Preston publicly touched him, gently, from time to time, with a goofy smile just to remind Leon that he was still there.

"Proud of you, Wolfie," the horse whispered as the group peeled off to gather for food. He tugged on the still tender scruff affectionately. The pain was worth the affection.

"Proud of you, too, Ponyboi. Remind me to nip the back of your neck later."

The drafter's ears darkened a bit with a blush that matched his own. They embraced and the horse's stomach rumbled loudly. "Sounds like its time to see if Aunt May-May's pecan pie is everything you say it is."

"It is… remember don't wolf down your food. Pace yourself."

"I will."

"Remember, you can't just vomit up bad choices anymore."

Smiling, the horse headed to the picnic tables. "Nag, nag, nag… Don't forget to eat something yourself. Go make some deliciously bad decisions, Wolfie. You deserve it."

***

Later that night, Leon slipped onto a bench near the pile of wood that would be the bonfire tomorrow. He wanted to eat his proteins alone. Turkey jerky hardly qualified as a deliciously bad decision but he recalled the odor being offensive to other horses. He had liked the scent of it then. Now the mere scent set him to drooling.

The wolf chased the jerky down with a local brew that appealed to his new sensitive palette.

He allowed himself to belch, enjoying the sensations his throat made to accomplish it. It tickled him nine ways to Sunday. Not to mention the way an equine's beer bottle was like drinking from an old-fashioned, milk glass quart bottle. His tongue splashed in its opening. Being smaller made him feel lighter and graceful.

Some of the children were fascinated by him, following him and giggling. Once he started eating, they left him alone. That was a thing about horses. Most of them couldn't bear to see another horse alone. Leon, however, had always been different. When he was alone, it was because he wanted to be alone. Wanted to stay alone. No one ever seemed to believe him.

Now that he was a wolf, they simply understood. He wanted to be alone.

And when he ate, they let him concentrate on just that.

He loved these people.

I just loved them better on the outside of the circle than the inside.

Leon folded up the empty wrappers into a napkin and shoved it into a pocket. He closed his eyes and let his ears soak up the reunion. He heard clicks of glass bottles, the clanks of thrown horse shoes, and the gentle murmur of a dozen different stories being told just on the other side of the woodpile. Then he caught his own voice on the twilight breeze.

Preston's voice now. His true voice.

A drafter's deep rich laugh. The mocking undertones that a younger Leon had always undermined his shared joy with were absent. The horse he might have been filled him with a strange sense of melancholy.

But he felt no sadness. Just as a new vista was opening up with Preston, a new, more focused future was opening for Leon. He didn't know if that distant path would still be with his old body and its new occupant. The Janus device had changed them. Their bodies might not maintain all their old memories. Pre-swap memories might leak back. So much of the mind was unknown.

At least, it seemed that their concept of self was fixed… if the horse stayed wanting to be a horse, and the wolf remained happy with his carnivore body, then that was really all that mattered.

He spent several minutes listening to the party. He couldn't hear his boyfriend's voice, and he briefly wondered if he should check up on his drafter. But then he realized that he was a little drunk.

A liter of beer is… how many bottles of 'normal' sized beers?
Four?
Five? Something like that.

That was probably twice as many beers as he should have had. The jerky sticks and two forkfuls of pecan pie, so sweet that it had burned his long, thin tongue, wasn't enough to soak up all that beer.

Good beer, though.

The urge to howl wandered into his head, but he squashed it instantly. Shepherds knew what the herd would have made of that sudden whimsy. It certainly wasn't from a tug of loneliness. He was going to have to watch his alcohol intake. That was all.

Leon opened his amber eyes as he heard unshod hooves on the path-stones on the other side of the towering pyre. Twilight was still hanging on, and tiki torches were being lit all across the church yard. He stood, forcing his hands to stop wringing themselves. The novelty of having claws and webbed fingers had not yet worn off. He only swayed a little.

A stallion in a baggy, tweed suit and white reunion shirt limped into view a second later. Tall and broad, even for the Hertsmere drafters, the old piebald was at once familiar and alien.

"Preston?" The voice rumbled out of the horse with all the undertones and vibrations of a train of freight cars casually moving through town.

Leon would not have recognized him if the horse hadn't spoken, but even for a moment he wasn't sure. The new ears – the new eyes – were part of it. But the other part of it was Howard himself. His step father seemed to have caught up to May-May's advanced age. Leon's tongue slipped from his jaws. It took a concentrated effort to put it back before the wolf realized his mouth was hanging open. He'd seen the old hoss three Yuletides ago. Or was it four? Either way, Howard was just about fifty. And judging by the way his favorite suit was hanging off him, the years hadn't treated him well.

"Yes, sir? That's me." His soft lupine voice broke like a teenager's. A vile bubble of air popped in his throat. He forced his hands into his pockets to keep them from wringing.

"You don't know me, I'm Howard Wheat. I'm Leon's step-father. I wanted to introduce myself."

An effort of will sent him taking a few quick steps with an out-stretched hand. A massive equine hand took his with an abundance of gentleness Leon had never experienced from the older stallion before.

The back of the gripping hand was furless, covered by a square, white, cotton bandage with a red-brown spot. The grasp was barely held before the older horse's hand fell open to release the black wolf's hand. The stallion's sleeve puffed out a cloud of short hairs in two tones. The acrid scent of disinfectant and strong medications stung the wolf's little black nose gently.

That's not gentleness; that's weakness.

"Leon sent me out to seek your approval."

Leon's black ears shot up against his wishes, but then this was an honest surprise. "My approval?"

The horse smiled almost shyly. "I don't know what Leon told you about me and his mother… or about my relationship with him. Thelma had a hard time trusting a man at first, after Leon's father done runaway from them. Thelma eventually learned to trust me. Leon, though, he never did really warm up to me."

Feeling trapped, Leon glanced around. No gray drafters were coming around the corner to save him. He cursed Preston and wondered what his ponyboi was up to. "Do you need to sit down? You look beat."

"I do, thank you. You solid enough to lean on, Preston?"

"I am," the wolf said. He and Preston had… tested their bodies' limits these last few months. "I won't be able to pick you up should you fall."

"If I fall, just leave me there." With a grunt, the large equine settled on the bench and let go of the wolf's shoulder. "I've been running around too much these days."

Black nails massaged blacker pads as Leon's mind raced for something to say. "I'm sorry to hear about your loss. I heard it was… unexpected."

The horse blew a gentle blast of air that might have been a laugh, but for the lack of humor. "Yes, it was. I was sick for the last two… three years. It was supposed to be me. We were prepared for that. There were so many medical bills. But it was her the shepherds came for. Sudden internal hemorrhage… that happens to horses sometimes."

His mind dull, the wolf could only nod.

The pinto drafter looked up at the wolf. From the wolf's sitting position, the drafter's large oval shaped nostrils lined up with Leon's eyes level as if they were the eye sockets of some fleshy skull. Instead of looking down, Howard turned his head sideways. A measuring look from his right brown eye. "Some of Leon's aunties took it upon themselves to call me and warn me that Leon had arrived with a gay wolf boyfriend. I think they were afraid I'd make a scene. I'm not going to. I feel like I should thank you for bringing Leon home."

Leon nodded again, wondering if he should have had less beer. Or more.

"You don't talk much for a wolf, do you?"

Leon felt his ears fold back. His step-father had always questioned his wolfishness.

Of course, I had been a horse at the time.

"I'm not your average wolf," Leon admitted. "I was raised by horses… more or less."

The big but frail stallion nodded once. "Well, that explains why you're with my step-son. And I already know why he's with you."

His blushing ears rang a klaxon in his head. "What do you mean?"

"Leon had boxes full of wolf and dog pornography 'hidden' under his bed. Don't tell him I always knew. I used to hide them when his mother was obsessed with spring cleaning."

The wolf swayed under the weight of his step-father's casual revelation. "You knew?"

"I figured he was either gay or BI… I hoped for BI because then he could have a normal life. Maybe." The horse seemed to notice the confused wolfish set of ears. "I don't know if your folks worried about that sort of thing, but homosexuals calling themselves gay seemed like such a cruel joke. Having to live in secret is a terrible thing. Such a terrible heart-breaking thing. We never wanted that for Leon."

Leon tried to suppress the urge to growl. He was only partially successful. "I don't think we called ourselves 'gay' first. Other people slapped that on us."

An apologetic cant to the horse's ears slid into a soft smile. "I'm sure you're right." The horse blew air for another measuring moment. "The important thing is that you all claimed it. Took it. Made it your own. Now you can be legally married and… gosh, even our last mayor was gay. If I had known that the world was going to change so much before he was even thirty, I would have… well, I would like to think that I would have been supportive."

His step-father was being reasonable.

Just how many giant beers did I have?

"I think Leon would be happy to hear that." Leon forced his hands into his pockets.

Pink ears stood up on the horse's head before bending awkwardly down. "I told him… and he said I should tell you."

Leon's own ears danced a little too. Of course Preston would send Howard to him. He was touched and confused all at once.

After a moment, Howard sighed. "I don't think Leon thought I'd be here. I think he thought that, with his mother dead, I'd have no reason to stick around. That, like his biological father, I'd just vanish in the night, never to be heard from again."

Leon nodded. "Maybe a little, he did. I think."

The horse shrugged and took off his oversize suit jacket. There were a lot of uncomfortable looking angles under the white t-shirt. "Well, I'll tell you, I really thought I might sell the house and run down to Florida. Especially when it looked like Thelma's son was blowing off her funeral. But May-May took me aside and asked me to stay. She told me that, 'Family wasn't just blood. It was a bond.' And CC – I heard you met her – CC told me that, 'Family was whoever stayed when the yelling started."

"That sounds like CC."

The older horse nodded and smiled. "So, like it or not, I'm a Hertsmere. I'm going to stay. I'm getting a trailer... there's just ten times as many steps in the house than I'm willing to deal with. I'm thinking I might rent the place out... CC says there's an app I can put on my phone to help with that. I'm not sure I want to be a landlord."

Leon smiled and nodded, feeling awkward in front of the man he once thought he hated. Now, it seemed lame to blame him for his unhappiness.

Into the lingering silence, the two men fought to find words. Thankfully, the horse did not ask how Leon and Preston had met, or the other niceties that the wolf would have to lie about.

Eventually, the horse cleared his throat. "Leon is... different. I mean, he almost seems like a different person. Happier. Content."

Leon's new wolf body had an easier time hiding a laugh. "He is. He is a different person, I mean."

"The accident? Can you talk about it? CC said something along the lines of you signing an NDA or something."

Leon wished he was a horse again so that he could properly kick his cousin. "Something like that. Yeah. Leon's memory from... before... is spotty. And what he remembers... it's literally as if someone else told him stories about his past."

Literally, Leon thought with a wolfish grin.

"How about you? You were in the same accident, too, weren't you?"

"I was... lucky. Really lucky. I only had to relearn how to walk... and talk. Life is too short to dwell."

"Ain't that right?" The horse seemed to squirm on the bench awkwardly. "Help me stand, Preston. I think it's time to see if my blood sugar is ready for a slice of May-May's pecan pie."

Leon allowed his lupine body to be used as a makeshift cane. His heart pounded with unexpected concern as the extent of his step-father's frailty was impressed on him. Even to his smaller wolf body, Howard seemed much too light. Then, suddenly, the horse's arms wrapped around Leon in a tight hug. The horse's muzzle was next to his, pulling in his jerky flavored breath as Leon gasped.

Habit and courtesy overwhelmed Leon, and he surrendered in defeat to the traditional sharing of breaths. Little wolf lungs expanded and drew Howard's moist air in. And…

And… it wasn't a bad thing. There were notes of illness, of chemicals, and the undertone of slightly cooked meat that a chemo patient sometimes emitted. It was comforting, in some odd way that Leon could never process before.

Howard straightened up and looked a bit apologetic. "That was a hug for Leon. He never liked them growing up much. Can you give it to him for me later?"

Leon smiled and began walking the larger drafter back around the unlit pyre. "Let's go give it to him now. I have a very strong feeling that he's going to like your hugs a lot better."

***

The little fillies that Preston had been introduced to earlier that day were braiding the horse's mane and tail. The drafter was pleased as punch. Sitting on a hay bale, the ex-wolf was not just tolerating the pulling and the chatter as the girls climbed over him, but encouraging them to weave in ribbons and wild flowers. For Howard, it was such a shocking scene that he stopped dead in his tracks, causing the wolf he was leaning into for support to nearly fall over.

Leon yipped a series of small barks that passed for his laughter these days. "Well, he really needed more color in his life."

Howard blew some air out of his lungs and then gave a rumbling guffaw. "He did, yes. Yes, he did."

His stepfather shifted and took his weight off the wolf's shoulders. "I'll be right back."

As the elderly horse gingerly made his way through the sea of colts, fillies, and yearlings that were gathering around the wayward son, CC wandered over to Leon. "He is really fitting in well. I did a good job of setting him up for his masquerade."

"It's not… I'm sorry that we lied to you. But it's very important."

The mare nodded, with a flick of her ears. "I can see that. So how long are staying?"

Leon looked up at her with a dog-like cock of the head. "The weekend. Like we said. Back to hot—"

"No, I mean, with your old body. How long are you going to stick around him before you run off to be with the wolves?"

Black eyebrows rose up and his ears stiffened. He turned his eyes back to his man. Preston was laughing and slowly spinning, trying to look at his braided tail, much to the laughter of the newest generation of Hertsmeres. Leon's lupine heart tightened and his tail decided to wave in the wind behind him.

He looked at his cousins and aunties, working over grilled corn, spiced apples, and salads of every stripe. Talking, hugging, and exchanging the breaths that made them one united herd. Some heated debates would flare up, here and there, but by the time his sharp wolf eyes could track it, the dispute was settled. Only CC liked to argue for its own sake. Leon knew she'd be the matron auntie of the herd in years to come.

I want to be here for that.

"Why are you panting like that? Are you over-heating?"

Leon laughed wolfishly then. It was the only way he laughed these days. "I'm smiling, CC. This is me smiling."

CC was not quite impressed. "You didn't answer the question."

Still wagging his tail, Leon nodded his head to the young horse he used to be. "I'm not my father, CC. I'm going to be with Preston as long as he wants me. As long as he'll have me."

The mare nodded. "He says the same about you. Not about not being his father, but you know."

CC shook her mane out and pursed her lips outwards, as if tasting the air and finding it wanting. "Howard's going to ask you to stay. Him. Preston. He's going to ask him to take over the Wheat house. It's been in the Wheat family almost 100 years, ain't no one going to say boo if he just sold it to strangers. Yet, what he's doing is worse. He's just going to give it away to a stranger, and he's not even going to know that's a stranger. There's no way Preston is going to want to say no. It's drafter scale. Ain't many places like that."

"I hope he says yes. I love it here, and its a wonderful house."

CC gave him a measuring look. "You aren't even going to be able to reach the kitchen counter."

"I'm as tall as I was when I was ten. I'll be fine." Leon stood up to his full wolfish height and then leaned heavily on his cousin.

"You hated it here."

Leon shrugged like a drafter, rolling his shoulders. "I resented Howard replacing my no good father. I resented being so much larger then the other horses."

"You were a fool, Leon."

"Maybe." The wolf stopped leaning and turned laughing amber eyes up to the taller mare. "But I do love these folks. I just could not stand that I could not be myself with them. I resented the whole idea that if I wanted to be part of the herd, I had to be a horse. I had to match what they thought a horse should be. That wasn't me."

"You think it's going to be easier being a wolf in a herd of horses?"

"I expect I might get kicked a few times, but to paraphrase something I heard from a wise old man, family is whoever sticks around when the kicking starts."

This is a powerful, important story about the simple need for connection and the darkness that one can fall into without it. (See the last page of the book for content warnings.)

Thoughts and Prayers

Thurston Howl

Tracker dog disease sucks.

Jason Ritts was a 23-year-old Doberman in Chicago, and on the cold day of January 7th, he received the news he had contracted tracker dog disease, or TDD. He had not asked for it. He had gotten it from an ex, a Dalmatian named Mark. Jason had known he had gotten a tick from Mark a couple of nights the year before, but Mark had sworn up and down that he was clean on everything. But here was the proof that was a lie. And as Mark later confessed, he had known he had had TDD for about eight years. Basically, TDD worked against his immune system, breaking it down and trying to kill him.

It had been two weeks since the diagnosis, and Jason was trying to move on. It was tough being a gay college student from a middle-lower class family living by himself in the suburbs. It was even tougher having all that with TDD. His meds cost $3,500 a month, and the insurance paperwork for all of that was work by itself.

What he needed most though wasn't money or even the drugs, he thought. It was contact. He needed some sense of community. That's what drove him to the decision to finally be open about his status. Completely open. He changed his dating profile info to say he was TDD positive. And now, he had drafted a post on Furbook: "Hi everyone, I know I don't post a lot here, and I know this may be a call for attention, but I need it right now. I just found out two weeks ago that I'm positive for TDD. I'm not going to die. The meds they have for it will keep me just as healthy as anyone else. But I just need any support I can get right now." He had written and re-written the post three times, and he was finally satisfied with it. But it still scared him. What if, throughout the day, he noticed people were just blocking him? What if his family saw, and they disowned him or something?

With a final exhale, he pressed the 'Post' button. The phone made a small beep, informing him that the post had been published successfully, and though regret pounded against his heart, he put his phone back in his pocket and finished getting ready for work.

He lived alone, and he was happy with that. He worked every day at the local Bears & Noble, which served as a general trade books store as well as the college bookstore, so it included a textbook department and an apparel store for all the college athletics fans. But Jason worked in the trade department. He liked to be paws deep in bookshelves. Customers would come in asking for recommendations based on their interests, or a specific book for which they only knew the shade of the cover, or even information on what happened to the bookstore that had been at the same location ten years ago and why it wasn't there anymore. Nine times out of ten, Jason could help. And it made him feel confident in himself. He knew books, and he liked feeling useful.

Today he had an opening shift. But as he finished getting dressed, he felt the phone start to buzz in his pocket. With a nervous twitch of his ears, he pulled it out, and sure enough, there were ten notifications from Furbook. He swiped to open the app, and there were zero likes on the post but ten comments. Most were short, all along the lines of, "I'm so sorry this happened to you. My prayers are with you." He smiled to himself. Maybe, just maybe, he wasn't alone. Maybe people wouldn't start hating him for this. Maybe he would beat this disease.

He put his phone back in his pocket and grabbed his keys before heading out into the Chicago snow for the second time that morning. His car had already been heating up, and he raced to get inside. Careful of the ice in the driveway, he pulled out of the apartment parking lot and plugged his phone in to the speakers so he could listen to some Ke$heep on his way.

Even while his phone kept buzzing, he made his way to work, his nose twitching throughout the ride. At the first stop light, he risked a glance down at his phone. Now up to 37 comments. He looked up—the light was still dark—and then swiped on his phone to look at some of the comments. A lot of the same. Some of the same words repeated before his eyes: "So sorry," "Wishing," "Prayers," and a new phrase, "You're very brave / strong." He snorted.

He appreciated that people were being supportive of him. Their comments indicated that they cared, that they wished well for him. Still, it kinda stressed him out. All the comments were more pitying than embracing. More prayers than invitations to connect. More well-wishes than people asking how he was doing. But those thoughts made him feel guilty, and he clenched the steering wheel tighter and exhaled. They were offering support the best they could. That's what he told himself. Most people didn't know shit about TDD, and he was probably the only person most of them knew who did have it.

***

A horn honked behind him. He glanced up to see the white light, and his ears flattened as he pressed on the gas. He tried to wave in front of the mirror to apologize to the driver behind him, but he had no way of knowing if the dog saw it. The phrase appeared in his mind's eye, just that line of sans-serif text: "You're very brave." He assumed they meant brave for being open about his status online. But he just didn't see it that way. Despite his somber face, he was terrified. He was lonely. Worse, he was desperate.

After a few minutes of driving, he made it to the bookstore and wheeled around to the small employee lot in back of the store. Jason grabbed his employee badge and left his warm car to shiver in the cold air outside. This store didn't have a door in the back as most buildings in the area did, just the one out front. It took him almost five minutes in the frigid air to get to it. By the time he did, his canines were clacking together in his muzzle. But once inside, he shivered again from the sudden warmth. It was empty except for a couple of store managers setting up the cash registers for the day. Jason made his way upstairs and put his coat up in the employees' office.

As he went to the trade desk, he saw his coworker, an old St. Bernard named Tom, was already logging in himself. "Oh, good morning, Jason!"

"Morning, Tom. How was your weekend, you old dog?"

Tom barked once and then laughed. "Oh, it was fine. Caught up on some reading and had a game night with my neighbor. Was a fun time."

"I'm sure. How drunk did you get?" Jason teased with a smile, his little nub of a tail wagging past the hole in the seat of his pants.

Tom barked again. "None ya' business, pup."

Jason moved past him and logged in to the computer. "Whatever. When's Ralph getting in?" The thought of the stern German shepherd manager put a stop to Jason's wagging, but he also didn't want to be seen messing around with Tom all morning by any of the other shift managers either.

"I think he's out sick today."

"Oh, cool," Jason said as he looked at the clock. Ten minutes till the store officially opened.

"So…" Tom said, "I saw your Furbook post."

Jason's heart froze. He didn't look up from the computer. "Oh yeah?"

"Yeah, how are you holding up?"

It was the first time Jason had been asked. Not even the nurse who had told him his diagnosis had asked. "I'm doing…" He had almost said "fine" out of habit. Even now, he wondered if that was the answer Tom was expecting. He chose to go with the truth. "I'm not doing great, Tom."

Tom waved a paw and caught Jason's attention. "Eh, I wouldn't worry about it if I were you."

Jason's eyes widened. "Huh?"

"Look, pup, it's not as bad as it used to be, yeah? It's not a death sentence. It's just a thing."

He couldn't believe how nonchalant Tom looked as he said it, as if they were still teasing each other. "It's just a—?"

"And besides, you know better. You shouldn't have been sleeping around. And if you do, always make sure you ask for someone's vet records."

Jason wanted to say it was a bit late for that advice, but even then it just wasn't how things had gone down. Jason *hadn't* been sleeping around. He had been in a committed relationship. He had been in a relationship with a dog he trusted. It was true he hadn't asked for Mark's vet records, but he hadn't thought he needed to. He thought if you loved someone, and that dog loved you, it was okay to trust them on their word.

"Hey, Tom," one of the shift managers called.

Jason's jaw hung as Tom walked away. That was all Tom said to him throughout the whole work day—no one else at work approached him about the topic—but the words haunted Jason. Even an older gay dog was saying it was Jason's fault he was positive. Could it be? Was he really the stupid one here? Did he… get what he deserved?

***

Once he got in the car on the way home, he heard his phone start to ring. He had received about a hundred comments on the Furbook post, but they were all more or less the same. But when he looked at the phone now, he saw it was his mom calling.

He swallowed, but his throat felt suddenly dry. Pulling out of the lot, he pressed 'Accept' and brought the phone up to his triangular ear. "H-Hi, Mom."

"Hi, sweetie." Her voice sounded soft and caring, like she was afraid for him. "I saw your post. I'm so sorry for you."

His heart sank. Her, too. "Yeah… thanks, Mom."

"How did you get it? Was it that Dalmatian last year?"

"Yeah, it was. He had told me he was clean, but… he lied."

"Oh my god. That son of a—"

Jason interrupted her as he pulled out onto the main road, "Mom, it's alright. I'm… not even mad at him. I just… really need to feel loved right now."

"Well, of course I love you!"

He smiled. "Good. I love you, too."

"But," his mom started again, her voice turning deep and somber, "I do have something I want you to keep in mind. But you're not gonna like to hear it."

A sinking feeling. "Yeah?"

"For fuck's sake, keep your legs closed in the future. TDD isn't the only thing you can get, and if you just focused on your job and getting back into school, you wouldn't have time to worry about guys."

Jason's jaw clenched, and his claws dug into the steering wheel. "Ok."

"Ok? You know I still love you, right? I just care about you and want to keep you safe."

"I love you too."

"Good. Talk to me later if you need. I gotta go."

"Bye, mom."

Click.

***

Still pissed from the phone call, Jason exited the car and walked the three yards to the front door of his apartment. He felt exhausted. Worse, he felt like iron chains were wrapped around the insides of his chest, pulling and weighing him down. Every breath felt thick and warm, his pulse ringing in his head. He felt lonelier than he had ever felt in his life.

Once inside the apartment, he turned on the living room light and stripped out of his clothes, letting the warm air of the apartment melt away the cold in his joints. The idea of turning on the TV disgusted him. The thought of food made him nauseated. He didn't even want to take a shower. He abandoned thoughts of being productive tonight and went straight to his bed. Instead of getting under the covers, he lay across the bed's side and grasped his phone between his paws. He considered the darkened screen for a good three or four minutes before making a decision.

With a sigh, he pulled up his Yiffr app. He needed company tonight. It didn't matter what kind. It could be kissing, petting, cuddling, just holding paws, whatever. Just something. He needed to be touched. Furred skin against his.

What he hadn't expected was that there would be messages waiting for him already. Not as many as on Furbook, but several. They were noticeably varied compared to Furbook, too:

TDD? No thanks. Not interested in getting diseased LOL.

Why is someone unclean even on this app? Go kill yourself.

TDD = Too Diseased, so Die.

Who pozzed you? Wish it could've been me ;)

Can't even get laid without worrying sick dogs like you will be around here.

What does TDD mean? Can I get it from kissing?

A tear splashed onto the screen and stopped him from being able to swipe anymore without drying it off. The messages kept on going though. Now that he was online, more kept coming. All of the same nature. Some fetishized the TDD. Some responded with pure, innocent confusion. Others with violence. One asked for his address so the dog could come kill him. One wanted to put all dogs with TDD on an island and blow it up. One said, "If I were you, I just wouldn't have sex with anyone. Just saying imho."

It all hurt. It all hurt so much. Everywhere. The loneliness felt visceral to him. Even with the heat in the apartment up to 75 degrees, it felt freezing. His whole body was shaking, and his muscles quaked with the intensity of his crying.

Shaking harder now, he let the phone fall to the sheets. He stood up and left the room, slamming the door behind him in the process. New words from the conversations flashed across his mind: *Unclean. Dirty. Die. Slut. Deserve. Filthy. Die. Poz. Just saying. Die.*

He turned on the light in the kitchen and slammed his paws into the counter. The impact jolted up his arms and shoulders, but he just held that position, clenching and unclenching his digits. He felt miserable, and his thoughts centered in on that feeling. His mind split into five directions, one for each of the stages of dealing with trauma and grief: denial—*This has to be wrong. I can't have TDD. I'm not the kind of guy who gets TDD.*—anger—*I don't deserve it. It's fucking Mark's fault! He should be the one suffering right now!*—bargaining—*I'll do anything to get rid of it. Someone, just tell me what I have to do. I'll do anything. I take it all back. Please.*—depression—*I'm so alone. I feel terrible. No one loves me. No one ever will love me.*—and acceptance—*I have this… and that's all there is. There is no escape for me. That's it.*

And in front of him, behind his pot of coffee grounds, there was his pill bottle. He had thrown away the label in case anyone happened to see it. It was half a month's pills for the TDD. He only had to take one a day. It was just a simple pill. TDD was a totally manageable disease. Wasn't even a big deal. Except to the world, it was the worst label a person could have.

Unclean. Slut. Dirty.

He made his way to the sink and turned on the cold water. He grabbed a clear glass from the cabinet above the sink and positioned it beneath the faucet, filling it almost to the brim. Then he set it on the counter beside the pill bottle.

While his mind still processed the five different emotions, his paws moved of their own accord. He opened the pill bottle and raised it to his snout. As the angle increased, each green pill landed on his tongue. He started counting them, but lost track after ten. He emptied the bottle into his maw and then set the bottle back down on the counter, his tongue holding all the pills still against the roof of his mouth.

With one quick movement, he brought the glass of water up to his muzzle. He downed the water and the pills. As he did so, tears continued to roll down through his fur and landed on the linoleum floor. He tried not to think about what he was doing. He tried not to think about what was going to happen. He just kept replaying the images of the messages he had received all day. He heard Tom telling him he shouldn't have slept around. He heard his mom telling him he should have kept his legs closed. He saw the pack of dogs on Yiffr telling him to kill himself.

He made his way to the couch. Within ten minutes, he was passed out. After four hours of internal bleeding, he was gone, his phone buzzing angrily in his room the whole time.

People who are diagnosed with HIV in America have twice the risk of suicide as the general population, with some sources saying it goes up to seven times the rate in the first year of diagnosis.

One major thing you can do for people living with HIV, people like me, is let us know that, no matter what, we are loved.

*One can measure the quality of a society by how well it
treats its werewolves.*

SCHISM
Anhedral

Seas have their source, and so have shallow springs,
And love is love, in beggars and in kings.

~ *Sir Edward Dyer (1543-1607)*

***

April, 2022

"Mum, we've already been through this, over and over. They need me up there, and I've made up my mind. I'm going."

Agnes Hargreaves stared back at her daughter across the breakfast table, the lines around her eyes deepening with her frown. Jean winced. Ten years ago, five—oh hell, even one—she'd have retreated immediately at the slightest suggestion of that stare. But she was twenty-four now, and just last week she'd finally received her GP certification. A flush of newfound confidence still coursed through her; this time, Jean would not back down.

Eventually her mother blinked, giving a minute shake of her head.

"I still say they need a vet up there more than they need a doctor—"

"I've read the physiological studies, Mum. *All* of them, I think. And although there's plenty that we still don't understand about what makes werewolves tick, everyone agrees on one thing: right now they need both doctors *and* vets to help them out."

Agnes sighed, glancing away. "And what if you get infected? What then?"

Jean resisted the urge to wag a finger at her mother. "Not likely, Mum. C'mon, you know about the new Galen laws, the ones that keep the rest of us safe. The mandatory separation distance, the masks. When was the last time you saw or even heard about a wolf ignoring those laws? There haven't been any confirmed cases of wolf-to-human infection since the original epidemic a year ago."

Ah yes, the epidemic. Some had argued that the virus responsible must have been concocted, for it seemed a little too perfect in its action to have evolved right out of the blue. Spread by any bodily fluid, even by the meagre aerosol contained in a single sneeze, it was so contagious that it rampaged around the world in weeks. Adults and the very young—they could carry it all right, though they showed no symptoms. But if you happened to be one of those unhappy five percent of adolescents that bore just the right mix of genetic markers in your DNA… well, chances were that, before you turned eighteen, you were going to wake up one day seeing the world through suddenly brighter, lupine eyes, to a world freshly brimming full with countless scents unknown.

'Spontaneous Adolescent Lycanthropy', or S.A.L. for short—that was the official euphemism. The tabloids mostly went with 'fur fever'. And once you'd changed, that was it: no cure, no reversion, never once again the naked ape. In three short months there were upwards of a hundred thousand very hairy, very frightened youngsters in Canada alone, each of them discovering first-hand exactly what it was like to be excised from humanity at a single stroke.

Even tolerant and open-minded Canada reeled and staggered as a nation. For every five were-children embraced by their human families, five others would be ostracised. The space of a few months wasn't anywhere near long enough for the country to get to grips, let alone to heal; indeed, there were days on which it seemed as if the wounds rent through society had barely begun to fester.

It certainly didn't help that new cases kept right on coming, as children from Halifax to Great Bear Lake aged into the demographic that could very well damn them instantly and forever. It helped even less when it turned out that newly-transformed weres could pass on the condition to pretty much any unaffected human, of whatever age.

A social sticking-plaster was the requirement of the day, even one that would do little more than cover up the most grievous of the wounds from public view. The Lycanthrope Communes represented one such palliative.

"North West Territories. Yellowknife, of all places." Her mother dropped an elbow on the table, letting her head sink down on one propped hand. "Seriously Jean, you'd rather head off into the wilds than kick off a great career at the practice right here in Toronto?"

"They've been advertising for a GP for *months* now, Mum. No one wants to go, not even with the financial incentives. And Yellowknife does have flights to Toronto, y'know; it's not like you're never going to see me again.

"In fact…"

This was going to be pushing it, she knew. But dammit, this time her mother was actually discussing her plans with her, not slamming the door shut in indignation. At least not yet.

Jean took a big breath.

"In fact, why not come and join me for a bit? You've never taken a sabbatical, not in, what is it now, twenty years?"

Her mother cocked her head and stared at her daughter as if she'd just sprouted fur and a tail herself. "And if I do that, Jean, then who's going to cover the surgery? Who's gonna look after the shelters downtown? Especially as, apparently, I'm gonna be down a doctor as it is?"

Jean didn't have a ready answer for that. Few and far between were the doctors who would give up their spare time to work at more of the same for free. It was seldom that they were unwilling, or lacked generosity; rather that a GP's work was intensive and stressful, so time off was essential for one's own well-being. But Jean's mother had always been made of sterner stuff. Her unpaid charity work at the homeless shelters had made her a local legend.

Mrs. Hargreaves, perhaps sensing her advantage, pressed on.

"And our church… its teachings? I always raised you to be strong in faith."

Ah, here we go, thought Jean. She'd always known the big guns would get wheeled out sooner or later; this would probably be her mother's final gambit. But with a sinking heart Jean knew it was also the subject that would mark the end of the conversation they were almost having. So much for the positivity.

The leaders of their church had declared werewolves to be soulless. 'Non-humans', they might as well have said, though they candied their condemnation with weasel words. And this was the real reason Mrs. Hargreaves objected to her daughter's choice; it wasn't the distance, or the dearth of career prospects, or the infection risk. No, not those things at all.

Agnes Hargreaves would happily treat men and women of any nation, sexuality or faith at her GP practice or at the shelters. But a frightened, furry youngster? Never.

***

There were as many different ways to characterise S.A.L. as there were commentators in broader society. However, few would argue that the virus was not completely egalitarian in the way it affected poor and rich alike. As she approached the settlement that she'd call home for the foreseeable future, Jean found herself admitting a grudging respect for the infection, at least in as much as this attribute was concerned.

For yes, much like the Black Death had proved centuries before, S.A.L. was showing itself now to be a great leveller. And one of the upshots of this was that a certain Samuel Parsons, just another billionaire upstart from Vancouver, came down to breakfast one fine spring morning in the year 2021 to find not one but both of his beloved daughters sobbing out their tears from newly wild and golden eyes, clutching onto one other in a desperate embrace.

Samuel Parsons hadn't gotten to where he was through indecision. And as he drew his children into his arms, as he marvelled at the softness of the dense dark pelt now covering their shoulders, he assured the two of them most fervently that he still loved them, that they were still every bit as much his family as they'd been the night before. As he spoke the words, he knew deep down that they were nothing more than truth.

Decisive? Why, certainly. Unaffected? No. By some small miracle a switch was flipped in the good Sam Parsons that day, and as the shining wolf-eyes of his progeny stared up at him, he felt a newfound empathy flood through him to his very core. He shuddered; his paper billions had never once provided such fulfilment in the gleaning.

Samuel Parsons, against the frenzied pleadings of his various advisors and hangers-on, liquidated all of his assets. His daughters would remain quite safe, close by his side; this at least he could guarantee. But if he had anything to say about it, all of the discarded waifs and strays who now took wolfish form would be catered for as well.

***

3 May 2022

The taxi stopped on the dirt track well short of the nearest line of chalets, and Jean stepped out into a crisp spring morning and the birdsong chorus of the boreal north. She'd barely had time to pull her big suitcase out of the boot before the driver was reversing into his turn and pulling promptly back the way he'd come.

Jean watched the dust cloud rising from the tyres with a rueful eye. Ah, well; no turning back now.

With its ranks and ranks of hastily flung up wooden huts, the brand-new Yellowknife Lycanthrope Commune resembled nothing so much as an old style prisoner-of-war camp. However, the two-thousand-odd young werewolves housed there were not incarcerated; there were no fences or guard towers to be seen. Rather, it was a place where they were safe, where they could get on with their new lives and their education with some semblance of normality, where those parents who had not completely severed ties could visit them in a controlled, risk-free environment.

"Your ride wasn't wasting any time, was he? I swear, one day he'll learn not to fear us. They all will."

The baritone voice managed to sound rough and curiously melodious both at once; the words themselves were perfectly clear. Jean had heard no footfall, but spinning on the spot she picked out the wolf pacing easily towards her, quite at home, thank you, on two legs. Jean couldn't quite suppress a gasp; the newcomer safely overtopped six feet and must, she estimated, have weighed at least two hundred pounds. All of which meant that he was either one of the older teens, or else an adult.

Toe-wise stance and hard, lean muscle. A wolfish tail. Distractedly she noticed he wore nothing but his pelt of mottled greys and blacks, in sharp contrast to those city-dwelling wolves who were obliged to cover up. A cage-like contraption with straps and buckles dangled from one big paw; without breaking stride the newcomer brought the device up to his muzzle and fixed it there with fingers quick and sure. He'd clearly carried out the action many times before.

"Doctor Jean Hargreaves?" He was practically upon her now, reaching out with arms held wide. The mask made it difficult to read his expression, but there was no mistaking the sharply perked ears, the enthusiasm in his voice. "Richard Fletcher, chair of the Yellowknife Commune Council."

Jean flinched only slightly before offering her own hand. It was immediately engulfed in two massive furry paws. The grip was firm, very firm; Jean dry-swallowed, and willed her heart to slow its manic pounding.

"Doctor Hargreaves, you are most welcome here!"

He snatched up the heavy case for her as if it contained naught but air.

***

6 *May 2022*

Dear Mum,

I know you have to deal with far too many e-mails when you're at work, and so, surprise! Good 'ol pen-and-paper is what you get from me today. Good grief, it's been a while since I wrote a letter longhand!

I'm all settled in at last. They've given me my own apartment, self-contained; it's a privilege for sure, because the kids all sleep in dorms and even the adult wolves are mostly sharing, two to a room.

The settlement is five miles out of Yellowknife, and there's no denying that the setting is picturesque. No maples this far north, of course—I'm going to miss those. But the pine and tamarack spread out as far as I can see, clinging onto thin poor soils, knolls of bedrock breaking through all over like so many gnarled and bony fists. Lots of little lakes and marshes around here, too; the cries of loons and willow-grouse are my alarm-clock every morning.

The Commune itself feels a lot like an old-style boarding school, with a curriculum much like mainstream human schools. Almost all of the teachers are wolves as well, infected as adults before the risks were understood; a few of the subject specialists are humans, but it seems they all get bussed in each day from town. I think I am the only human who's a full-time resident here.

I know you won't like hearing that. But I want to reassure you that all the wolves follow the Galen laws religiously. Every single wolf carries a mask at all times, and learning how to fit it and maintain it is the very first lesson every kid here learns. In fact, it's drilled into them so frequently that they can fit and remove the things as a reflex action, without a conscious thought. When they're wearing them they look like so many muzzled dogs.

Of course, if we're out in the street they can just choose to give me a wide berth, and not bother with the mask. After all the jostling I've been used to in Toronto's Chinatown or down Younge Street, it's a weird experience to have a crowd part around me like a grey-and-tan sea of fur, as if I were some Israelite bent on lone escape, or perhaps a leper from days of old, an untouchable. I know it's only for my own protection, but it's hard sometimes not to feel like an outsider, the unbelonging, *l'etranger*. I suppose I'll get used to it in time.

My duties so far have been routine. We're taking regular bloods from every werewolf here; they get taken daily to the new gene-sequencing lab in town. The researchers there are studying genetic drift, ongoing mutation, anything to help characterise the genome. Meanwhile, I've gradually been getting to know my new 'customers', as it were. The youngsters are as boisterous and healthy as any human children, and, well, it looks like werewolves age spectacularly well. An older wolf came in for a check-up yesterday; he's the French teacher here, infected in his classroom way out there in Quebec. He's seventy, and as strong and healthy as an ox.

What else to say? Oh yes—the rumours about their diet were only partly right. The bit that's true: werewolves really are obligate carnivores, and they prefer to eat their meals uncooked. But they don't go out in packs *en masse* to slaughter all the local wildlife; hunting here, in twos or threes, is a treat for special occasions. They do set traps for hares, but most of their food gets brought in daily, fresh from the abattoir in town.

I'll keep you posted as I find out more. For now I can confirm that the Commune is largely autonomous, with a very light-touch oversight at provincial level and most day-to-day decisions the responsibility of a locally-elected Council. Its current leader is a chap called Richard Fletcher, who really is a very individual fellow indeed. For instance, he vanishes off into the woods most evenings, and no one seems to understand exactly why…

***

10 May 2022

"…so yeah, I figure it was probably my own son Daniel who infected me back last spring." Richard set down his tools and glanced up at her. "Whoa. Last spring. Has it really been a whole year already?"

They were in one of the big site maintenance sheds that squatted on the outskirts of the township. A wide bench littered with hand tools lined one wall; mills and lathes ranged down another; and right there in the middle of the floor the leader of the settlement was down on his knees and getting his paws grimy. Hard at work amid a maze of steel and bright-hued glass, the big gruff wolf looked faintly ridiculous in his full-length fireproof apron.

"Daniel's fourteen now, and thoroughly dismayed to have big bad wolfy Daddy around twenty-four hours seven to tease him. Ha! He'll live. Oh, you don't mind if I carry on here while we talk, do you? Soldering iron's good 'n hot, and I'm due back in the surgery in half an hour."

Jean leant back against one of the benches, a good two metres from him; it was the minimum separation required by law, since he wasn't masked. She eyed him curiously. Twelve months ago he'd been a high-flying veterinarian in Ottawa. And now? An irrepressibly cheerful werewolf, a doctor of a sort to all his kind and quite comfortable as a leader to boot, daring to hurl a great brazen spear of self-confidence into an uncertain future.

"Oh, no," she said, smiling back at him and folding her arms across her chest. "I can see you're in the middle of things; please don't stop for me."

"I thank you, milady." He grabbed a shard of glass, turned it to and fro before offering it up to the lattice. There was a momentary cloud of smoke from melting flux and solder as he put the red-hot iron to use. "So, how's your own surgery shaping up? Finding everything you need in there?"

A sudden springtime hailstorm beat a quick tattoo upon the sheet-steel roof, and Jean had to wait for a lull before replying.

"Oh… yes, thanks. Everything is good."

But it was the wolf that paused then. He set down his tools, got to his feet, turned to face her. Jean blinked, shaking her head; she was still getting used to the strong empathic sensitivity that all the wolves of the Commune seemed to share.

"Something isn't right. Please Jean, whatever it is you need, just name it and it's yours."

Straight to the point was another wolfish trait. Oh well, if needs be she could be direct as well.

"I… I came across a box of masks in there. Standard surgical masks, for humans. And it got me thinking." She took a deep breath. "I want to start wearing one when I'm out and about, so that all you guys don't have to."

"Jean…"

"Hush for a moment, wouldya, and hear me out? I'm not talking about wearing it all the time; I know that there are other humans around here during the day, and I doubt that all of them would want to cover up. But in the evenings, it's only me. In the evenings, why should two thousand wolves have to put themselves to trouble on my account?"

He was frowning at her now. "This is dangerous talk, Jean. It's true, the Galen laws give us some flexibility within the Communes. But it's important that the kids get used to wearing their masks at any time of day. They can't stay in the Commune forever; as adults they're going to be moving back out into the big wide world, and that world is full of folk who'd rather do without the tail and fangs and fur."

"I—I understand all that. But things are going to change, aren't they? They *have* to change. Sooner or later we'll find out how to immunize humans, or else stop wolves from being quite as infectious as they are now. We can't be sending armies of young werewolves out into the world with the notion that they'll have to wear those damn masks forever!"

He was quiet for a moment, before starting to pick his way through the filigree of steel laid out there on the floor. His feet were wolf-proportioned, naturally, so extricating himself was no easy task; at last he reached the bench, ears up, great golden eyes meeting her own.

"I had no idea," he murmured across the distance that separated them, "that the masks bothered you so much."

Jean fidgeted. "Well—yeah. They do."

"I appreciate that sentiment, more than I can say." He sighed out a breath and glanced away. "But really, Jean… your decision to stay here, to live right here with us… I don't think you really understand just what it means to every single wolf that calls this place their home." He looked back to her, gave her the smallest nod. "The hope, I mean. The hope you give to all of us."

Jean flustered at that, not expecting his words and uncertain how to respond. Fortunately Richard was content to fill the gap.

"What I mean to say is this: when the wolves here meet with you, the inconvenience of putting on their masks or moving to one side is the very last thing on their minds."

It took Jean a few more seconds to process that. But then, and rather unsure of herself:

"You can blame my mother for how I feel, I think. She—she did a lot of voluntary work in Africa when she was younger, just after apartheid in South Africa was finally done away with for good. She got involved in getting basic healthcare out to a lot of the native peoples there." She stared back at the once-man, this bane of every childhood dream, this thing she had been taught she should abhor but never could. "She said she was the only white face amid a sea of dark ones, ignorant of their different cultures and all but a few words of their languages. She told me she felt like an alien, an impostor, no matter how much she wanted to help."

"I…" His long jaws gaped. They were monstrous, but she didn't flinch. Intellectually, she had understood well before today that he would never harm her; now, in this moment, she knew it with her heart. "I—"

"I don't want to feel that way, Richard. Not now, not ever." She forced her best, most winsome smile onto her face, but had to blink as well, because her eyes were unexpectedly full of water. "Just—please speak to the Council about this, would you?"

***

8 June 2022

Dear Mum,

I pestered and cajoled him, yes I did. Never knew I had it in me to be so stubborn; I think I must have inherited some of it from you. I like to think you might be proud.

Eventually he said I should come with him to address the whole Council myself about the masks, so that's exactly what I did. Was he testing me, I wonder? I cannot rule it out.

But the long and short of it is: they agreed. Evenings, or one-on-one in my surgery, it's me that wears a mask. And I swear it's already making a difference. It's like they've cracked apart a door for me that leads into their world.

Werewolves run their bodies hotter than we do—I guess you probably knew that already. But there's an infinity of distance between reading the dull fact of it in a textbook and feeling the raw heat of a young teenaged wolf as she clutches on to you, bawling out her tears for parents she may never see again. You can study all you like about werewolf reflexes and endurance, but that's nothing to actually witnessing the kick-boxing tournaments of which they are so fond, to see them take off into the wilds before sun-up on some sixty-mile orienteering jaunt, returning in the twilight with long tongues lolling from grinning jaws, and panting hard.

Other things that mark them out from us are more subtle. They have classrooms here, of course they do, and wolf teens have access to all of the same technology a human teenager would enjoy. But werewolves genuinely seem happiest when they're out of doors, and I've found that they'd rather be sniffing at the breeze for new scents than shuffling about with their eyes glued to their phones. I have to wonder how all those weres in more crowded countries are getting on.

And because they are still teenagers, I get to see all of the joys and all of the angst of young love, all of the catfights (or perhaps that should be 'dogfights'?) over stolen boyfriends. But at least the average wolf teen tends not to get as hung up on his or her own body as a human youngster might; there's a certain earthiness about them, a celebration of their physicality that perhaps explains their preference to go without any clothes. And if two young wolves in love should happen to slip off quietly into the pines of a fine midsummer evening, well, it seldom draws a comment, and so long as no one's getting hurt, the adult wolves here seem content to look the other way. At least they don't need to worry about unexpected pregnancies: under the Galen laws all female wolves have to get contraceptive implants, and that's one rule the Council doesn't get to waive.

I'm rambling on now, aren't I? I'll draw this letter to a close with this: in spite of all the prejudice they face, the masks, the prohibition on them ever having children of their own, there is a palpable optimism that clings to a lot of the wolves here that I've never seen before. At first I thought it was just the camaraderie of shared adversity, but no, it isn't that. Not that at all.

Because here's the thing. I've come to understand that when most humans look at werewolves, the unease they feel is not the legacy of centuries of lupophobia, or even the more general wariness that comes when facing the unknown. No, it's the very rational fear of being in the presence of beings that can smell you coming from half a mile away, can run faster and for much longer than you could ever hope to, could tear you limb from limb were they not all so damnably civilized.

And the wolves have come to realise all this as well.

***

24 June 2022

As a rule, Jean was very open with her mother as she settled into Commune life. However, there was one important subject that she withheld from discussion, and that involved the project Richard was embarked upon with the steel wire and the coloured glass, back in workshop that spring day.

He was constructing a stained-glass roundel window for Yellowknife Commune's new church.

"It's… it's *beautiful!* You have an amazing gift!"

Fully eight feet across, the finished piece was even now being offered up by four strong wolves to take its place in the opening prepared for it, high up in the gable of the nave. The central crucifix was familiar enough of course, rendered simply in glass of forest-green and edged all around with gold. But the motif that encircled it was what really drew the eye: the bodies of a human and a wolf artfully contorted so as to form a circle, jaws of the wolf forever snapping at the human's heels, an unfurred hand reaching out as if grasp the lupine tail. The arrangement reminded Jean forcibly of an ouroboros.

As the artwork was finally lifted into vertical the sun's midsummer rays struck it from behind, and in an instant Jean's vision exploded in a dizzying riot of colour.

Jean gasped, hardly knowing where first to turn her gaze. But soon more forms and shapes began to coalesce into familiarity: here a pair of chickadees, hopping about the thin branches of a springtime pine; here a grey jay with its bill open wide, so perfectly realized in steel and glass that she could almost hear its raucous call. Meanwhile, arrayed all round the lower half, she found the flora of the northern forest: blueberries, wild roses, the twisting vines of honeysuckle.

There was a burst of barks and shouts of affirmation from the expectant wolves gathered nearby, and Jean didn't hesitate to add her own applause. Richard flicked his ears at her, adding a little one-sided smile that was an oddly unsettling sight upon the wolf's long muzzle. Was he unused, she wondered then, to such unconditional praise?

"Oh," he muttered, "I was always toying with the stained glass as a hobby, ever since I was very young. First time with anything as big as this, though. I just hope the steel I used is strong enough to take the weight."

She was so awed by the revelations in the glass that she blurted out her next words all unthinking. "I never knew about any wolves that kept their faith! Did you keep yours, as well?"

"Huh," he grunted quietly, glancing aside with ears down flat. "Sorry to disappoint you, but… no. Still, there's plenty here that attended services before they changed, and would do so even now, if their church had not cast them out into the wilderness."

He turned again to face her with a shrug.

"To have a place to carry on their worship—it's still important to them. And so it's important to me as well."

The wolves were busy with clamps and bolts now, fixing the window into place. Richard squinted intently at it, as if to avert his eyes might prompt its immediate collapse. Jean, meanwhile, was still thinking about what he'd said.

"Wait a sec. The church banished them, so how—"

"New denomination," he grunted curtly. "Werewolf friendly. There's a working group set up across all the Communes, trying to come up with a revised, um, order of service. What do you call it now, what's the proper term…"

"A new liturgy," Jean confirmed with barely a whisper. "I wonder if that will be enough, though. Sounds like they might be needing a brand new theology."

Another grunt; he cared more about his handiwork and about his people than for this conversation. "I dare say."

Jean frowned; the ever-cheerful Richard she'd come to like and to respect had taken a leave of absence. She pondered on it for a second, hoping that the effect was temporary, and decided to take a stab in the dark with him.

"Y'know, Richard, I can't deny that the Good Book has more than a few unpleasant things to say about your kind. The wolf in sheep's clothing, savage and ravenous wolves, all of that."

"I'm familiar. Metaphors for the ills done by men is how those phrases were intended. Not to be taken literally."

Huh; he was not entirely uninformed, then. But there was a sullen resignation in his eyes, and Jean decided it was not a good look on him at all. She closed the distance until they were side by side, pulling on her own mask because he seemed too distracted right then to fix his own.

"Richard, I think I might know why some of those wolves standing right there have kept their faith."

His ears twitched and perked a bit at that, and his eyes flashed back at her. Jean couldn't fathom if he was merely curious, or issuing a challenge; and so it was in great daring that she reached up then to touch his shoulder. He flinched minutely, but did not pull away.

"Because, y'know, for all that the bible has precious little of any use to say about wolves, it's a bit more helpful when it comes to the subject of love. And I have seen more love in my few weeks in this place than I ever came across in all my years before."

He was silent for a second, nostrils flaring, and Jean feared that she had missed a step. But then his ears went up and his jowls cracked into a smile, a symmetrical one this time. She felt his arms go slowly around her, and all unresisting she let herself be drawn into his warm embrace.

"Jean," he whispered to her, whiskers tickling her ear. "There's something I would like for you to see."

***

Midsummer nights at sixty-two degrees north tend not to get properly dark, for at that latitude and time of year the sun's sojourn below the horizon is brief indeed. And thus it proved on this occasion too; the sky was cloudless and pellucid, already burnished for the coming day and brimming with incipient possibility. Only the brightest stars could be made out, and the Milky Way was but a faint and misty smear across the firmament. Jean found that she could easily see colours, and she certainly had no difficulty following the big wolf as he forged ahead between the pines, keeping to a thin track through the feathermoss and sphagnum that she'd never trod before. She was certain Richard was moderating his pace for her, but even so there was a tautness and an urgency to his movements, as if he were running late for a party he didn't want to miss.

"Richard—oof!" She had stumbled on a root. "Richard, where are you *taking* me?"

The big wolf paused, drawing deeply of the calm and humid air as he waited, no doubt taking in a myriad of different scents that she would never know.

"We're nearly there," he rumbled as she caught up with him at last. "Just up this little rise."

He had plainly come to accept a wolf's abilities as his new normality; what was a negligible climb for him became in truth a hard, shin-scraping scramble for his companion. But at least the granite of the crag offered

Jean firm footing, and she eschewed his proffered paw even on the steepest sections. She may not have been as agile or as fast as him, but she was determined to show she was still capable, and no wolf's weakling.

She crested the top at last, and gasped.

The ridge they had ascended overtopped all the pines, and now the taiga was laid out all before them, numinous and perfect, green-hued, brown-hued, bejewelled with water. The lilies spangled in the lake nearby just like so many stars.

"This is where I find the Lord now, Jean." He spread his paws out wide like some timeless guardian of a land long since revered. "The north, which by rights belongs to all the wolves… *this* is my church now. And look! Here come my fellow celebrants."

Thin dogwood scrub clung low upon the ridge. And it was there, just there and there that she discerned five ghostly lupine bodies weaving through, their forms revealed by little more than occlusion of the surrounding stems. The newcomers were not twenty feet away, and edging closer. So used had Jean become to seeing werewolves on two legs that it seemed perverse to find these fellows down upon all fours.

Wild wolves.

Jean hastened to Richard's side, barely remembering to strap on her mask as she did. But even as she put her hand up to his furry chest she felt it swell, the wolf drawing the night's air deep into his lungs. She glanced up at her protector, concern and curiosity oddly mingling inside her, to see that he had closed his eyes and tilted back his muzzle to the sky.

His howl started out so deep and low and *close* that it could be felt rather than heard. But it lifted swiftly, first in pitch and then in volume, until the very air around her rang with an untamed, primal resonance. The wild wolves, staring directly at her with the flicker-flash of eyeshine, drew breath as one and added each of their deep voices to Richard's own. Terrifying and beautiful, utterly mesmeric, it was a chorus that had serenaded the world long before mankind deigned to claim all creation for his own.

Brain decoupled, lost to the night-time and the sound, Jean clung onto Richard with both her hands. Had she been capable of rational thought, she might have concluded that it was her best and only option.

She didn't notice when one by one the voices dropped away, until the only ones remaining were those of Richard and the largest of the wild wolves. And she didn't notice when those two last voices came slowly into consonance, when the mingled tones did what any pair of close-matched sounds will do. Spawned of the slight difference between the parent howls a throbbing ululation was birthed there in that moment, a gently pulsing rhythm that sped and slowed; it seeped deep into the listener, entrancing her, flooding every vital part.

Jean's muscles fell to total relaxation. Though she didn't know it, Richard managed to catch her just before her body met the ground.

***

25 June 2022

Dear Mum,

Please excuse the shaky handwriting.

I have news. After you have read it, I pray that you might find it in your heart to forgive your daughter, too.

***

29 June 2022

"Delayed Onset Lycanthropy. *Seriously*, Richard? My body's new to science, apparently, and you're going with *D.O.L.?*" She nipped him, none so gently, on his ear. "I'm no one's *doll*, mister!"

"OW! Okay, okay, we'll come up with something better..."

Jean couldn't bring herself to be too upset with him. Not with the sweet blood of their last kill still lingering between her fangs. Not with Richard spooning back against her in the adorable way he did, the strong male's neck perversely vulnerable close by her muzzle. She hated to admit it, but the combination of the two traits turned her on no end. Or perhaps it was just the scent of him, maple syrup and smoky bonfires, that was messing with her better judgement. It was redolent of her Toronto childhood; over the past few days Jean had been trying not to over-think the coincidence of that.

They were lying here together under the pines, moss-bed soft beneath them, the brightening sky above; dawn wasn't terribly far away. Jean forced herself to concentrate on their conversation, because otherwise she'd be succumbing to him all over again, and in short order too. Dangerous for a female wolf, she knew, to give a male that kind of power—no matter how much she loved him. "Talking of new to science, what about this whole wolfsong... language... thing. What was the term we were going to use, hetero or something—"

"A heterodyne language. It's the interference between the voices of the singers that carries meaning; you can't speak it on your own. As a concept for communication, I still can't quite wrap my head around it."

"Neither you nor I, dear wolf. At least I know now what you've been up to all these evenings."

She moved her hand from his chest to touch his paw—the paw that held the little digital recorder with which he'd been taking down his 'conversations' with wild wolves. In the privacy of her apartment, he'd been showing her his acoustical analyses, and they'd begun collating stats on pattern repetition rates. They'd also started a crash-course in linguistics, studying together.

"Funny thing though. Humans have been studying wolf howls for years, but there's nothing in the literature that remotely resembles what we've heard. If wolves are choosing to keep their conversations quiet when humans are around, then why'd they make an exception for me that night?"

He turned slightly in her arms, reaching down a paw to stroke her flank. "I wonder if we'll ever know. But my best theory is that they sensed the wolf inside of you, just waiting to get out. The wolf that just needed the right kind of nudge to get her going."

Jean pondered it, strangely unconcerned. She laid her muzzle between his ears, knowing how much he liked it; sure enough, she was rewarded with a crooning growl, sounding deep within his throat. The evening was perfect, and she didn't want to spoil it; still, one further thing still needed to be said.

"Y'know," she muttered slowly. "Discovering that wild wolves may be sentient—this isn't going to help relations with humans at all, now is it?"

He let out a quiet snort at that. "No. No, it is not. One day—one day, maybe they'll be ready. But for now, well, I guess it's just one more secret to heap upon the pile."

He shifted again, and this time his finger-pads came to rest upon the little patch of shaved skin atop the forearm of his mate. So, so gently he pressed there, feeling for the half-inch length of plastic he'd injected just the day before—the contraceptive implant that, by the Galen laws, Jean was now compelled to bear.

Except that Jean had autoclaved her implant for three hours before Richard eased it underneath her skin. The treatment, by her estimation, had been quite sufficient to denature every last bit of progestin that the chip contained.

After all, it wasn't just the law regarding masks that Jean saw as criminally unjust. And she wasn't about to change her views on account of her newly bright-gold eyes and russet fur.

***

May, 2023

184

The taxi's tyres spun up a cloud of dust, and as her ride beat its swift retreat, Agnes Hargreaves took up her suitcase, set her jaw, and turned to the two masked wolves waiting for her nearby. One of them held a little swaddled bundle, so tiny in his vast grey paws.

"Doctor Agnes Hargreaves, welcome to Yellowknife Lycanthrope Commune. My name is—

"Richard Fletcher. Yes, I already know just who you are."

Richard's jaws snapped shut; he drew his bundle closer, turning slightly away. His body language was completely clear: if you intend ill deeds on what I'm holding here, you'll have to go through me.

The other wolf huffed, short and sharp, and set her hands upon her hips.

"*Mum.*"

The woman snapped her gaze over to the female wolf, and got an acid stare and a hint of fang from one curled lip, visible even through the mask. The snarl was not very far away. Agnes gasped and tried to move her legs, her arms; she found herself unable.

But her daughter softened then, and with that Agnes Hargreaves dropped her case and began to flick her eyes between the bundle and the female wolf.

"Oh Mum, come here already. Josh is sleeping anyway; he isn't going anywhere."

For long moments the mother hesitated. Eventually Jean strode right up to her and, before she could react, pulled her tight into her arms. And still Agnes Hargreaves did not make a move.

"I love you, Mum. And I am so very happy to see you now."

That was enough; that did the trick. Agnes flung her arms around her daughter and began to hack out great long sobs, body shaking, uncaring of spectacle or decorum. Her head came down to rest upon the lupine neck, the hot tears coursing; they fell gently on her daughter, matting fur.

The tale of a ship's cat, a magician's familiar, and a kitten between worlds.

A Scrappy Start

Cathy Smith

It wasn't a good day to travel, yet Master Wang couldn't afford to delay his journey any longer than he already had. He felt a tension in the air reflected as an ache in his joints. The pain hit him once he was away from the soothing Feng Shui energies he'd set up inside his hotel room. However, he no longer had a shield when he stepped onto the wharf looking for a ship to book his passage.

He would've thought the water dragons were about to raise a squall if he were back home. The feeling was more intense from some ships. His familiar Tum's fur was standing on end from the energies in the air inside his carrier.

Just when Master Wang was about to give up, he caught a cabin boy flipping a coin into the bay's waters. It took the vision from his third eye to see a hand with webbing between its fingers appear. The hand emerged from the waters to catch the coin.

The tension in the air evaporated, and the ache in his joints receded as if it'd never been. His brows came together at this.

The cabin boy said with a smile as he turned to face him, oblivious to the hand from the waters, "It's good to put a coin in the waters around Triton Island for luck."

"Luck?" Master Wang repeated.

"Triton Island is like our wishing well. Ilan sailors have been wishing for smooth sailing in this spot for centuries," the youth said.

"I see," Master Wang murmured. He saw that even Ilan's water spirits were of a prudent bent if they were easily assuaged by tolls. He didn't know if he envied the Ilanians or pitied them for the prosaicness of their lives.

At least he knew which ship he should book passage on. "What's this ship called?"

"The Tempest."

"I wish to book passage with you."

As far as the cabin boy knew, Tum gave a chirping purr of agreement; Master Wang heard, "This is good enough."

Master Wang caught a tabby giving Tum a hard look from the Tempest's top deck. The cat challenged his familiar with an intense stare. The fact that Tum didn't hiss back told him this cat was a female. He sighed.

***

Unlike most cats, Wench liked the sea air so much, she didn't care that it came with a fine mist that got brine in her fur. She was proud of being the Tempest's mascot. Her job was to boost morale and keep the mouse population down so they didn't ruin the crew's victuals. The cabin boy Bixby met her needs. He brushed her fur and saw that she was given a daily allotment of fresh water to drink. She loved her life, but sometimes she longed for the company of her own kind. She enjoyed shore leave as much as the sailors did and always came back with a new get.

The voyage to pick up Chin goods had been long even though they only transferred the goods and didn't go to Chin itself. They had only docked long enough to take their cargo and passengers on board. The crew had a night or two of carousing; Wench regretted that she hadn't gone along with them. Only the smell of a male of her species in a carrying case had made her stay onboard.

The scent of cinnamon incense clinging to his fur made him seem like some kind of delicacy. His meows were high-pitched as if he were in a constant state of irritation. She assumed it was a natural reaction to being cooped up in a carrier, but she soon discovered he was always fussy. He had an old man who wore yellow robes and whose head was bald except for a long braid to attend him.

Silken furnishings were set up for the old man and cat. The elderly human received five silk pillows while the cat received only one. A meal of steamed fish was prepared for them both. The old man was given his fish with vegetables. The cat received his fish with a fragrant sprig of herb. Wench watched this in a corner.

The old man was put to bed soon after he ate while the cat sat on his cushion. He yawned more out of boredom than out of tiredness.

What a life! I am given water but have to hunt for most of my food. The sailors will toss me fish guts sometimes if they are gutting their catches, but never give me a fillet.

Bixby swept the compartment. He was far more thorough than Wench expected him to be. She found herself chased out with the broom when he checked behind a curtain. "Scat, cat!" The cat on the cushion gave a hissing cackle as she was thrown out of the room. That should've been the end of it.

***

The fact that Wench missed out on her shore leave caught up with her a week into the voyage. Her blood boiled so badly she couldn't stop herself from giving plaintive cries.

"Shut the wench up, Bixby," Captain Hershell said. "Our passengers are complaining, and the crew doesn't like it either."

"She's in season! What am I supposed to do about it!" Bixby asked.

"Throw her overboard if you have to," the Captain said.

Wench sniffed. *You need your shore leave as much as I do! It's not fair!*

Bixby glanced at her and gave a loud sigh.

***

Master Wang laughed when Bixby approached him about his problem with Wench. "Our mascot is lonely, and it's making her noisy."

He carried Wench in his arms hoping the sight of her would stir Master Wang's sympathies.

"We heard the racket from here! There's no way I'll allow Tum to associate with such a female!"

The tomcat glanced at Wench. The hardness of her life kept her as hard and sinewy as his breed. Her skill as a huntress kept her from starving. He nodded as if to say 'yes'.

"Bring the female closer to Tum, so he can get a good look at her," Wang said.

Bixby placed Wench onto the floor of the cabin. Wench went up to Tum and touched noses with him. He gave a sneeze as if her dander was too coarse for his sensitivities.

Wench in turn hissed.

"I guess it's not happening," Bixby sighed.

The Siamese gave a yowl that was almost a bark in Wang's direction. "Not while there's an audience at least," Wang said. "He doesn't want to be seen with her."

Bixby couldn't help laughing. "If he's going to treat her like a dockside doxie does that mean I can charge him two bits for time alone with her?"

"Most of our temple's funding comes from stud fees for the temple cats," Wang said. "The wise men and magi of our land pay small fortunes to add them to their familiar's bloodlines."

There was a yowl from both of the cats, and Wang and Bixby thought it best to leave the room.

Master Wang stepped outside the cabin as Tum spent time with that breedless female.

***

Six months later Master Wang sought passage on the Tempest again. He wanted to travel on a vessel that propitiated the local water spirits for his return trip to Ilan's Chintown.

The Ilanians weren't militant skeptics, but their old beliefs had faded into folklore. Their elite believed the folklore was nothing more than tall tales.

The stories had been affordable entertainment for their peasant forebears, but they were no longer oppressed by Aristos stealing the fruits of their labor. There were other ways to amuse themselves nowadays. Magic practitioners hid in plain sight as parlor magicians and spiritualists. Their best clients were silly women with too much time and money on their hands.

Master Wang's decision pleased Tum. "Do you think the crew will provide me with companionship again?" Tum purred the question from his carrier.

The appearance of Wench with a cluster of kittens on the top deck made Master Wang laugh. He said in his first language, "That's all the companionship you could ever want in your old age."

"There's no telling if any one of them is mine what with her shore leaves," Tum grumbled.

One kitten had tabby coloring in a Siamese pattern. "That one's yours at least."

Tum stared at the kitten. "I want to see him in private."

Master Wang's brows drew together. "I never thought you cared about the kittens you sired."

"That's because they were raised in the Temple, not among savages!"

When Master Wang set up in his cabin, he said there was a mouse to get the kitten sent to him. Wench always took her kittens on her hunts, and he should be sent there too.

***

The mother cat and kittens were allowed almost free run of the ship to keep the vermin down. The captain's quarters and the better guest cabins were off limits most times. However, they weren't able to place the same limits on the ship's mice. That's why the ship's cat and her kittens were allowed inside the cabin to hunt for it.

Scrappy was shocked to find himself in the most luxurious room he'd ever seen in his life. The air was perfumed with a rich flowery scent he didn't think a flower could produce on its own. The fabrics were soft and shiny. The floor was clean to the point of shining instead of being worn and soaked with brine. He would never have imagined anyone could live like this. He was even more surprised to see a thin tan and brown cat lying on a cat-sized cushion and bed. The cat had a glittering yellow metal collar around his neck. There was some sparkly stone hanging from its middle that Scrappy wanted to play with.

"There's already a cat here, Momma! Why doesn't he catch the mouse?" Scrappy asked his mother.

"Your father doesn't catch mice. He's a rich man's pet," his mother hissed. She would've preferred another ship's tom to this spoiled plaything. The only reason she'd bred with him was because there had been no other tom when she was in season. That's why she was teaching her newest litter to be more practical.

Scrappy sniffed. "A 'pet'—what is that?"

"Being a pet is when all you have to do is lie around all day and allow a human to pet you occasionally to get food," Momma said.

"The sailors pet us sometimes," Scrappy said.

"Yes, but we are working cats, we earn our keep, which is what we should do now. Go find that mouse!"

Seeing that his mother wouldn't say more to him, Scrappy walked up to the tomcat on the cushion. "So, you're my father." The relationship meant nothing to Scrappy. He knew where kittens came from, of course, buthe only wanted his mother's attention. And he wanted it less as he got better at hunting.

When he came close to the tom, the cat caught his scent and sniffed his nose. "You smell of fish and mice. No magic." He sighed.

"What kind of cat lets himself get rubbed with spices," Scrappy said in return.

The tom settled down in his cushion. "It's incense. It helps me do my job, which is far more important than mousing. I am a magician's familiar."

"Familiar? What's a familiar?"

"You couldn't begin to understand the scope of my abilities or the wonders I've seen in my line of work. I'm the product of generations of careful breeding. I've got a certificate that proves it. My master paid a top price for me and even then, he had to prove himself worthy to my breeder. All you'll ever be is a ship's cat. Now go find that mouse and leave me in peace."

***

"Well," Master Wang said when he was alone with Tum.

"He's got my looks and his mother's strength. He's better off living with the savages rather than in the Temple," Tum meowed before he lay his head down for a nap.

Scrappy in turn would've forgotten his talk with the tomcat. However, his life took him down a path he never expected. Not that most cats expected or dreamed of anything. Scrappy planned no further than his next meal.

His mind was preoccupied with a green parrot that Captain Hershel kept in a golden cage. Each morning the parrot woke the crew up with its imitation of a cockcrow. The sound made Scrappy expect a chicken for breakfast.

"How long will it be before the chicken with green, yellow and orange feathers is fat enough to eat, Momma?" he asked Wench one day, thinking it was a chicken like the ones occasionally kept in coops by the crew.

"Doubloon is the captain's parrot, not a chicken, Scrappy."

"A bird's a bird. He'll taste just as good in my stomach."

Wench swatted Scrappy when he said this.

"It isn't fair for the Captain to keep such a juicy bird to himself!" The unfairness ate at Scrappy's mind. He decided he would get that bird.

***

"I don't like how the kitten looks at Doubloon, Bixby," the captain said.

"He's just young and nosy," Bixby said.

"I saw him lick his lips when Doubloon preened himself," Captain Hershell countered.

"Wench is civilized. Her son will be too."

***

Doubloon must've had some magpie blood in him for he loved to pick up shiny bits and gossip. The captain liked to let him out for exercise once a day. This gave the parrot a chance to scavenge for new treasures to add to a nest he kept on top of the ship's ballast.

Doubloon checked out new passengers to see if they brought anything he could use for his collection. It was no surprise when he found a ledge close to Master Wang's cabin and waited for an opening.

Scrappy followed the parrot in turn. He was nearby when Bixby came with a kettle of hot water for Master Wang's tea. Doubloon swooped into the room as soon as the door opened. Scrappy raced in to follow Doubloon.

Bixby was so startled, he spilled the hot water. An act that almost scalded him and Master Wang. All the while there were angry hisses and screams for "help!" from Doubloon who could speak the human tongue.

"What's happening?" Captain Hershell said as his pet screamed for help. He ran into the cabin to see Scrappy shaking Doubloon around in his jaws. "Stop that, you beast!"

He picked Scrappy up by the scruff of his neck. Scrappy dropped Doubloon on the floor as he hissed at the captain. Captain Hershell threw the cat out of the cabin. Scrappy would've been thrown overboard if Bixby hadn't caught him in mid-air.

Blood pooled under Doubloon's prone body, but he was still puffing for breath. He screeched in pain when Captain Hershell picked him up. Captain Hershell glared at Scrappy in Bixby's arms. "Get that animal out of my sight."

Tum watched from his cushion all the while. "There's no hope for this barbarian."

***

An hour later, Bixby put Scrappy into a water-tight barrel with fish heads and water. "I'm sorry, kitty."

Tum had stepped outside the cabin to watch, and Master Wang followed him. "What are you doing?" he asked Bixby

"The captain wants Scrappy off the ship for trying to eat his parrot. It's all I could do not to get Scrappy thrown overboard into the sea."

Tum looked at Master Wang. The man took a bronze disk with a square hole in the middle from off a chord that hung on his belt. "This is to pay for Scrappy's safe passage on this ship. We'll keep him locked in the cabin, so he'll stay away from the captain's bird," Master Wang said.

Bixby looked at the bronze coin piece. "I'll check with the captain first and see if he agrees to it."

***

Scrappy was taken into the cabin. The air was indolent with spices. Sometimes the cargo hold was full of this stuff, and he avoided those areas at much as possible. He sneezed when he was overwhelmed with strident aromas.

Tum sniffed at him. "Such behavior as you displayed would get you taken to the town pound."

Master Wang sighed. "That's what'll happen to him when we land in Ilan. I just wanted to make sure he made it to land and wasn't thrown overboard."

Tum sniffed. An act of bravery Scrappy admired, for he couldn't stand to breathe such pungent scents so deeply. "We hardly need to go to that extreme. No one knows of Scrappy's indiscretion on shore. He can start afresh."

Master Wang sighed. "Tum. He's a half-breed. Mutt cats fend for themselves."

"What about that shop you saw in Warlock's Weekly? You said it was outrageous of them to charge such high prices for inferior stock. They're too uncultured to know any better and Scrappy's a barbarian. He'll fit right in."

"I wouldn't trust any retailer that would advertise in that rag. Its weekly top ten of the divisions in the Trade are guilty pleasures for me."

Tum chuckled. "Just like Wench was to me."

That won the argument.

***

Scrappy wished he knew what a "boutique" was. He'd seen a fish market on shore once during one of the Tempest's stops. The sight of all the fish guts from the filleted fish had tempted him. Yet a wave of nausea had stopped him when he stepped on land. It had made him lose his appetite.

Bixby came back with news and a platter of steamed fish for the passengers. "The captain wants another bronze coin as a damage deposit. It'll be surety in case Scrappy escapes and gets Doubloon in his jaws again."

Master Wang sighed when Tum looked at him. "Tell your captain I will want the damage deposit back once we land on shore."

Bixby nodded. "I'll tell him."

Scrappy's ears perked at the mention of that juicy bird. His ears went to the sides of his head and curled like horns.

Tum snorted, and Master Wang caught the look on Scrappy's face. "I've got a plan."

The lid was kept on the tray of steamed fish while Master Wang rummaged in a chest. He took out a pouch of herbs and Tum's nose twitched.

"He's much too young for catnip."

"This is an emergency," Master Wang said. He took the platter and removed the lid. There were two fillets of fish on the platter. He mashed up both with a fork, though kept them separate. One fillet was mashed with green lime juice that was squeezed into it.

The other fillet was mashed with the herbs Scrappy was too young for.

The lime enhanced fish was placed before Tum. Scrappy got the mash with the herb. Scrappy sniffed it. Then his sight grew fuzzy and his world went back.

***

He woke up to Tum's chuckle. "Who knew catnip would have such a strong effect on you. It knocked you right out."

Scrappy gave a long stretch. "I've slept long enough. I want to check for mice."

"There's one in the right corner of the room, little one."

"And you just let it stay there without bothering to catch it yourself?" Scrappy never thought a cat would be so lazy. "Well, if you don't want it, then I do." So, he went to the corner of the room and found a lumpy sock stuffed in the loose shape of a floppy mouse. "This isn't a mouse! Some cat you are if you can't tell the difference."

He picked up the stuffed toy and threw it into the air in disgust. That's when he caught scent of that smell again.

***

His hunger pains woke him up next time.

"He's up again," Tum said to Master Wang who was smoking a pipe.

Master Wang took a puff and sighed. "I hoped he'd be out for another day, so we could reach the shore."

Scrappy's stomach growled.

"Give him some fresh food and water."

"Give me that juicy bird, so I know that nasty herb isn't in the food," Scrappy grumbled.

"That bird will be your last meal if you get what you want. You must make do with fish again," Master Wang said.

"No funny stuff?"

"The fish will be without the herb."

A salted fish from a barrel in the cargo hold was brought up to Scrappy. It was good, but the salt made his throat dry. He drank all his water in one gulp. The salt overrode his taste buds, so he didn't catch onto the fact the water was laced with the herb until too late.

"NO." He was out again.

***

This time he was in a cold, hard, black box when he awoke. He scratched at its surface to see if he could get a foothold. Light and air streamed in from airholes. The air was pungent with soot, and Scrappy gagged in response.

He howled and thrashed, but the lid was on the box securely. There was a loud sigh and a fabric mouse was squeezed into an airhole.

"UGH."

The scent of the catnip weighed down his eyelids. "It's not fair."

***

There was a ring of cats surrounding him when he came to. Scrappy was used to the company of his mother and littermates, but all these cats growled at him. "Smelly half-breed!"

He snarled back at them.

A human with leather gloves grabbed him by the scruff of his neck. He drew out his claws and swiped the air, trying to get at them.

"Our clients insist their animals be housebroken. Your creature obviously is NOT," a man with a nasal voice said.

Scrappy was placed back into Master Wang's lacquer box.

Then he caught a smell. Human but more refined than he was used to. Their scent was washed and tinged with grooming products. The mellow scent of tobacco came off him. But it smelled as if it was fresh from a pouch and not smoked. Scrappy was used to the old salts who smoked out of pipes on the ship. Bixby kept them supplied with tobacco but didn't smoke himself. Was this a cabin boy?

Scrappy found cabin boys the most trustworthy humans in his short life. He stopped flailing.

"Can I look inside?" a light tenor voice asked.

Master Wang grunted, "Yes."

The young man had hair the color of those shiny discs Bixby collected with such glee. The ones he called "coppers." His eyes were the shade of water in all its shifting lights. A light gray that shifted with the colors surrounding it.

"May I?" the young man asked.

Master Wang nodded.

A shiny rock passed over Scrappy. He growled when it lit up. Responding to it like a challenger. The stone got brighter. "He'll do." The words came out in a short laugh. The kind Scrappy heard when Bixby cleaned up after him so the Captain wouldn't find the latest mess he'd made.

Nasal Voice saw what was going on and interrupted. "Bestiary Boutique takes a fifty percent commission for all sales made in this store."

Master Wang spoke: "Scrappy is a half-breed."

"Then I want to pay half the price of a pedigreed cat in this store. And receive the equipment and supplies added to the purchase," Copper added.

There were grunts of acceptance all around.

The bills were paid out, a receipt written, and the bills split between Nasal Voice and Master Wang. Scrappy had seen such things happen when cargo was sold on land. He never thought he'd be the cargo that was being sold.

Master Wang spoke to Copper as Nasal Voice gathered the accessories and supplies. "Scrappy's father was a temple cat. His mother was the ship's mascot. He is an untrained barbarian but such robustness might serve you better in this land."

Copper nodded at this, and Scrappy knew his career as a familiar had just begun.

A sparkling vision of the future that reminds us, no matter how different we are, we are all members of one giant community, sharing this world.

The 180-Pound Gorilla

Tim Susman

They would mix up people with just about anything in the 23rd century. You had quartz people with jagged crystals of hair; you had poison ivy misanthropes who had to be barred from standing in the exits of sporting events. You had gold people and marigold people; ox people and fox people; you had tortoise people and porpoise people. And you had people-people as well, and the people-people still ran just about everything.

This was fine with the mixed-people. They thought that their future would resemble their present, and this was because one could not yet mix people with foresight. Some people did attempt to mix themselves with two extra eyes, but most often they put them in the backs of their heads, and this did not create foresight, but hindsight, and most of these people were miserable.

Not all the people-people were foresighted-people either, but the ones who were foresighted-people in a very narrow way often ended up in charge of things. These foresighted-people were considered very dull by just about everyone else, always talking about Future Good and Diminishing Marginal Returns and Sunk Cost Bias, but they were undeniably good at running things like companies and governments, and they assured the mixed-people that they would remain free to enjoy their mixed lives. And that seemed like a fair division, and so it was for many years.

There came a time when life became unexpected and difficult for the mixed-people, and they felt that perhaps they might do a better job than the people-people, even with their foresight, of running things the way they wanted. The general feeling among the people-people was that the mixed-people had gotten more or less what they wanted out of life already, and asking to be treated like normal people on top of that was just plain greedy.

Compromises came about in due time. The mixed-people were allowed to do some of the things they wanted, but not all; the people-people were allowed to keep some of the rules they wanted, but not all. The people-people called the compromises "mixed-laws," and the mixed-people called the compromises "bullshit," and this is how you know that they were good compromises.

And then the mixed-people started having children. And that is how Oliver was born.

Oliver's parents had met on a bar—not in a bar, but on a bar—at the 2248 Olympics on Mons Olympus on Mars. Oliver's mother represented the People's Republic of Antarctica in gymnastics, and Oliver's other mother represented Switzerland. They met while practicing their parallel bar routines in the gym, and kissed on the award podium (Oliver's Swiss mother came in second, his Antarctic mother third; they blamed their lower finishes on their love and did not mind at all). Oliver's Swiss mother convinced his Antarctic mother to come back home to Switzerland where they could retire to the steamy mountain jungles, and they decided that becoming gorilla-people would allow them full and unlimited enjoyment of the possibilities of those jungles.

So Oliver was born, and like all children of mixed-people, Oliver was a person, unmixed, because acquired traits are not passed on to progeny, despite the writings of Lamarck. But legally, Oliver was a gorilla-person because his mothers were gorilla-people; the law did not read scientific journals and had missed the debunking of Lamarck, and had gone on believing that people were whatever it said they were.

By and large, Oliver did not mind being a gorilla-person. He lacked the gifts of muscular arms which did not get tired of swinging, but he did not like swinging as much as his mothers did, and in fact he went to university in Omaha, in the United States, because it was the flattest university he could find, and also because it had an excellent law program. He took Sociological Theory of Extreme Body Modification (EBM) Adoption and Behavior one semester, did not see himself or his mothers in it, and thereafter focused on his pre-law studies. He wore a suit to most of his classes and ate corn flakes in the morning and protein paste in the evenings, and he got his law degree when he turned twenty-five.

He had hoped that by then, his native Switzerland would allow mixed-people to practice law, but all the lawyers were people-people, and they were not very interested in opening up their practices to competition from a sudden influx of new lawyers, whether or not they had fur or feathers or fronds. But the United States did allow Oliver to practice law, and even if in the eyes of the law he was a gorilla-person, his clients and friends mostly knew him as "Oliver the lawyer."

In 2281 Oliver's Swiss mother was rushed to the hospital with several broken ribs and a dislocated shoulder. His Antarctic mother was not allowed to visit her, because the hospitals too were run by people-people and they had very unmixed ideas, true or not, about the sterility and disease communicativity of mixed-people. People with foresight often saw only the future that suited their temperament. This was not fair, but as they were the people running things, they mostly got away with it.

Oliver's mother hooted and banged on the hospital door with her gorilla fists, which made for good holo-footage, but it did not help her case. So Oliver filed a suit on her behalf, which appeared in many newspapers read by his clients and friends. Oliver did not mind that. He flew back and forth to Switzerland and enlisted the help of another activist lawyer, as gorilla-people were still barred from practicing law in Switzerland. He did not mind that either. The court allowed him to make arguments as an Expert Consultant, which is something like being a mixed-lawyer. He argued that a compromise was not always the best way to make a law, when basic rights were being sacrificed in the compromise. And he argued that the love of steamy jungles was not a reason to punish a person who was in love with another person, mixed or not. And he argued that the foresighted-people had a responsibility to the mixed-people, as they had accepted responsibility for the institutions that served the mixed-people.

They argued the case for two years, during which time Oliver's Swiss mother was discharged and his Antarctic mother died of a stroke. The case was suspended for one week for Oliver to hold a funeral and grieve. He had set aside money for such an event and so was able to spend most of the week consoling his Swiss mother, who was taken completely by surprise.

At the end of the two years, the hospitals agreed to make accommodations for mixed-people. The case was hailed as a landmark and Oliver returned home to the jungle. He had worried that his clients and friends would not understand his gorilla heritage, but with the exception of one man who said that he wanted a real mixed-person lawyer—someone with lizard scales or fish fins or both—they all remained close to him.

The mixed-people continued to gain rights and gain status, and someone (perhaps it was Oliver) suggested that they simply refer to everyone as "people." Some years later (perhaps at a conference about just such this topic, but definitely not on an award podium), Oliver met someone attractive and interesting, and after some time, they fell in love and were married. Perhaps they decided to mix themselves with the same things, or different things, or nothing. The important thing was that they loved each other just the way they decided to be.

A glimmer of hope from the past—a shimmering vision of Camelot—gets thrust, unwittingly, unexpectedly, into the grim, grimy present.

THE CORVID KING

Amy Clare Fontaine

Arthur dreamed an endless dream.

He dreamed of sumptuous banquets with his comrades by his side, roast pheasants and bards and fire jugglers. Feasts where the wine and the laughter never ran dry, and the great hall rang with stories and songs all through the night. The hearth warmed his bones and the company warmed his heart…

He dreamed of dancing with Guinevere in the courtyard in the moonlight, the fragrance of the flowers in her hair…

He dreamed of chasing his falcon through the woods on a warm summer day, racing through the trees and laughing into the wind…

He dreamed of jousting with Lancelot again, a friendly practice duel. The snorts of their horses in the dusty yard, the stomping of hooves as they circled each other, the cheers of the crowd, the way his heart raced as he charged at last with his lance held high…

He dreamed of Guinevere dancing around the maypole with the village children in the spring, twirling colorful ribbons…

He dreamed of Camelot, the castle's towers tall and strong in the first light of dawn, her banners flapping proudly in the wind.

Camelot.

Arthur smiled, floating along on the river of his dreams. His heart leapt at the thought of his kingdom. Camelot, his crown jewel, his pride and joy, the bastion of chivalry and culture and magic that he had worked so hard to build all his life.

All his… life…

Arthur's brow furrowed as a dark memory intruded on his pleasant dreams.

***

He knelt upon the ashen ground, stabbed through the heart by an enemy sword. Blood leaked out of his chest. He coughed and sputtered, crawling across the earth on his knees.

"Lancelot," he whispered hoarsely. "Lancelot."

The noise of the battle raging around him echoed distantly in his head, as if all of it—the thundering hooves, the clashing swords, the triumphant shouts and pained cries of men—were no longer real to him. He fell back onto the ground, wheezing wetly, his eyes closing.

"Your Highness!"

That shout brought Arthur back from the brink, just barely. Lancelot knelt beside him, his armor dented and dirty. The normally strong and valiant knight now looked at him like a brokenhearted boy. Arthur reached towards him.

"Lancelot."

Arthur coughed violently, and his hand dropped to his side. Lancelot wiped the blood from his brow, his fingers as gentle as a nursemaid's.

"Shh, Arthur, be still."

For the first time, Arthur saw fear in Lancelot's eyes. Arthur choked on his words. "Tell… Guinevere… tell her I…"

Arthur erupted in another coughing fit that wracked his whole body. Then he fell still upon the earth. He felt Lancelot's hand upon his brow once more. The knight smiled sadly down at him.

"She knows, Arthur. She knows."

Arthur smiled back and closed his eyes.

When he opened them, silvery fingers were lifting his body. He was flying through the air, wind rushing all around him. His chest still burned and bled… and yet…

He sailed above his green, jolly, wooded, wild England, through a billowing veil of mist. He closed his eyes…

…And when he opened them once more, he lay on his back on a dais, Excalibur at his side, in the center of a temple whose walls did not reach the ceiling, leaving the room exposed to the elements. It was misty beyond the temple, wet and wild and cold. His pain was gone. Vines seeped in through the gaps between the walls and the ceiling, and he heard a strange bird cry out from somewhere far away. He also heard… was that a monkey…?

Arthur felt those silvery fingers that had carried him through the skies caress his skin, heard the melodic chanting of women as they danced around him. A fog rolled through his mind. Someone planted a kiss upon his brow.

"Sleep, Arthur," she said.

Arthur slept.

***

Arthur had been sleeping for such a long time, but he had not been aware that he was asleep—until now. Now a great rumbling shook the earth beneath him, and he awoke. He no longer wore his chainmail and his suit of armor, though Excalibur still lay at his side. He felt light as a cloud. He looked around him at the temple, which rumbled and moved like an animal, sending him and his sword flying across the dais. Squawking in alarm, he took to the air before he could think and flew through the damp, vine-laden jungle around the temple, which crumbled to dust as he passed. He sailed through a silvery void, and the moisture clung to his feathers like dew. He heard the haunting, beautiful female voice echo sadly in his mind.

"Goodbye, Arthur."

***

Arthur emerged from the mist into a very different world. The sun beat down on his black feathers from overhead. The land below him was still shrouded in a blanket of fog, but as he dove closer, its features slowly began to take shape. He shrieked in terror and anger.

His green, jolly, wooded, wild England was no more. Strange roads as black as night roiled through the countryside like snakes, like scars. Along the roads glided fierce metal beasts, which moved like ghosts but were much noisier. They belched smoke into the air that stung Arthur's lungs. Still flapping in midair, he screamed.

England had been overrun by demons!

Arthur flew and flew over the sorry country, his brain still lingering in a wounded daze. Beside a great river, he spied monstrous spires which he was sure belonged to the fortresses of the demons.

"The demon stronghold." Arthur clacked his beak. Folding his wings against his sides, he dove through the air, landing smack in the middle of one of the hellish roads between the huge, menacing towers. He looked around. A metal demon squealed toward him. He stood his ground, puffing out his feathers.

"I am King Arthur of Camelot. Stop terrorizing my kingdom, foul beast!"

The demon emitted a strange honking sound that rattled Arthur's bones, continuing to roll towards him.

"Idiot bird!" cried a voice. "Get out of the way!"

Startled, Arthur fluttered into the air—just in time, as the demon barreled over the spot he had just vacated. He perched upon the roof of a carriage parked beside the road and looked for the source of the voice. He found it quickly. A golden horse attached to the carriage was rolling her eyes at him.

"You're not from around here, are you, bird?"

Arthur bristled, ruffling his feathers.

"I am not a bird!" snapped Arthur, preening indignantly. "That is no way to address your king!"

The horse laughed, a gentle, flowing whinny that somehow reminded him of Guinevere.

"You're a bird, honey. Take a look at yourself." The horse inclined her head towards a puddle in the street. Jumping down from the top of the carriage, Arthur hopped over to the puddle and looked down at his reflection. A crow cocked his head jauntily back at him.

"Intriguing," said Arthur wonderingly. "Merlin must have thought this form would help me defeat the demons somehow." Arthur clacked his beak and flew back to the top of the carriage. Perching there, he looked around. People marched tiredly along the grimy street, as if they were sleepwalking. A gray fog hung over everything. Demonic screeches split the morning in two. None of the people said hello to each other. They just marched like ants toward their destinations, bundled in jackets to keep out the misty cold. Some of them entered the demons, which were hollow inside, and rode around in their bellies. Even the people outside the demons coordinated their activities around the movements of the demons, only walking where the demons permitted them to walk. Arthur shuddered. The humans were their slaves.

"Demons?" asked the horse.

With a full body shake that ruffled all his feathers, Arthur flew onto the back of the horse and perched there.

"Let us ride," commanded Arthur. "Bring me to my sword."

The horse bucked him off. He fluttered into the air, huffing.

"You're crazy, bird! Leave me alone!"

Arthur kept trying to perch on the horse's back, but she kept shaking him off. He clicked his beak angrily.

"You don't understand! They have brainwashed you all! You cannot even see your own enslavement!"

Alighting on the plush bench in the carriage, Arthur pointed his wing at the nearest demon. "Do you see that?" he hissed at the horse.

The horse looked from the demon to the crow, unimpressed. "Yes, I see it. That's a car."

Arthur laughed hysterically, a grating, cawing sound. The horse winced.

"Acar?" Arthur said. "You know your demons by name?"

The horse snorted and shook her head, her mane whipping around her. "Cars aren't demons. They're machines. Humans made them. They use them to travel."

Arthur stared at the nearest passing car with his beady eyes. "How long was I asleep?" he murmured. When the horse said nothing, he flew around the carriage and landed in front of her. He looked boldly up into her eyes, despite the fact that she towered over him. "What century after the death of Christ is this?" he demanded.

The horse swished her tail, shifting her weight from hoof to hoof. "The twenty-first," she said. "And I hope my master comes back with those carrots before it's the twenty-second."

Arthur fluffed his feathers and blinked. He alighted upon the roof of the carriage once more. He looked around at the wild, fast-paced, rushing world around him—the racing cars, the din in the streets, the sheer lack of sparkle to it all. His mind reeled. His heart sank, and he shivered.

"Guinevere," he murmured, closing his beady eyes for a moment.

"Oy, Penny! I'm here!"

A man had arrived and was patting the horse and feeding her carrots as she chuffed with contentment. Next the man gave her a bucket of water, which she eagerly began to drink. As the man leaned against the side of the carriage, looking around at the goings-on in the street with a distant, distracted air, Arthur hopped up and down on the top of the carriage and flapped his wings, trying to catch the man's attention.

"Excuse me, good man, can you tell me, are there any great ills plaguing England at present? Are there battles to be won, or dragons to be slain? Damsels in need of a good knight's assistance?"

The man just stared into space, looking right through Arthur. Glancing up from her bucket, the horse flared her nostrils at the bird.

"Quit your screeching, crow. It's quite dreadful."

Arthur's narrow head darted from side to side, assessing the flurry of motion and noise in the street. As the horse's man accepted money from a young couple and ushered them into the carriage, Arthur hopped on the horse's back again. She jerked her hindquarters and sent him flying into the air.

"I told you, stupid bird, go away!"

Hearing the horse's agitated whinny, the man went to the horse's side and patted her gently. "Easy, Penny. It's all right."

Arthur stood before the horse, Penny, and looked up at her pleadingly with an open-beaked gape.

"Please, I'm lost and alone in a strange place at a strange time, and no one here seems to know me. I need to at least get back to Avalon and find Excalibur. I seem to have left her behind there. Do you know where Avalon is?"

With direction from her master, Penny began to pull the carriage, her master, and the two passengers into the noisy street and the traffic. "I do know where Avalon is," the horse said softly as she trotted away.

"*What?*" squawked Arthur. Determined, he hurried to the roof of the carriage, clinging to it for dear life as it jostled through the streets.

"Yes," Penny said. "It's not too far from London, as the crow flies. Pardon the expression. I was born there. I miss it." Penny sighed wistfully, clopping through the dirty streets. Fog lay over everything like a death shroud, and austere brick buildings pressed in on the street from all sides. Cars screamed and lights blared.

"With… all… due… respect…" gasped Arthur as he bounced atop the carriage. Suddenly, the car in front of Penny and the lines of cars around her came to a stop, and she stopped too. Arthur caught his breath, found his bearings, and continued. "With all due respect, Lady Penny, this seems like no place for a noble steed from Avalon."

Penny grimaced. "It isn't." Nickering softly, she shifted her weight from hoof to hoof, waiting for the car in front of her to start moving again. Arthur hopped from foot to clawed foot, and suddenly an idea flickered through his bird brain.

"Would you like to return to Avalon?" asked Arthur. "With me?"

The light changed. The cars started moving forward through the intersection, and so did Penny. "Can't," Penny said.

Arthur flapped his wings frantically to stabilize his body and stay in one place. His stomach churned. He was really not enjoying this ride as much as the humans were. Launching his body into the air, he started flying alongside Penny instead.

"Why not?" asked Arthur.

Penny shot him a sidelong glance. "I have a job now, and a master who feeds me carrots. I have responsibilities. I can't just leave."

"What's this bird doing, squawking about?" muttered the coachman. He waved a hand at Arthur to shoo him away. "Go on. Get!"

"I am sorry to have disturbed you, good man," said Arthur politely. He flew a little higher, high enough to avoid the man's line of sight but low enough to still talk to Penny.

"He can't understand us, can he?" asked Arthur.

"Nope," said Penny. "Men don't understand naught but themselves."

Arthur glanced down at the coachman. "That's a pity," said Arthur. "My teacher, Merlin, understood the languages of all the birds and beasts, and even plants and stones. And stars."

"That's nice," said Penny, turning left at the next intersection.

Arthur tried to perch on the outer rail of the carriage, but the young couple shooed him away. The carriage went around several city blocks, past the towering spires of cathedrals and a huge clock tower, along a river that sparkled only weakly in the gray half-light. At last the carriage parked beside the curb at the place where Arthur had first found it. The coachman helped the couple out of the carriage. He patted Penny's head and fed her another carrot.

"Good girl," said Penny's master. "I'm going to go get you more carrots. And water."

The man walked off along the sidewalk, whistling a tune Arthur had never heard before. Arthur perched atop a phone booth beside the horse.

"So this is your life," Arthur said slowly. "You walk around the blocks and come back to where you started. Every day."

Penny sighed and looked up at him. "Why are you following me, crow?"

Arthur warbled and stretched out his wings. Suddenly, the fog covering the sky parted, and a ray of light shafted down upon the crow, making him look like more than a mere bird. Like an angel, even. Penny squinted at him. His black eyes blazed with righteous fire.

"My dear Lady Penny, where is your spirit of adventure? You don't have to be a mere carriage horse for the rest of your life!"

Penny shook her head. "What else can I do?"

The crow leapt into the air, soaring around Penny in excited circles. "You could be a hero!" he cried. "A legend! Noble steed of the king! You could go on quests to distant lands, see marvels you've never even dreamed of, far beyond this city's fog! We shall return to your green homeland of Avalon, and then… and then… who knows?"

Penny tossed her head. "I *would* like to go back to Avalon." Her coat twitched some flies away. "Will there be carrots?"

Arthur clacked his beak and bobbed his head. "My dear Lady Penny, once Camelot is restored to its former glory, I will see to it that we find you the finest carrots in all the land. As many as you can eat!"

Penny tossed her head and laughed, that surprisingly musical whinny that sent pangs through Arthur's heart as he thought, inexplicably, of Guinevere.

"I've gone nuts here in London! Why am I making deals with a crow who's spouting nonsense?"

Arthur flew down and perched on Penny's back. To his surprise, this time, she didn't shake him off.

"Because your heart yearns for greener pastures. For freedom. For adventure. For Avalon."

Penny blinked slowly at Arthur. "All right," she said. "Can that clever beak of yours get me out of this silly harness?"

The crow cawed with delight. When Penny's master returned, whistling, to his carriage, with an armful of carrots and a full bucket of water in tow, he found only a carriage, with no horse attached.

***

Penny trotted down the sidewalks of London, with Arthur the crow riding on her back. She had gotten so accustomed to human traffic by now that she knew how to obey the language of the signals, the lights. Arthur asked Penny an infinitude of questions and then listened, rapt, as she filled him in on all the major changes, events, upheavals, and advances in technology in England that she could think of, onward from the time period when Arthur imagined he had been put to sleep by the priestesses of Avalon.

"You are a very erudite horse," Arthur observed. "The brightest I have ever met."

Penny swished her tail bashfully. "Thank you."

They walked on the sidewalk on a bridge over the river. Cars streaked by beside them. All around them on the sidewalk, humans rushed past, but they all made adequate space for Penny as she moved through the crowd. One or two passersby gawked at the sight of a riderless horse with a crow on its back, but the vast majority paid no attention whatsoever. The skies, while still mostly cloudy, were now partly blue.

"Where did you learn so much about human history, Lady Penny?" asked Arthur.

Penny trotted across a crosswalk, past a cart Arthur now knew to be a burger stand.

"My master… well, now my former master, I suppose… anyway, he has a great fondness for history, especially the history of London. That is why he was giving visitors tours of the city in that carriage, to show them the sights and tell them stories about the history behind them."

Arthur shifted around on Penny's back. He hadn't been sure he could get accustomed to riding bareback on a horse in his new form, yet by now, after many hours of practice, he found himself managing quite well.

"And so much history there has been," Arthur mused. "You have told me so much about the events that have transpired in our great Mother

England during the past few centuries. But tell me, why no mention of King Arthur and Camelot in your history lesson? Are the people of England not aware of what became of them?"

Penny laughed. "King Arthur? Camelot?" She laughed harder and harder, a wild whinny that caused nearby pedestrians to stop and stare. Arthur screeched.

"How dare you insult my honor, miscreant?"

Reluctantly, Penny stopped laughing. "Sorry. It's just—King Arthur and Camelot are legends. They're not real. Most everyone knows that. Except you, I guess. Sorry."

Arthur croaked sadly and fluttered his wings. "It is a shame that the great kingdom of Camelot has passed into legend, however this grievous error occurred." Arthur looked up at the sun overhead, and then around him at the people passing by. "But it will be all right. I will set things right again, reclaim my throne, and bring the spirit of chivalry and the wonders of Camelot back to the people of England, and the world."

Penny walked more slowly after hearing these words. "Uh… huh," she said, hesitantly.

The crow shook himself furiously.

"The world is out of balance without Camelot as its guiding light. But I will make things right again. I will stand for chivalry and justice and goodness as king. I will not allow madmen like this monster you mentioned—Hitler, was that his name?—I will not allow men like that to rise to power ever again. Peace will reign once more. I'll make sure of it."

The horse snorted. "Oh? Tell me, how exactly do you plan to do that? In case you haven't noticed, you're a crow."

Arthur chortled. "Wait until we get to Avalon and I retrieve Excalibur. I will make this work somehow. You'll see."

***

"Here we are!" said Penny.

Arthur's beak gaped open in dismay.

They had wandered all the way through the city of London and its suburbs, foraging in dumpsters for produce and other scraps along the way to keep up their strength. They eventually escaped from the brick and concrete jungle into a countryside that looked at least somewhat more familiar to Arthur, albeit more marred by roads and houses than it had been when last he'd seen it. "So England's still alive," Arthur had murmured as they passed over green, rolling hills and dales, past farms and mills and fields and sparkling rivers, stone castles and quaint villages with thatched roofs. Penny had smiled and nodded at this comment, whinnying with contentment, clearly relieved to be back in the country at last.

But now… now that they had reached their destination, it wasn't quite what Arthur had been expecting.

There were acres of rolling pastures, flanked at their far edge by an old wood. A red barn stood in the center of the yard, along with a stable and a farmhouse. "Avalon Estate and Stables," read the wooden sign that swung cheerfully above the gate that opened to the part of the dirt road that led over to the farmhouse. Penny turned to Arthur, swishing her tail with relish.

"We made it!" cried Penny. "Isn't it wonderful?"

Arthur blinked his beady eyes and said nothing. The horse huffed at him.

"It… it is wonderful," Arthur said slowly. "But I'm afraid it is not the Avalon I am looking for."

"Oh?" Penny's face fell. Arthur sighed, turning his beak toward the paved road on which they had come.

"I am sorry, Lady Penny, but I must be on my way. Thank you for your good company, and the history lessons."

Arthur started flying back in the direction of the paved road.

"Where will you go?"

He heard her voice call softly after him, and the note of sadness in it. He stopped flying away and flapped in place in midair instead.

"To find Avalon," he said. "My Avalon. I have to retrieve my sword. I'm not sure where it is anymore, but I'm hoping my heart will lead the way."

He swiveled around in the air and looked at Penny. She pawed shyly at the ground. "Well, I wish you the best of luck, little crow. It's been fun to listen to your stories. You may be a little crazy, but I like you. I will miss you."

The crow's wingbeats stuttered in midair. He was surprised to hear this from the horse who had wanted nothing to do with him when they first met. He looked toward the farm, and the wood beyond it, which seemed to glow in the bright light of sunset. The sight stirred a memory. He closed his eyes…

***

He pictured his old friend Merlin the last time they had met. It had been sunset, and Merlin had had that twinkle of stardust in his eye. The wizard had been kneeling on the ground in an open field on the edge of the wood where he and Arthur had met, twirling a stick in his wizened fingers, looking at the twig as if it were the Holy Grail itself. Arthur strode up to Merlin wearing his full suit of armor and a serious frown.

"I'll be riding out soon, Merlin. We are heading to war."

"I know," said Merlin softly. Smiling like a child, he started drawing lines in the dirt with the stick, his blue robes billowing out from him on the ground like a lady's skirts.

Arthur looked down at the wizard's drawings. "Is that a spell?"

The wizard shook his head, not looking up from his task. Arthur stood beside Merlin, clasping his hands behind his back. "Won't you come with us, Merlin? You could help us win this fight."

Merlin shook his head. "You know I don't like fighting, Arthur."

"I don't, either." Arthur sighed. Merlin continued to draw lines in the dirt without looking up.

"It's the little things," Merlin said quietly.

Arthur blinked. "I'm sorry?"

Merlin continued to draw. The branches of the trees on the edge of the wood swayed in the evening breeze.

"Arthur, I know your men may love adventures, and quests, and great battles. But these are not the things we live for. We live for the little things. The sunset shining on this glade. A cool breeze. A friend's laugh. Music. A fire in the hearth. A good book. Waking up in the morning with someone you love. Drawing lines in the dirt for no reason at all. These are the things that make life worth living."

Arthur frowned as the breeze stirred around them. It didn't even touch him through his thick armor.

"But Merlin, we cannot continue to have the things of which you speak unless we ensure that our world remains a peaceful one. And we can only do that through quests and battles to keep the peace, to protect the things we hold dear."

Merlin put his stick down and stood, putting a hand on Arthur's shoulder. "Arthur, come down here and look at this." The old man knelt on the ground once more, gesturing for Arthur to do the same. Awkwardly, Arthur knelt beside Merlin in the dirt in his bulky armor. Merlin smiled and pointed. "Look, Arthur," he said in a reverent whisper, like a man in church. "Look there."

Arthur squinted at the spot Merlin had indicated. A fuzzy green caterpillar was crawling across the dirt. Arthur laughed out loud. "Stuff and nonsense! What's so special about that, Merlin?"

Merlin fixed Arthur with a steady gaze. "Don't you remember your boyhood lessons, when we changed into animals together, Wart?"

Arthur winced at the mention of his childhood nickname and continued to watch the caterpillar. Merlin went on, "There is much to be learned from even the simplest creatures. Being a king isn't just about glory and armies and swords and quests, you know. Remember?"

"Yes, I do remember," Arthur mumbled. "Sorry, Merlin." He got down on his belly and stared intently at the caterpillar. The caterpillar had made its way to a velvety fallen leaf and begun to gnaw at its edges.

"Remember this, Arthur. Remember that on the best quests, you often find what you were looking for where you least expect it. The wonder of stars in a caterpillar. Gold on the underside of a leaf."

Arthur nodded. "I will remember."

Merlin beamed. "That's my favorite pupil." Standing, Merlin turned and began to walk towards the woods. Arthur stood and watched the long shadow his friend cast across the glade, which was brilliant in the light of the setting sun. Pausing for a moment, Merlin turned on his heel and looked back at Arthur one last time. Arthur saw his tall blue form silhouetted in sharp contrast to the orange sky overhead and the dark outlines of the trees beyond. Merlin grinned at Arthur, and even from this distance, Arthur could see a knowing twinkle in the wizard's bright blue eyes.

"Oh, Arthur? One last thing. Go to the farm with the horse. She is your caterpillar."

***

Arthur awoke from his flashback. He was not in a suit of armor, talking to a wizard. He was a crow, flapping in place in the air and looking over at a golden horse who was trotting dejectedly towards stables that had once been familiar to her, alone.

"Penny, wait!" he croaked, flapping towards her.

Penny looked up and blinked. "Crow?"

Arthur smiled, alighting on the post of the gate she was about to pass through. "Please," he said. "Call me Arthur."

"Arthur." The horse rolled the word around on her tongue. "Arthur, don't you have to find your Avalon? And your… um, your sword?"

The crow bobbed his head. "A wise man once told me that we often find what we are looking for where we least expect it."

Penny's mouth twitched into a smile. "Are you coming to Avalon with me, then?"

Arthur nodded. Penny neighed with delight. "Great! I can't wait to show you around!"

The horse trotted through the gate and along the dirt path toward the stables. The crow looked toward the edge of the forest, a forest which looked miraculously familiar. He thought he spied a flash of blue between the trees.

***

"Hey, hey! Is the gang still here?"

Penny trotted down the aisle between the rows of stalls, peering in at the horses who were residents. They looked at her without any indication that they knew who she was. In fact, they seemed rather miffed that she was trotting around like she owned the place while they were cooped up in stalls. As it became clear that she didn't know any of these horses, Penny's face fell.

"Hmm. I guess my brothers and sisters and my mother and father were all sold long ago," she murmured to Arthur.

A dun mare peered out at Penny and Arthur suspiciously. "What are you doing here, strange horse? Why on Earth did you bring this bird with you?"

Arthur puffed out his feathered chest. "I am no mere bird. I am King Arthur of Camelot, on a quest to restore my kingdom and reclaim my throne!"

The dun horse guffawed with laughter. "You… what?"

Penny glared at the strange horse. "That is no way to treat my friend. He's a little not right in the head, but that doesn't mean he deserves your rudeness. Shame on you. I thought the horses of Avalon had better manners than this."

The horse stopped laughing and leveled a cool gaze at Penny. "The noble horses of Avalon do not affiliate with riffraff."

Arthur clacked his beak and swooped through the air. "I do not appreciate your tone, Lady Horse. Let us abandon this meanness of spirit and instead exchange pleasant introductions."

The horse's nostrils flared. "I am Winifred," she said stiffly, turning pointedly away.

"What are you doing out there? Huh? Huh? Who are you? Where did you come from?" piped a fast, excited, high-pitched voice from the opposite row of stalls. Turning, Penny and Arthur saw a young Shetland pony, jumping excitedly up and down to get a better look at the two newcomers. Winifred snorted. Penny walked up to the pony's stall and looked down at her with a friendly smile.

"I'm Penny, and the bird is my friend, Arthur. We came from London. What's your name?"

The pony squealed in delight, still bouncing up and down.

"I'm Dreamy Moon Pie! But you can just call me Dreamy!"

Penny chortled at this. The pony continued, as bright and bubbly as before, apparently unfazed by Penny's laughter.

"Those purebred studbook names, yeah, they're pretty funny, aren't they?" Now Dreamy giggled, too. Arthur stayed respectfully silent.

Penny stopped laughing and nodded. "Yeah, my studbook name's pretty embarrassing, too." Penny grinned sheepishly, swishing her tail.

Dreamy grinned back at her. "Hey, do you want to go play or something? We could go frolic in the meadow. The humans aren't around right now. It would be the perfect time to get away!"

Penny looked at the pony. "Won't you get in trouble?"

Dreamy shrugged. "I'm always up for an adventure, whatever happens!"

Penny looked around at Winifred and the other horses in their stalls. "Do you want to come with us? We could all spend time together, munch some grass, get to know each other."

Winifred turned her head away. "As I said before, we will not associate with riffraff."

Penny narrowed her eyes. "I'm just as high-bred as you. I'm from Avalon. This is my home. You have no right to…"

"Yippee!" Dreamy cried as Arthur opened the gate to her stall. She pranced up and down the aisle like a child hyped up on too much candy, and then she rushed out the double doors on the other side of the stable.

"If you change your mind later, you are welcome to join us," Arthur said to Winifred pleasantly. Then he flew after Dreamy, and Penny followed him out into the sunshine.

Evening dappled the fields before the forest with a rich orange glow. Dreamy raced across the grass, her mane whipping in the breeze. "Yay! This is so much fun! So, so fun! You're the best thing that's happened to me here! Thank you! Thank you!"

To Arthur's surprise, the pony got down on the grass and started rolling around on it like a dog. He had to laugh at the ridiculous scene. Feeling the wind in her mane, Penny started running, too—at first, with more restraint than the youthful pony, but eventually she gave in to the freedom and the joy in her heart at being out in an open space once more, and she danced across the field, a golden horse against the orange light of sunset, laughing into the breeze. Arthur flew in circles over the two equines, relishing the feeling of the cool breeze on his feathers. He felt a pang in his heart at Penny's laugh, as it reminded him of Guinevere. But they were all dancing and enjoying the moment. No need to think of a past that was gone, that had crumbled to dust somehow and he wasn't sure why…

Arthur landed on the grass and stood there, staring at nothing. Penny stopped her prancing and looked at him. "Arthur?" she asked, trotting up to him. "Are you all right?"

Dreamy still raced about the field crying, "Whee!"

Arthur looked towards the wood. Without a word to the worried horse, he took off for the forest.

***

Arthur flew through the tangled wood. Briars scratched him, but still he pressed on. He dodged around clawing, cloying branches, going ever deeper into the darkness.

He wasn't sure whether he was flying toward something or fleeing something else. Despite Merlin's advice all those centuries ago, he felt incomplete simply hanging around this estate with a bunch of equines. He felt like he should be doing something more.

He was so lost in his tangled web of restless thoughts that he almost flew smack into a gnarled oak tree. He paused for a moment, peering into the deep hole at the base of its trunk. It was so dark and wide that it looked like a cave. Suddenly understanding smacked him in the face like a stone wall.

He knew this tree. Merlin had been imprisoned here, lifetimes ago.

Descending to the forest floor, Arthur began hopping around the base of the tree. His beady eyes scanned the shadows, searching for something, though he wasn't sure what.

At last, a stray sunbeam glanced off the object of his search. It rested on a bed of fallen leaves against a thick root. Arthur carefully picked up the multifaceted sapphire jewel in his beak. It had an ancient inscription on it, etched faintly in silver. Arthur recognized the small, crazy handwriting.

"When the time comes," read the inscription, "you will find the words you need."

Arthur held the jewel in his beak, comforted by the feeling of Merlin's presence and the reassuring message. Even when a fierce wind whooshed through the branches overhead, causing the chance sunbeam to disappear and casting the forest in shadow once more, peace still washed through him. He didn't have all the answers yet. But when he needed to know what to do, he would find a way.

Arthur bowed his head and closed his eyes, saying a silent prayer of thanks.

"Oy! You! What you doin' in our wood?"

Startled, Arthur squawked a muffled squawk around the jewel in his beak and took to the air in a flurry of feathers. Wheeling around the tree, he spied a fox, a badger, and a polecat, standing together and looking at him suspiciously. They were larger than him, and what big teeth they had!

Arthur shifted the jewel into his talons and flapped in place in midair, staring down at the three carnivores.

"Hello, good comrades! I apologize. I did not mean to trespass, nor to disturb you. I was looking for something. A gift from a friend."

Just then, the fox spied the jewel in Arthur's talons. Instantly, his expression softened, his ears airplaning to the sides in a gesture of relief, his mouth open in an excited squeal.

"Oy, it's him! The gent Merlin told us to wait for!" The fox wagged his bushy tail. "You're a king, ain't ye?"

Arthur landed on a mossy stump near the base of the oak tree, still clutching the blue jewel.

"I *was* a king," Arthur replied, his heart sinking. "I'm not sure what I am now."

The polecat waddled towards him. "Bah! Once a king, always a king, eh?" she said cheerfully. She circled Arthur's stump, sniffing him in a friendly, curious manner. "You still smell like a king," she said, with a smile and a flick of her long tail.

"The once and future king," the badger agreed in a gravelly voice, with a solemn nod.

Just then, Arthur heard two worried equine voices calling his name. "Arthur! Arthur!" With the jewel in his grasp, he took to the air.

"It was good to meet you all, my fine forest folk. Did Merlin give you a message for me?"

The fox nodded. "Yes. When the time comes, we'll be here, waiting for you."

Arthur nodded, and the warmth and peace from the jewel washed over him again. Even though they were apart, his friend was still looking out for him.

"Thank you," said Arthur. "I will remember that."

And with that, Arthur flew back through the forest. Back toward Penny and Dreamy. Back toward his new Avalon.

***

Arthur had arrived at Avalon Estate and Stables at the ripe end of summer. He spent the next several months there. At first, he rested on the hazy edge between contentment and restlessness. He still felt like he should be doing something more with his life. After all, the priestesses of the *real* Avalon—no, he corrected himself, the *first* Avalon, the Avalon where he had begun his new life—the priestesses had whispered to him amid his fevered dreams that when the time came, when the world needed him, he would awaken to reclaim his throne, to restore honor to the world. Hopping around some farm as a crow—without his title, his kingdom, or even his sword—seemed like a far cry from saving the world.

Yet he heeded his old friend Merlin's advice from so long ago, and gradually, he learned to see the noble in the ordinary, the adventurous in the mundane. He learned this largely from watching Penny. The horse found joy in the simplest things. To her, running through the pasture seemed just as good as the grandest of quests, and a sweet apple on a crisp fall day was just as good as a sumptuous feast. When Arthur told her stories as she grazed in the sun, she listened. And it meant the world to him.

"Do you believe me?" he asked her one day, as she stood at the water trough at the edge of the pasture, taking a drink.

Penny looked up at him and smiled. "About what, Arthur?"

Arthur perched on a fencepost and looked down at her, fluttering his wings anxiously.

"About my stories. That Camelot existed. That I'm really King Arthur. That I've done all the things I say I've done."

Penny gazed thoughtfully into the distance. The breeze stirred her golden mane, which shone in the sun.

"They're lovely stories," Penny said evasively.

Arthur clacked his beak and hopped from foot to foot. Penny turned back to him and met his gaze.

"Listen, Arthur. I like you for who you are now, not whoever you were. You inspire me to be kind to everyone, even stuffy horses like Winifred who are mean to me sometimes. You inspire me to be brave, to take chances and explore new places, like that waterfall we found in the wood the other day. You make me feel like, even though I'm just a horse, I could also be a fine lady."

"You *are* a fine lady," Arthur said firmly.

Penny whinnied with laughter and tossed her head. "See, that's what I love about you, Arthur. You believe in what *could be*, the noble potential in everything and everyone. And that's what matters most."

Soon enough, Arthur stopped feeling restless. He came to love flying over the sun-dappled fields, racing through the air above Penny and Dreamy as they ran. He loved watching the family who owned Avalon Estate and Stables saying grace through one of the wide windows of the farmhouse before they dined. He loved watching the leaves of the wood change color as summer turned gracefully into fall. He loved following Penny as she gave horseback rides through the woods to humans embarking on simple little quests of their own. He loved trying to make Winifred laugh by hopping along the rail of her stall and croaking and clacking at her; at first, she was resistant to his "nonsense," but one day in October he got her to crack a smile. He even learned to love being a crow: croaking and cawing in a strangled symphony, scavenging in the wood and finding new things every day, sailing above the trees and pastures spreading his black wings wide against the sky and seeing England from the air.

Excalibur was not gone, he realized now. Camelot was not gone. Guinevere and his knights were not gone, nor was Merlin. He carried them all in his heart, and he knew he was still a king on the inside, no matter what anyone else saw or said. He kept the blue jewel tucked away in the rafters of the stable, and he watched fall turn to winter and the woods and fields get blanketed with pure white snow, and he waited patiently for his time to come.

Arthur noticed, as December wore on, that the heads of the estate put up a glittering Christmas tree in the window, that they strung twinkling lights all over the outside of the farmhouse and the stables. And then, one snowy day, Christmas arrived. Arthur felt it in his heart. The humans were celebrating in their bright, merry house, exchanging gifts and pleasantries, while the horses still stood in the dark, musty stable, which looked rather glum in comparison.

Arthur had an idea. "Will you let me ride you in a little while?" Arthur whispered to Dreamy. "For a show, of sorts?"

The pony giggled. "Oh boy! Sounds fun!"

With a clack of his beak, Arthur took off for the back door of the human kitchen. Slipping discreetly inside, Arthur spied two props that would serve his purpose perfectly: a metal strainer and a wooden ladle. He brought each object back to the stable over the course of two separate trips, for he lacked the strength to carry both items in his claws at once. With his nimble beak, Arthur released Dreamy from her stall. She trotted out into the aisle with an excited squeal. Placing the strainer on his head like a helmet and the ladle in his claws like a sword, Arthur rode Dreamy from one end of the stable to the other, crying, "Hear ye, hear ye, good horses of Avalon! It is I, King Arthur of Camelot, and my trusty sword Excalibur!" Arthur brandished the wooden ladle. Dreamy whinnied, rearing dramatically for emphasis.

"I have a Christmas pageant for you all today, to bring cheer to your hearts on this dark winter's day! For a child was born today who brought light into our world. He was a far greater king than I, but others have told his story far better than I ever could. Today, I would like to simply tell you the stories that are mine to tell: stories of the great kingdom of Camelot."

Penny and the other horses waited, listening. With a deep breath, Arthur began. Astride his trusty steed, Dreamy, Arthur told his stories, acting out scenes from his quests and adventures. He spoke of fair maidens rescued and great monsters vanquished. He told tales of each knight from his court, where each man came from, how he rose to greatness, his finest deeds as well as sweet, personal moments of friendship. In his croaking crow's voice, Arthur spoke of Merlin and Lancelot and Guinevere. He spoke of the peace and prosperity and leadership that was so hard-won and unexpected from a little boy named Wart who had been teased all his life, a boy who happened to be in the right place at the right time and pull a legendary sword from a stone.

"But it was never about the sword," Arthur said. "Not really. Nor about any of the other external trappings of being a king. Not greatness and luxuries, nor fine achievements and battles. Camelot was about…" Arthur choked on his words. "About who we were inside. What we believed in. Peace, prosperity, chivalry, beauty, courage, justice. Goodness. These virtues are what we stood for. They are…" Arthur croaked. "They are what we died for. My time as a king may have passed, but these dreams shall never pass from the world. Camelot is still in my heart, and I know how to see it even here, if I know where to look." Arthur bowed, with his wings spread wide. "Thank you all for your time."

Dreamy clopped her hooves as if in applause. "Yay!" she cried. "Bravo! Bravo!" The horses stood staring at Arthur for a long time in silence. Penny's eyes burned with tears, but there was a proud smile on her face.

Finally, the silence was broken by a derisive snort. Arthur turned and looked at Winifred.

"Nonsense," she scoffed. "Utter nonsense! You are not a king! You are merely a deranged crow! What are you still doing here? Shoo!"

The other horses, except for Penny, started laughing at him. Arthur clucked meekly and shrank into himself, hiding his head with his wing.

Perhaps Winifred was right. Perhaps he was merely a deranged crow. What proof did he have, after all? Arthur shivered at the cold winter air, a twisting feeling in his gut. All he had were his memories, and those had begun to fade around the edges like dreams.

Arthur closed his eyes and wished to die.

Suddenly, he heard a stall door bang and squeak. He startled and opened his eyes, his feathers ruffling in alarm. Penny stood beside him and Dreamy. Her stall door hung open on only one hinge. She had kicked it open with her hooves. Penny glared at the other horses, her mane tossing around her head in fury like an angry lion's.

"Don't listen to them, King Arthur. They may not believe in Camelot, but I do."

Arthur's heart swelled with pride. He saw a blue light glowing in the rafters. He flew up to the jewel, grabbed it in his beak, and descended back down to perch on Dreamy's back. The blue light enveloped him, and Dreamy, and Penny…

And suddenly the three of them stood in the wood at the base of the oak tree, snow falling around them almost silently, like moth wings. Arthur still stood on Dreamy's back, with the metal strainer on his head, the wooden ladle in his claws, and the jewel in his beak. The equines and the crow all shivered in the cold.

"Where are we?" whined Dreamy.

"At last," said a voice.

Penny, Dreamy, and Arthur turned to look. A fox, a polecat, and a badger stood beside the oak tree, watching them expectantly.

"Are you ready to go?" asked the fox.

Penny and Dreamy looked at Arthur, confused. Arthur nodded at the fox, with such self-assurance and regal bearing for a crow that Penny and Dreamy's fear and confusion lessened. The fox grinned a toothy grin. "Good," he said. He nodded to the polecat and the badger. Together, the three animals ran in complicated circles around the tree, as if tying Celtic knots around its trunk with their movements. A soft blue glow lit the opening in the tree with a flash, and then it vanished. The fox, the polecat, and the badger stopped moving and turned as one to face Arthur, standing in a line beside the oak tree.

"The way is opened," said the badger. "We will follow behind you."

Arthur nodded. Penny gazed at him. "Do you know what's going on, Arthur? Do you know where we're going?" she asked him quietly.

Arthur fluttered. "Not entirely. But I trust my heart. I trust Camelot." He cocked his head at Penny. "Do you?"

Penny stared back at him for a long time. Finally, she nodded. "I do."

"Oh boy!" giggled Dreamy, quivering with excitement beneath the crow. "An adventure!"

Arthur nodded, smiling. "Indeed." He nodded to the fox, polecat, and badger. "Thank you," he said. The animals nodded back. Arthur led Dreamy into the wide opening at the base of the oak's trunk, and the wood disappeared in a flash of blue light.

***

When the piercing blue light cleared at last, Arthur, Dreamy, Penny, the fox, the badger, and the polecat all stood at the foot of a tall statue of a man on a horse, between two stone lions near the steps leading up to the statue. People bustled past them on the sidewalks. Traffic screamed around them on all sides. Arthur turned to Penny. "Are we back in London?"

Penny nodded, looking around, her tail swishing restlessly.

"Yes. This looks like Trafalgar Square."

Dreamy trotted around for a while, taking in the sights, with Arthur riding on her back. Arthur saw the way people trudged past him through the gray, dismal fog and the snow, their hands jammed in their jacket pockets. None of them noticed him. They never even looked up. His heart hammered with fear. He was invisible. He was nothing. He was merely a deranged crow with a metal strainer on his head and a wooden ladle in his claws and a meaningless trinket in his beak, riding a silly pony. He clucked nervously. Then he shifted the blue jewel into his claws and looked at it.

"When the time comes, you will find the words you need."

Arthur turned to his animal companions. "Can you all please do something for me? I need you to dance around the base of this statue. To imagine, as you do, that you are going around some great, magical maypole, one last party at home before an adventure to come. Can you do that for me?"

The animals nodded. Dreamy giggled. Penny smiled. "Yes, Your Majesty."

Arthur smiled, too. Filled with strength, he flew towards the top of the statue with the strainer on his head, carrying the ladle and the jewel. He perched on the top of the statue, watching the comings and goings of the crowds and the cars. No one stopped to notice him.

"I am King Arthur of Camelot," croaked the crow.

The people moved on through the dismal gray fog, heedless of the bird on the statue. Arthur faltered. He cleared his throat with a hesitant caw. At first, no one stopped to look at him. But as the horse, pony, fox, badger, and polecat danced around the base of the statue as if it were a maypole, their motions attracted the attention of a handful of pedestrians, and the wide eyes of some of the onlookers eventually traveled up to the top of the statue.

King Arthur wasn't sure if they were listening to him, or if they'd understand him if they were. But regardless, he had to tell the tale in his heart that was burning to be told. So he did.

He spoke of sumptuous banquets with his comrades by his side, of roast pheasants and bards and fire jugglers, feasts where the wine and the laughter never ran dry, and the great hall rang with stories and songs all through the night, and the hearth warmed his bones and the company warmed his heart.

He spoke of dancing with Guinevere in the courtyard in the moonlight, the fragrance of the flowers in her hair…

He spoke of chasing his falcon through the woods on a warm summer day, racing through the trees and laughing into the wind…

He spoke of jousting with Lancelot, a friendly practice duel, the snorts of their horses in the dusty yard, the stomping of hooves as they circled each other, the cheers of the crowd, the way his heart raced as he charged at last with his lance held high…

He spoke of Guinevere dancing around the maypole with the village children in the spring, twirling colorful ribbons…

He spoke of Camelot, the castle's towers tall and strong in the first light of dawn, her banners flapping proudly in the wind.

Most of all, he spoke of his dream, the dream of a better world that had guided him all those years.

And suddenly, the blue jewel glowed, and the clouds above him parted, and sunlight shafted down upon King Arthur of Camelot. He spread his black wings wide, and his feathers refracted rainbows, and suddenly the whole city of London was looking up at him and the traffic of Trafalgar Square was still and silent and everyone was dreaming of Camelot together. Strangers smiled and greeted each other. Some even embraced. A soft rainbow glow bathed the grimy streets. People saw the crow and the horse and the pony and the fox and the badger and the polecat, and they remembered that there was wild magic in everything, and *everyone*—even in a plain, black, ordinary bird.

King Arthur cawed and gazed down at the people of England.

"Good people of England," said King Arthur, his wings still lit from above with a bright rainbow glow, "remember this day. Be chivalrous with each other, find nobility in the ordinary, and remember the wild spirit of this green country. Remember our stories. Remember magic. Remember… remember Camelot."

The people nodded. The rainbow light shivered around them, like a pearlescent reflection of ocean waves. Suddenly, there was one last flash, and the rainbow was gone. The jewel was gone, too. All that remained was a crow in a metal strainer, holding a wooden ladle.

The people of London resumed their hurried bustling to nowhere. The traffic flowed on. But King Arthur still stood proudly and happily at the top of the statue, Excalibur in his grasp and Camelot in his heart.

***

Penny was found by her old master and started giving carriage tours around London again. She is much happier about her job now, for there are greener pastures even than the ones of Avalon in her mind. She keeps the rainbow dream of Camelot close to her heart and gives every crow she sees a second glance.

Dreamy was adopted by a traveling circus, and now she goes on many adventures of her own. She babbles excitedly about her time with King Arthur to anyone who will listen.

The fox, badger, and polecat slunk back to their wild wood. They live there still, roving through the trees, guarded by a wizard with a twinkle in his eye.

And King Arthur? Well...

King Arthur still roams London as a crow. To the rest of the world, it might seem as though England has forgotten his message, the great stories he told on that fateful day. For, on the surface, it seems as though nothing has changed. But King Arthur knows better. He has learned to see Camelot in the little things: in flowers brought to a tired cleaning lady after a long work day, in a father pushing a child on a swing set at the playground. He finds rainbow traces of Camelot everywhere he looks: even in gutters, even in his simple life as a crow. And he is happy.

Someday, while you are in London, take a second look at an ordinary black feather that has fallen on the ground on some grimy street. You may see an echo of Camelot there, a shivering rainbow light to brighten even your darkest days.

*When a cat gives you an appraising look, like you're
failing to meet even their most lenient standards, they may
well be composing an academic essay in their head about
how foolish all of us humans are.*

THE HUMAN-ENGLISH LEXICON: NOTES FROM AN ANTHRO-XENO-BIOLOGIST

A. Humphrey Lanham

The human-English lexicon—for whatever inane reason—has ascribed a unique collective noun for all manner of animals. And as always, the humans have done so in an incredibly bizarre and opportunistic way. As an anthro-xeno-biologist and accomplished feline, I am submitting my notes for review.

Some animals, naturally, have and deserve their descriptors, for they are in need of organization and someone telling them what to do. Wolves, for example, and especially their domesticated *lesser* cousins are described in collection as a pack.

And dogs, to their credit, have taken this title to heart, collecting anyone and everyone that resides in their master's domain as their "pack" and making all sorts of ruckus to protect said "pack" from intruders such as the mailman, the suspicious squirrel, and the unscheduled gust of wind.

Sheep in turn have the descriptor of flock. A term used to describe both the wooly beasts on four legs and the "sheeple" of various political and religious leanings. Herd seems to be a common descriptor for at least two dozen different animal species from elephants to asses.

Beyond the sensical collective nouns, humans decided to get "punny" coming up with all sorts of unnecessary terms, created in the name of cleverness. A chatter of budgies, a zeal of zebras, and a glimmer of goldfish all replace pre-established and perfectly acceptable terms such as flock, herd, and school.

But one of the most insulting terms they have ascribed must surely be a murder of crows. As a highly read cat, I can tell you, while crows are known to congregate around dead things, they are no better than the common venue of vultures circling around a rotting carcass. They are more closely related to dental floss, extricating bits of gristle from betwixt teeth, than to anything to which the word *murder* ought to be applied.

At the same time, cats are denoted in plural as a clowder. Really? Surely our species is far more deserving of the collective noun, murder, than the scavenging crow. We are fierce monsters. Hunters of moths and mice and laser beams. We are the silent bringers of death. And when our humans attach those dreadful bells to our necks, we are the bell that tolls.

No. For whatever reason, the human species has taken it upon itself to name things with such human whimsy as to be absurd. But a collective noun they have neglected to define is one for their own species. A presumptuous lapse in judgement if you ask me.

They have lofty terms for themselves: a people, a culture, a society. But these are as separative and divisive as they are descriptive. A crowd might suffice. But, again, the term crowd has a variety of denotations and connotations that affect the meaning in any number of ways. And in general, a crowd is large and overwhelming in number.

So, as an anthro-xeno-biologist, I submit for the record three suggestions to add to the human-English lexicon that should be satisfactorily descriptive and punny enough for the human ear. I believe after four years of observation that these terms could arguably apply to as few as three humans in *my* house and as many as the entire population of Earth.

And they are: a confusion of humans, an argument of humans, or, dare I say, a clusterfuck of humans.

Take a journey with Shadowpaw Jones into the dark side of Kittytown to see if he can find a ray of light, among all the shades of gray.

CURIOSITY KILLS
Blake Hutchins

When Zozo Linn slipped onto the barstool next to me at *Mouthfriends*, a felian pub on the west side of Kittytown, I sniffed something was up. His ears rotated back to monitor the rest of the room and he smelled of fear. He growled at the bartender to bring him a pint of the IPA on tap and a shot of Maker's 45. It was a little after eleven a.m., but I was drinking my lunch too, so I didn't judge.

Zozo was an acquaintance from the early days of the Change. I'd have said friend, but he wasn't the kind of lick who tolerated others well enough to have friends. His irascible streak made my alley cat attitude look like sunshine and mariachi bands. I'd heard he was into making software these days. If it kept him from interacting with people, it was a win-win for the world.

He cut straight to the pounce. "Shadowpaw Jones. I wanna hire you. Right freakin' now. Can we talk?" Black-framed acetate glasses made his silver-green eyes huge. Staring at a screen all day must have been murder on them.

"We're talking now." I poked a claw tip at the cardboard coaster in front of me. It sported a woodcut cartoon of a beaming cat face holding a dead rat in its jaws.

I'd come by for a quick bite and a break from the crowd of sign-wavers and chanters occupying the sidewalks outside my office. The pub was quiet other than a couple licks sharing a basket of chicken strips near the door, and a few others watching a Blazers game on a small TV set up in the opposite corner. It smelled of craft beer, bacon, and disinfectant. Lighting was dim, just the way our kind liked it.

I wasn't interested in company. At the same time, I was curious, which has gotten me into endless buckets of trouble.

Zozo eyed the bartender. "Maybe I don't wanna discuss things in public."

"I have an office. Make an appointment."

His lip curled. "Fine. We can talk here, but keep it down."

"You got a problem with my office?"

"No, I just don't want to walk through the Bast-be-damned protestors. It's all over the news."

"So take the back way in." I tipped the glass to lap up the last of my tequila, then turned it upside down on the bar's scarred wood surface, carefully avoiding the cheery little coaster. "You picking up the tab?"

A pause. "If I have to."

"How about that. My schedule just opened up." I gave him my full attention.

Zozo had put on a little weight since I saw him last. His light gray and silver fur practically glowed next to my black striped tabby coat, not to mention the inky black mitts that had inspired my name. The glasses made him look respectable until you spotted the fire engine red Death Tuna T-shirt under his plaid jacket. A pinstriped trilby hat and a laptop bag slung over his shoulder completed the hipster look. If he'd been an Ape, he'd have sported one of those giant chin fur monstrosities they called beards in this town. I called them chipmunk nests without the benefit of actual chipmunks.

Me, I wore a nondescript black wool coat over the usual Goodwill leftovers pulled from the kid rack. I preferred my trusty bomber jacket, but had found out the hard way that leather creaked too much for investigative work in K-town. Felian ears were too sharp.

I tapped my glass with a meaningful claw. The barkeep nodded. He was a brown and ginger tom with a pierced lip and one of those fake tails all the kittens were wearing these days, since whatever was behind the Change hadn't seen fit to leave us our originals. The fake waggled like a lime green dust-mop at his back as he clambered up the ladder to fetch the Cuervo off the wall of bottles. Most Kitties were toddler-sized compared to Apes, hence the necessity of ladders or catwalks in these joints. I wasn't a regular here, or he'd have known to keep the Cuervo at sea level.

"Tell me what's eating you," I said to Zozo.

"Jesus Bast-lickin' Christ, what makes you think something's eating me?"

"Something's always eating you. You smell spooked."

"Fine. Yeah. Whatever. I need help, smart ass." He put his hat on the table, licked his handpaw and ran it over his head a couple of times. "I started a tech co-op last year. Code Tygers. Got a leg up from FFEA tax credits." At my blank look, he explained, "Federal Felian Employment Act."

I yawned. He didn't like that.

"Go to hell, lick," he snarled. "We're in the same building as you. Just moved in, so we're neighbors. You want the job, show a little respect."

"You're the master of irony. How about I listen nice and quiet as long as I'm drinking your booze?"

"Fine, be that way. Where was I?"

"You're about to tell me what wants to eat you."

"Alright, yeah. So I've been mentoring this young queen, Blaze Hawthorne. She's real good, a natural coder, damn smart. I taught her a bunch, showed her the ropes. She's cute too, which never hurts. She helped me set up the network security for Code Tygers."

He took a swig of beer, wiped his mouth on a napkin, and fished a folded piece of paper out of his laptop bag. "This is her." He flipped it down on the bar in front of me like he was a blackjack dealer. I opened it with one handpaw while enjoying a lap of tequila from the glass in my other.

The picture was printed out on low-quality paper. Resolution was grainy, the colors muted. None of that mattered for Blaze Hawthorne. Wide green eyes and a brilliant white-fanged smile shone out at me like a burst of sunlight. Her coat was black with a white throat and a matching white streak that shot from between delicate ears to the tip of her nose like a comet. She wore a pale blue fringed top and a pink ball cap tipped back. The top sported a grinning cartoon monkey face with X's for eyes. A piece of indistinct jewelry gleamed on her chest.

I liked her right away. She was the kind of queen I'd have fought a hundred toms over back in the cat days.

"Damn cute," I murmured. "Where'd you meet her?"

"Ah, you know. A dancer at Kit-Kat Blue, near Ross Island." By that, he meant the Ross Island Bridge, Portland's working-class hood on the east side of the Willamette River. The west side was high-end apartments and office space for people who made their coffee with little plastic pods. Kit Kat Blue was a felian strip club.

I wrinkled my nose. "You're a regular Pygmalion, Zo. What's the problem with her you want me to fix?"

"She stole something from me. I want it back, and I want it fast."

"Owe someone money?"

"You could say that, yeah."

Zozo downed his shot, closed his eyes to soak it up, then eyed the glass as if he were considering a refill. When he spoke again, his voice was quiet. "A few days ago, Blaze took off. I didn't find out until yesterday what she'd taken." He made a face like he'd eaten a spider—which I've done, by the way. They taste terrible.

"How do you know it was her?"

"She's the only one who knew what it was."

"You want me to track her down for you," I said.

"Yeah. But no charges, none of that cop bullshit. I just want my property back, nice and quiet."

"What'd she swipe?"

He licked his lips, as if his mouth had gone dry. "Jewelry."

"Jewelry. A ring?" I figured it must be valuable and sentimental, though I had a hard time imagining a Kitty like Zozo being sentimental about anything.

"A pendant. A little gold rectangle with a tiger that has ruby eyes."

"Actual rubies? Is it valuable?"

"Yeah," he breathed. "Damn valuable. I—" He bit off what he was going to say, then blurted, "She was my Bast-be-damned assistant, Shady! How could she do this to me?"

"You were sleeping with her, weren't you? And she rolled you." I patted his shoulder. "It wouldn't be the first time a pretty face made a tom stupid."

The silence pouring off him spoke volumes. I sensed the attention of the other felians in the room, and the bartender started humming to himself in a polite pretense of not hearing every word of our conversation.

Zozo took his glasses off and did some vigorous grooming to settle down. When he was done, he replaced the glasses on his mug and glared at me.

"So you gonna do this?" he asked.

"Got a home address for this queenie?"

"Yeah. Hold on." He showed me a street address on his phone. I copied it down on a napkin, along with Blaze Hawthorne's phone number.

"You been over there since the theft?"

He scratched his neck. "You kidding me? She'd see me coming and high-tail it so fast I wouldn't even sniff her vapor trail."

"Alright, I'll sniff around there to start. Anything else you can tell me about her? Drugs? A monster brother? Concealed carry?"

"Nah, she's a freakin' pacifist, a real do-gooder. Sticks her nose into everything, just like you. You'd like her. Hell, *I* liked her, and you know I don't like anybody. All-around gold star social justice warrior, that's her, always on a crusade about some bullshit."

I didn't like the way this was shaping up. Blaze Hawthorne looked like a manipulative thief on the one hand and a decent person on the other. The easy way I reconciled those two stories came at Zozo's expense. I wondered what he wasn't telling me.

"Nothing illegal here?" I said.

He hesitated before saying, "I swear to Bast."

"Not real credible, buddy."

"Look, it's a flash drive, holding data. Proprietary stuff, OK? Worth a lot to my business. We made… commitments." Fear smelled thick on him.

"Who's after you, Zo?"

"After me? Nobody. But… I *need* that tiger pendant back. Like yesterday."

I waited, but he didn't spill any more info. Clearly he was in trouble from somebody sketchy who would be unhappy if they knew this data of his had gotten loose. But equally clearly, he wasn't ready to say more about it yet.

A job is a job. I wasn't so flush I could tell him to go chase birds.

"Alright," I told him. "My rates are two-fifty a day plus expenses. Two days up front as a retainer."

"Jesus Cats, that's robbery."

"Almost half what you'd cough up for an Ape P.I., lick."

After a pause long enough to give himself face, Zozo grunted agreement and fished out his Visa to pay the tab. I tossed a few bills onto the bar for a tip and told him to send the retainer via PayPal. On the way out, I used one of the courtesy scratching posts set up for customers. It always paid to keep your claws sharp in this town.

***

I figured I'd start the hunt at the most obvious entry point, which was also the least likely place I'd find Blaze Hawthorne: her home. Assuming she really lived there.

The address Zozo texted me was on Frampton and 68th, far enough I didn't feel like walking. I hiked back to my office and took my scooter, a street-legal Mao Mao with a 50cc engine and a seat sized for felians.

It was typical March weather for Stumptown. Slivers of blue sky showed through the tumbledown cloud pattern like rips in a cocktail dress. The rain had mostly let up, which was an improvement, but the wind was being an asshole. I fought the scooter twenty blocks down Sandy before I gave up, parked it at a Jack in the Box, and padded it the rest of the way. I envied the detectives from the old days who could look up phone numbers attached to actual houses, then call and ask if someone lived there before you trekked out to try to find them. There wasn't an app for that, though.

Actually, there probably was. The human world moved faster than a panicked mouse on a parquet floor. And with about as much thought, if you asked me.

Like most of K-town, this neighborhood had been pretty nice once upon a time, before the Change. I'd seen the pictures. Now pushing three hundred thousand Kitties packed into close quarters amid converted housing and hastily thrown up cinder block apartments, Kittytown had become, not to put too fine a point on it, a densely packed ghetto. Kittens were out playing on porches under eaves, toms and queens crouched practically anywhere that offered shelter from the weather. I felt a hundred pairs of eyes tracking me. That was an uncomfortable reality of felian psychology. We liked to observe, not be observed. And like anyplace in K-town, everywhere was somebody's territory. Every doorway, phone pole, and fence corner carried a dozen different scent markings alongside felian gang tags sprayed on fences and walls in Ape rather than Kitty fashion.

The Apes wondered why we fought so much amongst ourselves. Something had to give, eventually. There was talk of a second Kittytown going up in Southeast, but those plans were stalled in city government last I'd heard.

By the time I walked up the path to an olive-green bungalow with a porch that spanned the entire front of the house, it was just after noon. The yard was lush and overgrown, with grass up to my hips and an overly optimistic cherry tree pumping out pink blossoms and enough scent to overpower territory scent markings. The paint on the sidings was flaking, and a dirty-sock smell of mold threaded its way in among the cherry blossoms' perfume. Typical K-town, in other words: scungier the closer you sniffed it.

A rangy ginger-and-white tabby wearing a denim jacket and cargo pants lounged in a scratched-up recliner on the porch, smoking a cigarette and reading a paperback. I approved of the latter activity. He was a younger tom, maybe a bit over five in old cat years, a kitten at the time of the Change. His left ear held three hoops, the right only one. A red and black Blazers logo peeked out from the open jacket. The book was titled *Strategies for Resistance: The New War*. Five black mailboxes were screwed onto the siding outside the door.

"Yo," the tom said, not looking up from the page he was pretending to read. "What's your biz, catty cat?"

"Looking for Blaze Hawthorne," I replied. "Know her?"

"Who you with?"

I didn't like his tone. "Santa Claws. He's coming early this year and I'm checking his list."

He did look up at that, yellow eyes flaring as smoke plumed from his mouth. "Beat it, asslicker."

"Make me."

He tossed the cigarette aside, dropped the book on an upside-down bucket, and jumped up. We stared at each other, ears flattened. He was taller, but I was bulkier. A low growl built in his throat, rising in pitch, and I bared my fangs. He feinted a claw slash. Resisting the desire to flay his pink nosepad open, I stepped inside and punched him in the gut, like my former cop buddy Flanagan taught me back when we were on friendly terms. The lick doubled over. I grabbed him by the scruff, twisted his arm, and jammed him over the porch balustrade to give him a chance to catch his breath and reconsider his social strategy. He had one of those fake tails like the bartender, except this one was black with a bright red tuft that reminded me of a blood-dipped flag. It pressed against my belly in an irritating way.

"Let's try again, now that we're comfortable," I said. "I popped by to look in on Blaze."

"She… she ain't home," he gasped. "Motherfucker!"

I twisted again. "Manners."

"She ain't home, I said!" This time he didn't add anything unhelpful.

"See? That was easy. You going to behave?"

"Yeah." He sounded surly, but he wasn't fighting me. Felian dominance, once established, tended to stick for the duration.

I let him go and stepped back in case he'd lied and wanted to take it to claws. He didn't. Instead, he massaged his forearm. His body language was a lot more respectful. We made introductions. His name was Skeets Glisan, another stray.

"You know Blaze?" I asked.

"Everyone knows Blaze," he said. "She in trouble?"

"Maybe. That's what I'm trying to find out."

"You a cop?"

"C'mon, there are no Kitty cops."

He chewed on that for a second. "Yeah, that's right. OK, Roxy's up there now. I better take you up."

"Roxy your girlfriend?"

That produced a grimace. "Not mine."

I twitched a whisker at that, but he didn't explain, just led me inside. What was once the entrance to a living room was now a dark, enclosed hallway with three doors to the ground floor apartments, and a fourth sporting the universal bathroom sign. Someone had used a Sharpie to add cat ears and whiskers to the little human icons. There was just enough room left over for a narrow set of stairs leading up. I doubted anything here was up to code.

I followed Skeets up the creaking staircase to a landing so tight it needed grease for two felians to squeeze past each other. Neither of us was hampered by the lack of lighting. Two doors led off the landing. The first was ajar. Skeets pushed it open and motioned for me to enter. There was no sign of forced entry.

I slid by him into a tiny studio barely big enough to hold a beat up paisley love seat and a narrow dresser bland enough to look coughed up from IKEA. The former had seen better days, given that its guts were strewn all over the scratched hardwood floor. A bright green rubber raincoat was draped over one arm. Behind the sofa was a tiny window shaded by gauzy yellow curtains. The place smelled of lemon, catnip, felians, and pot. The dresser drawers were scattered on the floor amid a chaotic jumble of clothes and other items. A brick and cinder block bookcase was wedged up against the wall opposite the couch, its shelves swept clean.

A tough-looking gray and white tabby queen whirled at my entrance and hissed. Her eyes were the color of new pennies. I held my handpaws up, palms out, claws in. "Easy. I'm a family friend of Blaze's. Shadowpaw Jones. You must be Roxy."

"He says Blaze is in trouble," added the oh-so-helpful Skeets from behind me. I resisted the urge to cuff him and his stupid plastic and wire tail out the window. It wasn't high enough of a drop to make it count.

The queen nodded. She was wearing a faded gray blouse, lots of arm bangles, a striped green headband, and a long, beaded necklace. Her jeans were fashionably ripped, showing bright patches of fur. A blue tail with a feathery texture stuck out behind her. What was it with these kittens and their fake tails? She was pretty, though not in Blaze's class.

"I don't actually know for sure she's in real trouble." I gestured at the room. "Or didn't before now. It's obvious she's in a jam. You must be Roxy."

She took a posture of agreement. Skeets leaned over and tried to lay a comforting handpaw on her shoulder, but she shrugged him off, ears back. I gave her a little space to collect herself.

A quick scan confirmed the obvious: place had been ransacked. The kitchenette's drawers had been dumped onto the floor, along with the contents of two tiny cupboards and a mini-fridge. They hadn't been gentle, whoever it was. Broken glass and spilled food were part of the mess. A partial paw print in hummus told me it wasn't Apes, and that the perps had been in a hurry. At the same time, they'd been methodical. Whoever had done this knew what they were looking for: something small enough to be easily hidden. I noticed a few claw scratches where that someone had tested the baseboard molding. They'd been thorough.

The couch was more interesting. The cushions showed three long, straight slashes, equally spaced. They hadn't been torn open, which meant the searcher had used a knife rather than felian claws. A sharp knife. That might mean a human. Or a savvy felian who didn't want to leave traces of paw scent or claw scales behind.

After what I figured was a decent interval, I introduced myself to the queen, showed her my PI license, and gave her my business card. Her full name turned out to be Roxy Stark, the street name-as-surname telling me she was strayborn, like Blaze. And me.

She groomed to calm herself, applying dainty licks to her wrist and paw and a few daubs at her cheek and temple. I tried not to stare. No hummus on her feet, so I ruled her out as the source of the kitchen print.

"How do you know Blaze?" I asked.

"She's my girlfriend." She glanced at me. "Does that shock you?"

I shrugged. Nothing really shocked me anymore.

She dropped her gaze. "She's always busy, but I haven't heard from her in a couple days. So yeah, I'm worried."

"You live together?"

"Sometimes. I mean, I got my own place."

Skeets made a strangled noise. She shot him an irate look.

"Hey buddy," I said. "A little privacy, OK?"

He was smart enough to take the hint, though he shot me a glare on his way out that told me we'd tangle again sometime. After I heard the door close behind him at the bottom of the stairs, I turned my ears toward Roxy.

"Sorry about that," she said. "Skeets puffs up a lot." She gave me the once-over, her pupils dilating a little. "He doesn't have your strut."

"You embarrassed about your relationship with Blaze?" I asked, dragging the conversation back on track.

She blinked. "Nah, I wasn't. Blaze wasn't real public about it, though. Same sex relationships are new for us. You know."

"I thought she had a boyfriend."

To my surprise, she said, "I wouldn't be surprised."

"You're not jealous?"

"Why would I be? That's for Apes."

That checked out. Felians would fight over someone in the moment at the drop of a hat, but didn't seem to have the same kind of attachment patterns as Apes. One more reason humans stereotyped us as promiscuous and flaky. Sometimes we did get jealous, though.

"What brought you here?" I gestured at the room.

She turned those bright penny eyes onto me. "I told you. I was worried. The place was like this when I got here. What do you think?"

I glanced around. "Well, Blaze wasn't here when it happened. This has all the earmarks of a search, not an abduction. Stuff's all over, but it's methodical. No sign of a fight. See, the lamps aren't knocked over, things are spread out as if someone was going through it all. There's no smell of blood or signs of stress shedding. They knew what they were looking for. Was the door open when you got here?"

"Unlocked, but closed." She frowned. "You think she wasn't here?"

"Not since this morning at least. Bedding still looks partly folded, so either she'd put it away or she wasn't here to start with."

"Oh, OK. That makes sense."

"Any idea where she might go?" I asked.

She laughed. "Me? No, I wish. She had her paws in a lot of pies. She was working with someone on the resistance, volunteering—"

"The resistance?" That term made my ears perk up. "You mean the protests?"

"Right. The Save Kittytown scrap. She liked to call it 'the community resistance.' She's intense like that. Always going on about 'the community' this, 'the community' that."

"Yeah, I heard she liked to volunteer. What was she doing for the 'resistance?'"

She folded her arms. "Lots of stuff. I don't know, community organizing, door to door stuff maybe. Lots of meetings."

"Did she seem scared?"

"Blaze wasn't scared of anything."

"I guess not."

I did a closer scan of the room, stepping carefully to avoid the broken glass and foodstuffs, sniffing at the drawer pulls to see if the intruders left anything. All I got was more Blaze scent, Roxy's lavender, a bit of Skeets, some random shedding that could have come from any of them or another kitty. The hummus smelled like hummus, and it was room temperature, but still fresh. The intruders had to have been here in the last few hours, but I wasn't picking up their scent, which meant they'd been damned careful. Whoever had stepped in that hummus, it wasn't Roxy or Skeets.

A small framed photo on the floor caught my eye, and I crouched for a closer look. It showed Blaze outside somewhere, in the rain, smiling up at the camera as drops glittered on her fur. She looked happy. Her apple green eyes reminded me of spring. I slipped the photo into my coat pocket, then went over and lifted the gauzy curtain to peer out toward the street.

The porch roof made it impossible to see if Skeets was still there, but the rain was coming down for real now, like a long exhale.

I let the curtain fall. "You got somewhere else to go? Not your den, somewhere else safe."

"I have friends." Roxy laughed. "You don't think I'm—"

"Someone tore up this place looking for something Blaze has. If they figure you know something, they might come for you, either to see if you have it, or as leverage."

"Oh, I… yeah, I have someone I can hang with." A pause. "You sure you're not a cop?"

"Anything but, kitten. You have my card. Call if you feel like you're in trouble."

She said she would. I made sure she texted her friend, then waited while she called Uber for a ride. She threw a few small items of clothing into a plastic shopping bag, along with toiletries scavenged from the floor. I did a little more snooping while she was busy. Next to the couch in a chunk of ripped foam and cotton quilting, I found something interesting: a couple of fresh twenty-two rounds in their brass casing. They smelled faintly of Blaze. I pocketed them and straightened when the cessation of air movement in the room told me Roxy was ready. I wondered where the pistol was.

"This might sound odd," I said, "but did Blaze have any way of protecting herself? Like a knife or a gun?"

She frowned. "She had a concealed carry permit. She said she owned a gun, but she never showed it to me."

"Probably smart of her. Thanks. Sounds like she can take care of herself."

Roxy shook her head. "You could say that. She's got a temper, that one. Her name fit her. She was on fire about everything." She flashed those bright penny eyes at me and purred, "That's what I loved about her."

"You ready?" I asked, and Roxy nodded. She was acting brave, but I smelled her anxiety. It made me feel protective. The sooner she was somewhere else—somewhere safe—the better.

When we walked outside onto the damp porch, Skeets and his book were nowhere in sight or sniff. An orange flyer peeked out from under the couch where he'd been sitting. I snagged it with a claw. It had a crease indicating it'd been folded in half, and sported a cat that was half white skeleton on a black backdrop and half a black cat on a white background. The paper held a whisker of Skeets's scent. It read *Alive and Dead*, and gave an address far up on Northeast. A live show featuring a bunch of bands I'd never heard of, with names that ranged from the absurd to the just plain dumb. I snorted and dropped it on the couch.

Roxy took an inquiring pose.

"Someone forgot his bookmark," I told her.

She rolled her eyes. "He's always reading that political stuff. I don't get it."

"You're not political?"

"I got dreams, mister. They come first."

A maroon Volvo with an Uber sticker in the window pulled up to the curb. Roxy gave me a curt nod and trotted through the rain to her ride, fake tail bobbing behind her. I watched her go and wondered what it'd be like to be a younger lick. This generation that hadn't been cats long enough for it to stick, along with the kittens being born who were never cats at all, they were something new I didn't understand. Nobody did, Apes included. Me, I was a loner who still remembered when life was about fighting, fucking, hunting, and sleeping in the sun. On the two days every year when Portland had sun, that is. Sometimes I felt like the world was leaving me behind, like I was part of a species going extinct. After my generation died, who would remember the the yowling, red-clawed dreams of cats?

Rain pelted the yard and sidewalk with thick, cold drops. A gauzy curtain of water trailed out of the bungalow's blocked gutters, and the wind slapped some of it into my face. I pulled out my hip flask and took a bracing nip. It was going to be a wet, chilly slog back to the scooter. From the couch, the half-dead cat on the flyer seemed to regard me with amusement.

"You ain't kidding, brother," I told it before stepping into the weather. "I'll be lucky to be only half-dead before I get home."

***

The rain didn't change to hail on me until a couple of blocks away from the old school building that housed my office. The Save Kittytown protesters weren't waiting outside, which meant they had the common sense to stay out of the rain. Since the building had been converted to a Felian Enterprise Zone post-Change, it had served as a poster child for the kind of investment the community supposedly wanted, so I guessed it made sense as a rallying point for protest. I sympathized, but I wasn't a joiner. The protests had been murder on my already decrepit customer traffic. No one liked to run a gauntlet, especially when they wanted to keep a low profile. I'd been using the back entrance myself, and I lived there.

A half-dozen posters had been taped to the building's main doors. They displayed slogans like *Save Kittytown from the MAN*, and *Stop Unjust Eviction!* You saw that kind of thing all over Portland these days. Political causes bred in this town like mice in a pantry.

But someone had tagged the wall nearby with the message FLF NOW. That bothered me.

Soon after the Change, the Felian Liberation Front had cropped up as an organization of Kitty revolutionaries who hunted down the worst of the Ape speciesists, using guns, arson, and pipe bombs to take out their prey. Ape law enforcement labeled "the Fluff"—as some comedian had dubbed the FLF—an active domestic terror organization. Even though it hadn't been active in years, humans still considered FLF *the* big felian boogeyman. The painted letters here smelled relatively fresh. I went inside to shake hail pebbles out of my wet fur and grab a quick catnap before going out again to look for Blaze. I'd have to pick up my own can of spray paint to cover up the FLF tags. Ape paranoia already had a huge appetite. I didn't want it in my yard.

Once inside, I hung my wet coat on the hook by the door and peeled down to fur, tossing the soggy stuff in the hamper. The school had working locker rooms and bathrooms, so I didn't see the need to keep a separate residence, though I didn't advertise that I lived in my business space. I toweled off and brushed my fur. After I was done, I grabbed dry clothes from the cardboard boxes in the closet. I wasn't exactly the most finicky Kitty in terms of housekeeping. Once I was comfortable, I settled at my desk with the photo of Blaze I'd taken from the apartment and brought José out of his drawer for a business meeting, along with a strip of jerky I kept there for reasons. I wasn't a total barbarian, so I poured the tequila into a shot glass and toasted José's bottle before I took my first lap. Señor Cuervo was a good partner for helping me think through a case.

I didn't like how this job was shaping up. Someone had done a thorough job tearing up the apartment, which meant Blaze definitely had something someone wanted real bad, most likely that damned tiger pendant. Zozo wasn't being straight with me. The next time I saw him, I figured I'd tell him to loosen up his tongue if he didn't want to wear it for a tie. I needed to know why the pendant was so important, and why he was afraid.

Roxy seemed mostly on the level, but her presence in the apartment bugged me for reasons I couldn't put a claw into. She didn't seem Blaze's type. I wanted more info before I braced her. And Skeets had been on the porch keeping a watch, I was pretty sure. More questions than answers so far.

Blaze. I regarded her picture as I dabbed my tongue into the tequila. Her face didn't strike me as that of a duplicitous thief. Zozo said she was a do-gooder. Roxy had mentioned her being active with "the resistance" and helping the K-town community. Stealing from a mentor didn't square up with that kind of idealism.

Unless what she stole from Zo made it square.

Careful, Shady, I told myself. You're a bit too interested in this queen.

A peek through the blinds confirmed the rain had started again. Across the street, a shiny black sedan with tinted windows and hubcaps so new you could eat off them had pulled up. In this neighborhood, it stuck out like a tank in a playground. I watched it for a few minutes. No one got out, and I let the blinds snap shut. The gloom of the office suited my felian eyes just fine, though an Ape would have found it too dark.

I was missing something; I was sure of it.

I didn't know where Roxy was, but I needed to know what Zozo thought was so important on that thumb drive. That made my next step pretty damn clear. Time to go visit my new neighbors.

***

It was almost four o'clock when I stepped into Code Tygers. Zozo's outfit was located on the other side of the school's main entrance, in a couple of adjoining classrooms that had at one time been separated by a sliding room divider set in ceiling tracks and opened accordion-style. The window curtains were open to let in Portland's anemic daylight through a wall of windows. Zozo had put down a gray berber carpet and covered the walls with art prints mounted on canvas, most of which appeared to be moonlit paintings of streets and alleys, subtle shapes and shadowy close ups of doorways. I thought I recognized the artist, a local lick who went by Grindlebeet. The layout was a kitbash of surplus, Ape-sized laminate desks interspersed with pots of ferns, catnip plants, and chewing grass, plus a couple of water coolers that stood like goalposts at opposite ends of the room. A few cheap wood and rice paper folding dividers broke up the wide open feel. In one corner, floor-to-ceiling cubical walls cordoned off what I assumed was a meeting space. A few cardboard boxes were stacked next to a big whiteboard. A half-dozen felians, almost all of them wearing glasses, peered intently at their laptops. At the very back of the room, Zozo waited behind a huge glossy desk with two big monitors squatting on the cherry finish, the pinstriped trilby tipped back on his silver tabby head.

"You find it?" he demanded as I drew near.

"Nice place," I countered, hopping up on the chair before his beast of a desk. "You must have gotten a deal on the furnishings."

He ignored the comment, his posture and gaze staying interrogatory.

I leaned back and braced a footpaw on the edge of his desk. "You want to talk here?" I rotated my ears back to indicate the rest of the room.

"Conference room," he grumbled. He led me to the space cordoned off in the corner, where the tall soundproofing dividers barely enclosed a mahogany-finish conference table the shape of a medicine capsule with a speaker phone that looked like a black cough drop. Humans would have found the room uncomfortably cramped, but it was just about right for felians. There was still the oversized furniture to deal with, but we were used to that.

Once the door closed and we'd seated ourselves, I started. "I haven't found it yet, but there's been some interesting developments. Someone tore up Blaze's digs."

He winced. "Shit. Any idea who?"

"Someone who wanted to find that pendant real bad. What did Blaze really steal?"

"Data."

"Mouse-shit. There's more to it than that. Give."

There was a long pause. I waited. Silence can be your friend in a negotiation—or an interrogation. A lot of people get uncomfortable and end up talking to fill the quiet.

"Alright," Zozo said at last, gaze fixed on his clenched handpaws. "You know the New Sunrise Project?"

"I might have an inkling. Let's see… is it the construction project in K-town everyone's fluffed up over? The reason protesters are waving Bast-be-damned signs outside my building?"

"*Our* building, smart ass. But yeah, that's it. Scumbag real estate speculators, probably from Taiwan or China. They wanna rezone North K-town, throw up a couple super-pricey thirty-story brick hairballs nobody will occupy, surround them with yuppie strip malls and Starbucks, drive rents into orbit—fuck those sons of bitches. Apes, they don't give a rat's ass about us, am I right?"

I shrugged off the rant. It was an old story in the Portland metro region. Skyrocketing rents were forcing Apes and Kitties alike into the burbs. Like with other cities around the country, Portland's K-town had been a special set-aside in the chaos following the Change. Humans had been terrified that whatever power, God or aliens or whatever, had transformed every cat in the world into fuzzy little humanoids overnight would turn all the Apes back into monkeys if they stepped out of line. So we got all kinds of juicy federal and state programs, subsidies, and education thrown at us right out of the gate. Instant civil rights, no strings attached.

Now, six years later, Ape memories were short. Strings happened.

"Go on," I prompted.

"Blaze and I are part of the K-town community organizing to fight this bullshit, OK? Protests, petition to city hall, referendum signatures, letter writing. Save Kittytown."

"I've heard of it. Sniffed the entrance of a meeting once. That was it. You know me, I'm not a joiner."

"Well, it's all above-board stuff, I swear to Bast. Research, library visits, records offices. Rallies. Web searches. Talking with people."

"What kind of people?"

"C'mon, you know. *Apes*. They're the ones who run everything." He spat the word like a rat had crapped in his mouth. "We wanted to figure out who's really behind the New Sunrise project. We know it's going through Phenom Bank. Commercial real estate investment biz is the big thing right now. Land doesn't go anywhere, unless you're on the Cali coast. And the city council is totally corrupt. Money doesn't just talk, Shadowpaw. It sings like a Bast-pissed siren."

"Old story."

"So what are you gonna do now?"

"Like I said, I have a few more leads. But I notice you still haven't told me what's on the drive. Don't tell me it's just data. That cat won't scratch."

"It's… shit, it's authentication to an online account. With money, OK? A lot of money. That's all you need to know."

"How much money?"

"A *lot*. Trust me. The actual amount's unimportant."

"The hell it is. If it's that much, what are the odds Blaze isn't even in P-town anymore? What do you bet she hasn't just flown off to a new life in Cabo?"

We were both quiet for a bit. Finally he said, "She's not that kind of queen. Trust me, she just ain't."

"You are feeding me a line, Zozo. A bunch of lines. I don't like it."

"Fuck you. A line? What are you talking about?"

I leaned forward, locked my gaze with his. "You've been hiding the ball on this since you hit me up in Mouthfriends. Tell me this: why did she steal it in the first place?"

"I don't get you."

"Tell me, or I walk. I'll refund the retainer and you are on your own."

After a short staredown, his gaze dropped. "She stole it because it's a lot of money, and she's a greedy—"

"Cut it," I said. "You know that's not true. You just got done telling me she's not that kind of queen. You've painted her like a young felian Mother Teresa. What did you plan to do with the money that got her so upset?"

He started to bluster, but I talked over him, feeling hotter by the second. "OK, let's try this theory on for size: Blaze is a social justice warrior with a big heart. You come into a 'lot of money,' and you get excited like a weasel in a cage full of hamsters. You tell her exactly what you're going to do with the money. If it was just a matter of keeping the lion's share for yourself and donating a hefty chunk to worthy causes, I bet she'd be good with that. But that wasn't it, was it? Because you're an angry, Ape-hating son of a bitch. You have different ideas, the kind of ideas that would choke a social justice warrior's conscience like a Bast-pissed noose. The kind of ideas that convince her everyone will be better off if she takes the money and runs."

My mouth tasted bitter, and I paused for a swig of José to clear my palate. "How about it, Zo? Am I on the right track?"

His silence was plenty confirmation. I sniffed I was, indeed, on the money here.

"So," I continued, "the question is what you planned that had her so rattled. From what I know of her, the one thing that seems like it'd get up in her grill hard is violence. So I'm guessing you shared as how you were planning on using those funds to spin up the FLF again, or something like it. Get a bunch of young pissed-off Kitties to start packing heat, train 'em up as hit-cats, form cells and a network, maybe even learn how to make bombs."

"You're nuts," he said, claws out on the mahogany finish. "Hiring you was a huge fuckup." He was about as convincing as a Monopoly money twenty.

I laughed in his face and stretched. "Fine, I'm off the case. Officially, anyway."

"Wait, shit, I didn't say that. Listen, lick, I… I still want you to find Blaze, see if we can fix this."

"I dunno, Zo. Seems like she's in the right here. Or more than you are, anyway."

"I don't want her hurt," he said, his voice quiet. The claws retracted.

"My rate just doubled if you want to stay in the loop."

He sat there and digested this, seething, before his whiskers flattened against his cheeks. "Fine. OK. No more than three days, though."

"Fair enough. Any idea who else might know about this money? You haven't exactly been careful."

"Just me and Blaze were the only ones supposed to know. Maybe she told someone?"

"Maybe so. Someone tore up her lair looking for the tiger, though. Do you know where she did volunteer work?"

"Buncha places. Kittytown flops, Rose City Mission, soup kitchens. I think she's on a river cleanup group too. She goes to a lot of City Council meetings too. I dunno how she has the time."

"She sounds pretty focused."

"Yeah, her politics are..." He bit off what he was going to say, but I could fill in the blanks. Scowling, he added, "She mentioned a friend at the Mission, someone named Becky."

I widened my eyes in mock surprise. "Bast strike me down. You can actually be helpful."

I left him in the conference room and went to find my next hunting spot for Blaze Hawthorne. The fact that this was ultimately about money provided a familiar spoor. Greed offered a pretty clear motive, one I found oddly comforting.

***

The Kittytown flops yielded nothing that evening, no scent whatsoever of Blaze. There was a lot of turnover among volunteers, and not much monitoring of the occupants. It was an outfit run by some humane group just to put a roof over felians' heads, operating out of a warehouse on the northeast side near I-84, so the sounds and smells of freeway traffic provided background ambiance. Aside from separating toms and queens and providing clean bedding, it was a free-for-all. I witnessed two catfights while I was there, and had to stare down one aggro young feral built like a tangle of sticks. His language skills were rudimentary. I could have snapped his neck with a single swat, but to my relief, we came to an understanding without throwing claw. None of the dozen licks I interviewed recognized Blaze from the photo. Feeling relieved to get out of there, I gave them each a few bucks and called it quits.

The next day, after throwing down some coffee, I headed for the next place on my list.

Rose City Mission was a building only its mother could love, a collection of beige blocks lacking windows on the first floor. A tall chain-link fence surrounded a modest parking lot that smelled of wet soil and asphalt, metal, and smoke. The big white wooden cross affixed to the front of the tallest chunk of building looked to me like a single coat of paint slapped over plywood. The sign in the parking lot sported a cheery little red rose next to blue block letters, because one of the architects had slipped up and included a splash of color. I parked the scooter near the entrance and locked my helmet in the pannier.

A few Apes in coats and knit caps stood outside smoking cigarettes. Two Kitties huddled against the wall near the entrance, shivering, but under the overhang and mostly out of the wind. I passed them with a respectful nod, dug into my wallet and pulled out a fiver, handed it to the nearest one, a scruffy lick with matted orange fur. He accepted it with a dignified silence, flicking his ears in thanks, and I continued on my way.

"Yo, furball!" one of the Apes called, "Doors ain't open until five!"

A sign taped to the outside of the door confirmed he was right as far as the rule went. But the door opened anyway, and I went in. I had my sling and a couple of steel balls in my coat pocket. Since I was coming to what amounted to a chapel, I figured it'd be better if I left the hand cannon at home, concealed carry permit or no.

I made my way down a hallway until I came to a reception area like a ticket booth, with a Dutch door painted aircraft carrier gray. Both top and bottom were closed, so I pulled out one of the steel balls and rapped.

After a minute, the top half opened, and an old Ape male with short-cropped gray hair and skin the color of tobacco poked his head out. He wore metal glasses with the big teardrop-shaped lenses cops and military types seemed to love, and a neat checkered shirt under a windbreaker. He smelled a little sour, but not horribly so.

It took him a second to look down and notice me. "We ain't open yet," he pronounced in a voice like a cement mixer. "Another hour."

"I'm not here for your services," I said, holding up the picture I'd taken from Blaze's apartment. "I'm looking for this Kitty."

"Don't know her." He leaned out to get a better look, peering at me suspiciously. "You with the police?"

I shook my head.

"Social services? Immigration?"

"Nope. I just need to find her. People are worried about her. I want to help."

He let out a sigh and his demeanor changed. "Well, that's good of you. You better come to my office. Name's Sipes. I'm the pastor here."

"Shadowpaw Jones," I said. He leaned out and extended a meaty hand. We shook, and I followed him behind the ticket booth down a hallway into a plain white room big enough for a very small desk and two chairs. He settled into the chair behind the desk. The only indication of religious trappings was a frayed poster on the wall behind him that read "Let go, Let GOD" in rainbow letters.

I wasn't impressed by the sentiment, but by the persistence. The Change had cratered a lot of Apes' faith. In this, they suffered almost more psychological trauma than we did. Whole new schools of thought were still popping up as professors and theologians argued about the purpose of the Change, and who or what might be responsible. Everyone was trying to hash out the theological implications or figure out what the aliens' agenda was. Me, I just figured something out there was screwing with us and having a good laugh, like the kind of Ape who used to turn garden hoses on me or toss firecrackers in my cat days.

I showed Pastor Sipes my P.I. license. He examined it closely, handed it back. "Well…" he rumbled. "I guess you're on the level. What can I do for you?"

"There's a person named Becky here who knows this Kitty."

He gave me a slow blink that would have been a friendly gesture of trust and affection from a felian, but for Apes, it was just a sign of the monkey wheels turning.

"There's a lot of women named Becky, son." He gave me a shrewd look. "But it might be you're looking for Rebecca Flores."

I nodded. "Might be."

"She and her kids oughta be here now. Becky has been here since Fall. We don't turn out moms and kids during the day, 'specially in weather."

"Can I see them? Just want to ask a few questions."

He took a slow breath and let it out while he regarded me. "What questions might those be?"

"I'm trying to track down Blaze Hawthorne—" I paused. Something about Sipes's body language tipped me off. A minute stillness in his posture, a flare of his nostrils when I mentioned her name.

"You know her," I said.

"Maybe you better go, Mr. Jones," he said, standing.

I stood on the chair so I could look him straight in the eye. "I have reason to believe this Kitty is in real trouble. I need to find her. You are not helping her by kicking me out. I don't have the answers as to why, but I'm sure I can help." I realized in that moment that I didn't think Blaze was the villain here. My intuition told me there was something else going on, and she was in danger.

He paused, considering, then grunted. "Alright, fine. Guess I gotta trust in the Lord here. You can talk with Becky. But you best be respectful." He cracked a meaty red knuckle and gave me a pointed look. Something was going on here. He was being protective of something.

Or someone.

He escorted me down a cream-colored hallway to a larger room filled with rows of white-framed double bunks, unmade. The mattresses were covered in thick plastic covers and included pillows with similar protection. A few people in there were moving down the rows distributing sheets and blankets onto the beds. They seemed efficient enough. A few beds had already been made up, a few human females on them fussing with young children. I smelled sanitizer, soap, and a bunch of reasonably clean Ape bodies. I caught a whiff of a couple of felians too, but distant. I didn't see any.

"No Kitties?" I asked.

"Felians don't come in until later," Sipes said. "We have a room set aside for them too, queens and kittens apart from toms. We're talking about making rooms for couples, but this was a tough winter. We just make do. Normally we don't let people stay in here during the day, but with moms and kids, we make an exception. Becky's kids have been sick lately, so we gave them some extra privacy."

He spotted who he was looking for and gave my shoulder a little tug. "Come on, Mr. Jones, I see Becky." He led me to a bunkbed where a woman was sorting through a small pile of clothes. A floor fan purred nearby, adding a little false freshness to the air in the room.

I was terrible at telling exact Ape age in years, but I could tell Becky Flores was a young mother. She had medium-length dark hair that needed serious grooming, light brown skin, and wore a plum-colored sweatshirt on over jeans. I spied a suitcase under the bed. A floor fan purred nearby, making a little breeze. Two little girls with similar headfur and coloration peered down at me curiously from the top bunk amid a pile of bedding. They were cute by Ape standards, I supposed. I gave them a little wave, and they giggled, then pulled their heads back.

"This is Rebecca Flores," Sipes said. "Becky, this is Mr. Jones. He's here to ask questions about Miss Hawthorne."

She brushed hair back from her forehead and tucked it behind her ear. "Sure," she said. "I guess."

Sipes stood there with his hands folded in front of him, and I sniffed the discomfort coming off Rebecca Flores. Maybe she was just being shy, or maybe there was an angle here I didn't see yet. He wasn't leaving, but I figured I'd see what I could get out of her before I had to roust him out of there.

"Thanks, Ms. Flores." I put on a smile that didn't show too much fang, and showed her the picture. "I guess you knew Blaze?"

"Yeah."

"Can you tell me what she was like?"

"Nice." Rebecca's gaze kept darting toward Sipes. "Kind."

"Did she talk about herself? Friends, places she liked to go?"

"I dunno. She liked the rain."

"What about the rain?" I wanted to keep her talking.

Rebecca played with her hair behind her ear. "She just liked how it smelled. She had a word for it. I don't remember what it was."

"Damp?" Reverend Sipes suggested. "Mossy?"

Rebecca shook her heard. "No. It was… kind of fancy. I don't know."

"Petrichor, maybe," I said.

"Yeah, that sounds right," she said. "She in trouble?"

Before I could answer, Sipes did. "Mr. Jones is here to help."

"I was just wondering," she said, her eyes focused on me. "The other man and all."

"The other man?" I glanced at Sipes.

He produced a handkerchief and mopped his neck. "Yeah, well. Yesterday evening, another fellow said he wanted to find Ms. Hawthorne. We turned him away. Smelled fishy."

"Good call," I said. "Listen, do you mind if I talk a little more with Ms. Flores alone? I won't take long."

His smile faltered, but after a moment, he nodded. "Of course, of course. I'll be back in the office." He lumbered off, lingering at the door as if he was about to say something, then thought better of it. I waited while his footsteps receded, until I heard him close the door to his office.

As soon as he was gone, the tension bled out of Rebecca Flores. She sat on the lower bunk.

"You with the cops?" she asked.

"Nope."

"Good." She glanced in the direction of the office. "Reverend Sipes, he's a good man, but he…"

"He makes you nervous."

"I don't want to talk about some things in front of him. Wouldn't be proper."

"What kinds of things?"

"He don't know where she works."

"The strip club," I said, and she nodded. "She doesn't work there anymore, right?"

"She had stories, too. About that." She put her finger to her lips, stood and looked into the top bunk. I heard a soft patter of Spanish, high voices answering. The only words I understood were "mama" and "gato." I was pretty sure only one of them referred to me.

When she came down, she seemed more relaxed. "The girls listen to their music on their radio." She pointed at her ears. "They got headphones, so I can talk."

"Thanks. Tell me about this other man."

"I was there when the pastor talked with him. He was nice at first, then got loud. I didn't like him, and the pastor made him leave. I don't think the guy wanted to talk to Blaze about a job. He reminded me of a cop. Before he left, he gave me his phone number, told me to call him if Blaze came around, said there was a reward."

"I'd like to get that number. He give you a name?"

"Wylie. I didn't get no first name." She found her purse, a fake leather thing that smelled of tobacco and cinnamon gum, produced a folded piece of yellow paper with a phone number in blue ballpoint ink and handed it over without hesitation. I tucked it into my coat pocket.

"He say why he was looking for Blaze?" I asked.

She shrugged. "Said she stole something expensive, and he needed to talk to her."

I nodded, kept eye contact, but said nothing, letting the silence draw her out.

"I didn't trust him. He was a big dude, you know? He did the kind of thing big dudes like to do: they crowd you. He got all up in the pastor's face. Made me scared. I played dumb, just talked Spanish, and he gave up."

She stood up to check on her kids, sat again on the lower bunk, chewing her lip. There was something she wanted to say, probably whatever she didn't want Sipes to hear.

"Is it something about the club?" I prompted.

"Some of the other girl Kitties kind of bothered her. They were friendly with dudes, you know."

"At the club? Not a big surprise."

"*Dudes*," she said, holding her hands out wider than any felian body.

The dime dropped. "Ah. OK. Why are you telling me?" I didn't care what consenting adults did with each other, though cross-species relations struck me as another new thing neither felians nor Apes really knew how to talk about yet.

"That wasn't Blaze. She was real nice. She cared about people, wanted to make a difference. But she didn't cross that line."

I was starting to feel like I was trying to hunt down a saint. It sure didn't sound like the kind of person who would steal from her mentor or displayed a hot temper. Unless, maybe, she had a damned good reason.

"She wore a piece of jewelry, right?" I pointed at my chest.

"Oh yeah, a tiger pendant. Real pretty. The girls love it."

"Did she tell you where she spends time when she isn't here? Besides the club."

Rebecca looked at her shoes. "She said she had an apartment…"

"Say she's not going back there."

"She has a friend she stays with sometimes, when it's real late or the weather's real bad. Bartender from her club. A human. I think they live near it."

"This person have a name?"

"Chandra. I didn't get the last name."

"Gracias." I turned to go, but paused. "Why did you tell me all this? I'm a stranger."

"You're a *gato*, like her. I think she needs help. Plus you waved at my kids. This Wylie dude acted like they weren't there. When you don't have a home… you get good at noticing when people don't give a shit, you know? You're nice."

I snorted. "Sister, you sure you've got the right Kitty?"

Her voice conveyed certainty. "My grandmother says you can tell a lot about someone from how they treat kids. She likes you."

"Likes me?"

Rebecca touched the little cross around her neck and gave me a wan smile. "She still watches over us, Mr. Jones."

"I see." And I did, sort of, but a shiver went through my whiskers. "Thanks again for your time, Ms. Flores. You've been really helpful."

Three sets of eyes watched me all the way to the door.

***

I headed back to the office, grabbed a quick catnap, did some grooming, and consulted some more with José. It was a walking meeting, not a sitting one. After a couple laps of tequila, I felt ready to do a little follow-up.

Rebecca Flores had given me a lot of information to think through. Seemed like my next best bet would be to hit Kit-Kat Blue and see if Blaze was there. If she was on the lam, I doubted I'd see her. Zozo would find her there easy as scratchin'. But I might find her friend Chandra, maybe other people who could shed light on where Blaze had gone to ground.

I peered through the blinds. The black sedan with tinted windows was still there, parked across the street behind my neighbor's dusty pickup. The driver had a good view of the school's front entrance and also my office window. He'd been there since noon, at least. This was painfully unsubtle, practically an invitation. I decided to accept.

After I put on my jacket, I walked outside and sauntered over to the sedan. It was a black Lexus Infiniti, the kind of car an Ape drives when they want to show off how classy they are, but can't afford a Porsche. I took note of the license number.

I'm considered tall for a felian, yet the top of my head barely crested the window. I rapped on the glass, and the window whined down, revealing a bullet-shaped Ape head bolted on top of a brown suit. A dusty caterpillar had died on his upper lip. He smelled of gun oil, pork tacos, and bay rum with a touch of lime. That last was his aftershave. He'd have been better off using it on his tacos. I sniffed he was alone in the car, also that it was a rental. So much for the plate giving up his identity easily.

There was something else… the barest trace of a felian scent. If he hadn't been putting out so much other nasal static, I might have picked up more detail. I doubted he'd let me stick my head in for a closer whiff.

"Can I help you?" he said. His voice was higher than I expected, but he managed to grate it out so it sounded acceptably threatening.

"You've been parked outside my office for an hour and a half," I replied. "Need to come use the bathroom?"

"Get lost," he said. The window started to whine back up, but not before I held up my phone and snapped a pic.

"Hey, asshole!" he said. "You can't do that!" The door swung open fast, but I danced out of the way and bounded onto the hood. By the time he was halfway out of the car, I had a steel ball loaded in the sling hanging from my handpaw. He froze, which told me he knew damn well what felians could do with slings. I just let the ball hang there, casually. But my footpaws were braced. I wouldn't be able to let fly at this range, but whipped overhead, the steel ball was plenty capable of cracking open a thick skull or breaking a limb.

"Why don't you put your hands out where I can see them, nice and friendly," I said.

His face was red, but he put them up, one on the roof; the other white-knuckled the top of the door.

"See? Now that's friendly," I said.

"This is menacing. That's a crime," he said, trying to sound indignant and failing.

"Aww, I'm just a little Kitty scared by a big, bad human. But see, I sure as hell can take pictures of strangers staking out my workplace. Why are you covering me?"

He looked smug. "You? You ain't that important, buddy."

"So you're waiting on someone else. Let's see, there's only one other business here. You're staking out the tech geeks. Who you working for?"

"Go fuck yourself." He ducked back into the car. The door slammed and the engine turned over a second later while the window whined back up.

Not wanting to stick around as a hood ornament and roadkill candidate, I jumped into the bed of my neighbor's pickup truck. I didn't think the Ape would try anything. He was here for a stakeout, and he'd been made. Sure enough, he pulled out with a squeal and accelerated south toward Sandy Boulevard with a vengeance, leaving rubber behind. I thought about putting out one of his taillights on principle, but the cops viewed felian slings as real close to firearms. I didn't blame them, and also didn't need to complicate my life with assault charges.

Still, I had a pic. Maybe Flanagan would run it if I tossed him a treat.

***

My call went to Flanagan's voicemail. A curt recording simply said, "Detective Flanagan, Portland Police. Leave a message." So I did, asking for a check on the license plate of the Lexus, and whether a Blaze Hawthorne had a concealed carry permit. Multnomah County wouldn't cough up that last bit of info to the general public, meaning me, but they would to a police inquiry. If Flanagan even bothered. We weren't on personal speaking terms, but I was still a felian consultant contracted with the Portland Police Bureau, so we ran into each other on business. He'd never forgiven me for killing dogs he'd trained when they attacked me on a previous case, and I'd never forgiven him for being dirty. We called it even, and worked together under an uneasy truce.

I needed an angle on this case. Rebecca Flores had mentioned Blaze's friend Chandra, so I started there. Looking for Chandras in the online people finder websites didn't turn up anything but too many Chandras to chase down. It added up to the same big zero, and nobody had an address in Southeast near the Kit Kat Club Zozo had mentioned. I was drawing a big zero.

I changed tack and started looking into whether there were any news stories about security breaches at banks locally. Nothing in the news, which meant if Zozo was on the level, it'd been enough money that the bank he hit wasn't publicizing the loss yet, probably because they were still trying to fix their security and figure out what to say in their announcement. I started wondering where Zo had moved the money, and why the tiger thumb drive was so important. I don't do that much tech, so I needed to talk with someone savvy about it. Fortunately, I had someone other than Zozo to consult with.

The Pharaoh was a plugged-in cat who made his lair in a rickety add-on room practically stapled onto an old brick building that probably used to be a hardware store, located in one of the densest areas of K-town. I'd gotten useful info out of him a few times in return for favors. I don't know if he was in Zozo's league as a coder, but he sure seemed to know computers. He went by "The Pharaoh," but I knew him by his first name Moopsy, which he only used with friends. The fact he considered an ornery loner like me one of them said a lot about his social life.

It was about a five-minute scoot to get there after a quick stop for an offering. The sky was producing a light drizzle most Portlanders didn't dignify with open umbrellas. I parked a block away next to a hitching rack of rental bicycles and walked through a passel of rangy kittens trying to look tough with their fake tails, backward facing ball caps, and vape pens. Bast knew we didn't know what we were in this Ape world, so most of us just copied the Apes. Me included, though I was more retro about it. I blame watching *The Maltese Falcon* right after my Change.

Moopsy kept his lair like a ball of yarn tangled with a box of nails. Wires and cables snaked everywhere, connecting a couple of violet-lighted computer cases and a trio of huge monitors bolted to one wall. Pizza boxes littered the floor. Facing the monitors was a huge recliner that practically filled the cramped space. Moopsy sprawled on this with a keyboard on his corpulent lap, a blanket wrapped around him. He was a Sphinx, which meant he was furless, a wrinkled felian the Apes found grotesque instead of cute and enticing. Sphinxes had it rough. Felians found them freakish as well. As a result, he'd become neurotically self-conscious. Moopsy was a hustler, though, made decent swag playing videogames and posting his playbacks to YouTube as "The Pharaoh." He'd initially wanted to go by "Baron something or other" that sounded like coughing up a hairball, but I'd talked him out of it in favor of tying into his breed association.

Ignoring the smell of unwashed felian and dry pizza crusts, I stepped over a couple of dead pizza boxes and put my offering of a six-pack of Dr. Pepper on the coffee table next to the recliner. Moopsy was busy playing something, the two screens flashing and flipping with a riot of shapes and colors. I thought I saw a giant parakeet puking fire at a cartoon skeleton with a top hat, but couldn't be sure. Just looking made my eyes water.

"Hey Moops," I said.

After a couple of seconds, he paused the games and turned to me, his pupils dilated. "Shady? Hey, Catmandoo, what's the pounce?" His eyes were a watery green with gold flecks, and as they focused on me, the pupils shrank to something less suggestive of violence.

"I need a consult, buddy," I said. "Got a problem I'm trying to figure out." I gave him the basic rundown, omitting names.

"Huh," he said when I was done. "Weird."

"If there's money, how's it connected to that thumb drive?"

"Well, could be your guy just moved the funds into an online bank account and the thief set another password. But then he could go to the bank for a reset."

"Right, so maybe a safe deposit box?"

He peered at me like I was drooling, chuckled. "Lick. Please. We're in the twenty-first century." He scratched behind an ear. "I tell you what. I think we're talking about cryptocurrency."

"Say again?"

"Cryptocurrency. You know, Bitcoin?"

I showed him my best blank look. He snorted. "Bast's thousand flaming tits, Shady. How do you even get by in this world? Look, cryptocurrency is the thing—well, it was the thing. It's kind of floundering now, but it's still a great vehicle for money laundering."

"Explain."

"You know—well, obviously you don't—it's digital currency, just exists online, but trades like dollars or pounds sterling or rubles. The cool thing, though, is any account can only be unlocked with a unique, very strong password keyed to that account and that account only. Lose the password, you are one unlucky shit-mouse, I tell you what."

"Customer service?" I asked. He grinned and shook his head, eyes full of glee.

"Shit out of luck," he repeated. "No way in if you don't got the password. Super secure."

"So the thumb drive might have the password to a cryptocurrency account? How's that work?"

"Like any other online banking account. You got one, right?"

I twitched my ears yes.

"Cool, so that's basically it. Simple transfer of funds to where you want the money to go. Prolly have to use an actual bank account to buy things online."

"Alright. One more thing. You said it was good for money laundering?"

"Yeah, if the person knows what they're doing. It's not anonymous, but there are enough unregulated currency exchanges and dark web brokers that if you bounce it around long enough, you can muddy the trail and then exchange the funds for fiat currency." At my blank look, he added, "Real money."

"So you think the password to the cryptocurrency is on the thumb drive?"

"Yeah, and the account number, obviously. If it was a regular bank account, I bet your guy could still access it."

"K, thanks, lick. You've been awesome. I owe you one."

He gave me a lopsided grin. "'S cool, Shadester. Thanks for the pop."

As I showed myself out, I heard the caterwaul of the game start up again behind me. The outside air tasted extra sweet, but Moopsy had given me plenty to think about.

***

On impulse, I swung by Blaze's apartment to see if there was anything I could sniff out, or maybe catch a break and find her there. Nothing. No one answered my knocks. The porch was empty, a few cigarette butts ground out in an old soup can still gave off a faint smell of nicotine and smoke. The half-dead cat poster was still there, a little wrinkled from the damp air. I picked it up, gave it a sniff. It had a faint whiff of that lick Skeets Glisan's scent on it. The date of the event was tonight. The hunter's instinct started ringing bells.

I could think of a few more questions for that Kitty. Maybe it was time for me to get out more, do a little yowling. And get straight answers out of a young lick.

***

I'd spent a lot of in time dive bars during my short post-Change life. The rougher and less pretentious they were, the more my inner alley cat felt at home. Alive and Dead catered to the rougher kind of felian all right, but went all the way around the bend on the other side to take the steaming prize of being rough and pretentious all at once. As soon as I passed over the threshold, my fur started to itch. I had to cover my ears with my handpaws.

The band called themselves Anal Distillation, and they sounded pretty much like you'd expect from the name, only with more deafening bass. The dance floor was a mosh pit done Kitty-style, meaning it reminded me of a continuous low-grade catfight featuring a few dozen felians driven insane by the agonizing wall of noise that blasted out of the speakers. Everything was painted black in one room, white in the next. Tables resembled giant nails driven into a concrete floor. Everything was designed around a play on "alive" with cat angels and unicorn cats, or "dead," with cat skulls and cartoon tombstones. The bar evidently only served two things: PBR in cans, and green jello shots they called "the radioactive pellet" served in plastic shotglasses. It smelled like cough medicine to me. For some unexplainable reason, jumbles of black and white pillows nobody seemed to be using were piled in corners.

Felian culture had a long way to go. I wasn't encouraged.

I bought a PBR for camouflage and prowled through the place looking for Skeets. In one of the back rooms—one of the "dead" ones far enough from the dance floor that the music didn't have the volume of dueling leaf-blowers—I found him packed around a table with four other Kitties. The table was a graveyard for beer cans and little shot glasses with green residue inside. All drunk toms, which meant a few ruffs were going to get scruffed up before I got what I wanted. That was fine with me. I wanted answers, and I wasn't going to go easy this time if Skeets threw down.

Five sets of dilated felian eyes noted my approach, and their owners went quiet. Their body language was sloppy but not welcoming.

"It's the private eye," Skeets slurred. "Got a bone to pick with you, mouse-dick."

The direct approach seemed like the way to go. I lobbed my beer to one of his friends, who caught it by reflex, befuddled. While his buddies were distracted by the motion of the can through the air, I leaned over and grabbed Skeets by the whiskers. These are very tender parts of a felian. He flailed in confusion and yowled as I yanked him over the table and dragged him away. There was a convenient wall nearby, into which he slammed quite nicely.

His friends started to stand up like they were ready to be tough.

"Sit your fake tails back down, licks," I snarled. "Skeets and I are going to have a chat. But you frost me, he's going to be donating his whiskers to the Wayward Whisker Home along with half his face." I tightened my grip for emphasis, and Skeets whined. I must have been convincing, or his buddies realized they were too drunk to make a play. They sat, fixing me with unblinking hostile glares. At some point, they were going to remember basic math, and then they'd find their courage.

Keeping an ear on them, I addressed Skeets. "I have a couple of questions. Answer them, I'm out of your fur, get me?"

"Leggo my whiskers…"

"Answer my questions first."

His ears flicked.

"Right," I said. "First, who really tore up that apartment?"

"I don't—" he began. I tightened my grip and he winced.

"Window was locked," I said. "Hummus on the floor smelled fresh. You were on that porch long enough to know Roxy had gone in. The way I see it, you had to have seen or sniffed something or someone else. You were gone when I left, or we'd have had this talk earlier."

"Aright, aright, I'll tell you…!"

A bunch of Kitties hurrying through from another room jostled me as they squeezed by. With a sharp hiss, Skeets took advantage of the distraction to free himself, grabbing my handpaws with his own, claws out. I had to slide in close to keep him from getting his footpaws up to rake my belly. As we wrestled against the wall, he gave a push, and we tipped over a nearby table and slammed into the Kitties seated around it. Confusion reigned as Skeets tore himself loose and staggered away from me. A calico stumbled into me, and I shoved her aside.

There was a deafening crack-crack and a couple of blinding flashes in my peripheral vision, followed by the unmistakable smell of blood and the faint acrid odor of propellant. Someone yowled.

The room exploded in full-on Kitty panic as felians scattered for the exits in sudden, utter silence other than the sound of breaking glass or pattering footpaws. I crouched, Glock in hand, which didn't help reassure anyone. But instinct is instinct. All I could hear was the ringing in my ears from the gunshot. It hurt like blazes. The room cleared. I tried to catch any familiar scent, but there were too many felians for me to sift anything out of the nasal static, which included blood.

A black Kitty with a slashed denim vest and black t-shirt and jeans eyed me warily from the bar in the adjoining room, his eyes all pupils. As I looked up, he spied the gun in my hand and took a powder, springing over a table in a single bound. A pack of Lucky Strikes fell from his sleeve and hit the floor.

Skeets was slumped on the corner over a couple of white pillows, fake tail thrusting out like an awkward red-tufted flag. I sniffed he was gone, even if the spreading dark patch on his chest and the crimson smear on the wall above him weren't enough to clue me in.

I put the Glock away and crouched over him. The hole in his chest suggested a small caliber round. I thought of the .22 rounds I'd picked up from Blaze's apartment and grimaced.

It wasn't the first time I'd been close to death, far from it. But it always left a mark. If I hadn't come here, maybe, or if I'd been more alert, this young lick wouldn't be dead. Maybe. I got out my cell and snapped a pic of him. What had he known that someone—another felian—was willing to kill to keep me from learning? Why didn't they pop me in the first place? Seems like that would have been simpler.

Practical P.I. habits took over, and I quickly went through his pockets. My scent and fur was all over Skeets from our tussle, so there wasn't any danger of incriminating myself any more than I already had.

I snagged his phone right away and tucked it into my coat pocket. His wallet had an Oregon ID card with a surly photo, a little money, and a folded piece of blue paper I pocketed along with the phone. I barely had time to replace the wallet and close Skeets's eyes before the bouncer lumbered up to clap a size eight handpaw on my shoulder and haul me to my feet.

"Cops are on their way," he said. "You ain't going anywhere."

I flashed him my third-best smile. "Wouldn't dream of it."

***

The first cop on the scene was a uniform I knew from my work with Detective Flanagan, and he snorted as soon as he saw me.

"Officer Arriera." I nodded.

"Jones." He jerked a chin at the body. "You got a bad habit of showing up at these things, man. Flanagan ain't gonna be happy."

I offered a big, tongue-curling yawn. "Flanagan's never happy except around dogs."

"You know the drill," Arriera said as he began to unspool the yellow tape to cordon off the crime scene. "Stick around for a statement, stay outta the way."

"You don't think I did it?"

He snorted. "Did you?"

I shook my head and let him do his job.

An unopened can of PBR beckoned to me from the foot of a table. Waste not, want not. I needed something to wash Skeets's death out of my palate.

I was halfway through the beer when Flanagan got there about twenty minutes later, and as predicted, wasn't happy to see me. He was a burly Ape in civilian duds under a charcoal raincoat. Red hair was receding from his forehead, and a cigarette plumed smoke from a russet-stubbled face. His pinched expression when he saw me was the new normal since we'd fallen out over a previous case. He headed Portland's Kittytown beat, which meant we ran into each other professionally more often than either of us liked.

"Shady," he muttered. "You keep showing up around dead vics like a dedicated pain in the ass. What's the bullshit you've gotten me into now?"

I gave him a cool nod. "Maybe just bad karma."

"You know this lick?" He indicated Skeets's body.

I took a swig of lukewarm PBR. "Skeets Glisan. Met him on a case I'm working on."

"Any idea what went down here?"

I gave him the bare details of what I'd seen and heard. He grunted when I was done, and crouched over the body, his bulk making Glisan look like an Ape child. Up close, Flanagan smelled like pastrami on rye with a sweat aftertaste and some peppermint candy I detected in his jacket pocket. It added up to a fun scent cocktail, especially with how Skeets's death still dominated the air. I'd smelled worse, but this was going to put me off pastrami for awhile.

"Low caliber rounds," he said. "Two to the chest, probably close range. You sure you didn't smell anything?"

I shook my head. "Too many other scents in the air. Then the gunpowder and noise drowned everything out."

"You get anything from him?"

"Nah," I lied.

"Alright. Come outside and we'll take a statement."

Skeets's phone and the paper felt like they were burning holes in my coat pocket. "Am I free to go then?"

"Yeah, we both know the routine."

"You never got back to me about that plate I called in," I said.

He shrugged. "I only do favors for friends."

"Or bribes," I pitched my words so only we could hear them. His face twitched.

"Rental car," he said. "Name of Carl Wylie. That's all you get."

"Thanks," I said, and meant it.

As we stepped through the crime scene tape, another detective I didn't recognize came up to Flanagan holding a sealed plastic baggie that contained a small revolver. Looked like a .22, and I would have bet dollars to donuts it belonged to one Blaze Hawthorne.

Dammit. Everything I'd learned about Blaze rubbed against her being the one pulling the trigger. Whoever popped Skeets did it in cold blood.

The new detective was a she-Ape a head shorter than Flanagan, with pale skin and hair so blonde it looked white, pulled into a stubby ponytail. Maybe pretty by Ape standards, but what struck me was her light gray eyes. They reminded me of a predator's, a look of which I approved. She wore a zip-up, black, hooded raincoat over a jacket, black slacks, and thick-soled boots. She smelled all right to me, meaning no perfume or weird flower soaps. I appreciated humans who didn't make my eyes water.

"Found this by the bar, Detective," she said. "Twenty-two, Ruger double-action. Two shots fired, six in the cylinder."

He grunted again, accepting the baggie and peering into it before handing it back. "Good work. Send it to ATF, see if we can get a trace. Unless…" He side-eyed me. "Mr. Jones here has any idea who this might belong to."

I examined a dewclaw. "Gonna have to take a pass on that one."

"That's not the same as not knowing."

"If I find out anything solid, I'll let you know."

D'Amico extended a hand to me, smiling. "Detective Katie D'Amico. I'm new to the K-town detail."

We shook hands. "Shadowpaw Jones. I'm Flanagan's personal pain in the ass."

"I've heard," she said, still smiling along with that predator's gaze. I wasn't quite used to that from an Ape, but I decided I liked her. Provisionally.

"You haven't heard enough, obviously," Flanagan growled. "Jones here turns up practically every time something fucked up happens in K-town. Like a bad penny. But he can be a whole bunch of helpful if you get past the snark. It's going to take a few days before we hear anything on that gun. Take his statement. I'm going to see if this dump has coffee." He stomped toward the bar while I followed D'Amico outside to the squad cars.

I was running a risk not sharing my suspicions about the gun with Flanagan, but I didn't know for sure it belonged to Blaze, and I wasn't about to have an APB put out on her until I knew more. Ape cops in K-town were like the proverbial bulls in China shops. They might drive her deeper into hiding—or even skipping town if she hadn't already. Or they might just shoot her.

Bottom line was I needed to find Blaze. This game had just turned deadly. And there was one obvious place I hadn't visited yet.

***

Once upon a time, Portland had a rep as the Sin City of the Pacific Northwest, and it still boasted the highest per capita number of strip clubs in the country. The Change had only added to that stat. Kit-Kat Blue was, like most establishments in its line of business, not much to look at from the outside. This was by design; it was the kind of place that didn't want to make its activities or patrons easily visible to the public, resulting in a windowless shoebox with a square spray of gravel for a parking lot. A tall wooden fence fringed with a string of LED lights enclosed an attached open space for customers who smoked. There was no other outside lighting other than a single bulb over the entrance and the electronic sign that spelled out the club name on high in blue neon retro script, the latter accompanied by a silhouette of a nude felian queen with a full-on cat face and tail. The clouds looked pregnant with moonlight. The wind was blowing steadily from the direction of the Willamette River, a few blocks to the west. I appreciated not being drenched, though the wet city smell filled my snoot with a cocktail mix of asphalt and rubber, spiced with a musky organic thread not quite dirt and not quite animal.

The bouncer was a big former angora, long white fur bursting out of a black Hozer t-shirt that read *Take Me to Church*. I showed him my P.I. license. "I'm here to see Blaze Hawthorne. Just asking a few questions."

He sniffed me pretty thoroughly and let me pass. His stance told me if I wasn't on the level, he'd use my face to give the gravel outside a good scrubbing. I held his gaze just long enough to suggest that might not be a good career move for him. We arrived at an understanding.

Inside the box, the lights were low other than colored spots illuminating a mirrored stage. A half-dozen felian toms had their heads down in a serious poker game at a large table to one side, seemingly indifferent to the naked calico queen gyrating on stage. Behind the bar, a gray queen with tired eyes swiped at the counter with a dishcloth, and a weak-chinned human woman with pink-dyed hair was pulling beer into a pint glass. The music was louder than comfortable for my ears, a sedate volume for Apes. A couple of shifty looking Ape males hunkered into their coats at the back of the room, staring at the stage with hungry eyes.

I made my way back to where the musk of felian queens mingled with the cigarette stink drifting in from the door to the enclosed yard. I appreciated how the latter helped make the former less distracting. A couple of the strippers gave me appraising looks, and they were sleek enough to turn my head, but this wasn't a venue for yowling. Sometimes I wondered why we copied the Apes in so many broken ways, but we were barely out of nursery school as a species, and humans weren't the best role models. Maybe we'd learn better.

"Looking for Blaze Hawthorne." Keeping my gaze on their faces, I showed the two queens the photo I'd snagged from the apartment. One queen was a marmalade tabby, the other a silky Korat blue with hot jade eyes trying to burn a hole in mine. They both wore short, sleeveless dresses tied at the shoulders.

The tabby shook her head. "She ain't here. Haven't seen her this week."

The Korat scowled at her. "Shut it, Zinkie. We don't know who this lick works for."

"What makes you think I work for anyone?" I asked.

"You got a look." She narrowed her jade eyes. "You're not trawlin' here for your health." She turned an ear toward the stage. "Or the dancers. Why don't you get lost, OK?"

I put the picture away. "Why don't you tell me who else came around asking for Blaze, and why they scared you?"

Zinkie the tabby gasped, a handpaw flying to her lips. The Korat flattened her whiskers, her regard shifting from hostile to evaluating.

"Follow me," she said at last, and led me to a door set in the wall next to the stage. Zinkie followed close behind, clearly anxious.

The door opened into a decent-sized green room that pulled double duty as storage space. A three-shelf rack with cleaning supplies occupied the wall space to my left. To my right, a low end table flanked three felian-sized chairs. A couple of full-length mirrors were mounted horizontally along the wall. Bundles of clothes topped off by purses and a few umbrellas were stacked to the side, out of the way.

A svelte Bengal queen stood before the mirror, checking her lingerie. She glanced at me with curiosity as I entered behind the Korat, then gave me a more thorough appraisal. I returned the attention. Whatever was behind the Change, it totally reworked feline physiology, grafting cat features onto a distinctly hominid shape. Nowhere was this more evident than with the female body. Mammaries were now located on the ribcage in a pair like an Ape's, instead of along the belly, and the hips were wider. At the same time, we were different. Newborn kittens were much smaller relative to human babies, so queens still produced litters of three to five without as much discomfort as human women.

That fecundity explained the giant push for felian birth control, full stop.

The Bengal locked her gaze with the Korat and wrinkled her nose in inquiry.

The Korat said, "He's looking for Blaze. Says he's not a cop." Turning to me, she held out a handpaw. "I'm Liz. The spotcoat over there is Sheba Rae."

"Get lost, tailmunch," the Bengal said, but there was no rancor in her tone. "He's cute, anyway."

Liz and I shook. "Shadowpaw Jones," I said. "This shouldn't take long. What can you tell me about Blaze? Has she been here in the last couple of days?"

"No," Sheba Rae said. "But she should show up tonight if she wants to pick up her paycheck. And keep her job."

"She missed last night," Zinkie put in, her striped face tight with concern.

"When was the last time you saw her?" I asked.

"Two days ago," Liz said. "She was in and out. Said she wasn't feeling well." She stretched her handpaw, letting the claws extend for a moment before retracting them.

Now that sounded like it fit right into what I'd been sniffing. If Blaze was spooked and looking for a safe lair, she wouldn't want to stick around where she was known to work. "You believe her?"

"Why shouldn't I?"

"She seem nervous? Like she was keeping an ear out for someone?"

Zinkie's ears perked up for a moment, but Liz put a handpaw on her, and she relaxed. I was onto something.

"Maybe," Liz admitted. "Once she got paid, she scrambled."

I decided to pounce a little. "She go to Chandra's, maybe?"

Liz flattened her ears. "You're awful nosy, flatpaw."

"Hold on, ladies." Sheba Rae came over, having thrown a robe over her lithe Bengal form. She smelled nice, a clean scent of heather and jasmine with a hint of lime. Most felians who used perfumes diluted it by at least a factor of five so it wouldn't overpower our snoots, as opposed to deadnose Apes, who practically bathed in the full-strength stuff.

She regarded me carefully with slitted eyes and took in my scent while I tried to keep my composure around hers. She was tall for a queen, her eyes level with my chin. Memories of a mating scrap with a brown and white bruiser of a tom flashed through my mind's eye. I'd almost lost an eye on that one, but that spotted queen had been worth it. After a long moment, Sheba Rae's pupils relaxed and she nodded.

"I think this tom's feeding us straight. I say we level with him." Her gaze hardened. "But if you're lying to us, buddy, I'll make sure you regret it."

I let out my breath, impressed by her ferocity. "Noted."

"Chandra Mara is the fake name on an apartment we all lease together. Kind of a safe house. It's right across the boulevard, about a block and a half away."

I widened my eyes, the felian equivalent in this context of raising an eyebrow and inviting further comment. "That must have taken some doing."

Liz curled her lip. "Landlord's not picky so long as they're paid. We have a dozen dancers between Kit Kat and Diavolo's chipping in. It's pretty barebones, just a couple of Goodwill mattresses, sleeping bags, coffee pot in the kitchen."

I nodded. "OK, and you all go there when…?"

"Late night when the weather sucks," Sheba Rae said. "Or if there's a weirdo patron hanging around."

"Apes, mostly," Liz said. "You know the type."

Something unspoken passed between them. Zinkie looked like she was about to say something, but a glance from Liz shut her down.

"Can't you just ditch 'em?" I asked. "Most Apes can't keep an eye on us at night." This was true. Felians were quick and small. Most of us possessed a natural talent for stealth, especially if we were cat-born. But even the new Change-born were able to move around on little cat feet when it suited them. And Apes couldn't track by scent, which meant all we had to do was get out of their sight.

All three queens glanced at each other. Sheba Rae shook her head. "We could, but we'd have to head out to the river a bit and double back. Too much street light otherwise."

"A lot of nights it's not worth the trouble," Zinkie chimed in. The others nodded.

"After a long night of dancing, you kinda want to crash," Liz said, twitching a silky gray ear. "Most of us, anyway."

"You mean you're not party animals?" I said, affecting shock.

Sheba Rae uttered a short laugh. Liz scowled. Zinkie produced a wan smile.

"You gotta be kidding me," Sheba Rae said. "Who has time?"

Time to cut to the chase. "So when are you going to tell me about what's really going on with Blaze?"

Liz's eyes narrowed. Sheba Rae became very still.

"What do you mean?" Zinkie asked, eyes wide.

"Well," I said. "It's pretty clear you know more than you're saying. Is she at Chandra's, or would I find her somewhere else? Because I think she's in real trouble."

Zinkie started. "Oh, I'm on next. Bye!" She darted toward the door that led to the stage, closed it behind her as she left.

There was a long beat of silence. Both queens had gone still and tense.

"What kind of trouble, flatpaw?" Liz asked, ears flat.

Sheba Rae showed me a little claw. "Don't think we need to call Rooter to handle you, buddy. Zinkie might not know how to throw down, but we're both cats."

I took a step back, handpaws up with claws retracted. "Easy, I really do want to help her. She's in trouble. People are looking for her. Someone's already been murdered over it."

The tone of their tension shifted, became brittle. Sheba Rae relaxed her claws.

"Who?" she asked.

I put my cards on the table. "A lick by name of Skeets Glisan. Shot in the Dead and Alive Club a couple hours ago. I don't know how he's connected to her exactly, but he is."

Liz slumped. "Bast be damned."

Sheba Rae put an arm around her. "Sorry, honey. I know you liked him."

"He's been here?" I asked.

"Yeah," Sheba Rae said while Liz closed her eyes the way felians did when they grieved. We didn't shed tears the way humans did. "He was a regular. Liz thought he was cute, but he liked another queen."

"Blaze?"

"No, a different dancer. He stopped coming here after that other tom friend of his picked up Blaze."

A sneaking suspicion started scratching in my gut. "That other tom? Tell me about him."

Sheba Rae made a small noise and exposed her neck in a graceful shrug that threatened to distract me from my line of questioning. It'd been awhile since I'd been this long in such close quarters with attractive queens. Their scent was all around me. I took a hard mental grip on the scruff of my neck. Felian instincts weren't shy, and the queens knew it. This queen did, anyway.

More gruffly, I repeated my question.

Sheba Rae smiled, amused at my discomfort. "Older lick, bulky build, silver and gray fur. Always wore a hat…" She trailed off at the expression on my face.

Son of a bitch. A bunch of puzzle pieces fell into place. My discomfort with the queens vanished, replaced by a slow, hot lick of anger.

"Cut the scamper and take me to Blaze," I growled. "Right ruttin' *now*—if you want to save her life."

***

Sheba Rae and Liz held a hasty conference and picked Sheba Rae to come with me. I wasn't complaining, but my patience had run thin, and I was no longer distracted. My hackles were up.

After this was over, I was going to have words and probably claws with that Bast-be-cursed, lying bag of mouse farts who called himself Zozo.

The apartment was two blocks south, across the four-lane asphalt monster of Powell Avenue, which ran by the club. We slipped in silence down a tree-lined street to a small duplex with a porch over a pair of narrow garages. It had two stories perched atop a garage that opened to the street but was flanked by a raised yard that made the second story its own ground level. A trio of plastic trash cans stood at the curb. The place looked like the housing equivalent of someone who'd had a few too many drinks and needed a fresh change of clothes. Paint was peeling off the siding, and the bushes looked like they hadn't been trimmed this decade. Concrete steps on the right side led up past a concrete retainer that supported a plot of weed-entangled rosebushes.

We took the steps up and came to the front door. Sheba Rae produced a key and opened it. I perked my ears forward and listened hard, my handpaw poised over the gun under my jacket. I nodded to Sheba Rae, and we went in.

There were no lights on inside, but our felian eyes had plenty to work with from the streetlight filtering in around the sheets someone had hung over the windows. After a miniscule mud space with a cracked vinyl floor, we came into an empty room with dark wood panel walls and a carpet the color of coffee backwash. It sucked the soul out of me just to stand there. It smelled strongly of queens and faintly of coffee. I sniffed carefully, detected a familiar felian scent from Blaze's apartment. Recent, so she was here. One doorway opened to the kitchen, another probably to either a closet or a bathroom. A set of equally carpet-cursed stairs led up to the third story. I heard soft movement from upstairs, the faint creak of a floorboard, the scuff of a footpaw against carpet, the faint hum characteristic of a space heater. There was no way Blaze hadn't heard the latch turn. She knew we were here.

Sheba Rae called out, "Blaze, honey? It's me." She regarded me with a curious expression before heading up the stairs. I followed, stepping softly out of habit, but giving Sheba Rae a little room to warn Blaze before I poked my nose into her presence.

The third story could have competed with a postage stamp for floorspace. Blaze Hawthorne and Sheba Rae were sitting on a mattress with a sleeping bag spread over it. A compact Black and Decker radiant heater cranked out heat under the window next to a mammoth radiator with enough metal to stop a high-caliber bullet. As I came into the room, Blaze sprang to her feet. She wore a mid-length plaid skirt and a pale yellow blouse.

Blaze was even more striking in person. It was more than just her looks. She had presence. I stood gawping for a second or two, until I remembered how to work my mouth parts.

"Ms. Hawthorne?" I kept my voice steady and offered my handpaw. "Shadowpaw Jones."

She glared at me, claws out although her handpaws remained by her side. After a moment, I let mine drop.

From the mattress, Sheba Rae drawled, "This handsome tom says you're in danger. He was very convincing."

"I'm a friend," I added quickly, palms out, no claws. "And yeah, I do think you're in danger, and I want to help."

Blaze and I held each other's gaze for a few moments before she gave Sheba Rae a slow blink to let her know she believed me. She glanced at Sheba Rae, and something passed between them. My guess was that Blaze hadn't filled her friends in on what she'd been up to, and wanted to keep it that way for now.

The Bengal snorted and said, "I'll be on the porch smoking a bowl and keeping an eye out. Call me if you need anything." She said this with a pointed look at me and a claw tap on my shoulder that threatened serious repercussions if anything went sideways. Her scent warred with Blaze's in an intriguing way, and I focused on the terrible decor to dampen the sizzling in my blood.

After she was gone, I crouched down to seem less threatening. "Alright, kitten. You heard about Skeets?"

She shook her head.

"You knew him, though?"

"Yeah. Not well, but I know him from the club. Wait. You said 'knew.' Does that mean—"

"He's dead. Shot in the Dead and Alive earlier tonight. I don't know who the shooter was. I'm sorry."

Her eyes widened in shock, and she let out a hiss. It was a moment before she could speak. "It's my fault."

"Your fault?"

"If I hadn't… It's… Sweet Bast, *why?*"

"That's what I'm trying to find out."

"You said I'm in danger."

"Yeah, too many coincidences," I said, my stomach tight with anger. "Turns out the lick who hired me to find you knew Skeets. And I'm pretty sure your gun will turn out to be the murder weapon. When did you see it last?"

"I… sorry, this is all too much. Who hired you?"

"Zozo Linn. And I think he might have motive here. He might be gunning for you."

"Zozo?" She stared at me with an incredulous expression on her face. "No way."

"He's mixed up with Skeets, hired me to find you. Skeets was at your apartment that same day."

She shook her head. "No, you're wrong. Zozo would never…"

"Someone took your gun."

Downstairs, the door opened and closed softly as Sheba Rae came in from her puff. Blaze pulled a fold of sheet aside and peered out the window, eyes half-lidded in felian contemplation. At last she said, "I left the gun at the apartment. I don't carry it anywhere."

"You have a permit."

"At the time I thought that was the thing to do, but… I just never felt comfortable taking it with me. Turns out I don't like guns. They scare me. Should never have bought it. So yeah, it stayed at home. Never even loaded it." She chuckled ruefully. "So stupid."

Sheba Rae was coming up the stairs. I didn't know how that would impact the conversation. She could already hear what we were saying. I pressed on.

"Anyone else know about it?"

A shrug. "My friends, probably. It wasn't a secret."

"Zozo?"

"Sure." She let out a snort. "Probably. He was there once—not for what you might think."

"OK, I believe you. What about your girlfriend? She's worried about you."

She frowned. "Girlfriend? I don't have a girlfriend."

That stopped me cold. A final piece dropped into place.

Damn it, I'd been played. A soft scrape on the stair behind me preceded a familiar scent by a heartbeat.

"Step away from Blaze, Mr. Jones, and keep your handpaws where I can see 'em," a soft voice said behind us. Roxy Stark stood in the doorway, a snub-nosed .22 in her handpaw. The muzzle was pointed at my chest, nice and steady. She was about six feet away. One good leap, yeah, but she had point blank range in her favor. And one look at the copper eyes told me she wasn't the kind of felian who would hesitate in pulling the trigger. I wondered how I'd missed their coldness the first time. Stupid hormones, damsel in distress chivalry.

"Well, this is a surprise," I said, and meant it. "Where's Sheba Rae?"

Roxy gave a little silver chuckle. "Stupid stoner's taking a nap on the porch. She'll be fine aside from a headache for a few days."

The last piece fell into place. "You shot Skeets, tried to pin the blame on Blaze here. Nice touch using Blaze's gun."

"You are a sharp one," she said. "Go to the head of the class."

"Skeets loved you!" Blaze burst out. "How could you do that?"

Roxy snorted. "Please. The idiot was going to blow everything wide open. He wanted to put the money into *politics*. Can you believe that?" She licked her handpaw and rubbed her cheek in a single graceful motion. "Besides, I already have a lover."

Blaze's claws were out, though she kept her handpaws still. "Yeah? Which one of the regulars? Benny? Tabasco? Curlicue?"

"Carl Wylie," I said.

A look of confusion from Blaze. "Carl? But he's…"

"A human. Yeah." I grinned at Roxy. "Want to hear my theory?"

"This ought to be good," Roxy said. The gun muzzle never wavered from the line it drew to the center of my torso. "But make it quick. I don't necessarily need to shoot you, but I don't particularly need to keep you alive either."

I didn't take my eyes off her, but when I spoke, it was to Blaze. "Blaze, Zozo was the one who hired me to find you. Why? Because you worked with him to hunt for dirt on the source of New Sunrise financing. He showed you what he was doing when he hacked into Phenom Bank's network. He found access keys to the New Sunrise business account, and used that access to transfer a bunch of money into a fake ID internet account, using fake invoices, then converted that to untraceable crypto-currency. That was really slick. Unfortunately, now it was all about the money. Zozo confided to you he planned to get the FLF up and running again as a well-funded organization. That's when you decided to steal the crypto-currency password."

Blaze gave me a slow blink. "Yes."

"So Zozo went to your apartment with Skeets, hoping to find you. They tore the place up looking for the thumb drive. A little later, Roxy found out about the money from Skeets, who was trying to impress her because he had a thing for her. That's when things really started going pear-shaped. Roxy told her boyfriend Wylie, and the two of them hatched a scheme to lean on Zozo, threatening to go to the police and the bank if they weren't dealt into the payout. Half to them, something like that? And the land speculation money he ripped off must have come from very well-connected people in China, maybe even tongs interested in money laundering. No wonder Zozo was shedding tufts."

I'd tried to edge a little toward Roxy while I spoke, but she jerked the muzzle a fraction in warning. "Whatever. Keep your distance, flatpaw."

"Zozo freaked out," I continued, now addressing Roxy. "Wylie thought Zozo was double-crossing you two. Blaze had gone to ground, so Zozo hired me to find her. After I met you and Skeets at Blaze's apartment, you told Wylie, who figured he could stake me out and follow. Skeets was jealous of him, and threatened to go to the police. So you killed him with Blaze's gun."

"Gold star, detective," Roxy purred. "Skeets was a nip-brain." Blaze's ears went straight back at that.

"So here we are," I said. "You lovebirds probably worked out some story about shooting me and framing Blaze, same way you did with Skeets."

Her eyes glittered with malice. "What a marvelous idea."

I tensed to jump her, but Blaze jumped in front of me. "No. No more! I'm not letting anyone else die because of me!"

Roxy drew back and snarled. "Bitch, you looking to get shot?"

Blaze didn't listen. "I'm the only one who knows the password. It's not on the flash drive. You kill me, that's it. No money." She took a step forward.

Roxy pointed the pistol at Blaze's head and snarled, "You're lying."

"Hey, put away the gun," I cut in. I'd considered going for my own piece, but Blaze was in the way. I slipped my handpaw into my pocket and took hold of one of my steel sling balls.

"Nope." Blaze took another step. Roxy's arm trembled. I was worried she might panic and start shooting. Instead, she charged and swung the pistol at Blaze's head.

She never made contact. My steel ball whizzed by her ear to crack against the wall behind her. She flinched, and Blaze grabbed her wrist with both handpaws. The two queens wrestled over the gun. Roxy clawed at Blaze with her free handpaw while Blaze kept her grip on the gun arm. Both hissed and spat the whole time. Fur tufts drifted around them.

I started forward to intervene and strip the gun away, when Roxy stumbled and Blaze drove her to the floor. There was a muffled report, and both queens jerked.

Fearing the worst, I pulled them part, looking for the gun. It lay in Roxy's loosening grip. The queen's eyes were wide open in shock. She shuddered and went still. I knelt by her side, saw the neat hole going up beneath her sternum, sniffed her death.

Blaze scrambled to her footpaws and leaned against a table, handpaws over her mouth, blood on her chest. "Oh Bast. Is she—?"

"Gone." I closed Roxy's penny-colored eyes, feeling heavy. "That was a damn brave thing you did just now, kitten. Also dumb, but the two kind of go together."

That summer green gaze locked on me, and electricity raced up my spine.

"I wasn't going to let her hurt anyone else," she said, lowering her handpaws. "But I didn't mean... didn't want...!"

"Shhh. I know." I went over and held her. "It wasn't your fault."

"Of course it's my fault!" she said, pulling back. "If I hadn't stolen the password, she and Skeets would still be alive!"

"You didn't make the choices she made."

"No. You're right. I didn't." The way she said it, I caught a glimpse of the steely felian who'd made off with a fortune because she thought it was the right thing to do. This Kitty was not to be trifled with. "That still doesn't make it right. Two people dead because of me."

"Come on, let's catch a breath outside, clear our heads. Give me your side of the story, then we'll call the cops," I said. "They'll put out an APB for Wylie."

"Alright." She gave me a reproachful look. "But first let's check on Sheba Rae."

***

Sheba Rae would probably be fine, aside from the lump on her head. She was breathing OK, and seemed responsive when we woke her. We were going to have to get her to the ER tonight to be sure. Notwithstanding what the movies showed, concussions were serious business. We bundled her up in a sleeping bag and went outside. I told Blaze we'd call an Uber in a few minutes. But first I needed answers.

Steering her by the elbow, I led her down the steps by the rose jungle, and we took a walk around the block. Felian senses gave us a different view of the city after sunset. The world didn't contract the way it did for Apes. We could see the mist coming in over the hills, sending feelers onto the river. The checkered glow of streetlights filtered between the trees and houses. Everything retained detail unscrubbed by darkness. The air smelled of damp earth and wet asphalt and exhaust. Night traffic rumbled by on Powell, a few blocks north. An owl flew by overhead; mice squeaked to each other as they crept through yards and sniffed at trash cans. For a pair of stray cat types like us, it was a beautiful night. Under other circumstances with a queen like this, I'd have different thoughts on my mind. But this wasn't the time.

We stopped under a tree, in the shadow of a van that blocked the glare of the nearby streetlamp.

"Far enough. Tell me about the rest," I said.

Her eyes narrowed. "The rest?"

"Don't play dumb, Ms. Hawthorne. How much did you lift from Zozo? He said it was a lot."

She bit her lip. "What are you going to do?"

"That depends on what you tell me. Way I figure it, we need to make an executive decision before the cops get here. So spill. How much we talking?"

"About two million, depending on the exchange rate." Her expression was defiant.

I let out a hiss of surprise. No wonder everyone was going Ape. That was a lot of scratch.

"I'm so, so sorry I did it. It's not worth anyone's life." She hugged herself. In the dark, the bright patch of white on her forehead that was her namesake did, in fact, seem to blaze in my view. "I only took it because Zozo was going to—"

"I know."

She nodded. "I couldn't let that happen. They were terrorists. We can do better. Violence isn't the answer. You have to stand for something. You have to stand with someone. That's what community means. And there are so many people trying to do good. They need help." She looked at me earnestly, then reached up behind her neck and unhooked her pendant. "There's a spreadsheet on here that explains it all."

She pressed it into my handpaw, a little gold rectangle with a decorative tiger sculpture. Crystals on its back twinkled in the hazy light coming from the city around us. Fine silver chain slithered between my fingers. I tried not to get lost in Blaze's green eyes.

"Why are you giving me this?" I asked.

She gave me a wan smile. "Bast's bright paws, I don't want to be responsible anymore. It's been so horrible, such a terrible mistake. Everything went wrong, and now Skeets is dead… and Roxy…" She trailed off, and I put an arm around her. We started walking back to the duplex.

"Are you going to give the money back to Zozo?" she asked.

I slipped the little tiger into my pocket. "He's my client." Her eyes widened with reproach, and I added, "It won't go to the FLF. I promise."

She gave a little mew and hugged me. I let her. It was nice.

Too nice. A shoe scraped ahead of us. A big human sprang out from the duplex's concrete steps, about fifteen feet away. He had a gun in hand; his face was twisted. Carl Wylie, the bullet-headed Ape from the car stakeout. He'd been downwind, so we hadn't scented him, and we'd been too preoccupied with each other to pay attention. Even Apes can move quietly sometimes. Especially when they're motivated by two million reasons and vengeance.

"Jones!" He thrust a gun at me, and everything shifted into slow motion, the seconds crawling like a dying mouse. I scrambled to pull my piece and get Blaze behind me. I wasn't going to make it; he had the drop on us.

His gun blasted flame as Blaze slammed into me, shoving me aside. I came down on one knee with the Glock out. The pistol bucked twice in my hand, bright muzzle flashes spearing my vision, the noise deafening. Wylie stumbled and fired again, wide this time. His mouth opened as if he were trying to shout but couldn't get words out. He took a step, tried to raise his arm for another shot. It sagged as if too heavy to hold up. He folded into a slow-motion crumple onto the sidewalk, his cheek coming to rest at the edge of the grassy strip by the trash cans.

I was breathing hard, fangs bared, ears ringing, but kept him in my sights for another beat, resisting the urge to empty my magazine into the son of a bitch. He didn't move. Acrid gunsmoke filled my nose, but under that I smelled blood, a lot of it.

Wylie was still downwind.

Blaze lay next to me, arms extended from the shove she'd given me. She didn't move either. I dropped the Glock and turned her over, but she was gone. The exit wound wasn't pretty.

When I could think again, I called 911 and held her while I waited for the sirens to arrive. The thumb drive sat in my pocket like a hot coal.

***

The cops took my gun and my statement at the scene and had me repeat the latter twice more at the station. I didn't tell them about the drive, but let them run with the story of jealous lovers they jumped onto right away. They were grilling me for the fourth time when Flanagan came in and called them off. I confirmed Sheba Rae was OK, told him we still weren't friends, and went home to the office, where three shots of José didn't help me sleep at all. I had too much of Blaze on me: her scent, the feel of her fur, the stench of her death in my brain. I got up, cleaned the Glock and put it away, and did my best to scrub the dried blood out of my wool coat.

I thought about Blaze, and all the things that went wrong for good people who tried to make a difference.

Eventually, my tequila-fogged brain remembered the flash drive. I plugged it into my beat-up laptop and took a gander. It included a weblink to the cryptocurrency wallet login page, but none of the files on the drive included a password. Most of them were selfies of her visiting places around Portland, and there were a couple of files of poetry presumably written by Blaze herself. They weren't that good, but reading them made my heart ache anyway. Kittens and idealism. There was also a spreadsheet on which she'd planned out her donations. Unsurprisingly, she hadn't set aside anything for herself. I felt old and useless. I could have told her not to waste her life on a cynical alley cat tom like me.

Eventually I dozed.

When I woke, my cheek fur was flat on the keyboard, and someone had packed my mouth and eyeballs in sand. I pushed myself up and checked the time. Six-fifteen.

The night's events came back to me like a hammer blow. A glance out the window showed cracks in the dark metal cloud cover, indicating the coming day might be more sun than wet. I thought about how wrong it felt that this would be a day without a Blaze Hawthorne to witness it, and hot rage ignited in my chest. She'd lived for everything, died for nothing, and she had loved the rain. That was all I could think of for an epitaph: she'd loved the smell of rain. Half her poetry went on about it. I reached for José, and my handpaw froze an inch from the bottle.

The smell of rain. There was a word for it.

I didn't know why that idea struck me just then. Maybe the subconscious popped it out of the pressure cooker of fatigue and grief and guilt. Maybe it was just the dumb, stupid luck of a half-awake hungover brain. When I went back to the laptop and entered *petrichor* for the cryptocurrency password with trembling handpaws, I found myself looking at an account balance. The number in cryptocurrency wasn't impressive, but a quick search showed the dollar exchange total came to over two million. That'd buy a lot of kibble.

My chair creaked as I leaned back, mouth as dry as a dead rat baked on asphalt. It was more money than I'd ever seen, ever dreamed of seeing. I could buy a house, see the world, pack the rest of my nine lives with queens and caviar.

I hadn't ever thought about what *I* wanted. Since the Change, I was just doing what I thought was right, surviving, trying to make sense of this new existence. Like most felians, I didn't have childhood dreams. Cats had existed in an eternal present. Considering the new possibilities put me into mental vapor lock.

After awhile, the screen went dark. A little after that, my brain came unstuck and I made a decision.

***

The weather turned out decent, with patches of blue sky and enough sunlight to make the wet street shine. I called Zozo to tell him I had the drive and that I'd meet him at Code Tygers after lunch. He squawked about the protesters, and I told him to cat up if he wanted the drive. He shut up and said he'd be there.

He looked up as I stalked over to his desk. My anger must have warned off the other Kitties, because they kept their ears down and didn't meet my eyes as I passed them.

"You look like shit, lick," Zozo said.

"You want to do this out here?" I snarled, leaning into his space. "Or somewhere private?" Behind me, the room filled with silence.

His fur fluffed, and his ears flicked back, but he mastered himself. I was a little disappointed we didn't throw down on the spot.

"Conference room," he growled. He led me into the walled-off space with the goliath table and shut the door behind him. We both took our seats and glared at each other.

"What you got?" Zozo demanded.

"Blaze is dead," I replied. "But before she died, she gave me the drive and put the pieces together for me. You were right. She was special."

He took his glasses off and put them on the table, then started grooming his arm.

"You don't get off the hook so easy," I said. "Let me lay it out for you. You didn't figure Save Kittytown was getting enough traction, so you went hunting for better leverage on New Sunrise. Turned out they had a security flaw, a big one. You hacked their business accounts and lifted a bunch of money, probably through fake invoices and the like. Then you converted it to crypto-currency so it couldn't be traced."

I tossed the thumb drive onto the table. The little gold tiger with the ruby eyes seemed even smaller in the fluorescent light. Zozo twitched, but made no move to scoop it up.

"Blaze wasn't involved with the FLF. But *you* are."

"I know licks who were," he said, not meeting my gaze. "Let's leave it at that. What about—"

"The password? Forget it. The wallet's empty. She donated the whole kit and caboodle."

"You're kidding me!" He jerked in disbelief. "Two million bucks?"

"Like you said the other day, she was a real do-gooder. No dough for you to fund a resurgent FLF, sorry. Or line your own pocket."

"Where'd it go?" He held up a handpaw. "Wait, son of a bitch, don't tell me. Soup kitchens, SPCA, Save Kittytown… Jesus Bast-licking Christ."

"And a dozen other groups. She spread it around generously."

He slumped in his seat. "Well, fuck. What happens now? The cops on their way?"

"Why would they be? There's no evidence of theft. Your name's not attached to this." I pulled out the phone I'd taken off Skeets. "On the other hand, the messages on this might make things more complicated for you. The cops don't have a sense of humor about felian 'resistance fighters.'"

He sat up straight.

"You met Skeets through Blaze, right?" I asked. "Talking about activism and resistance."

Zozo regarded me with hatred. "Fuck you. Yeah, that's how it happened. He was a young, angry lick ready to tear things up. He reminded me of me. We hit it off. I told a bunch of war stories from the old days. When I got the money, I got excited, told him and Blaze we'd start up the FLF again. The name has cachet. It's a fuckin' *brand*. But I was thinking hacktivists, not terrorists, I swear to Bast. But Blaze turned out be a Bast-be-damned pacifist. We argued, and I thought—"

"You figured she'd go along."

His ears twitched yes.

"But she didn't. She changed the password to the wallet and took off. And the nature of cryptocurrency meant there was no way you could regain access. She stayed in the Mission, cycled through a couple of other shelters. You tore up her apartment."

Zozo just stared defiantly at me, so I went on. "Skeets was tagging places around P-town with FLF graffiti. Bragging about the FLF comeback to anyone who'd listen. Word got around, and when that investigator started getting close to him, there was a good chance he'd get real dirt on *you*. You're lucky Roxy took him out, huh? Cause if she hadn't, you might have decided to tie off a loose end."

He let out a low growl. "What a fuckin' idiot."

We both knew his last comment was pointed at himself as much as at the young, dumb tom. My anger was still there, still hot, but it started to cool, a little. Nothing was going to bring Blaze back from the dead. Or Skeets.

"So we went through all this bullshit for nothing," he spat.

"Except for three licks dead."

"Three?"

"Roxy too. And her Ape lover."

"Jesus…" Ears flattened, he put his face in his handpaws. "I swear to Bast I didn't mean for that to happen."

"I wouldn't say it was for nothing," I continued. "Blaze planned all her donations in detail, where she thought they'd do the most good." I paused. "The transfers happened this morning, just like she wanted."

The lights went on. "Wait. She didn't? You… *you*…?" He stared at me in disbelief. "How'd you manage…"

"I got friends." Moopsy had come through for a modest cut, though it had taken him all morning to finagle the transfers to fiat currency in small enough amounts not to raise suspicion. Then we transferred everything to Blaze's beneficiaries. Zozo had already evidently bounced the funds around enough to tangle up the trail.

I stood. "There was a hundred grand set aside for Code Tygers. She didn't forget you." I nodded at the tiger pendant. "However, I made a donation in your name to the Rose City Mission. Because of course you wouldn't want to profit off the deaths of Kitties, would you? If you can figure out how to take the tax write-off, be my guest."

"You had two mil," he breathed. "Right in your handpaws."

"It wasn't mine."

Glassy eyed, he fixed his gaze on the jeweled tiger pendant. I went to the door, opened it.

"What about Skeets's phone?" he said. "The cops?"

I tossed the phone onto the table. "You weren't worthy of her bequest, Zozo," I said. "Make it up to her. And the felian community. Do better, because I have my nose on you, and I will tear you a new mouth through your nutsack if you pull scat like this again, or if I get even a tiny sniff you're messing with Fluff."

He didn't answer, just stared at the phone.

As I waded out through the desks and ferns and the coders stalking their projects, I could see the protesters were outside already, a few dozen humans and felians standing together in the drizzle, waving their ridiculous signs outside the school. I stopped and watched them for a minute. I figured they were wasting their time, but then I thought of Blaze, what she'd done and wanted to do. *You have to stand for something,* she'd said. *You have to stand with someone.*

I wasn't a cat anymore. No matter how much I maybe wanted to be. To fit into this world, felians had to become something different. Something better than the Apes, if we could.

I ripped a flap off one of the cardboard boxes stacked in the corner. Using a marker from a whiteboard, I scrawled *SAVE THE CAT* in big block letters on the cardboard, tossed the marker on a desk, and headed outside to join something bigger than myself.

About the Authors

Linnea Capps is a bubbly ball of fluff with an insatiable wanderlust. When not seeking out adventures and experiences, she happily plays songs on her ukulele and writes the stories she dreams up every night before bed.

Pete Butler-Davis lives in Pittsburgh PA, where he works in the infamous and deadly code foundries where molten ones and zeros are poured into the logic ingots used to build the interwebs. When not writing stories about dragons, Pete and his wife Jasmine make games together.

Madison Keller is the author of the epic fantasy *Flower's Fang* series of young adult fantasy novels, the humorous fantasy *Dragonsbane Saga* novella series, as well as numerous short stories. Their work has won both a Cóyotl and Leo Literary Award. They live in Oregon with their partner and their pack of adorable Chihuahua mixes, and when not writing can be found sewing plushies.

Twitter - @maddiekellerr

Website – http://MadisonKeller.net

Kyell Gold has won twelve Ursa Major awards and a Cóyotl Award for his stories and novels, and his acclaimed novel *Out of Position* co-won the Rainbow Award for Best Gay Novel of 2009. He helped create RAWR, the first residential furry writing workshop, and has instructed at each of its sessions through 2019.

He lives in California, loves to travel and dine out with his partners, and can be seen at furry conventions around the world enjoying the creative spirit of the furry community. More information about him and his books is available at http://www.kyellgold.com, and you can follow him on Twitter at @KyellGold.

Having been a conscript in the army for two years, **Mikasi Wolf** hopes that readers will appreciate the efforts of those who've lived, fought and died. We don't always have a choice of what we do, but we have a choice of what we choose to believe in. Believing in the power of words and stories, through them, Mikasi hopes that we may see through another's eyes.

Aside from writing dismal narratives, Mikasi also writes fantasy and stories based on his observations of the world, some of them actually humorous. His stories have appeared in several publications, including FurPlanet's *The Furry Future* (2015), *Gods With Fur* (2016), Jaffa Books' *Claw the Way to Victory* (2016), *Dogs of War* (2017), *Dogs of War II* (2017), *Exploring New Places* (2018) Thurston Howl Publications' *What the Fox* (2018), *BREEDS: Foxes* (2018), *SLASHERS* (2018), Rabbit Valley's *Furry Trash* (2018), and the upcoming *BREEDS: Wildcats.*

When he isn't writing other people's lives, watching movies or going on local tours, Mikasi does research as a Materials Engineering PhD student. He hopes that he doesn't get drafted just yet, because that would totally ruin his study and work plans.

An idea of his existence can be gleaned in the following declassified directories:
https://twitter.com/MikasiWolf
http://www.furaffinity.net/user/mikasiwolf

Frances Pauli writes across multiple genres, usually with anthropomorphic animal characters. She lives in the drier part of Washington State, where she writes obsessively, builds fursuits, crochets, and collects reptiles, spiders, and hairless dogs. You can find all her works on her website at: francespauli.com and many of her stories in furry anthologies. She also posts free work on various furry sites as Mamma Bear. She's been nominated for a Cóyotl award and won a Leo Literary Award in 2018.

Alice "**Huskyteer**" Dryden has been writing furry fiction since 2010. Her short stories have appeared in anthologies including *Heat*, *ROAR*, *Inhuman Acts* and *The Furry Future*, and have won two Cóyotl Awards, two Ursa Major Awards, and one Leo Literary Award. You can find a complete list of her published works at huskyteer.co.uk/bibliography

She lives in south London, owns a motorbike and too many books, and is a black belt in karate. She can bark well enough to confuse most dogs, but has no idea what she's saying to them. She enjoys travelling to other countries to sample their alcohol, cheese, and aviation museums.

Come and say hello on Twitter, where she's @Huskyteer. She doesn't bite.

Lloyd Yaeger is a horned owl made of equal parts fluff and sour gummy worms. By day, he is a sleepy grad student and writing teacher, and by night, he likes to write fiction, usually in the furry and sci-fi genres. He lives in Los Angeles with his loving partner and his pet, both of whom are cats, though only one of them walks on all fours. He studies English, and is currently writing a dissertation on something or other. With luck, and enough coffee, he may finish it someday. A list of his favorite things would have to include espresso, rabbits, roller coasters, queerness, cooking, cyberpunk, rye, and sushi. At night, he dreams of going to space. His work has appeared in *The Rabbit Dies First* (2019).

Bill Kieffer's only admitted vice is being himself on the internet (where he is a 6 foot tall—which Bill is convinced makes him very tall—anthropomorphic draft horse that types as Greyflank. He is ever-so grateful to his wife of over 25 years for putting up with him. Recently, he became a manager at a virtual reality company that totally groks that he's a furry.

He is a member of the Furry Writers Guild, a social media volunteer for the NJ LGBT Chamber of Commerce, the Democratic County Committee Man for his section of town, and is considering running for town council. Past fiction credits include the Cóyotl Award winning *THE GOAT: Building The Perfect Victim* from Red Ferret Press and *COLD BLOOD: Fatal Fables*, a collection of stories from Jaffa Books. More recent publications include short stories in *In Flux*, *Sinister Sheets*, and *ROAR 9!*

"Folding In The Wolf," the story in this book, came from the horse inside of him that looks in the mirror and just doesn't see itself. Ever. This story is dedicated to everyone that knows the mirror to be a liar and is only one impossible miracle away from being their best, true selves.

Thurston Howl is an LGBT journalist for the state of Michigan. His recent TED Talk, "Being Positive" tackles issues of HIV today, and his upcoming book on HIV in 21st century America will be coming out through Weasel Press this December. Despite living with HIV himself, Howl does not spend all his time working on HIV writing. He is the editor-in-chief of Thurston Howl Publications, an editor for Weasel Press, a copyeditor for Armoured Fox Press, founder of the Furry Book Review program and Leo Literary Awards, and a PhD student in English and Animal Studies at Michigan State University.

Proud Canuck by birth, Brit by chance of fate, **Anhedral** trained as a zoologist before making a career in ecology. In the name of science he's studied the unsavoury habits of Soay sheep on St. Kilda, radio-tracked seals across the Moray Firth, and counted seabirds in the remotest bits of Orkney and Shetland. Anhedral still lives in Scotland; these days he's a music teacher, and he's *loving* it.

Shamefully, Anhedral remained ignorant of the creative maelstrom that is furry until 2012. Some fuzzy friends helped him to catch up, and their kindness and generosity showed the fandom at its truest and its best. His wife suffers his newfound addiction with bemused tolerance, and for her love and support he remains extremely grateful.

When he's not wrangling unruly sentences or scaring his flute students with unplayable duets, Anhedral loves cycling, hill-walking, and carting his camera to out-of-the-way places. He drinks too much coffee for his own good, will never have time to get through all of the brilliant fantasy and science fiction on his bucket list, and loves most any critter that can fly. 'Schism' is his first published piece, but his other scribbles can be found over at http://www.furaffinity.net/user/anhedral/

Cathy Smith is an aboriginal writer who lives on an Indian Reservation within Canada. She has twelve publication credits. She has also won an honorable mention from the L. Ron Hubbard's Writers of the Future contest and was a co-winner of the 2016 Imagining Indigenous Futurism Contest. You can follow her latest projects at:
Wordpress: bit.ly/2e41qWT
Facebook: bit.ly/2dP3rXd
Twitter: @khiatons

Instagram: @cathy2891
Tumblr: http://bit.ly/2G3dEjo

Tim Susman started a novel in college and didn't finish one until almost twenty years later. In that time, he earned a degree in Zoology, worked with Jane Goodall, co-founded Sofawolf Press, and moved to California, where he lives with his two partners. Since publishing *Common and Precious*, he has attended Clarion in 2011 (arooo Narwolves!), published short stories in *Apex*, *Lightspeed*, and *ROAR*, among others, and recently released the second book in his Revolutionary War-era fantasy series, *The Demon and the Fox*. He's won a Cóyotl Award and a Leo Literary Award, and under the name Kyell Gold, he has published multiple novels and won several more awards for his furry fiction. You can find out more about his stories at timsusman.wordpress.com and www.kyellgold.com, and follow him on Twitter at @WriterFox.

Amy Clare Fontaine is a wildlife biologist by day and a fantasy/science fiction author by night. Her stories have been published in *ROAR* Volumes 6 through 10 and *Cosmic Roots and Eldritch Shores*, and her fiction was nominated for a Cóyotl Award and two Leo Literary Awards. By spinning magical tales and releasing them into the wild, she hopes to kindle a sense of optimism and wonder in her readers.

Amy has studied hyenas in Kenya, wolves in Yellowstone National Park, and nilgai antelope in Texas. When she isn't writing or researching animals, she enjoys drawing, playing guitar, traveling, and dreaming about what the world could be. The Furry Writers' Guild has been a very supportive community for her. To find Amy's other published work, including books, short stories, poems, and games, check out her website, https://amyclarefontaine.com.

A. Humphrey Lanham is a fantasy, science fantasy, and YA writer. She reads and writes a wide range of fiction but prefers strong female characters who refuse to cater to patriarchal social structures, expectations of romance, or cultural gender norms and stereotypes.

She is chair of Wordos, an internationally renowned writers' workshop in Eugene, Oregon. Her interests outside of the literary realm include kombucha kitcheneering, cat herding, and language learning.

Her cat, Ru, is an anthro-xeno-biologist and PhD candidate researching humans with a focus on their inexplicable, hydrophilic proclivities. Unfortunately, everyone keeps saying he is just a common Earth cat.

Follow their adventures on Twitter @ahumphreylanham and @ thecupcakebeast.

Blake Hutchins lives in the green hills of Eugene, Oregon with two mostly responsible cats who help him raise two free-spirited teenage girls. A member of the Wordos writing group, his publication history includes *ROAR 9, ROAR 6, Writers of the Future Vol. XXII, Polyphony, Shimmer, Blood, Blade & Thruster,* and credit as Lead Writer on the videogame titles *Starsiege: Tribes, Tribes 2, Starsiege, Night at the Museum 2,* and *Enigma: Rising Tide.* When not writing, single-parenting, or studying for yet another degree, he practices yoga, medieval European sword-fighting, and bodyweight training, and finds time to participate in local community activism.

About the Artist

Teagan Gavet is a professional illustrator, graphic novelist, and freelance rambler. Find more at: http://www.teagangavet.com
http://www.furaffinity.net/user/blackteagan

About the Editor

Your fearless editor, **Mary E. Lowd**, is a science-fiction and furry author in Oregon. She's had more than 130 short stories published, as well as several novels, including the *Otters In Space* trilogy, several spin-offs, and *The Snake's Song: A Labyrinth of Souls Novel.* This is the fifth volume of *ROAR* she has edited. She is also the editor and founder of *Zooscape.*

Content Warning: This story contains explicit depictions of self-harm, drug over-dose, and suicide.